Dis grace ful

Rachel Fox McLeod

SIMON &
SCHUSTER

New York · Amsterdam/Antwerp · London · Toronto · Sydney/Melbourne · New Delhi

DISGRACEFUL
First published in Australia in 2026 by
Simon & Schuster (Australia) Pty Limited
Level 4, 32 York St, Sydney NSW 2000

10 9 8 7 6 5 4 3 2 1

New York Amsterdam/Antwerp London Toronto Sydney/Melbourne New Delhi
Visit our website at www.simonandschuster.com.au

NATIONAL LIBRARY OF AUSTRALIA

A catalogue record for this book is available from the National Library of Australia

ISBN: 9781761634147

Cover design and illustrations: Emily O'Neill
Typeset by Midland Typesetters, Australia
Printed and bound in Australia by Griffin Press

FSC www.fsc.org MIX Paper | Supporting responsible forestry FSC® C018684

The paper this book is printed on is certified against the Forest Stewardship Council® Standards. Griffin Press holds chain of custody certification SCS-COC-001185. FSC® promotes environmentally responsible, socially beneficial and economically viable management of the world's forests.

'Rachel Fox McLeod's warm and witty prose had me hooked from page one. This refreshingly honest debut moves seamlessly from laugh-out-loud funny to quietly devastating before reaching its emotionally satisfying conclusion. With fabulously flawed characters and real emotional resonance, *Disgraceful* is my favourite kind of read. An exciting new voice in Australian fiction!' **Lisa Ireland**

'Full of raw honesty and heart, *Disgraceful* is a wild and dazzling debut. Fox McLeod has knocked it out of the park.' **Emma Grey, international bestselling author of *Pictures of You***

'A delicious read in every way. Hilarious, heartfelt, raw and real.' **Natalie Bassingthwaighte**

'Balls-to-the-wall fearless, funny as hell, and all the feels. This book broke my heart then put it back together again. An unforgettable read.' **Bianca Dye, radio and TV personality**

'Come for the laughs, but stay for the heart and wisdom that abounds in Rachel Fox McLeod's highly entertaining debut, *Disgraceful*. This is wonderful, car-crash storytelling – just try to look away as Grace Miller's mid-life implosion takes us from the confines of church to the wild abandon of the sex dungeon and the pure terror of the delivery suite. This is the mid-life rollercoaster in all its glorious mess – and I say Amen to that!' **Cassie Hamer**

'*Disgraceful* is a witty yet unflinching exploration of women's sacrifice, desire, and the quiet violence of being a good girl. Balancing playfulness with pathos, Fox McLeod's debut is a bold interrogation of generational trauma, the cost of self-erasure, and what women owe to the world and each other. *Disgraceful* is a complex and frequently funny journey through the awkward stumbles of self-reinvention and facing yourself anew. While the story is ticklish with smart humour, make no mistake: you'll close this book with a bruise in your heart. And maybe a to-do list.' **Sommer Tothill**

‘*Disgraceful* is a wild, witty and expansive novel that thrilled me from the first page to the last. It offers a rich, deep and sometimes disturbing examination of what happens when women step outside the bounds of expected behaviour, never once straying into saccharine territory or shying away from difficult truths. Brava, Rachel Fox McLeod.’ **Nina D. Campbell**

‘Rachel Fox McLeod writes with humour and sharp insight, but always with care. It is at different times heartbreaking, horrifying, exciting and genuinely funny. *Disgraceful* feels lived-in and truthful, not theoretical. Proving that sometimes the so-called bad decisions – the one that crack everything open – are the very choices that save us. *Disgraceful* is a confident, confronting and emotionally intelligent debut, and a true page-turner.’ **Fiona Horne**

‘We devoured *Disgraceful* and each chapter left us wanting more. It’s a fierce, funny story of resilience and self-discovery that flips the bird to anyone who tries to label us and toasts the sisterhood that keeps us standing.’ **Mez & Fonz – *The Midlifers podcast***

‘Wise, funny and unflinchingly honest, *Disgraceful* asks us to consider the true self we might find if we shed the layers life has asked us to don. Grace’s undulating path back to herself is a lesson in self-reflection and an inspiring reminder that beauty can sprout in the darkest times. A brilliant debut.’ **Brooke Crawford, author of *Better than the Real Thing***

‘Rachel gives us such an insightful portrayal of loss, recovery and acceptance. The importance of friendship, the mother–daughter and sister relationships shine through and are so beautifully and richly drawn. Most of all it speaks so eloquently to the experience of being female; I felt a true camaraderie with Grace and already miss her.’ **Katie Hoskins, author of *When the Party’s Over***

‘One of those fearless storytellers with the ability to transport the reader so truthfully into someone else’s life that they can’t help but recognise themselves, or someone they love, in the story – I’m calling it now . . . Rachel Fox McLeod is about to become your new favourite author.’ **Rebecca Sparrow, author and co-founder of Birds of a Feather Bookclub**

For Nikita, who taught me that being a mother is complex but loving is easy.

For Peyton and Maggie, who showed me that joy is in the small moments.

And for Lola, who was always the goodest girl and still walks beside me.

This story is for you.

A NOTE FROM THE AUTHOR

To my readers – should you wish to be forewarned of sensitive themes portrayed in this book and practise self-care around your reading experience, you'll find a list on page 389.

Looking for an immersive reading experience?

Listen to the *Disgraceful* playlist here:

Prologue

And you shall do what is right and good in the sight of the Lord

– Deuteronomy 6:18

The Bible has a lot to say about what it means to be a decent person. Don't murder people. Don't fuck your neighbour's wife. Don't let people fall off your roof. Don't eat owls. I've come to learn most of it is rubbish. No offense to God – let's face it, he was working with some crappy editors.

I'm not supposed to say that aloud, naturally. Not in my position. But – if they're honest – most people who claim to live by the Bible's tenets are stretching the truth. Sometimes a little. Sometimes a lot. Not that they'll admit it.

But what happens if you live your whole life by the book only to realise you've been wearing somebody else's skin? (Not in a serial killer kind of way – I'm being metaphorical, obviously.) And what happens when that skin suddenly doesn't fit so well? Maybe it's gotten a bit tight around the armpits, or it's starting to chafe your inner thighs. Maybe the seams are starting to split from the pressure of holding everything in and you need to find a new skin to wear or at least work out where you left your original one. The point is, sometimes your life doesn't turn out the way you thought it would. And you can't help but wonder whether it's too late to start over.

Often you don't have a choice. Life is full of surprises after all – good and bad. Some are tiny shocks that punctuate your day like a pinprick and disappear just as quickly. Others are bombshells that knock you completely off your axis. Your shoe heel might snap right as you're about to go into that important meeting. You might slice open an avocado and for once it'll be perfectly ripe. No mushy brown bits, not even one. Other times you might turn on the news to find someone famous – like Shane Warne – has unexpectedly died and even though you care little about cricket, you can't help being inexplicably grief-stricken. And then sometimes – just sometimes – your husband tells you he accidentally slipped and put his penis inside a pretty twenty-five-year-old and now he's in love with her, which on the scale of avocado to bombshell, is pretty nuclear.

The thing about surprises is they're entirely unexpected, so it can be hard to know what the appropriate reaction should be. If anybody had told me that by the end of my forty-ninth birthday my life would be crumbling around me and that I, Grace Miller – respected church leader, devoted wife and mother, dependable friend and committed recycler – would be on my knees in my equally dependable underwear, staring at a complete stranger's erection, well, quite frankly, I'd have laughed.

But we're getting a little bit ahead of ourselves. Pun intended.

1

shiny happy

This morning started the same way most weekday mornings have started for as long as I can remember, which makes it sound boring, but there's something to be said for predictability. It was an early winter Tuesday, which meant thirty chilly laps in the Icebergs pool, followed immediately by a 7 am yoga class on the deck to warm up, while Daniel worked out whatever demons he needed to work out on a nearby squash court.

I know it's odd talking about demons when my husband is *you know who* – but anybody who plays any kind of racquet sport will tell you it's saved them a mint in therapy. Besides, being responsible for the moral compass of an entire congregation is not without its stresses.

I'd sealed my yoga practice with my hands to prayer and a deep exhale, face upturned to the sun as the instructor brought the class to a close. Rolling my mat up, I'd glanced to my left. Lucinda hadn't even broken a sweat, but I guess that's to be expected when you're barely forty.

'How are you as fresh as a daisy after that many downward dogs when I look like a tomato?'

Lucinda had stood, deftly wrapping her hair into a topknot. 'Stop it. You always look immaculate.' We'd fallen into step, heading for the exit. 'Speaking of immaculate, are you wearing something fabulous tonight? I can't believe the concert's being televised. Are you nervous?'

'I'm not the one who has to deliver a sermon to potentially hundreds of thousands of people.' I'd shrugged. 'I've been too busy with the conference program to think about clothes, to be honest.' *That's a lie.* 'Nobody'll be looking at me anyway.' *Also a lie.* 'I'm focused on making sure everything runs smoothly for Daniel – no hiccups.' I must have seemed worried because she'd peered at me, squeezing my arm.

'If it runs anything like this week has, I've no doubt it'll be perfect, Grace. You two are like a well-oiled machine. It's been months since any of us have spent any real time with you.'

'I know.' I'd shaken out the tension knotting my shoulders. So much for yoga relaxing you. 'I'm so out of the loop. Sorry I haven't been around.'

Lucinda had touched my arm. 'Don't be silly. You're a literal rock any other time of year. I don't know what we'd all do without you.' Then she'd laughed. 'Now, let me see, what earth-shatteringly important things have you missed? Tom got his promotion – which is just as well. Celia's pregnant again . . .'

I'd pressed a hand to my chest. 'Praise the Lord. Another miracle baby.'

'I'd pray for a nanny if I were her. Four kids?' Then she'd gasped, 'Ooh, you know Peter and Monica's boy – Felix? In trouble at St. Benedict's again. Bullying this time.' She'd shot me a knowing look. 'Of course, they're denying it.'

'Where there's smoke—' I'd felt guilty for gossiping; it wasn't exactly charitable. But I've been living and breathing our annual church conference for the better part of five months, with this year's the biggest it's ever been, so it was nice to know what was going on with my friends, even if it was second-hand.

'Before I forget, dinner on Sunday is at Todd and Glenda's, not Sam and Tara's, because the plumbing in their kitchen is broken. The garbage disposal is giving off a God-awful smell.' She'd wrinkled her nose. 'Excuse the blasphemy. Anyway—' Before Lucinda could continue, a sweaty face had appeared in my eyeline.

'Happy birthday, Grace.' Ben – a class regular with acne-pocked skin and dreadlocks – beamed at me. He was also shirtless and somewhat pungent. *Behold a leper came to him and knelt before him, saying, 'Lord, if you will, you can make me clean.'*

'Thanks, Ben, you're so sweet—'

'You don't look a day over twenty-five.'

'—and going straight to hell for lying. How's your sister doing? Did you manage to get her in to see Dr Wallace?'

Ben had nodded. 'Dropped your name and *boom* – she had an appointment straight away. She said to say thank you.'

'See . . . a saint,' Lucinda had said, once he was out of earshot. 'You're basically Mother Teresa. I don't know how you do it.'

'Oh, you know, mostly prayer, a lot of faith, and a little caffeine.' Lucinda had raised her eyebrows. 'What am I saying? I'm forty-nine, it's mostly caffeine. But don't tell Daniel I said that.'

She'd made a quick 'my lips are sealed' motion. 'Chris and I will see you both afterwards. There's that wine bar, Veritas, opposite the arena. You deserve to celebrate.' Her expression had shifted – a change so tiny I might have imagined it. 'I hope Daniel appreciates everything you do. He'd better be spoiling you.' Then it was gone. She'd air-kissed my cheeks before peeling off with a breezy, 'Happy birthday, darling.'

I'd blinked at her retreating back, an unexpected lump constricting my throat.

'Shiny Happy People' burbled from the car stereo as I manoeuvred Daniel's Range Rover through traffic, nursing a long black for Daniel and a latte for myself. We always carpool after working out – it's our bit for the environment. Daniel gets picked up from the house before I'm awake by whoever he's playing squash with, and I collect him once I've finished yoga. It's a well-worn routine and the drive gives me a chance to catch up on calls.

'Siri – call Minette.' The phone rang for a second before a harried voice shouted over an alarming amount of noise. It sounded like an engine revving.

'Stars Fold Ministry, God is watching!'

'Minette, it's Grace.'

'Hi, Mrs Miller. Sorry for yelling. I'm down at the loading dock. Everything okay?'

'You tell me.' I'd winced at a metallic screeching sound.

'All good. Bump-in's underway, soundcheck's at two. Mr Miller sent the updated run sheet through overnight.' Minette had hollered again, 'Whoa! You can't do that. It's bloody sacrilegious, mate.' She'd returned to the phone, 'Sorry. Lucky I'm here or the neon Jesus'd be crucified with cable ties.'

I'd fought the urge to ask for details, having made the decision months ago to leave most of the concert logistics to Daniel and Minette and focus on the conference. Short of cloning myself, managing everything would have been impossible, but the lack of control made me twitch. 'What about Pastor Evans?'

'All settled into his hotel. Sasha's set to go live on TikTok once everything's underway.'

'Who?'

'Sasha *Mason*,' she emphasised. I had no clue who she was talking about. 'The influencer? Almost a million followers?' Minette had sounded exasperated. 'She's performing with the choir . . .'

'Oh, right.' The name sounded vaguely familiar. Apparently my patchy memory comes as a package deal with the hot flashes. I'd hoped medication would fix both problems but clearly not. At least I was no longer permanently on fire – small mercies I supposed. I just needed to do something about the intermittent rage. 'Sorry. I do remember Daniel mentioning her, now that I think about it.'

'Everything's under control, don't worry.' Her tone was annoyingly placating. A stab of irritation had poked me in the back.

'You know what they say, Minette,' I'd snapped. 'Even the laziest king flees wildly in the face of a double check.' Now Minette was the one baffled. *Yep. Definitely needed to sort out the whole rage thing.* 'Look, Daniel will be there after nine. Now the conference has wrapped up, I'm back at the school today . . . but I'll check in later. The slightest hitch, you call me.'

'I'm sure we'll be fine. And Mrs Miller? Happy birth—'

I'd hung up, cutting her off as I pulled up outside the sports centre. Daniel was in his usual spot, juggling a racquet. He'd thrown the door open and folded himself into the car as I'd leaned in, holding out his coffee.

'Good game, darling?'

Usually Daniel gifts me a sweaty kiss on the cheek and I make a show of wiping my face in disgust. But this morning he'd simply taken his coffee, barely looking up, and started scrolling on his phone.

'Aren't you forgetting something?' I'd probed.

'No.' Daniel had glanced at the back seat. 'I've got everything.' He went back to his phone. 'Did Minette get the new run sheet?'

'Sure did.' I'd hidden my disappointment and pulled away from the kerb.

We wound our way in silence through the traffic towards Vaucluse. Something was definitely up. The morning drive home is usually our scheduled chat time, before the day takes over. It always follows the same pattern. First, Abbey. She calls us regularly to catch us up; her father more than me. I try not to take it personally. Daniel fills me in so it's not like I'm missing out on anything. She's a grown woman and she's busy. I understand what that's like. It's fine, really.

Our social circle comes next. All our friends are couples and belong to the church, which makes it easy to keep up with any news. Stars Fold Ministry business typically takes up the rest of the drive – fundraising, hospice visits, the youth group, anything needed for upcoming services. See what I mean – predictable.

I'm not complaining. Our life needs to be organised – regimented, even. It's a lot of work supporting Daniel's vision. *Our* vision, I should say. It's not as though I merely stand by his side looking pretty. Truth be told, if it wasn't for me – especially in the early years – doing all the admin, taking care of fundraising, staying home with Abbey while Daniel was away on pilgrimages, I doubt we'd be where we are.

Things have sky-rocketed beyond expectation recently, especially with the church's profile exploding thanks to one of our youth group kids, Jonah, winning *The Voice* last year. It continually astounds me that the tiny community church we founded twenty years ago has grown so much, although I cringe when people call it a 'mega-church'. It sounds so . . . *American.*

I sometimes wonder whether the kids who bullied me in school have seen our faces plastered on the sides of buses trundling around the city. *Not such a loser now, am I?* I check myself. *Have some humility, Grace. Practise forgiveness.*

Still, I really hope they've seen them.

I'm under no illusion that Daniel is the real shining light, especially to our congregation. He's their pastor after all. But you know what they say: 'Behind every great man—', etc. Although I sometimes wonder whether the second half of that proverb should be '—is a woman who needs to get her own life'.

I'd glanced down at my knuckles. They were white. Loosening my grip, I'd forced my shoulders down. 'I didn't hear you leave this morning.' Daniel hadn't looked up from his phone. Another minute ticked past. 'Do you want to go over tonight's sermon?'

'No.' He'd looked up briefly. 'It's under control.'

'But we always—'

'It's fine, Grace. I've got it.'

I hadn't known what to do with that – apart from wonder what I'd done wrong. It had to be something because – preoccupation aside – Daniel is nothing if not exceptional with dates.

By the time we arrive home, I've run through every possible explanation for why my husband of nearly thirty years hasn't wished me a happy birthday. We drive through a pair of wrought iron gates and pull up outside the house – a seamless union of original art deco sandstone and more recent glass-panelled extensions, all clean lines and hard, glossy surfaces.

As I close the front door, the tiled entrance rings with the sound of Daniel's footsteps on the timber staircase as he takes the stairs two at a time like a fifteen-year-old basketballer instead of the silver-haired fifty-two-year-old he is. I place my bag down, kick off my sandals, and hang the keys on their usual hook. He's like a tornado lately and I have no idea where he gets his energy. My knees hurt just watching him.

Dexter waddles excitedly out of the kitchen, claws skittering. He bumps against my legs and rolls on his back, tongue lolling. Dexter is nine and – considering that's sixty-three in dog years and golden retrievers are cursed with joint problems – I have more in common with my dog than my husband.

'Meet you down here in twenty for breakfast, then I'll drop you to the school.' Daniel strips off his t-shirt before I have a chance to answer, head down and thumbing his phone as he strides into his bathroom and closes the door.

I scratch Dexter's belly then climb the stairs like a forty-nine-year-old woman who's just taken an intense yoga class and needs a lie down. At the top of the stairs, I turn the opposite way to Daniel and head towards what used to be our room, until Abbey moved out and it became only mine. Daniel chose to move into Abbey's room on account of his snoring, or more specifically my complaining about his snoring, which sounds like a pterodactyl having an asthma attack. I like to think God guided his disciple into a separate room because, if he hadn't, I might have stabbed Daniel in his sleep by now, and then where would we be?

It's not like our sex life has suffered. Mainly because we don't have one. Sex has never been the driver of our relationship and things petered out completely years ago. I'm not one of those women who need passionate lovemaking to know my relationship is solid. Our marriage is built on a foundation of mutual respect, shared goals and parenting our daughter. The important things. It's not perfect, but what marriage is?

I close the door, slip out of my tracksuit and pad into the bathroom. The air still holds a chill, and the tiles are frigid underfoot. My skin erupts in goosebumps. Regardless, I swivel the tap to the left until icy needles shoot from the showerhead, making me gasp. I read once that a cold shower improves circulation and skin elasticity, and you'd have to think every bit helps once you reach a certain age. Between this and the ocean laps, I should be positively prepubescent.

I towel off and line up what Daniel calls my 'cauldron'; A complex collection of serums and creams – patented repair this, vitamin C that, AHAs, some French moisturiser with algae that's approximately the price of a flat screen TV, and enough retinol to skin a cat – all of which *has* to be applied in a very particular order, some in the morning, some at night, but every day without fail. Otherwise, my skin will apparently dry up like some kind of decrepit lizard and peel right off.

Then there's the army of tablets tasked with trying to keep this body working the way it's supposed to. Omega 3, vitamin B complex, evening primrose oil, glucosamine and turmeric for my joints, and magnesium to help the muscle cramps. And let's not forget the HRT. It's a wonder I don't rattle when I walk.

I smooth moisturiser across my cheeks, unable to resist pulling the skin back in front of my ears. The corners of my mouth lift – only a fraction, but enough that I'm dissatisfied when I let go. It's ridiculous, I know, but it's part of the deal. We are the faces of Stars Fold Ministry. It comes with expectations – constantly *on*, constantly smiling – and more than a little effort. Daniel says people look to us for hope, as proof that a life lived with God brings you joy. Which is a lot of pressure because, to be honest, this face does not look joyful when left to its own devices. Unfortunately, that's not something Botox can fix.

I straighten a photograph of Abbey on the dresser. It was taken on her eleventh birthday, at the skating rink in Penrith. She'd been obsessed with rollerskating for months and had insisted on a roller disco party, despite my safety concerns and doubts I'd be able to convince the other St. Agnes' parents to trek all the way to the Western suburbs for a Woolworths mud cake, 80s music and the prospect of bruises. I told Abbey it was about the driving distance but really it was because I found it hard to go back there. Too many memories I wanted to avoid.

Trying to convince her a pool party would be just as much fun didn't work. Abbey was desperate to see her cousins and I knew there was no way Liz would bring the boys over this way. She always said Vaucluse 'smelled like money and bullshit'. In the end, I refused to be drawn into the inevitable drama of passive-aggressive hurt feelings and thinly veiled accusations of snobbery from my family if I said no. It was easier to agree and bite my tongue.

In the photo, her blonde hair is tied into a side ponytail and she's wearing a pink t-shirt with bumblebee leggings. She's mid-skate, glitter gel sparkling on her flushed cheeks, her grin marred by two missing teeth. It was a happy moment, but I also remember the tears that book-ended the day.

As we got ready to leave for the rink, Abbey had asked if she looked pretty. I'd given my usual answer, the one I thought led to self-assurance and a grounded perspective. I told her there were things far more valuable than being pretty. Mainly that she was clever and kind and funny.

Abbey had promptly burst into tears. It took us a while to coax what was wrong out of her, but finally she'd whispered, 'You say that every time.'

'Because it's true, sweetheart.'

Abbey had scrubbed at her face, spreading glitter up her arms. 'It's because I'm ugly, isn't it?'

'What?' I'd reeled back, alarmed. 'No. Abbey, you're not ugly. Don't be silly. Where is this coming from?'

'You never tell me I'm pretty.'

I'd exchanged a worried look with Daniel, and he'd stood up.

'I might leave you girls to it.' He'd kissed Abbey's head. 'You are the prettiest girl in the entire world.' She'd looked up at him gratefully as he left the room and I squashed a flicker of annoyance. I'd turned Abbey to me and cupped her chin, gently forcing her to look at me. How could I have been so stupid?

'You're so much more than just pretty, honey.' Her forehead crinkled as she searched my face, looking for a scrap of validation that shouldn't matter, but clearly did.

'If it's not important, why do you try so hard to look nice all the time?'

I didn't have an answer.

Later that day, after too many party pies, a frenetic game of Red Rover and 'Stupid Girls' by P!nk on repeat, there were more tears. This time due to a physical fracture instead of an emotional one. As the doctor set Abbey's wrist at the hospital, the day's guilt was cemented into my own bones.

Abbey's twenty-eight now and a solicitor. The years in between have slipped through my fingers. One minute Abbey was mucking around with Play-Doh, the next she was mooning over boys; now she's expertly juggling a heavy case load and a somewhat robotic fiancé named Tobias, who under no circumstances should we *ever* call Toby.

She says she's happy and perhaps she is. I don't think she'd tell me if she wasn't. I should be proud. She's worked hard and accomplished so much. But I can't help thinking I dropped the ball somehow.

There's no time to blow out the mess yoga has made of my hair, so I scrape it back into a tight bun. I stare at myself in the mirror. *Forty-nine*. How did that happen?

'Alexa, play "Morning Affirmations".'

'*Now playing "Morning Affirmations".*'

I count vitamins into handfuls as ethereal music and a disembodied voice fill the room. I wash the first lot down, gagging slightly.

'*I am grateful for the blessings in my life.*'

'I am grateful for the blessings in my life.' I repeat the mantras with as much conviction as I can through mouthfuls of coated capsules. 'God provides everything I need.' Another mouthful. 'I am aligned with my higher purpose.'

'*I am worthy and I am loved.*'

My conviction wanes. 'I am worthy and I am loved.'

'*My life is a complete success.*'

'My life is a complete . . .' I look down at my wedding ring as I lift it from the soap dish and slide it on, 'success'. I twist it absently, unable to fight the gnawing sensation in my stomach. Then something inside me snaps. I fix my reflection with a hard look. *Get it together, Grace. You're being ridiculous. God has more than looked after you. You have everything you ever wanted. You chose this, so suck it up.*

I close my eyes and take a deep breath. When I open them, I force a smile until it almost reaches my eyes. *Okay, Grace – reset. Nothing is wrong, you're imagining things. It's probably your silly hormones.*

I keep the internal pep talk going. Maybe Daniel's planning something for my birthday and wants me to *think* he's forgotten. He's probably downstairs right this second making me a birthday breakfast.

Smile plastered on, I push aside the plastic-wrapped dress hanging ready for tonight and duck into the walk-in, dressing quickly. Black pants, a grey t-shirt and ballet flats – I always dress down on the days I'm at the school. I never know what kind of mess I'm going to get into and it's best to be prepared. Pausing at the door, I square my shoulders and take another deep breath, willing myself to believe that it's going to be a blessed day.

I trot eagerly down the stairs and find Daniel waiting in the entrance way, jingling the car keys. He's edgy, and I can't put my finger on whether it's nerves or excitement. I stop on the bottom step and eye him cautiously. 'I thought we were having breakfast before we left?'

'I said "meet you down here in twenty", Grace. That was nearly forty minutes ago. I honestly don't know why getting ready takes you so long. It's not like you need to do much; you always look great.' I stare at him, caught off guard by the unexpected compliment, and he blinks as though equally surprised. 'Besides, I've already eaten.'

'Oh.'

'There's still some bacon left if you're hungry. But you'll have to grab it to go, I need to be at the conference centre by 9.30 and if I'm dropping you at the school first—'

I consider the bacon, then remember someone telling me once that TV cameras add five kilos. 'No, that's fine. We can—'

'Okay, great. Let's go.'

2

baby did a bad bad thing

By the time we've driven a few blocks, the rhythmic thud of Daniel's fingers on the leather steering wheel in the otherwise silent car is torture. I sit straight-backed in the passenger seat with my bag on my lap – like a fawn about to bolt – unable to shake the creeping sense I'm being driven to my doom.

My phone pings with a text:

Abbey: Happy birthday, Mum. I love you, call you later.

Warmth floods my chest. I smile and glance at Daniel, but he stares fixedly ahead. 'Are you alright?' I touch his leg and his head jerks with the stricken look of a person who thinks you've been talking for a while but they haven't heard a word.

'Sorry, what?'

'I said, are you alright, darling? You've been a bit funny all morning.'

'Oh, right.' He glances at me. 'I'm fine, Grace. Today's a big day, you know that.'

I'm not convinced, but I know better than to push. Daniel doesn't work that way. If something is bothering him, I'll have to put my misgivings aside and coax it out; slowly and gently, carefully pinpointing which insecurity is niggling and tending to it like you would a child. And like with a child, there'll be tears and recriminations – it'll build, explode, then it'll be over. He'll apologise and tell me he doesn't know what he'd do without me. I'll be left ragged while he takes the strength I give him to do the job he's called to. It's simply the way of things, although it amazes me that someone who's a life raft for others often finds it hard to keep his own head above water.

'I know. It's a lot.' I sit back, giving Daniel one last look before shifting my focus to the streets rushing past outside.

I used to think it was my calling too – or at least it was my cross to bear – because I committed to this life, whatever it took. Nobody made the choice for me. I often find myself repeating in my head – *God wouldn't have led us to one another, and given us Abbey, if it isn't where I'm meant to be.* But no matter how many times I say it, deep down I know the truth. I didn't do it for God. God was never part of the plan, he was simply part of the package. I opened myself to God because it was what Daniel wanted. I do wonder whether God knows what the bloody hell he's doing though. Not that I'd tell Daniel that. I definitely wouldn't say 'bloody hell'. It doesn't align with our brand.

I am fine; everything is fine. Repeat ad nauseum. I should take Daniel's mood at face value. Like he says to me, not everything has to be a drama. I'm clearly oversensitive because of the whole birthday thing.

'So, what's on the agenda today?' Daniel cuts into my thoughts, oddly upbeat. 'Cooking up anything exciting?' It takes me a moment to recover from the whiplash.

'Um – actually, yes. Apparently, the Mid-Autumn Festival in parts of Southeast Asia falls over the weekend, so some of our

Chinese and Vietnamese students are teaching the class how to make mooncakes.' I laugh at the quizzical look on his face. 'They're little pies filled with lotus paste.'

I've been volunteering at St. Agnes' as a teacher's aide since Abbey graduated. The school was so good for Abbey, especially through Year 9. The bullying had gone on for months and I doubt she'd have gotten through it if they hadn't been so supportive. So one day a week I assist Alice, the home economics teacher. Even as the church grew, I refused to give it up – a commitment is a commitment.

If I'm truthful, I like that the school is separate from Daniel and the church. I love being there for our community. Don't get me wrong, it means the world to me. But my work at the school is something of my own and, if nothing else, I know something about making a home.

'Lotus paste? Sounds delicious.' Daniel grimaces.

'It'll be great.' Then I can't help myself. 'I also heard a rumour there might be special cupcakes for someone . . .' I wait for the penny to drop. It doesn't.

'A class load of teenagers hopped up on sugar. Good luck with that.'

We drive a bit further in silence. I slip back into disappointment and Daniel appears to be deep in thought as traffic slows to a crawl. As the tangle of cars snarls around us, Daniel's mood follows suit. Suddenly he treads the brakes, jerking us forward. He hits the horn, gesturing wildly out of the window.

'Daniel!' I gawp at him as he blows out a shaky breath. He rakes his fingers through his hair as the traffic starts moving.

'Sorry. It's just—'

'Hey, take a breath.' I touch his arm, finally knowing what to do. I have to talk him off the ledge. 'Tonight will be fine. I know there's a lot riding on it – people are watching – but we've got this. Everything's under control.'

'Yes, but—' he keeps his eyes firmly on the road.

'No *buts*. There's a reason we hired Minette – so we could step back from the small stuff.' I keep my voice modulated, approaching him like a skittish horse – *no sudden moves.*

Daniel draws a deep inhale as he slides the car to a stop outside the school.

'Grace—'

'No, let me finish.' I know the drill; I've done it enough times. 'You, my darling, will be amazing.' I wave at a couple of kids walking past, smiling brightly at them before looking earnestly back at Daniel. 'Somehow the right words always come to you – you know exactly what they need to hear. You have to know you were born for this. He speaks through you. He *chose* you. I truly believe that, and I believe in you. I'll be right beside—'

'Grace, stop!' His tone pulls me up sharply. 'I'm not worried about tonight.'

'Oh. You're not?'

'No.'

Now I'm puzzled. 'Then, what's the—'

'Gracie, I need to tell you something.' I sit back, immediately wary. Daniel hardly ever calls me *Gracie*, because he knows how much I hate it. 'I wasn't planning to tell you this morning, I was going to wait until after tonight. I know this is the worst possible timing.' He looks down at his hands as if struggling to find the words. 'But . . .'

I freeze. My first thought is, *this does not sound like a surprise party*. My second thought? *He's sick.* What else could make him so worried about talking to his wife? *Dear God, please don't let it be cancer.*

He looks up at me, a brief pained look crossing his face before he sets his expression to unreadable. 'I want a divorce.'

'What?' I fleetingly think I've misheard him, but what rhymes with 'divorce'? Nothing that makes sense. *Sauce. Force. Horse? He wants a horse?* I don't think he knows how to ride, but okay.

I stare at him as he keeps talking but something weird is going on with my ears because there's this intense rushing coming from inside my head. I only hear snatches of what he's saying . . . something about *motions.* He's asking me a question, *don't you think?* I nod blankly. Should I have nodded? It seems like the thing to do . . . *met someone* . . . oh . . . right. *Sasha* . . . *the choir.* Of course – the TikTok girl . . . *shown the way* . . . the way where? *Leaving.* And then I can't hear anything and there's something stuck in my throat, something big – like a fist. There has to be, because I can't breathe. Why does my chest hurt so much? Am I dying? And why, on God's green earth, can I NOT. STOP. FUCKING. STARING. AT. HIM? *Language, Grace!*

'Gracie?' He touches my hand and I withdraw it reflexively, clinging with both hands to my handbag like an old lady who thinks she's about to be mugged. My eyes sting but I can't blink; I try to swallow. 'Grace, can you please say something?'

I manage to squeeze my eyes shut for a second and clear my throat.

'It's my birthday.'

'What?' His eyes dart in several directions, which would be comical if the situation wasn't so dreadful.

'Today is my birthday.'

'Oh. Uh—' To his credit, Daniel looks panicked for at least three seconds before he coughs, his cheeks flushing. He can't meet my eyes. 'Like I said, I know the timing's not the best.'

I let out a sharp laugh and my hand flies to my mouth. I have no idea how the sound escaped from me. My head is light – like it's filled with pillow stuffing – and my heart is trying to punch its way out from behind my sternum.

'For who?'

'Is that all you're going to say?' Daniel straightens, defensive. We glare at each other across the car, for what seems like an eternity, until a vague calm settles over me.

'What else would you like me to say?' I feel sort of floaty – almost out-of-body – but I'm acutely aware of the air from the car's vents brushing my skin and my hair follicles standing on end. I shiver. This must be what it's like to be on drugs, the kind all the young people take that makes everything amazing even when it's not. I smile and Daniel recoils slightly.

'Are you okay?'

'I'm dandy.' I've never used the word *dandy* in my life. Daniel eyes me, clearly nervous. As he probably should be, to be fair.

'O-kaay.'

'Okay.'

'Grace—' Daniel shifts uncomfortably '—I need to know you're not going to make a scene later, that we're still a team. I know this is difficult but tonight's too important. We've got to be a united front. Our congregation is counting on us. Remember, the greatest gift under God is selflessness.' He touches my knee and I flinch. 'Right.' He pulls his hand back and rubs at his face. 'I thought I should tell you now . . . because I'm not coming home tonight.'

And there it is, in startling clarity.

'When will you be coming home?' The steadiness of my voice astonishes me.

'Can we not talk about this now?' Daniel makes the fatal mistake of looking at his watch and the hairs on the back of my neck prickle.

'I'm sorry, am I keeping you?'

Daniel sighs, as if the entire conversation is a chore, then looks at me with one of those patronisingly paternal '*come now child, don't be silly*' expressions.

'Grace, you know this is a bigger conversation than we can have sitting in the school carpark. We've both got a job to do. I'll see you tonight and we can talk tomorrow. And—' he looks suddenly awkward '—I'll leave it to you to tell Abbey. I don't want her to hate me and you're so good at explaining difficult situations.'

Typical of Daniel to drop the bomb and expect me to clean up the rubble. I've always done it – why would he expect any different now? He knows this will devastate her. But if it comes from me, I'll bear the brunt of it.

I glare at him for an uncomfortable beat then gather my bag and get out of the car. Despite wanting to lash out, I close the door deliberately. I'm not giving him the satisfaction of slamming it. Stalking towards the gate, I hear the buzz of the window sliding down behind me. I spin around, pre-empting him.

'I'll handle Abbey. Your *Father of the Year* trophy won't be tarnished. And don't worry about tonight – I don't want a scene any more than you do.' I lift my chin and give him a tight smile. 'Like you said, we have a congregation to think of. It's bigger than you and me.'

Daniel exhales visibly. 'Okay, good,' he says, giving me a tentative smile. 'See, selfless. Still the dream team, huh.' He holds my gaze for a moment, a funny look on his face. I can't tell if it's concern, regret, or something else. But it's enough that I soften slightly, for just a second. 'God always has a plan, Grace. You've just got to have a little faith.' Then he ruins it. He slaps his hand on the car door several times like it's a horse, deftly pushes his sunglasses back on and starts to pull away, his elbow hanging out of the window. At the last second, he brakes and sticks his head back out. 'I forgot. My suit. It's—'

'Under control,' I snap. Then I turn and march through the gate without looking back – a single thought running through my head.

God can shove his plan right up his arse.

3

burn it down

The fire doesn't take long to extinguish but it's enough to blacken the wall in the home economics kitchen, set off the sprinkler system and send an entire class of screaming teenaged girls stampeding into the quad. Twenty minutes later, I'm pacing in front of the principal's desk, chewing my thumbnail and rapidly changing direction.

'I don't know, Andrew.' I'm completely soaked, a wet tea towel wrapping my hand. Hair is plastered to my face and neck and I'm not sure how much of my eyebrows are left. 'It all happened so quickly.'

Andrew looks as though he's watching an intense tennis match.

'Grace,' he says, as he steeples his fingers under his chin and swivels in his seat. 'Can you stop pacing? You're making me seasick.' I sit, tensed like a schoolgirl about to get a detention. 'Thank you. Now take a breath and try to calm down. Everything's okay. All the girls are fine and as far as I can tell, it's minor damage. We're insured, of course.' He peers at me over his glasses. 'Right now, I'm more worried about you.'

I close my eyes and breathe slowly and deliberately, my shoulders creeping away from my ears. 'I'm *so* sorry. One minute I was heating the custard and the next minute everything was on fire.' I blink rapidly at the memory. 'I honestly don't know what happened.'

I'm lying. I know exactly what happened. I was standing by one of the cooktops, where I was supposed to be keeping my eye on a pan for one of the Year 10 girls. My head had felt tight, like it was circled with an elastic band. Jammed full of Daniel and Sasha. Imagining what she looked like – I mean, it's not like I'd had time to check her socials. She had to be pretty. She was all of what, twenty-something? *Please, God, if she's pretty, at least let her be stupid or a bitch. Don't let her be perfect.* Anything but that.

Then the pan was on fire. I'd stared at it as the flames got bigger until one of the girls nearby screeched. I'd jolted and immediately done exactly what you're not supposed to do – flap a tea towel at it. The pan combusted, flames climbing in seconds above the range hood and catching the tea towel alight. I'd launched it away from me in alarm – and it landed on the open rubbish bin, naturally full of discarded packaging.

In mounting horror, I'd gawked as the girls screamed and ran in all directions like excited mice, until Alice herded them towards the door. The sprinklers came on and I'd stood there – ignoring Alice's frantic shouts – as the flames diminished, with the sense I was getting smaller myself, until they finally went out.

'You don't seem yourself.' Andrew studies me carefully. 'Are you alright?'

I don't know how to answer that. How can I possibly seem like myself? 'Grace Miller' is on precarious ground. I don't know who I am without Daniel, the church, my family.

'No,' I say. 'I'm really not alright.'

'What's going on, Grace?' I stare at him for a long moment, trembling and on the verge of cracking open to spill my guts all over the desk. My mouth tightens.

'Just some unexpected stress at home.' I'm not exactly lying, but it's not the truth either. I'm not ready for it to be real, that's what it is. If I don't talk about it, maybe it'll all go away.

'Is Abbey okay?' There's genuine concern in Andrew's voice.

'Abbey's fine.' I can see his mind working overtime, trying to figure out what to do with me. The familiar urge to placate rises. 'Honestly, Andrew. It'll be fine, it always is.' I attempt a bright smile but my face refuses to cooperate.

'Go home.' He says it bluntly, but kindly. 'Take some time to sort out whatever's going on.'

'I really don't need—'

'It's not a suggestion, Grace. You've clearly got a lot going on at the moment. I'd like you to go home and rest.'

'Okay.'

'In fact,' Andrew clears his throat, 'take all the time you need. I wasn't planning on letting you know like this – and I realise this probably isn't the best timing, but—'

I stiffen. Why do people keep saying that? As if it makes the awful thing they're about to say any better. 'If it's bad timing, how about you don't tell me. Maybe wait until it's good timing. Or you know – never.' I try to turn it into a joke but I've never been more serious. 'Never would be better.'

Andrew's expression pushes me close to breaking. *Come now, child, don't be silly.* I want to poke him in the eye. I'm sure he doesn't mean to be condescending, he's never been anything but kind to me, but molten lava is pooling at the base of my spine. I push it down.

'It's only a couple of months until the end of the school year.' He straightens his glasses, not relishing the conversation. 'We can manage without you until then. But we've been in consultation with the Education Department for a while about the school's direction. Unfortunately, the decision's been made to remove home economics from the curriculum, starting in the new term. Alice, of course, will be staying on with us to teach English, but—'

'Oh . . . right.' I should have questions, but my mind is blank. He could be forgiven for thinking I'm stunned, but nope – no discernible feelings whatsoever. The whole day has been surreal and it's barely 11 am.

'I'm so sorry, Grace. There was a lot of discussion about the skills our young ladies need when they leave us – in the current climate. Home economics doesn't have the relevancy it used to. I'm sure you understand.'

Irrelevant. I know what it means.

'It's fine. Thanks for letting me know, Andrew.' My voice seems to be coming from across the room – calm, robotic. 'It's disappointing, but what can you do?'

Andrew reaches across the desk and pats my hand. I fold my fingers into a fist to avoid flinching. 'Look at it like a holiday, time to spend with the family.' He sits back. 'Maybe we can talk in the new year about other ways you can be involved with the school; we don't want to lose you. You've been such an asset.'

'I'd like that.'

'Okay then.'

'Okay.' I stand and tuck my hair behind my ears in an attempt to pull myself together. 'Thank you, Andrew. For everything. I'll, uh—' I gesture to the door.

'Make sure you get some dressing on that hand.'

'It's fine, only a little singed.'

'Take care.' He smiles and nods. I'm dismissed. 'Oh, and Grace—'

I turn, my hand on the doorknob.

'Yes?'

'Happy Birthday.'

I walk down Edgecliff Road in a daze, carrying a box packed with the few odd belongings I'd kept at the school. A framed photo of me and Abbey, a stack of old CDs, and a large silver crucifix set into a marble base that someone had gifted us years ago. It's heavy and ugly. I don't know why I want to keep it.

Daniel's suit – I'd picked it up yesterday – dangles from the box on its hanger. I'd thought about leaving it at the school but couldn't bring myself to be that petty. *You have heard it said, eye for eye and tooth for tooth. But if anyone slaps you on the right cheek, turn to them the other cheek also – Matthew 5:38*. A voice in my head whispers that the fleeting thrill of pettiness would be better than being a complete sucker.

I don't know how I lost control of the day with such ferocity. 'I'm fine. It's fine. This is totally fine.' I've been muttering the mantra since I decided to walk all the way home to stop myself spiralling. It's not long before my arms are aching, so it's with relief that I spot a bus stop a hundred metres ahead, near a small park. I cover the remaining ground rapidly and offload my cargo, rubbing my arms as I collapse onto the bench seat.

I can't even cry. There must be something wrong with me. In the space of a few hours, I've been rendered useless. No more husband, no more school. I have no idea what's going to happen with the church. I have no purpose. I should be bereft, inconsolable. But all I can do is stare at the ground in front of me like some kind of gormless twit.

The squeal of heavy-duty brakes shatters my trance and I look up. It takes me a moment to recognise our faces – ten feet tall, all shining eyes and teeth – staring back at me from the side of the bus idling at the kerb. *'Reach for the stars, because Heaven holds no limits . . . Welcome to the Fold'* is emblazoned down the side of the vehicle and I blink. Am I still in the fold? Do I have to leave the fold now? But it's my fold, I helped build it. *Fold. Fold. Fold.* What a stupid word. *Stars Fold*. It sounds like a cult.

Our giant faces look too airbrushed. The tiny holes in the vinyl wrap pixelate the pupils of our eyes. I decide that Daniel looks untrustworthy, definitely not the kind of man you'd want guiding your everlasting soul. Had he always looked so smug?

Anger flares through me like a lightning strike and, before I know what I'm doing, I'm on my feet, wrenching the crucifix out of the box with both hands. With an almighty yell, I swing it over my head, aiming right between Daniel's untrustworthy and pixelated eyes. The base bounces off the bus with a clang. Using the symbol of our Lord and Saviour's death to deface a council bus is probably sacrilegious, but considering the circumstances, I'm sure I have argument enough to reframe it as the sword of the righteous. I vaguely register the pneumatic hiss of the doors opening as I ready myself to swing again.

'Hey, lady! What do you think you're doing?' The bus driver, who doesn't look old enough to be out of school let alone driving a bus, glares at me. He's wearing the faintly ridiculous bus driver uniform of Bermuda shorts, a short-sleeved shirt and knee-high socks – but he's clearly more put out by having to deal with an unhinged, middle-aged woman when it's probably time for his tea break. 'This bus is council property.'

I glance at him, my attack thwarted – even I know it's not good to have an audience when you're committing vandalism – but the rage has to go somewhere. I let out one final screech as I turn and hurl the crucifix into the park. It pinwheels through the air and lands in a prickle bush, hanging lop-sided like a psychotic Christmas tree ornament.

'Whoa!' The driver recoils, staring at me like I'm a wild animal that might charge if he moves too quickly. Then he looks at the side of the bus and back at me. 'Far out, it's you. I mean, you're her.'

Great.

'I—uh—yes, that's me.' I put my hand on my heart. 'I'm *so* sorry.' I scramble for an explanation. 'I don't really like that picture of me.' *What? I sound deranged.*

He stares at me, uncertain. Clearly, they don't cover this kind of thing in bus driver training. He settles for a terse, 'Right then . . . well, don't do it again,' before retreating into the bus. He pops his head back out. 'Have a nice day.'

'You too, young man. And God bless.' *Shut up, Grace.*

The door hisses closed and the bus rumbles away, leaving me standing in a cloud of exhaust. Stunned by my behaviour, I turn back to the bus stop. The box and the suit taunt me from the bench. I don't want to look at them for another second. Calmly, I gather them up and heave them into the road. The picture frame shatters on the tarmac and several CDs jettison from their cases, rolling into the gutter as a truck hurtles past, the driver leaning heavily on the horn as he runs over Daniel's suit and flattens the box. *I guess that's that then.*

I consider leaving it all there. What does it matter? But I change my mind and wait for a gap in the traffic before darting to retrieve the picture of me and Abbey. Forlorn and dishevelled, I slump back on the bench clutching the photograph. *What now?* I reach into my handbag for my phone. I have no idea who to call but know I don't want an Uber. I can't go back to the house alone – not yet – and I don't know where else to go.

Should I call Daniel and tell him what happened? No, I'm not calling Daniel. I tell myself I'm not calling him because I know how much is riding on tonight and I don't want to bother him. Ever the dutiful wife. But truthfully, I'm not calling him because I'm scared he won't answer. I stare fixedly at my phone and jump when the screen illuminates. *Abbey*. I hold my breath and let it ring out. I'm not ready to tell her. I'm not in the right state of mind. I just attacked a bus with a crucifix like something out of *The Exorcist*. My ability to converse in a rational manner with my child about the demise of my marriage can't be trusted.

If I can't call Daniel—

I try Lucinda, twice. No answer. Glenda. No answer either. Tara's number goes straight to message. *Strange*. Where is everybody? Foreboding skitters up the back of my neck. What if they already know? Am I the pariah already? Surely not after everything I've done for them. I've always been there for every one of them and none of this is my fault. Shouldn't they be on my side?

I scroll through my contacts, anxiety clutching at me, until I land on a number. *Susie*. No. I can't do it. I put my phone face down on the bench.

Susie. It's been years. Too many. Will she want to speak to me? I have no idea. I simply know she's the only friend I have – if I can still call her that – who knows what it's like to be discarded and alone.

I pick up my phone, hesitating before hitting her name. My heart punches into my throat when she answers. She sounds the same and instantly I'm back there. Tears threaten and I squash them down so I can speak. 'It's me.' My voice thickens. 'I need you.'

A long, deep breath on the other end of the line.

'Tell me where you are. I'm coming.'

4

an eye for an eye

Susie drives an old VH Holden Commodore, but I don't notice her car at first. My attention is held by a scrappy dog that has dragged Daniel's suit into the gutter and is humping it enthusiastically. It seems a fitting end to the garment and I'm laughing hysterically as she pulls up. Susie winds the window down, taking in the dog, the suit, the carnage on the road, and me.

She whistles, impressed. 'Grace Emilia Miller, I don't know what the fuck is going on but if you keep sitting there laughing like a bloody hyena, you're going to get hauled off to the nuthouse. Get in the fucking car before I change my mind.'

I sober instantly and we lock eyes across the footpath – across the years – both wary. Tension crackles in the air as we study each other, looking for signs of difference. Signs we're still the same. She's blonder than I remember, her hair shorter. Her face is harder, but that's not a surprise. She's still Susie though, it's evident in the way she talks and in the way she takes a drag of her cigarette, blowing the smoke out while she looks me up and down. 'You look like shit.'

'Nice to see you too, Susie.'

An eyebrow lifts and her eyes are daggers. 'You want me to lie to you?' And there it is. First shot fired. *I can't do this.*

'This was a mistake.' I shove the photo of me and Abbey into my bag, on the verge of walking away.

'I'm kidding. Bloody hell, Grace, where's your sense of humour?'

'That wasn't funny. Not today.'

Her face softens. 'Okay. Not today.' Then the sympathy is gone. She takes a quick drag of her smoke. 'Get in the car, dickhead.'

I do as I'm told. The passenger door sticks, wrenching open with a metallic groan. Empty drink cans crowd the foot well and a pile of laundry camps where I'm supposed to sit. Susie leans over. 'Chuck all that in the back.' I sink into the front seat like a puddle. I've been hanging by a thread for hours and it's unravelling at speed. I'm not sure I can hold on. Susie covers my hand with hers. 'Where are we going?'

'I don't care. As long as there's alcohol and I won't see anybody I know.'

Susie revs the engine. 'I know the perfect place.'

The public bar at The Queen's Arms Hotel in Newtown is packed before lunchtime on a Tuesday, and that should tell you all you need to know. Perched on a corner, two streets back from the trendy main thoroughfare, it has so far managed to dodge the gentrification bullets that have hit other pockets of the suburb fatally in the chest.

Peeling layers of faded posters line the walls outside, touting gigs by bands with obscene names who have long since grown up and gotten soul-destroying jobs. Inside, it's clear the last time it saw a refurbishment was around 1985 and the same goes for the people lining the bar. The air hangs heavy with the musk of beer-soaked carpet mingled with hot chips and stale cigarettes. Unsurprisingly, the floor is sticky underfoot. The sound of Hunters and Collectors' 'Everything is on Fire' pumping valiantly from tinny speakers does little to drown out the jangle of the pokies from next door.

It's the antithesis of Vaucluse, and I'm strangely comforted by the fact. It reminds me of my first years at university, before I met Daniel – when I was a different person. A person I'd thought I wanted to run away from. I haven't thought about her in years.

'This is . . . nice.'

'You said somewhere you wouldn't see anyone. I figured your fancy friends wouldn't be caught dead in Newie, so . . .' She sweeps an arm.

'I wasn't complaining.'

'You didn't have to. Your face has subtitles.' She's still eyeing me, all hackles and uncertainty, and I can't blame her. 'What'll you have? My shout.'

'Oh, gosh. I don't even know anymore. I'm not really a drinker these days.'

Her brow furrows. 'You said you wanted alcohol.'

'It seemed like the thing to say.'

'And did you say "gosh"?' When I nod, she mutters *fucking hell* under her breath. 'Why don't I surprise you while you go to the bathroom and clean yourself up, you've got a little—' She gestures in the direction of my head '—I don't know what. Then you can fill me in on whatever the fuck it is Daniel's done.'

I flinch. 'How did you know?' Susie's look says *are you kidding?* and I feel stupid. It irritates me more than it should. I turn away, then turn back. 'I'll have a gin martini, thanks. Dirty, three olives.'

Susie smirks. 'Of course you will.'

The bathroom is pokey with black walls and exposed pipes. I glance in the mirror above the sink and immediately wish I hadn't.

A sooty mark from the fire mars one cheek, matching my smudged mascara, and a clump of hair sticks up from the top of my head. My burned hand throbs painfully. I run the cold tap and hold it under the water, resting my forehead on the glass before rummaging through my bag for a hairbrush, face wipes and lipstick.

Five minutes later, I steel myself and emerge from the bathroom. My smile is plastered on like armour but it doesn't protect me from the knot in my stomach. 'There.' I sit opposite Susie. 'That's better.' I sip at the waiting martini to delay the onset of conversation, trying not to grimace as it burns my throat. 'Mmm, yummy.'

The discomfort between us is so palpable it might as well be a third person. Susie glances at me in between staring out of the window, tapping her fingers on the table, and flipping her cigarette packet over and over. I study every corner of the room to avoid looking at her and manage to finish my drink in a few minutes flat. Another round arrives. 'I told the bar girl to keep them coming,' Susie says. 'I'm pretty sure we're gonna need them.'

I don't answer, instead taking a big mouthful of the second drink. Susie watches me, nonplussed.

'So, how are you?' I ask finally.

'Fuck no, we're not doing that.'

Another stab of annoyance. 'I forgot how much you swear.'

'I forgot how big a pole you have up your arse.'

'Are we really going to do this?'

'I don't know, Grace,' Susie says. 'I don't know what we're doing. You call me out of the blue after fifteen years – after that entire shitshow – saying you need me. Now you want to do pleasantries?'

'I guess not.'

Susie puts her elbows on the table. 'How about I save us some time. Life is fine as far as life goes. No kids. Never really part of the plan, but a little bout of cervical cancer stuffed that up for good anyway. Divorced Andy, he was a piece of shit. But you knew that, considering. Got off the gear when it started ruining my teeth, been clean ever since. Married Mick, that was alright for a while but he decided he liked the horses more than me – except when he was pissed. Husband number three now. Rob's a good bloke, got his life together, so we'll see.'

I reach out to touch her hand. 'I'm so—'

She withdraws it sharply. 'Bit late to feel sorry for me now. Life is fine, like I said.'

'Susie.'

'I've gone back to school. Bet you never thought you'd see that.'

I prickle. 'To be honest, I never thought I'd see you again full stop.'

'Touché.'

It's clear she doesn't want to get deep, which is fine. My insides are already on the verge of being my outsides without the added trauma of reopening old wounds. I down the rest of the second martini, a light buzz creeping up behind my ears.

'You're not hairdressing anymore?'

'Nah, gave that away years ago. Been doing some "spiritual development".' She makes air quotes and I raise an eyebrow. 'Not your kind of spiritual. Fuck that. I'm studying to be a life coach. Turns out I have a decent brain and it's not like I haven't been through enough shit.' She grins at me unexpectedly. 'If I can sort *my* life out, I reckon I can help anyone.'

Sort your life out. The phrase echoes across the years. 'Even me?'

She eyes me for a second then sits back, finishing off her drink and signalling the bar. 'I don't know. From where I'm sitting, it looks like everything turned out the way you wanted it.'

'The morning I've had would seem to demonstrate otherwise.'

Susie laughs. 'Listen to you. You can't just say, *my life has turned to shit.* You used to swear as much as I do before you got all rich and Christian. That's the Grace I remember.'

'I haven't been that Grace for a long time.'

'I know that,' she snorts. 'But you know what they say, you can take the girl out of Mount Druitt but you can't take Mount Druitt out of the girl.'

'I'm beginning to think that's part of the problem,' I say, half to myself and half to her.

When she asks how Mum and Liz are doing, I brush it off with a brief, 'Fine, same old.' I don't have the bandwidth to get into that. When I look up, she's staring at me with a funny look on her face. It passes like a shadow and she clears her throat.

'Are you gonna tell me what happened so I can break the arsehole's kneecaps?'

This time I can't help but smile back.

Susie's not surprised by my husband's revelation. She doesn't even bat an eyelid, as if it's expected and only surprising it didn't happen sooner. I go off on tangent after incoherent tangent: the fact I'm old and irrelevant; how much I miss Abbey; mine and Daniel's non-existent sex life; the pressures of the church.

Some of it I don't realise bothers me until it comes out of my mouth. Susie doesn't interject; she keeps signalling for drinks and lets me talk. Except when I tell her how long it's been since Daniel and I had sex. She doesn't connect the dots – *why would she?* – but exclaims loudly, 'Bloody hell. It's probably closed up by now.' I still don't cry. Finally, I tell her I didn't see it coming because I'd convinced myself nothing could go wrong if I was the perfect wife. Susie shakes her head.

'You realise it's never been about you?' She says it as if explaining something to a child and it's clear I've been either wilfully blind or stupid. Possibly both.

I blink at her like an owl. I'm quite drunk and regretting not getting some hot chips. 'I didn't think you'd come, you know.'

'When?'

'When I called. I was sure you'd hang up on me.'

'You still called.'

I nod. 'It was always going to be you in the end.'

'Mate, we could not see each other again for another twenty years and, if you called me to say you'd murdered somebody and needed help burying the body, I'd be there in a heartbeat.'

'Morbid, but good to know.'

'Morbid or not, I've got you.'

'Even though—'

'Even though.' She doesn't let me finish and the tears finally arrive.

'Suse, you know I never wanted to—'

'Yes, you did.' She smiles but it doesn't reach her eyes. 'But that was a long time ago and I might not have stopped using if you hadn't. I guess you did me a favour.' I sniffle and she makes a *pssht* sound. 'We're not doing the crying thing. Give it a rest. We'll talk about it eventually, but not now. You're drunk, I'm drunk; you've had a shitty day.'

She's right. My head swims but it's not unpleasant. Everything's numb, like I have a protective bubble around me. The pain of this morning is still there, stabbing at me and trying to slice through to my insides, but its blade is dulled and glances right off.

'You know what it is?' I slur slightly. 'It's a travesty.'

'Which part?'

'All the parts. Every parts.'

'Okay.' Susie seems to be finding my inebriation amusing.

'Actually, no. It's more than that. It's a . . . *fucking* travesty.'

'There she is.'

'It's true. And Daniel is an absolute cu—'

'Okay,' Susie cuts me off. 'Don't hurt yourself.'

'How could he do this?' I blink back tears again. The martinis obviously aren't working because the pain is suddenly more stabby. 'What am I going to do?'

'I wish I had the answer for you, babe,' she says. 'All I know is, when push comes to shove, the only way to get over someone is to get under someone else.'

'Where'd you learn that? Life coach school?'

Susie shrugs, as if the advice is indisputable. 'Think of it as a circuit breaker. And let's face it, a good old revenge fuck never goes astray when your hubby's a cheater.'

In this moment – this shining martini-drenched moment – it all makes sense. I turn and peruse the room, much to Susie's horror.

'Shit, Grace. I don't mean today. I'm not sure *now,* when you're upset and drunk, is the right time.' She glances around, perturbed. 'And bloody well not here.'

She's probably right. Clearly the motley crew assembled at the bar provides slim pickings for a revenge fu— sexual encounter. But I don't care. Call it hurt, call it anger, call it righteousness or plain drunk stupidity – I'm a woman on a mission.

If Daniel can have sex with someone else, so can I.

His name is Gerry and he looks more like a sad spaniel than a silver fox. I don't say that to be critical, only to point out that he wouldn't be my first choice if I wasn't six martinis in and knee-deep in emotional trauma.

He isn't unattractive. He has a nice smile and eyes the colour of denim that's been through the wash too many times. In fact, everything about him looks like it's been through the wash too many times. He's kind of rumpled. But the most important thing about Gerry is that when I approached him and said, 'Excuse me, sorry to bother you, but my husband left me this morning and it's pretty awful. I'd like to take you home to make myself feel better. Is that okay?' He said yes.

Susie was less than happy about it, so I told her loudly and in no uncertain terms that she might be my friend but I'm a grown woman and if I want to have a revenge fuck with a middle-aged stranger, I will bloody well have a revenge fuck with a middle-aged stranger. Everyone in the bar cheered and she threw her hands up saying, 'Fine, you're a big girl. Don't blame me once you're sober.'

Gerry tries to hold my hand in the Uber and it's weird, so I pretend to look for something in my handbag. Then I feel bad. I attempt small talk so he knows I'm at least making an effort to get to know him as a person and not seeing him as a piece of meat.

'What do you do, Gerry?' I try to focus my eyes on him but the driver is driving quite fast and my equilibrium is having trouble keeping pace around the bends.

'I'm in traffic control,' he says.

'How interesting.'

A long pause. 'What about you, Tracey?'

I don't bother correcting him; I'm just glad he doesn't recognise me. Mostly because I've already decided I'm going to do very bad things to him. I lie and tell him I'm in veterinary sales. When we get to the house, I put Dexter outside as Gerry turns in circles in the foyer. He whistles and says, 'Wow, veterinary sales must be lucrative.'

'It's a growth industry,' I reply, looking at the clock. Honestly, what kind of person has drunk sex at four o'clock in the afternoon? I hunt around in the dining room because I'm sure there's a bottle of red tucked away somewhere that somebody brought to our last dinner party. When I find it, I drink two glasses in quick succession before Gerry has finished his one.

Then we're in the kitchen and Gerry is kissing me. He is all teeth and hands and wet lips but he tells me I'm beautiful, which is quite nice, so I kiss him back. He tastes sour, but I still let him put his hands up my shirt. The transition from there to both being in our underwear is a blur but mostly involves my t-shirt getting stuck on my earring and Gerry headbutting my nose before our clothes end up on the kitchen floor.

Gerry backs me up against the counter and awkwardly clambers to his knees. It takes me a moment to realise what he's planning on doing and instantly my palm slaps to his forehead. Daniel doesn't even do that to me. 'You really don't need to—'

'Oh. Okay.' Gerry looks confused and gets back up again.

'We can just . . . I mean, I want you to, uh—' *Say it, Grace, come on, you can do it!* '—fuck me.' All the sound drops out of the room. I swear I hear crickets. 'Please.'

'Right then,' he says, and we stare at each other awkwardly before he adds, 'I think I'm going to need a bit of help.' My eyes widen in alarm.

'With?'

He looks down at his crotch and back up at me. 'You know. Just a little bit.'

The kitchen tiles are cold and hurt my knees, but comfortability for fellatio isn't generally a consideration when remodelling a kitchen. My head spins and I grip the front of Gerry's thighs for balance. His legs are unexpectedly hairy but I try to focus on the task at hand instead of wondering why men can be as hirsute as they like but we're expected to get all of ours ripped out at the follicle like some kind of punishment for being a woman.

Gerry is wearing green underpants with MONDAY written on the waistband. Maybe I should tell him it's Tuesday. I look up and he's staring expectantly at me so I decide to put a pin in it. *Okay, Grace. Time to do bad things to Gerry.*

His crotch is bulging. I know that sounds like one of those ridiculous erotic novels, but it is. Intimidatingly so. I don't think Gerry was being honest when he said he needed help. My fingers hook into his waistband and I lean back. Nobody wants to be poked in the eye with an erect penis. Pulling down on the elastic, I release him. And there it is. Ready. Needing literally no help at all.

Liar.

I wrap my left hand around him and three things happen at once. Gerry moans. It occurs to me that my mouth is dry. And the sun shining through the window glints off my wedding ring. I freeze. What am I doing? I'm married. And I love my husband.

Daniel.

What if he changes his mind? What if he realises he's made a mistake, rushes home and walks in to find me on my knees in the kitchen with a rumpled stranger's penis in my hand? The horrific thought cuts through the alcohol haze in an instant. 'I can't do this.'

'What?' Gerry's entire body slackens.

'I can't do this,' I repeat, as I let go of him and scramble up.

'Oh.' He's like a puppy that's been kicked. 'Why not?' We face each other and suddenly I'm cold. And far too drunk.

'This isn't me,' I say. 'I'm upset and confused, and I wanted to get back at my husband. I mean, you're lovely. If this was any other time, I'm sure . . . it's just, I don't think this will make me feel better.'

Gerry tucks himself back into his underpants, which I appreciate. 'I understand. My wife left me for my brother last year and it took me a while to get back on the horse.'

The minute it takes for us to dress is interminable. I walk him to the front door.

'It was nice to meet you, Tracey.' he says.

'You too, *Gary*, thank you so much for your time. I really appreciate it.'

I sag against the closed door. I can't believe I nearly had sex with a stranger. I must be out of my mind. I'm beginning to wonder if today is even real or if I'm trapped in some kind of upside-down nightmare. A wave of nausea hits me like a train and I double over, vomiting into the peace lily that sits by the door. It's not pretty and I want to wake up before things get worse. Although I can't imagine how they could.

I hear my phone ring – Miley Cyrus's 'The Climb'. I lurch to the kitchen and rummage in my handbag, trying not to wretch. It's Daniel.

'Hi—' I try to sound normal but my heart is hammering and I can't see straight. Gerry's aftershave still lingers sickeningly on my skin.

'Where are you?' Daniel snaps. 'You were supposed to be here half an hour ago.'

FUCK.

5

look what you made me do

It's after six by the time the Uber drops me off. I race towards the side entrance, holding my shoes and dodging latecomers and rows of feather banners emblazoned with our logo. I'm not sure what I'm doing here apart from to pretend everything's normal, because heaven forbid anyone thinks we – *Daniel* – might have made a misstep.

Obviously, I don't have Daniel's suit. It has probably had puppies by now. I'd grabbed an old suit from his wardrobe. He's going to be furious, and I don't know why I care. I'm the one who should be angry, but all I can think is *I can still fix this.* My anxiety is skyrocketing, despite the two valium I popped in the Uber to try to centre myself.

I spot Minette pacing by the door, speaking frantically into her headset. Built like a bird, her energy levels carry a surprising punch and she's the most organised person I've ever met. I stop and slip my shoes on and make an attempt at smoothing out my hair, trying not to dwell on the fact that not only am I still drunk, but my dress isn't properly done up because I can't reach the zipper. I walk towards her in what I hope is a calm and controlled manner but is really me trying to focus enough to walk straight.

'Mrs Miller, there you are!' Minette launches at me with a lanyard and venue pass. She recoils, probably from alcohol fumes, and eyes me curiously. 'I was getting worried. Mr Miller said he didn't know where you were, we didn't have his suit and—'

'I'm sorry, Minette.' I try to sound officious, but my voice comes out too high. 'I was unavoidably detained, couldn't be helped. Had to see a man about a—' *Penis!* '—dog.'

She gives me a funny look, starts to say something, then thinks better of it. *Excellent choice, Minette.* Instead, she marches me across the foyer and up a set of escalators towards a side door, deftly manoeuvring me between stragglers buying *I Love Jesus* t-shirts from the merch stand and a group of teenagers holding hands in an impromptu praise session. Loud synth-pop pumps from inside the arena and I hear the crowd starting to chant. This is not good. 'Anyway, here's the suit.' I offload it into her arms and she juggles it with her clipboard, frowning.

'This isn't—'

'I'm aware it's not the one we planned,' I interrupt, 'but Daniel likes this one. Couldn't be helped, like I said.'

Minette yanks her lanyard from her neck and swipes her pass at the card reader. 'That's fine, Mrs Miller. It's too late anyway, he's about to go on.'

'Shit.' I clock Minette's startled look. 'I mean, *oh dear.* How about you just get me to the stage. I'll handle Daniel.'

Efficient as ever, Minette guides me down multiple corridors as she barks instructions into her headset. I never would have found my way alone. We turn left and then right until I'm dizzy. I register people calling my name, shouting *Praise be!* but the faces are a blur. I ask Minette about catering for the speakers, so I appear coherent, but the pounding in my temples drowns out her reply.

Nausea sweeps over me and I break out in a sweat as my head fills with replays of Daniel in the car, the fire at the school, and me on my knees in the kitchen. *Pull yourself together*. I grab Minette's arm, taking a deep breath and leaning against the wall.

'Are you okay, Mrs Miller?'

I nod, squeezing my eyes shut. 'A bit unfit, Minette, I'll be fine in a minute.' My lips feel all floppy and I have the vague sense I said that the wrong way around. 'Minute. Min-otte. I'll be fine in a minuit.'

'You don't seem well.'

I open my eyes to find her staring at me in alarm. She also has two heads. 'I possibly have food poisoning, my Mini-Minutia.' I snort and drop my head back. *Her name is so funny.*

'I feel like you shouldn't be here,' she says, worriedly. When I don't respond, she pats my hand. 'Mrs Miller? *Grace*?'

I straighten to the sound of the crowd cheering. 'And miss this spectacle?'

She doesn't know what to say to that. Instead, she leads me across the corridor and into the side-of-stage area, fetching a stool for me. 'I'm going to get you some water. Don't go anywhere.'

I'm not sure where she thinks I'll go because, at this point, I don't know where my legs have gone. I won't get far without them. I register Daniel's amplified voice, calm and confident, ringing out around the arena. The crowd lulls and I'm drawn to the edge of the curtain.

The stage is dark, save for a spotlight on Daniel. He's standing on a dais, arms outstretched like the Messiah. The band clusters upstage left and I can make out a group of people taking their places upstage right. A throng of photographers huddle between the TV cameras that stand like sentries either side of the stage. The rigging overhead is festooned with lights, glittering like stars over the crowd – thousands of enthralled people holding up their phones.

'—and so, we have been commanded to go into the world and preach the gospel. We have been called by our Father to bring others to Christ—' Daniel turns his head and sees me. We lock eyes. I smile encouragingly and he pauses, his face hardening before he turns away, his charismatic smile directed back to the worshipping crowd, the cameras. '—and we ask for your strength, Lord, to lift us up so we can take the word of God—' The darkened stage closes in on me.

The first time I saw Daniel speak, I was nineteen and a year into university. Dad had stopped drinking by then but regardless, I'd taken the first opportunity I could to get out of that house. I'd moved into a dorm and thrown myself headlong into my Visual Arts degree, committed to setting the art world ablaze. Daniel was completing a Masters in Theology at another college nearby, convinced he knew what the world needed to heal and that he was the person to provide it.

We had nothing in common on paper – I thought myself progressive; Daniel definitely skewed conservative – but there was an undeniable attraction. We hadn't been seeing each other long but I was so smitten that my studies were suffering. Night after night, we'd talk into the small hours. Despite our differences, he made me feel safe, always knew the right thing to say. It was easy to reveal my soft innards, offer up my wounds.

Witnessing my parents' marriage had made me cynical, but Daniel was attentive and caring. His own parents had been anything but. He'd lost them in a car accident at seventeen, leaving him with a sizeable inheritance, including our house in Vaucluse and enough money to kickstart whatever he wanted to do with his life.

Daniel was determined to be different to his parents, to find *the one*. He mixed the Kool Aid and I drank it without a second thought.

About to deliver his first sermon, I knew Daniel was suffering terrible stage fright. But when I arrived to support him, he was cold and uninterested – naturally I assumed I'd done something wrong. Things came to a head minutes before he went on. He said he didn't think things were going to work. We were too different, wanted different things.

I hadn't understood. All I wanted was him and, if my first real relationship was going to fall apart after only weeks, what good was I? I talked until he had no choice but be convinced that we were meant to be. Eventually he relented, told me he was sorry, that he was broken and trying to be better. He'd said he knew that I *saw* him. That he loved me. Needed me.

When he kissed me before walking to the pulpit, I knew I'd done it. *I* had fixed things. He wanted *me*. I watched him take that audience in his hands and make believers of them. They weren't the only ones. He'd made a believer of me too. I walked right into it.

I blink and am back in the now.

'—music gives us new ways to express ourselves to God. New ways to feel the power of our Lord move through us, *connect* us . . .' Daniel strides to the front of the stage, encouraging people to clap as the lights rise and the drummer stamps out a beat. 'Please welcome, the Stars Fold Ministry Gospel Choir!'

The lights flash with such intensity that I stumble backwards. By the time I steady myself, the stage is alive with people and the crowd has pressed forward, arms high, a sea of shining faces raised in rapture. This is anything but a church service. It's as slick and high energy as any pop concert. Even I'm impressed, and it's not my first rodeo.

Then I see her. *It has to be her.* A young woman emerges from the choir to take her solo, like Venus from that clam shell. Cameras flash like strobe lights, partially blinding me. But I can't escape her – she's projected on the giant screen at the back of the stage, standing out from the rest like a diamond among coal, petite with long, dark hair and the flattest stomach I've ever seen. Sasha Mason is flawless and overflowing with the kind of sparkling energy I don't remember ever having. I don't know which I hate more – her or the look on my husband's face.

Daniel is enraptured. He has stepped to the side of the stage, but he can't take his eyes off her. I don't exist. He hasn't looked at me like that for decades.

The lights and music are making me sick. Minette looks at me from across the stage before speaking rapidly into her headset and disappearing. The song finishes and Daniel takes the dais again and he can't help himself. He calls Sasha out, rhapsodising over her – *a God-given gift* – making her bow again, clapping his hands raw. He glances towards me then away just as quickly, guilt shadowing his face before the plastered smile is back.

He might as well have slapped me. Two choir members whisper as they move offstage, and I swear they're pointing at me. Someone behind me laughs but when I turn, they've stopped. Maybe I'm imagining it. My head hurts.

How can he appear so together when our life is crumbling? When he's taken a sledgehammer to it. *I know how.* Daniel is a good actor; he always has been. Over the years I've watched him say and do whatever he has to in order to get what he needs: at home, in business, to get his point across in sermons. I didn't think it would ever be at my expense. He starts speaking again but it's hard to follow the thread. I'm splintered but my edges are numb.

As I try to make sense of what he's saying, my insides bubble with lava again.

'—the difference between how we see ourselves and who we are in God's eyes, can be difficult to accept. When we're on a journey of redemption, sometimes it takes us away from the path we thought we were on.' His voice rises. 'The Lord can call you to a new path and you have no choice but to go. The truth is—'

You've got to be kidding me. If Daniel thinks I'm going to stand by like a good wife and pretend everything is fine while he dismantles everything *we* have worked to build, he has another thing coming. I'm not invisible and I am not *irrelevant.*

Turning to one of the choir kids, I grab the microphone out of his hand. 'Is this thing on?' I tap the grille hard before blowing on it. A deep thud is followed by a loud squeal. *It's on.* Daniel peers around the stage, startled and signalling the sound desk. Before he can speak again, I march unsteadily onto the stage and his face drops. This is not on the run sheet.

The crowd and the cameras erupt, their praise washing over me like a wave. It's the only thing that keeps me standing. That and the lava that has now reached my chest, threatening to spill out. I put my hand up to acknowledge them, staring at Daniel until they fall quiet.

'Did you say something about truth?' I hold the mic too close and it feeds back again, harsh and deafening. I recoil and glance upstage, simultaneously registering that not only is Sasha watching me with wide eyes, but I'm fifty feet tall on the screen. I look like hell. *Oh well, too late now.*

I turn to the crowd. 'Hey, Sydney! Do you want to talk about the truth?' I hold the mic out and the arena explodes into impassioned shouts of *Praise Jesus! Yes! The truth!* I have them in the palm of my hand. I take a few wobbly steps towards Daniel – he's a deer in the headlights – look him dead in the eyes, pause dramatically, then punch the air and scream into the microphone like David Lee Roth. 'Then, let's talk about the fucking truth!'

And that's the last thing I remember.

6

be a good girl

I used to dream about Dad a lot. When I first moved out of home, after I married Daniel, and after I had Abbey. Then the dreams stopped, as if completing my own family meant I didn't have to prove myself anymore.

They started again after his funeral. For months I had the same recurring dream and I'd wake crying in the dark. My psychologist told me the dreams would stop when I let go of not having cleared the air before he died.

In the dream, I'm outside the front door of the old house in Mt Druitt. The door is open and Dad is inside, in the hallway, with a group of people. Mum and Lizzie are there. So is my English teacher from school and several friends of my parents. They're all staring at me, and Dad is introducing me like nobody knows who I am. He's telling them I'm his special girl, that I'm smart and exceptional at art, and that my reading level is years above my age.

'I love my little Gracie. Didn't I do a good job with this one?'

I'm happy because I love it when Dad calls me Gracie. And because I know if I give him a nice drawing, or get an A+ or one of those little paper awards you stick on the fridge, it means walking to the shop to get lemonade and he'll maybe let me ride on his shoulders, or he'll read to me at bedtime and kiss me on the head goodnight and say 'sweet dreams, kiddo'.

Then he says to show everyone my picture but I can't find it. I'm sure I was just holding it. He's disappointed and some of the people leave but he says, 'That's okay Gracie, do some numbers for us instead.' So I say, 'nine times nine is eighty-one' but he tells me that's wrong and now he's a bit angry and everyone leaves, except for Mum and Lizzie.

Dad hands me a big red book and says 'read to us'. I feel better because I really am a good reader, but when I open the book, the pages are blank. I tell him I can't read it if there aren't any words, but all he does is shake his head and say, 'you're supposed to be my special girl, Gracie'. And now Mum and Lizzie are at the other end of the hallway with their backs to me. They're scared of something. Maybe if I can do better, it'll go away.

I tell Dad I want to come inside and try again. He says I'm only allowed in if I can spell 'chiaroscuro', but I don't know what that word means. I start to cry and he says, 'Only special girls can come inside, you know that.' Then he closes the door. I can hear Mum and Lizzie crying too but no matter how much I knock and cry, he doesn't open the door – and I'm left outside. Alone.

7

it's all downhill from here

I wake, disoriented. It takes me longer than it should to work out I'm lying on my bathroom floor, partially clothed, my face pressed against cold tiles. The pressure in my head is unbearable. I hear Dexter barking and struggle into a sitting position tugging my dress up. There's someone knocking at the front door. How did they get through the gate without buzzing? Could I have left it open last night? I don't remember getting home. Everything's a complete blank after . . .

Yesterday rushes back in a tumble of disjointed fragments. Daniel, the fire, Susie. *Oh, my God* – that man. *I'm going to throw up.* I remember getting dressed and trying not to vomit in the Uber. Talking to Minette. *Sasha.* The memory of her is a sucker punch. A vague image of the crowd, from the stage. I'm holding a microphone. *That can't be right.* I reach desperately for what happened next but it's like plunging my hands into quicksand. The knocking comes again, and Dexter is going ballistic.

'For fuck's sake, Dexter!' It bursts from me and I taste acid. I don't know whether to cry, scream or run. My body makes the decision. I scramble for the toilet and puke up the contents of my stomach along with what little is left of my dignity.

I haven't thrown up this hard since I was pregnant. Once spent, I slide back to the floor, my forehead against the tiles. It's too close to the toilet to be sanitary but I couldn't care less. Surely I didn't drink enough to black out? I might not be a big drinker but still, this seems extreme. I remember the valium. *Christ.* What was I thinking?

I head downstairs, needing water and painkillers. My handbag, keys and phone sit neatly in the middle of the kitchen bench, which is unlike me. I check my phone. It's 4 pm. Apparently, I've been passed out for almost twenty-four hours. There are two missed calls from Daniel, two from Minette, and three from Abbey. Two text messages:

Abbey: Mum, please answer your phone.
Susie: You alright?

I flick the phone to silent, unable to formulate a coherent thought, let alone have a conversation. At least Dexter has stopped barking. I just want to make my head stop hurting, crawl into bed, and stay there until the world ends. A perfunctory search of the kitchen tells me I'm out of anything that could make a dent in this pounding. It seems an unnecessary insult.

Tap-tap-tap-tap-tap.

I jump, turning to find Liz's face peering at me through the window. She waves and gestures for me to let her in as I stare at her in confusion. What is my sister doing here? Now I know the world is ending.

———

I ask if she wants tea, forgetting in my haze that Liz doesn't drink tea, maintaining that it tastes like 'mud watered down with piss'. She raises her eyebrows.

'I know it's been a while, but you have met me, right?'

I rub my face. 'Sorry. I'm a bit out of it.'

'No shit.' She sits and looks me up and down, absently scratching Dexter's back with her foot. I'm aware my dress is undone but have no idea what state my head is in. I think I can assume from her expression that I look like I've been dragged through a hedge backwards. 'What's going on?'

I grab a glass from the cupboard and fill it with tap water, placing it in front of her even though she hadn't asked for it. 'What are you doing here, Liz. Is something wrong? Is Mum okay?'

She studies me briefly as if she's going to push it, then changes her mind. 'What? I can't drop in if I'm passing by?'

I shoot her a look. 'You live an hour away. When are you ever just passing by?'

'I had to pick something up in the city. Thought I'd take a punt and see if you were home.'

I don't believe her for a second. 'I thought the snotty air over this way gave you hives?' Liz shrugs as if to say, *what can I tell you?* and I prickle with annoyance. 'Look, can you just tell me what's up, please? I'm hungover and not having the best time of it right now.' My voice cracks. I give her a forced smile and she frowns.

'You're really not okay, are you?'

I huddle into myself. 'Daniel's leaving me.'

She lets out a low whistle. 'Wow, I didn't see that coming. I thought you two were rock solid. Power couple of the century.' I must look miserable because she softens. 'I'm sorry, Grace. What happened?'

I give her the Cliffs Notes, which is all I have. Daniel thinks our marriage has gone stale and his solution is to run off and bang the first dewy-eyed ingenue he could find. A tale as old as time. I tell her about the school and the fire. I don't mention Susie or my horrifying attempt at getting back at Daniel with Whatshisname. I do share that I got horrendously drunk, was late for the concert, and think I might have made a complete fool of myself.

'You don't remember?'

'Not a thing.'

'Bit off-brand, isn't it?' She stifles a smile.

'It's not funny.'

'I'm not laughing,' she says. 'You're entitled to be mad. Your holier-than-thou husband dipped his wick into one of the choir girls. I'm sure you've got people who can smooth it over for you though. I wouldn't worry.'

I bridle. I don't know why I expected anything other than our usual dynamic. Somehow, we always end up meeting each other cross-ways. 'Glad you think my life imploding can be so easily managed.'

'Well . . .'

'Thanks a lot, Liz. Appreciate the support.'

'Don't be dramatic.'

I'm done. 'Can we not do this? My head is splitting and I'm certain you didn't turn up unannounced just to needle me, so what's going on?'

The walls go up immediately. Any tenuous thread of connection that had unspooled, is broken. It doesn't take much for either of us to get defensive, every reaction coloured by innate misunderstanding of each other and our own insecurities.

'All good.' She pushes her stool back. 'It's not that important it can't wait.'

'For pity's sake, really?' I sigh heavily. 'Is everything okay with you and Colin? With Mum? Is she still forgetting stuff?'

'Maybe if you visited more than once a year you'd know.'

'I'm busy.'

'Yeah, Grace, we all know how busy and important you are.'

'What does that mean?'

'Nothing. Forget it. But let's just say I know your voicemail message off by heart.' Liz picks up her bag and starts towards the door. I have no choice but to follow. 'Mum's getting worse, so we need to talk at some point – about the future.'

Why does she always do this? 'If that's the case, talk to me now.'

'I said it can wait. You've got a lot on your plate and it's not a good time.' She pauses. 'A visit wouldn't go astray though. Just give me some notice.'

'Okay.'

'Have you spoken to Abbey?'

'She's tried to call a few times, but I don't know what to say.'

'Right.'

'Why?'

'No reason,' Liz shrugs it off. I give her a quizzical look but she doesn't bite. 'I'm just asking. You'll be fine, Grace.' She puts her hand on my arm and squeezes it gently, and for a brief second, I imagine sisterly warmth. 'You always are.'

I close the door and lean back against it, unable to shake Liz's question. *Have you spoken to Abbey?* Maybe I'm being paranoid because of everything that's going on, but there was something she wasn't saying. A hint of maternal protectiveness radiating from her that made my defences stir.

Liz and Abbey have always been close – always laughing at the same in-jokes, liking the same TV shows. With Liz and Col having three boys – and losing their daughter Chloe to stillbirth a month before she was due – it's understandable. But it doesn't mean it doesn't rankle sometimes. After all, Liz is the only person with any idea of the truth.

She'd never say it in so many words, but it's always been there, simmering across the years underneath her easy relationship with my daughter. *You were going to give her up.* I haven't set a foot wrong since. I've done everything possible to be the best mother I could.

But I've never been allowed to forget it.

8

not a monster

October, 1999

I have cabin fever. Six days without leaving the house and another two until Daniel is home from the conference. It couldn't have come at a worse time, Abbey having chickenpox. Mum and Dad are away and I can't keep asking Liz for help. She's already helped so much, despite everything on her own plate.

Day care says she can't go back until the blisters have crusted over and she's not contagious. No new lesions for twenty-four hours. But how would I know? It's not like I've counted them. She's definitely crusty though. Not that it matters. She can't go back to day care because – on top of the pox – she also has a cold that she's passed on to me, plus she's teething, to cap things off nicely.

Being sick and trapped in a confined space with a scabby and feverish snot-monster is not my idea of a good time. It's not her fault, poor kid. When you're two, you don't know what's going on. All you know is that you're hot and itchy and everything hurts. But even dosed up with paracetamol, she's grizzly and wearing my patience. Nothing I do is right. If Daniel were here, she'd quieten for him.

Groceries are low. Unless I want to add starvation into the mix, I've no choice but to venture to the shops. No need to shower, I tell myself, just throw on a tracksuit. I'll only be half an hour. Fresh air will be good for us both. And it'll stop me losing the plot, although it might be a little late for that. Yesterday I cried for half an hour because I couldn't get my bra done up. But at least I'd managed to get out of bed, so that was an improvement.

There's nothing I can do about how rotten Abbey looks. Every inch of her is daubed with calamine lotion, she won't let me brush her hair, and she's producing more mucus than I can keep up with. She fights me as I haul her out of the car and manoeuvre her into a trolley. I'm hoping I'll be recognisable to other mothers as under duress and not the proud owner of a feral child. I hand her a fruit roll-up, aware that bribing your child is not best practice, but these are desperate times.

Surprisingly, we make it around Woolworths without incident. It's not until I think I can slip quickly into Kmart that things go sideways. I blame Blue's Clues. *Abbey spots the cartoon dog from across the store and tries to climb out of the trolley.*

'No, sweetheart. Stay in the trolley please.' I rummage in my bag and hand her another roll-up. Abbey's not having a bar of it. She tosses it on the floor and arches backwards, trying to pull one leg out of the seat. Her shoe falls off. When I try to slip it back on, she kicks out, hitting me in the nose. I reel back, only just managing to bite my tongue.

'No.' She howls, stricken, and I shove the shoe in my handbag. 'Blue! Want Blue.'

'You're not having Blue.' I swing around and head away from the toys. If they're out of sight, maybe she'll calm down. But even at two, Abbey's nothing if not resolute. She throws herself sideways, screaming louder. Other shoppers stare and shake their heads, as if I have any control over the writhing creature in the trolley. I give a woman a tight smile and roll my eyes as if to say, 'Kids, right?' but she purses her lips in disapproval.

I grip Abbey under the arms, trying to sit her up. 'Come on, sweetie, be good for Mummy.' Abbey struggles against me, tears and snot flowing freely, and

I mutter under my breath, 'Fine, if I get you Blue's Clues, will you stop crying?' She reins in her sobs with a hiccup and nods.

With the over-priced plush toy acquired, Abbey is appeased for about thirty seconds.

Now she's determined to climb out of the trolley. 'Dowwwwn.' She's already displaying a frightening independent streak, so I think maybe if I let her walk beside me, she'll behave. Big mistake. As soon as her feet hit the ground, she tears away from me with only one shoe on.

You've got to be kidding me.

I catch up to her in the women's underwear section. She sees me coming and pre-emptively throws herself and the toy on the ground, screeching. Anybody would think I'm trying to murder her. I scoop her up, but she refuses to stand. She goes limp instead, a dramatic dead weight. Her skin clammy and hot, I nearly drop her. I feel terrible for even bringing her out of the house.

A woman in her thirties – with a perfectly behaved, spot-free four-year-old in tow – shakes her head across the aisle and I glare at her.

'What? Haven't you seen an upset child before?' The woman pulls her offspring in front of her and marches away with a loud tut. My own skin erupts into mortified flames as I try to get Abbey under control. Why is this so hard? Do other mothers go through this or is it just me? Maybe kids are like animals – they can smell fear. Abbey can sense my hopelessness, that I don't know what the hell I'm doing. I let go of her and stand up.

'Abbey, please. Can you stand up for Mummy?' I'm pleading now. 'Come on. Let's take Blue and go home.' But she's too far gone. There's no helping me.

Abbey is on her back now, shunting herself violently across the carpet with both feet, like an upside-down caterpillar. I watch in abject horror. She lets out a strangled screech with every thrust until she's lying underneath a rack of beige maternity bras. Not content with her progress, she uses the bras as leverage, yanking them from the hangers and down onto herself until all I can see is her chubby pockmarked legs sticking out from underneath the rack. I snap.

'Fine. If you can't be a good girl, you can stay here by your bloody self. I'm going home without you.' I turn on my heel and march out of Kmart. Without the groceries. Without my child.

I don't know where I think I'm going. Obviously, I'm not intending to leave my daughter behind – am I? What kind of parent threatens to leave their child? But my feet move of their own accord. I'm in tears before I reach the food court. None of this is how I thought it would be. Then my mind goes blank.

I'm a zombie as I shuffle towards a seat at the far end of the shopping centre and sit. When a hand eventually gently touches my shoulder, it barely registers. It's an older woman with tinted glasses.

'Are you alright, love?'

I stare at her. I don't know how long I've been sitting here.

'I'm fine.' I blink, trying to clear my head. 'My little girl's sick and being a bit of a handf—'

Oh, my God. Abbey! WHERE'S ABBEY? My heart punches into my throat. And then I hear it. Loud and accusatory over the centre PA system.

'Attention, customers. We have a lost child. If you have misplaced your child, please come immediately to Centre Management.'

Misplaced? I didn't misplace her. I ran away from her. What the fuck is wrong with me? I launch from the seat and sprint past alarmed strangers, sudden sobs threatening to swallow me whole. One thought runs through my head: You are a terrible mother. *I hear her crying from the corridor. It's a heart-rending wail, like a siren.*

Bursting through the office door, I ramble something about having only turned my back for a second. Abbey looks up, takes a moment to register my presence, then careens towards me. She looks like a psychotic troll doll – red-faced and wild, hair and face sticky with tears and snot. The plush toy is nowhere to be seen. I drop to my knees as she launches herself into my arms and buries her face in my neck. She smells like calamine lotion and sweat and fruit roll-ups and I'm crying as I hold on to her tightly and stroke her hair.

'Oh, thank God,' I say out loud, but my thoughts are saying something else . . . I can't do this. I can't do this to her. I'm not okay.

Then Abbey puts her hot little hand on my cheek and I lean back to look at her.

'Yes, sweetheart?'

'I want Blue.'

9

you oughta know

When I get home from the pharmacy – loaded up with ibuprofen, Hydralyte and Berocca – Daniel's car is in the driveway. I'm immediately caught between fight or flight. My heart pounds hard and fast in my chest like there's an actual bird stuck inside my rib cage. I'm not talking a sparrow. It's at least a magpie. Maybe even a crow. I'm so tired of this heightened state of anxiety, of holding my breath. Part of me wishes my heart would give out, so everything can be quiet. Guilt floods me the instant the thought crosses my mind. *What kind of mother does that make me?*

Daniel's upstairs in his bedroom when I finally go inside. I can hear him opening and closing drawers and his footfall tracking across the room. He can only be doing one thing – packing. The realisation almost brings me to my knees. *Please, God.* But before the prayer has the chance to fully form, I get the unmistakeable sensation that I'm reaching into nothing. God is not listening. How can he be, with everything that's happened? I'm on my own.

I stand by the stairs with the front door wide open, keys in hand and my heart in my mouth, so when he comes out of his bedroom I can pretend I just walked through the door. Daniel strides onto the landing carrying a bulging duffle bag. He pauses when he sees me, then trots easily down the stairs.

'I tried calling you.' His face gives nothing away. I make a show of rattling my keys and closing the door.

'I was sleeping. I wasn't feeling well.'

'I'm not surprised.' He stalks past me towards the kitchen. I'm on the back foot already. I hear the thud of his bag on the floor. When I reach the kitchen, Daniel is leaning on the bench, staring at me expectantly. Dexter has retreated to his bed near the window. He's sitting bolt upright, quivering the way dogs do when they sense a storm coming.

Suppressed anger simmers from Daniel like heatwaves above hot tarmac as I perch on a kitchen stool. It makes my skin prickle. I'm not sure which of us is supposed to speak first, or which of us is more aggrieved.

'I don't know what to say, Grace.' He has that 'I'm not mad I'm disappointed' tone. Ordinarily it would push my buttons, but I still don't know what I've done. Daniel has skilfully managed to shift the balance of blame, and I'm no longer allowed to be the wounded wife. 'What happened to not causing a scene?'

'If I tell you I don't remember much, would it make a difference?'

'I'd say that's very convenient.'

'I really don't remember.' I will him to register my wretchedness. 'It's a complete blank.'

He frowns. 'You're serious?'

I attempt to explain, leaving out Susie and the worst parts. I tell him about the fire, holding up my blistered hand. 'I ended up at a bar and had too much to drink. I just wanted to make it all go away. When I realised I was late, I panicked.' When I mention the valium, I'm mollified by the look of consternation on his face.

'Good grief.' He rubs a hand across his face, suddenly looking tired. 'What a mess.'

'If I said something or did something . . .' I reach to touch his arm but he puts his head in his hands and I withdraw.

'That's not the half of it, Grace. Do you have any idea how much damage—'

'*Christ, Daniel!* I don't even know what I did!'

He recoils. 'What's gotten into you? I thought that gel stuff was supposed to help with the mood swings?'

My head jerks back. 'Mood swings? Are you fucking kidding me?'

He shakes his head. 'When did you start talking like this? You want to know what you did? You commandeered a microphone and screamed profanity at the entire congregation.'

I stare at him, horrified. 'I what?'

'You accused me of infidelity in front of thousands of people.'

'I mean, that's not inaccurate—'

'You told them I was "*balls deep in that Instagram slut*".'

'I did not.'

He gives me an incredulous look. 'Yes. You did.' I want the floor to open up and swallow me. 'Then you challenged Sasha to a "hymn battle" and started singing "You Oughta Know".'

'That's not a hymn, that's Alanis Morrisette.'

'I know.'

'Well, that's not so bad . . .'

'It was the "*are you thinking of me when you fuck her*" verse.'

'Oh. That's bad.'

'You think?'

'Please tell me that's all.'

'You dropped the mic, then threw up in the holy water.' He gives me a weird shrug, which I think means he's done. I groan and lay my flaming face on the cool bench top. 'Luckily that's when you passed out. We had security take care of you.'

I lift my head. 'Take care of me'? And what do you mean, *we*?'

'*We* – Me. Minette. And yes. The place was in an uproar. Security helped get you backstage so the paramedics could check you over. I'm not the Mob. I didn't have them *take care of you.* I got Minette to bring you home and carried on with the concert. It's not like I could leave.'

I can't help myself. 'Oh, *no* – your wife might have been collapsing from alcohol poisoning or a bloody overdose, but you couldn't possibly leave your shining star.'

'That's not fair.'

I shrink back into myself. 'I can't believe I did all of that.'

'Don't take my word for it.' Daniel holds up his phone. 'Plenty of evidence on TikTok.'

I'm about to ask since when has he been on TikTok – which in hindsight is a stupid question – when he taps the screen. Some bright spark has made a video loop of me punching the air and screaming 'Let's talk about the fucking truth!' over and over. I look wasted, like those videos from the 90s of out-of-control rock stars like Courtney Love. Except I have zero cool cachet. It's mortifying and I cover my face.

'Turn it off.'

'You embarrassed me and you embarrassed yourself. This is going to damage us, Gracie. And so far, I haven't heard an apology.'

'Don't call me that.' The pet name snaps me firmly back onto my front foot. 'Is that all you're worried about? How this looks for the church? Maybe you should have thought about that before you had an affair with a girl younger than Abbey. Did you think I was going to play nice last night and watch you fawn all over her while everybody laughed behind my back? *Good little Gracie*, never making waves.' I shove my stool back, pointing my finger. 'And you know what? I'm not the one in the wrong, so I am not fucking sorry!'

People sometimes say that when something difficult is spoken aloud, the words hang in the air, frozen and waiting for a response. But my words unspool from deep inside me and coil like snakes on the floor between us, thick and black and venomous. Daniel puts both hands up against the barrage.

'*Whoa*. I wanted to take our time, figure out how to handle things,' he says. 'Stars Fold means a great deal to people. We have a responsibility to behave with integrity and treat each other with respect – to lead by example. This was not the way to go about things.'

I choke on my laughter. 'Are you listening to yourself? You've been lying to your wife's face for what I assume is months. You go on about compassion and truth, and *God's fucking plan.* You're so full of shit.' Sober, I'm hyperaware of how foreign the swear words feel, firing from my lips.

I'm no stranger to profanity. Far from it. When Liz and I were growing up, the word *fuck* adorned nearly every sentence that came out of our parents' mouths. As a noun. An adjective. A term of endearment. Sometimes all in the one sentence.

It wasn't a wonder we picked up a nasty case of potty-mouth. But God forbid we ever got caught. To this day, the smell of Imperial Leather soap makes me gag. Once I met Daniel, curse words dropped completely out of my vocabulary. The church wasn't the place for a well-timed F-bomb. After decades of restraint, letting them off the leash is delicious – the expletives crackling ferociously on my tongue like exploding candy.

'I should go,' Daniel says.

'Were things that bad?'

He shrugs. 'We haven't had sex in nearly fifteen years. That's not exactly normal.'

'So, this is my fault?' I bristle.

'That's not what I meant. I can't explain it. I feel . . . *alive*, for the first time in years. Like there's an adventure out there waiting for me.' He might as well be wielding a blade in each hand. 'It's exciting, spontaneous. She makes me feel virile and—'

'Okay, that's enough,' I interrupt. 'You're right. I think you should go.'

'Grace—'

'Before I spontaneously remove your *virile* testicles with that spatula.' I cross my arms protectively across my body.

'Fine. This isn't getting us anywhere.' He picks up the duffle bag. 'Look, it's probably a good idea if you stay away from the church for now.'

'That's alright by me.'

'It'll give me and Minette a chance to work out how to spin this.'

'I'm sure you'll figure it out.' The words are brittle in my mouth, sugar glass with a bitter aftertaste. He doesn't say goodbye. He gives me a long, searching look then walks out of the kitchen. I watch him go with a sense of rising panic. I know once he walks out the door, it's done. Despite everything, I'm not ready for that.

I can still fix this.

I race after him. 'Daniel!'

He stops in the doorway. 'What?'

'Stay.'

This single word is loaded with *I'm sorry* and *I forgive you* and *I'm terrified* and *please, I'll do anything, just please don't leave me* – and behind it all is a voice, screaming in my head that I've failed. In the end, I have simply failed.

He refuses to meet my eyes. 'No, I need to go.'

I can't help myself – one last desperate grasp. 'But I love you.'

Daniel finally looks at me. 'I know.'

He closes the door.

10

wallow

Oh Lord, why hast thou forsaken me? The days that follow the confrontation with Daniel blur into one. After he's gone, I crawl into bed with Dexter curled behind my knees. When I wake at 3 am, he's disappeared. I stumble in the dark to Daniel's room and bury myself among his rumpled sheets. The bed smells of him. I try not to think about how pathetic I must seem. Dusk bleeds into the dark hours, into dawn and so on and again.

I drift between wake and sleep, curled into a ball, protecting my tender underbelly from further attack. I imagine spines protruding from my back. I can't take more wounding. I sleep until my body won't sleep any more then lay face up, tracing a crack in the ceiling for hours.

I stare until my mind makes a living thing of it, crawling inch by inch until it cleaves the room across and widens like a yawn, splitting my life into two distinct pieces. Before and after. On one side, my previous life unfurls like a faded map. Recognisable, as familiar as breath. Easy to navigate. My life on the other side is unknown and uncharted – blank and full of terrors.

You are not good enough.

It's all my fault. If only I'd been better. If I was better, Daniel would want me. If I was better, Abbey would love me more and perhaps my sister wouldn't hate me so much. If I was better, maybe Dad wouldn't have died. If I was better, I wouldn't be alone.

Oh Lord, why hast thou forsaken me?

The self-pity is as alien to me as that man in my kitchen. I'm usually the one with optimism running through my veins, ever ready with a hopeful solution, a call to resilience. Now there's sand under my skin.

I'm the one who can call scripture to hand for any occasion, offering the right words at exactly the right time. I know the Bible front to back – I'm nothing if not thorough when I commit – but nothing I reach for is the right shape. Not Job nor Jeremiah, not the Gospels or even Philemon. The faith that became a safety net as the years passed is now empty words wrapped around me, like someone else's coat.

But despite the fallout, I can't deny a thrill at the first terrifying flickers of freedom, in discarding care of consequence. Saying what I think, my language loose and unmoderated. I've been clinging that stranger's coat for so long, it's an unexpected relief to strip it from my back, even if it leaves me naked.

Oh Lord, why the fuck hast thou forsaken me?

Don't take the Lord's name in vain. But where's the vanity in thinking of myself for once? I've put Daniel and Abbey, the congregation, and everybody else first, for as long as I can remember. I've tried to be selfless. *The greatest gift under God*. It occurs to me what that word really means – without myself. Why? And for what?

You know what.

Daniel and I weren't together when I found out I was pregnant with Abbey. We'd been dating for almost a year but had broken up a month prior. It was my choice. Instinct told me our relationship wasn't the fairytale I'd hoped. The regular cycle of Daniel withdrawing and me scrambling to make things right was taking its toll. Susie tried to distract me for weeks, but I missed Daniel. Even fairytales weren't perfect all the time – and he needed me.

My period had always been irregular, and we'd been careful, so it took me a while to realise I was late. When I did, I had no idea what to do. I was twenty. I had a year of my degree left. Liz had already put Mum and Dad through the wringer falling pregnant the year before at the age of fifteen, refusing to tell them who the father was and moving into a share house in Blacktown. Nate was a few months old by then and they adored him, but things were still fractious.

That was not going to be me. I got as far as calling the women's health clinic in Chatswood. I had thought myself a feminist. Pro-choice. I thought the decision would be easy. It wasn't, and I was scared.

The woman on the phone was kind but pragmatic. If I wanted a counsellor, I could have one. But I didn't want to talk about my feelings. I needed someone to give me the answer to the only question that mattered: What if I regretted it? The woman assumed I meant the abortion.

You see, people only talk about the regret of ending a pregnancy, like it's something indelible and inescapable that your heart will remind you of daily until you die. And maybe it is that way for some women. Mostly it's not. Perhaps that's what other people have a problem with.

But what's worse? A woman choosing to empty her womb and live with her decision – whether it's easy, whether it's right, or whether it turns out to be neither – her reconciliation personal and tucked away, deep in her chest, or the potential regrets that come with the more socially acceptable choice?

It's easy to feel compassion for women who dream of having a baby but cannot, who feel like the love they have to give has nowhere to go. Or for grieving mothers who have suffered the unspeakable loss of a child. But nobody talks about the pain of having a child who isn't truly wanted. Of giving up everything for something that was never part of the plan. There are rarely conversations about the resulting resentment, of distance and disappointment and the damage it can do – to you and to them. Why aren't more people worried about that? I guess it's easier to blame the mother after the fact, for somehow falling short.

In the end, I couldn't do it – to this day I can't articulate why, it had nothing to do with religion or the Bible. I just couldn't. So I chose to risk the regret and did the only thing that made sense to me. I told nobody, and I ran back to Daniel. He proposed to me on the spot, proclaiming there would never be anybody for him but me. We were married a month later.

I never told anybody how close I came to ending it all.

Those who would call me mercenary are looking at it all wrong – I loved Daniel, I did. Marriage, motherhood and fidelity are indoctrinated into us as something we should desperately want – ideals sold to us in pretty packaging as markers of our success as a woman. Whether I really wanted it was irrelevant. But if I was going to do it, I would do it perfectly. I would be the best wife and mother possible. I would get it *right.* It couldn't be that hard. Millions of women did it every day.

So, I quit university. As Daniel had often pointed out, the chances of me being a successful artist were marginal at best. In the end, Daniel offered me – *us* – a way out and the chance at a better future.

I don't regret having Abbey. Wondering hypothetically whether I'd make a different decision if I went back in time is pointless. I've had twenty-eight years of knowing and loving my daughter. Desperately so sometimes. I wouldn't be without her for anything.

I do not regret *her.* But I don't think I was supposed to be a mother. Or a wife. Now none of it matters. I appear to have failed across the board.

There's an adventure out there waiting for me. Daniel's words echo in my head, sly and injurious. The worst thing is, it wasn't said with malice – there was a genuine spark of excitement. That's what guts me. Does he think there weren't times I wondered what my life might have been if I *had* made a different decision. Would I have made it out of the suburbs, as an artist – or something else? Where would I be? *Who* would I be?

I have to get out of Daniel's bed. I can still smell him, but it's not comforting any more. Looking around the room in the light, it's suddenly unfamiliar. I don't want to be here. I sit cross-legged in the bottom of my shower for an age, letting the water cascade over me, plastering my hair to my head and running in rivulets down my back.

I feel alive, he said.

When was the last time I felt alive, like *really alive*? I struggle to remember because, up until a few days ago, I was still convincing myself that the life we'd built was a good life, that it was enough for me. Maybe when Abbey was first born? Those early months when everything is a blur of exhaustion and you can't help but experience the intensity of every tiny moment, like your heart is trying to keep up. I felt alive then.

Thoughts of Abbey are the only thing stopping my life feeling like a waste. I thought I was doing it all for her, sticking to the plan even as I found everything that came with motherhood more difficult than it was supposed to be. Even as – over the years – she drifted closer to Daniel. But what if it was for me all along? To prove I was worth something.

I'm going to have to talk to her. But I don't have the right words. I picture her often serious expression, the one that belies her quick wit and raucous sense of humour. I think about how articulate she can be, but how she always defers to Daniel when she's around him, suddenly ten again – shy and tongue-tied. I recognise myself in her, in those moments. With my own dad.

Whichever version of her I tell, she'll be shattered, and I don't know how to make that right. What kind of mother am I, if I can't make this right? It's what I've always done. I have to shield her from this.

The hot water runs out and I barely blink. It takes a minute for sense to finally hit, the cold water puddling around me, chilling me through. I could easily stay here, staring morbidly at the bathroom tiles until my extremities turn blue and my nipples snap off, or lie in bed berating myself and sniffing Daniel's pillow until I waste away from starvation. But what would be the point? So I can live out the rest of my days as a sad and bitter middle-aged divorcee, while Daniel is off living his best Marco Polo life with his sparkly pop tart?

Fuck that. I want to feel alive.

11

welcome to the jungle

The Hip Joint in Newtown is several steps up from The Queens Arms. A row of red leather booths lines the wall opposite a long, narrow bar and the charcoaled beams in the roof are threaded through with devil's ivy. A smattering of Saturday night drinkers keeps the sole bartender occupied, but not so busy he can't stand and amiably chat.

Beyond the bar, several people skirt a battered pool table that sits on one side of the dance floor. As I arrive, some kind of rock band – two guys with guitars and a drummer – is in the throes of a raucous sound check on a low stage in the corner.

'*Chhhhhh-ECK! Check check.*' One of the young guitarists stands out from the others. He's tall, blond and muscular – clean-cut in jeans, sneakers and a tight white t-shirt. He's more Bondi than Bon Scott and a mismatch for the rest of the band, who look like they've been booted out of a Foo Fighters concert for headbutting someone. He riffs expertly for a few seconds, all flying fingers and quiet confidence.

Susie waits in one of the booths, already two beers in and eyeing off the shaggy-haired drummer, who's doing a stellar impression of Animal from *The Muppets*. She spots me and her eyebrows raise.

'Michael Hutchence called,' she yells. 'He wants his leather jacket back.'

I look down, self-conscious. 'What's wrong with my jacket?'

'Nothing. If you plan on being in an INXS film clip.'

I frown. 'Here I was feeling good about myself.'

'I'm giving you shit, settle down.' She grins. 'You look great – different.' I'm not sure whether it's a compliment. My post-shower epiphany had led to a deep dive into the recesses of my wardrobe – and a box of Abbey's uni-era cast-offs – culminating in an outfit made up of a red cocktail dress, a pair of strappy stilettos, and the aforementioned biker jacket.

Daniel had always preferred my hair up and my makeup 'natural', so I'd left my hair loose and dug out a red lipstick I hadn't worn in years. It's as far away as I could get from black pants, ballet flats and a plain t-shirt. The point being to not look anything like the dull, predictable kind of woman a husband would find it easy to leave.

Susie pushes a glass of wine across the table as the band starts playing. 'Let's pace ourselves, shall we? I don't want to have to peel you off another sad-eyed middle-aged man.'

'Very funny.'

'How was he by the way? Did he give you a good seeing to?'

I turn a deep shade of beetroot and decide against providing details. I'm never going to be able to look at the word *Monday* the same way as it is.

'Couldn't go through with it.'

'I did try to warn you. I was beginning to think he might have cut you up and dumped you in the harbour, he had that look about him. Nondescript on the outside, psycho on the inside.'

'Nice to know you were concerned.'

'You were in bad shape. What kind of friend would I be otherwise?'

It's a loaded comment but I'm all trauma'd out. That's a conversation for another night, when I'm not trying to be brand new. 'I'm guessing you know how bad things got?'

'Huh?'

'You haven't heard about the very public fuck up?' I'm relieved, maybe the news hasn't spread. 'Apparently, it's all over TikTok.'

Susie's eyes widen. 'Whey-hey, who are you and what have you done with my stuck-up friend? I don't do socials, love. It's all dopey nineteen-year-olds who like the sound of their own voice and argumentative boomers. Seeing as I'm neither of those things, I don't see the point.' She leans back. 'You're going to have to fill me in the old-fashioned way.'

I lay it out as briefly as possible, but she knows me too well. 'Bit light on the details,' she says. 'Kudos for throwing up on stage but come on, I want the juice. Don't make me google.' I reluctantly fill in the gaps and she laughs so hard she nearly slides out of the booth. 'You're kidding me. "*Balls deep*"?'

'Yep.'

'In front of thousands of bible thumpers?'

'Yep.'

'You're definitely going to hell.' She cackles. 'I could not love you more.'

'Glad you're happy to be seen with me. I've been deserted otherwise. Not a single person from the church has reached out.'

'How very Christian of them.' Susie shakes her head. 'All that "love thy neighbour" crap. It's only ever when it suits them. I could never understand why you went in for it.'

'You know why.'

'Yeah, Mr Second Coming.' She snorts. 'Although, I'll bet you a million dollars he was too busy thinking about himself to give you even one.'

I rack my brain for the last time Daniel made me orgasm, but who remembers sex from more than a decade ago? It always took me so long to get aroused that, not long after Daniel made a flip comment about RSI on our honeymoon, I'd gotten into the habit of faking it. I guess he never thought he needed to do anything differently. Why would he? I gave him the impression he was doing a bang-up job.

'I don't have a million dollars, so you're out of luck,' I say. Susie eyes me disbelievingly. 'Anyway, it wasn't just about Daniel. It was at first – but then I liked being seen as a good person. I liked knowing *I* was making a difference in people's lives.'

'Sounds very altruistic.'

I point upwards. 'The idea that *He* loved me unconditionally . . . I needed that.' I don't need to continue. Susie's face tells me she gets it. 'It made me feel safe, for a long time. But I think I made a mistake.' I clock her expression. 'Go on, say it.'

'What?'

'You have *I told you so* face.'

'I don't need to say it then, do I?' Then she shrugs. 'Took you long enough.'

She's right. How has it taken me decades to realise I took the wrong path? I think I've always known – after all, I took it deliberately. Maybe that's why I focused on putting everybody else first; if I didn't think about what *I* really wanted, I wouldn't have to admit my error. The air sucks out of me.

'I've been on my best behaviour for thirty years.'

'You get less than that for murder.'

I gape at her as it hits me fully. It's like I've woken from a coma to find the world has passed me by. 'There's so much I could have done with my life.'

'Let's not get carried away, babe.' Susie swigs her beer. 'It's not like you were destined to be a rebel.'

'But what if I was? I was nineteen when I met Daniel. I missed out on the crazy stuff you're supposed to do in your twenties. I could have been, uh—' I search my mind for a suitable example then bang the table. '—a dominatrix.'

She nearly chokes on her last mouthful. 'Steady on.'

'What? I'm good at rules. How do we know? If I'd never met Daniel—' I'm warming to my topic '—I could have been anybody. It's like that Gwyneth Paltrow movie. I'm one missed train away from spanking an accountant with mummy issues, wearing thigh-high latex boots.'

'You had me at spanking. But if you're going to make me imagine you in latex—' she holds up her empty glass, '—we're gonna need a bigger boat.'

The bartender is wearing a name tag, which I find odd. Why would you want a bunch of drunk people calling your name all night? I squeeze between a group of people and lean across the bar to make it out. *Travis.* Average height and dressed in black, he looks to be early thirties. He wears an unruly mop of curly brown hair and a scruff of stubble with the first appealing signs of grey. He's cute and navigates the bar with zero urgency, like nothing is a drama.

'Travis!' I shout, realising too late that the band has stopped and my raised voice is redundant. He turns, signalling me to wait and I worry I'm being rude. *Christ, am I so conditioned to be nice,*

I can't even call someone's name loudly without thinking I'm taking up too much space? When Travis approaches, I smile apologetically. 'Sorry, didn't mean to yell at you.'

'All good.' He grins. 'I've had worse things screamed at me across the bar than my name. What can I get you?'

I haven't got that far. I turn and catch Susie's eye across the room, making a drinking motion. She repeats it back to me which is no help. 'I think that means shots. Eight please.' I place my credit card on the bar.

'Quick Fuck?'

'Excuse me?'

He flicks his cloth over his shoulder and leans on the bar. 'The shots – would you like Quick Fucks, Slippery Nipples, Cocksucking Cowboys . . . ?' I blink rapidly. Whatever I'm ordering, it clearly comes with a side of porn.

'Just tequila.'

'I had a feeling you were a no-frills kind of girl. Lemon and salt?'

Is there any other way? I might be out of practice, but I'm not so old I've forgotten how to drink tequila. I watch as he deftly lines up the shot glasses and pours the tequila in a continuous stream without spilling a drop. He deals the lemon wedges like he's playing poker, whacks a salt shaker on the tray, and bows with a flourish. *Show off.*

I pull two shots towards me. I need fortifying before heading back to Susie. I sprinkle salt on my hand and load up with the lemon and a shot glass.

'Nice jacket.' The voice is close to my ear and sounds like warm butterscotch. When I turn – unfortunately with my tongue sticking out – the blond guitarist is smiling down at me. He has to be at least six foot four, and up close he has startling green eyes and the biggest set of dimples I've ever seen. He's also all of twenty-five, if he's a day. I have no idea why he's talking to *me*. I down one shot and shove the lemon in my mouth, trying to keep my face straight and failing miserably.

He leans a casual elbow on the bar, bringing those eyes closer to my level. 'What're ye drinking to?' The musical lilt in his voice is definitely Irish. I look over my shoulder to make sure he's not talking to some perky young thing behind me.

'My husband leaving me for a fetus,' I say, readying another shot. He looks down at my feet before his eyes travel lazily up to meet mine. I don't know what to make of it, so I go ahead and down the second shot of tequila.

'Clearly he's a fecking eejit.' He winks at me and I choke on a lemon pip. 'The name's Liam.' He's far too beautiful for his own good. He must think I'm someone else. He cocks an eyebrow. 'This is the part where ye tell me yer name.'

'Oh. Sure.' I'm still confused. 'I'm Grace.' I pick up the tray of shots. 'I have to get back to my friend.' I scoot away from the bar. *What on earth was that about?*

'Nice teh meet ye, Grace.' His words stroke the back of my neck. A thrill runs through me at the same time as my inner voice chirps – *don't even think about it.*

12

fuck it

I plonk the shots on the table. Susie downs one immediately and gives me a sly look. 'You took your sweet time,' Susie says. I concentrate on sprinkling some more salt on my hand.

'I don't know what you mean.'

'Come on – if you stood at the bar any longer there was going to be a cock fight.'

'What? Between who?'

'Seriously? Band dude was drooling into your cleavage and bar dude couldn't have been peacocking harder.'

'Don't be silly.' I glance at the bar. Liam has departed but I can see him preparing to get back on stage. Travis is busy pouring several beers. He catches me looking, flashes a grin. Susie follows my gaze and smirks.

'If you say so.'

'I'm old enough to be their mother.'

'Suit yourself.' Susie grabs another shot and salutes me. 'So, before you get arrested for perving on young boys, let's get back to your life imploding in spectacular fashion!' She's too gleeful for my liking. 'Have you spoken to Fuckface since it happened.'

Reluctantly, I run through the horrible conversation with Daniel. It takes up the entire tray of tequila. The next lot arrives with some variation.

'Thought I'd surprise you.' Travis deposits the shots with another flourish. What did Susie call it? *Peacocking?* 'Tequila and a few QFs and cowboys.'

'See?' Susie hisses at me as he departs. I'm beginning to think she has a point.

'You know, he tried to tell me I'm not a sexual person.'

'Who? The bartender?' Susie bristles. 'That little shit.'

'No, Daniel. I'll have you know . . . I have the potential to be a *very* sexual person.'

'I'm sure you do. Look, even if you weren't interested in sex, it's not like Daniel is a sex god.' She laughs. 'I know I'm biased – I always thought he was creepy – but can you honestly say he's the best you've had?'

'I wouldn't know. Daniel's the only person I've had.'

Susie cracks up. 'Very funny.' I stare at her, straight-faced. 'You're serious? This is worse than I thought.' She hands me a shot. 'You really have wasted your life.'

'I thought you were supposed to make me feel better?'

'I'm trying babe, but this is dire. We need to get you laid.'

'That's the furthest thing from my mind.' My eyes flick to the stage, where Liam is mid sweaty solo. 'I'm forty-nine and I don't have a clue who I am. Everything that I am is wrapped up in what I am to other people. It's pathetic. You know, I haven't even cried properly – that's weird right? I think I'm in shock.'

'I'm not surprised.'

'How did this happen? I can understand him being unhappy

with the lack of sex, but I thought everything else was fine. I've done everything right, Suse. *Everything.*'

Susie studies me. 'That's your problem. Life isn't about doing everything right. It's about making mistakes, falling on your arse and getting back up.'

'I haven't intentionally made a bad decision in my life.' I snort. 'Except marrying Daniel apparently.'

'You need to get messy, my love. Start giving zero fucks.'

I shoot her a look. *Does she know me at all?* 'It's not as easy as flicking a switch from giving *all* the fucks to no fucks at all.'

Susie makes a *psssht* sound. 'Stop trying to be so bloody perfect. Just do the things. Screw everybody else.'

'Maybe you're right.' There's no 'maybe'. The truth thrums deep in my bones. 'I am so tired of being there for everyone else and getting nothing back.' Her expression changes – it's slight, but I catch it – she's biting her tongue. I squash the flicker of guilt. 'I'm tired of worrying about what people are going to say. And I've had it with being *nice*, of never saying no because I'm scared to let anybody down. It's gotten me nowhere – except tossed on the scrap heap.'

'Daniel's not the only one who can have an adventure.' Susie hands me the last tequila on the tray, which I'm happy about because those QF things are awful.

'I know. But I wouldn't know where to start. It's not like there's a travel agency specialising in adventure tours for angry, menopausal divorcees. Wait – is there?'

'You could have a perfectly good adventure right here. You just need to create a brand-new life for yourself.'

'I liked my old life.'

'You did not.'

No, I didn't. *John 8:32. And you will know the truth and the truth will set you free.*

'What kind of life do you have in mind?'

'That's up to you, darl. I'm merely the facilitator. But this course I'm doing talks about how important goal setting is.' She nods her head sagely – like Yoda. 'Which makes sense; how are you supposed to change your life if you're dithering around and don't know what you want?'

'Are you seriously life coaching me now?' She shoots me a withering look. 'Okay, fine. I'll be right back.' I clamber out of the booth and lean over the bar. 'Hey, Travis. Do you have paper and a pen?'

'Is it for your phone number?'

'Funny.'

He produces a pad and biro from his back pocket. 'What makes you think I was joking?'

'The fact I own shoes older than you.'

When I get back to the booth, Susie is all business, a woman on a mission. 'So, Grace—the best goals are smart goals.'

I pull a face. 'Obviously. Why would I want stupid goals?'

'S.M.A.R.T.' She smacks me on the forehead. 'Specific. Measurable. Achievable. Realistic. Timely. You need clear goals – which means you need a list.'

'Of what?'

Susie looks at me like I'm an idiot. 'Of things you want to do, dummy.'

What if I don't know what I want to do? *This is hard.* A light bulb goes off and I slap her shoulder. 'How about bad decisions?'

'Now you're talking. But bad according to who? My definition of bad is very different to yours.' *I don't doubt that for a second.*

'Isn't that the point? Lots of things that boring, straitlaced people say are bad are not that bad at all. I've spent long enough being one of those people.'

We decide to brainstorm and settle on the parameters that a 'bad decision' means anything my 'friends' would clutch their pearls over, anything Daniel would be horrified by, and anything the old me wouldn't have done in a thousand years. If it feels like a 'sin', do it. If my first thought is, *this is not a good idea* – absolutely do it. We high five and do another shot.

My life is going to be my own from here – selfless is no longer in my vocabulary. *I come first* is my new mantra, to which Susie yells 'Damn straight!' – because, of course, she's solely standing up for my vagina, whereas I'm thinking a much more holistic approach.

How many bad decisions? Twenty doesn't seem to be enough to change my life. I need to commit. The way I committed to learning scripture. One hundred? That's setting me up for failure. Fifty is a nice round number – *done*.

The timeframe is easy. Fifty bad decisions before my fiftieth birthday. I'm not sure how seriously I'm taking it, but warmed by laughter, tequila and Susie cheering me on, it doesn't seem to matter.

'Excellent,' says Susie. 'That ticks off measurable and timely. It'll be like a gap year.'

Right, because those never end in calamity.

'You're really good at this.'

'I told you! So? What do you want to do?

'Umm . . . I could stop going to church?'

'I thought this was supposed to be bad decisions?'

'Right, of course. Uh, I could take up smoking?'

Susie sighs and puts the pen down. 'Really? This is what we're doing? Come on, Grace. You can be spicier than that.'

She's right and I know what she's getting at. I sit up straighter. 'Okay. What about a threesome?'

Susie punches the air. 'Atta girl. How about an orgy?'

'How about I start with a threesome and work my way up? An orgy seems like a lot of multitasking.'

'Fine. I'll put it at the bottom.' She shakes her head, disappointed with my slow start. But once I get the hang of it, the rest of the list is a riot. 'Why don't you get a sugar daddy?' Susie chews on her pen, struck by the idea.

I bristle. 'I can pay for my own things, thank you.'

'It is a *bad idea.*'

'I'm nearly fifty, Suse. He'd have to be at least seventy. There's a line.' I pause, thinking. 'I could be a cougar?'

'Indeed you could.'

'What about a sex dungeon?'

She wags her pen at me. 'You did say you're good at rules.'

'Except it sounds terrifying. What if I just watched?'

She rolls her eyes. 'Boring.'

The list expands at a cracking pace. Sleep with an artist, a teacher, a doctor, a lawyer and a fireman. Maybe even a police officer. *Oooh, I like uniforms.*

Have sex with somebody famous.

'Jon Bon Jovi!' I clap my hands.

'S.M.A.R.T., remember? Jon Bon Jovi is neither realistic *or* achievable.'

I make a sad face. 'Spoil sport.'

'Okay, but you might have to compromise.'

'Yay!' I grab a celebratory tequila.

Susie dutifully writes on the list – '*Fuck Jon Bon Jovi (Disclaimer: can substitute for other celebrity)*' – then looks up. 'Next?'

Have sex in public, on a plane, *in a church!* I can't help it, I reflexively cross myself. Old habits die hard. *Lord, forgive me.*

'You have to join Tinder,' says Susie, matter-of-factly. 'And you'll need to learn all the acronyms.' I look at her blankly. 'ONS, FWB, DTF, DP—' she suddenly backtracks. 'Actually, I'll put that last one at the bottom of the list too.'

I make a mental note to check Google later, God knows what she's signing me up for. Scratch that, God probably has his fingers in his ears going '*LA-LA-LA-LA-LA*'. I check the list. 'Why is it all sexual?'

'Because the sum total of your experience is one cock – and probably not a very good one.' I flash involuntarily back to number two – poor old Gerry – whose member was quite impressive, but that isn't the point. 'You need to widen your . . . horizons.' She snorts, amused with herself.

'It's not like being a bit slutty is going to change my life.'

'How do you know?'

'Because I know. There needs to be other things as well. I've got thirty years of *life* to make up for.'

'You should cut off all your hair.'

'Why would I do that?'

'Because you're going through a traumatic break-up. It's what you're supposed to do.'

'This isn't a movie – besides, I like my hair.'

'Really?' She scrunches her nose and I pretend to be offended. 'Suit yourself. Oh! I know. You should swim with sharks.'

My eyes widen in alarm. 'That's a terrible idea.'

'Exactly.'

'But I might get eaten. What about a dolphin instead? Dolphins are nice.'

Susie rolls her eyes. 'How is floating about with Flipper a bad decision? Besides, dolphins just have a good publicist. I've read that they're a bit rapey and murdery.'

'Oh. Eww,' I say, screwing up my face. 'Sharks it is then.'

'What about skydiving?'

'No way.' My resistance is so immediate and strident that she cocks her head at me.

'Shit, you're scared of heights.'

I shoot her a scathing look, then relent. 'Fine, I'm scared of heights. But honestly, that's boring. Anybody can go skydiving. Also, I might die, and then where would I be?'

'Probably in hell if this list is anything to go by. What else do you want to do?'

I chew my fingernail. 'Maybe I could pose nude for an artist? Oh!' I point at her excitedly. 'Get a tattoo.'

'Why didn't I think of that, *yes*! What would you get?'

'Something *big*.'

Susie narrows her eyes, nodding in approval. 'Nice.'

'Shoplifting!' I exclaim. 'That's definitely a terrible idea. Maybe I can get arrested?' I picture myself in an orange jumpsuit. I did enjoy *Orange is the New Black*. I have so many questions and a burning desire to answer them all. Is skinny-dipping illegal? Do swingers' parties actually have swings? What even is molly, and do I need to be at a music festival to take it? 'What number are we up to?'

'Only twenty-five.'

'Oh.' We fall silent, struggling to come up with new additions. 'Well, this is pathetic.'

'Give yourself a break, you're new at this,' says Susie, patting my hand. 'I think you're doing great. You did come up with sex dungeon.'

'That's true.'

'You don't need to have the whole list worked out. It can evolve organically, a living document.' She gasps. 'I can make you a spreadsheet.'

I have a sudden thought. 'What about rules?'

Susie frowns at me, exasperated. 'Haven't you had enough of rules?'

'Yes, but this feels so—' panic creeps in and I desperately want to shut it down before its greedy fingers take hold, '—untethered. Maybe a couple of tiny guard rails, for security.'

She rolls her eyes. 'Fine. How about this? You're not allowed to fall in love. No complications.'

'I can work with that.'

BANG! She slaps both hands on the table, startling me and making several people turn around. 'Do you know what this is?'

'A recipe for disaster? Comedy of errors?'

Susie leans forward. 'This is not a bucket list.' She pans her hands dramatically in front of her face. 'It's a *Fuck-it List.*'

We scream with laughter until our sides hurt. It's that shared and reactive laughter, the kind that moves in delirious cycles, subsiding only to be set off again by the slightest smirk or look. I can't remember the last time I laughed this hard, but I'll lay money on the fact it was with Susie. Despite everything, there's nobody else I'd rather be sitting here with. I pick up the last two tequila shots and hand one to her.

'To fifty by fifty,' I say.

'Fifty by fifty.'

I knock the tequila back, slam the shot glass on the table and turn to look across the bar towards Liam. A smile creeps across my face. 'I think I know where to start.'

13

lucky charm

Kissing Liam is a world away from kissing Gerry. He smells like fresh rain and tastes like peppermint. I don't offer him a drink or make small talk. I take his hand and lead him upstairs to my bedroom. Nerves flutter under my ribs but I've lost the tangle of confusion that knotted my chest a few nights ago. I'm no longer spiralling.

We stand in the middle of the room. He towers over me, but there's no sense of threat as he cups my face and kisses me again, slowly and deeply. I close my eyes and am consumed by burning clarity. Despite the tequila.

I want to see him. I pull at his t-shirt and he steps back, yanking it over his head in haste and making his hair stick up. He's all big hands, tanned skin and hard body and I can't help but think of that scene in *Crazy, Stupid, Love* where Emma Stone tells Ryan Gosling that he looks like he's been photoshopped. I make an involuntary sound and Liam grins and says, 'are ye alright?' I flush, worried I'm being creepy. The shadow of my former self whispers in my ear that I should feel dirty and lecherous, and somehow wrong. But I don't.

I give myself permission to look at him and he submits to my exploratory gaze without an ounce of arrogance or posturing. I run my fingers down his stomach. He flinches and tells me he's ticklish, so I do it again and we laugh. Then he reaches behind me with both hands and unzips my dress. It pools on the carpet and I step out of it as he raises an eyebrow. Then he kicks it across the room. It's supposed to be sexy and devil-may-care, but he's overcooked it and my dress lands on the bedside lamp.

'Shit. Sorry.'

I consider leaving it there but have a precognitive flash of it combusting while we're in the throes of passion. Literal *flagrante delicto*. 'Hold that thought,' I say. I crab walk to remove the fire hazard then awkwardly reposition myself in front of him. 'Where were we?'

'Right about here.' He traces my collar bone and I shiver.

Glancing down at his jeans, I say, 'I think you're overdressed,' and he sheds himself of them in a few seconds flat with a directness that testifies to the differences between men and women. The smallest things are the starkest reminder of how and what we're taught to perform.

'Better?' There's something about the way he pronounces his *r*'s – at once both hard and soft on his tongue – that does something to my insides. I'm not sure any woman can fully explain the visceral effect a Celtic accent has on arousal.

'I haven't been with anybody else since my husband.'

He leans back. 'Are you sure you want to?'

I nod. 'It's just . . . I might be out of practice.'

'Don't worry.' He touches the side of my face. 'I'll take care of you.'

Take care of you. Those very words can be taken in a variety of ways, entirely dependent on circumstance and intent. But in this moment, I understand him without a doubt. I look at him with a mix of wonder and puzzlement. 'How old are you?'

'Does it matter?'

'No.'

Leaning down, he circles my waist with one arm, scoops my body against his then kisses my neck. I am loose-limbed and heady with desire when he picks me up with no effort at all. The tumble to the bed isn't as smooth as intended. I bounce and our bodies collide and there's that laughter again. Kissing me, he unclips my bra with one hand like a magic trick. I wonder how many hours of practise it took to master such erotic sleight of hand.

Liam's tongue journeys my skin in languid circles as he pays lip service to one breast then the other before working his way downwards. My body is on fire. But as his tongue traces my belly, cool air hits wet skin and I shiver. I close my eyes, pressing back on the pillow, my breathing shallow. He removes my briefs with a playful flourish and tosses them over his shoulder, dimples flashing. Then he asks, 'Is this okay?' and I smother the voice that echoes, *Daniel doesn't even do that to me*, and let him hook my knees over his shoulders. One of his arms wraps around my hipbone, his hand pressed to my belly – palm flat, fingers splayed – pinning me like a butterfly to card.

'You should know, I probably won't c—' The rest of the sentence is lost as his mouth makes contact.

Within minutes he has melted me. I am liquid – arms and legs flung across the bed with abandon. I neither know nor care whether it's a case of Jedi-level expertise or simply an enlivening of nerve endings that have long been starved of attention. When I come, the sound that splits me open is like the yowl of a feral cat. I rise, body taut, forcing him to grasp my hips with both hands. It occurs to me that I might accidentally snap his neck or rip his head off with my thighs like a female praying mantis. It strikes me as macabrely funny. I start laughing and then something else overwhelms me. *Oh God, I'm going to cry.* I fling my arm across my face. *I've finally lost the plot.*

As soon as I relax, he disappears from the bed. I hear the jangle of his belt, still threaded in the loops of his discarded jeans and instantly assume he's decided to leave – that he thinks I'm weird for laughing or that I taste bad or that my orgasm face is ugly. Maybe he's put off by my stretch marks or saggy boobs. I sit up uncertainly, formulating a glib comment that implies I'm not upset by the abrupt abandonment. *Thanks for coming . . . oh, wait, that was me.*

But he's not leaving. He's standing with his boxers around his ankles, wrestling with a condom. I can't believe protection hadn't occurred to me. Not that being unfortunate enough to catch gonorrhoea from the first person I sleep with after Daniel would surprise me. Considering the trajectory of the past few days, it would be par for the course.

Liam clambers back onto the bed. 'I thought ye were gonna suffocate me, but what a way to go, eh?' He grins. I laugh again and then he's kissing me before I can object. I taste myself, tangy on his tongue. Then he's above me and inside me and we are only bodies – mouths and hands and tangled limbs. Bursts of laughter, sliding skin and panting breath.

His skin tastes of salt and sweat and I lose track of seconds and minutes. *How have I gone without this for so long?* I didn't realise how starved of physical touch I've been. Or how hungry for it I am. Maybe because it was never like this with Daniel. I let myself fall into it, head thrown back, thinking of nothing but how good it feels.

Afterwards, we lie face to face, our legs entwined. We talk about music, dogs, the Ricky Gervais special on Netflix. We doze and wake, kiss some more – slowly and drowsily. He tells me about

Ireland and how he misses his family. I tell him I miss being close to Abbey, that I don't know what my family looks like anymore. I tell him about the list and make a joke of it and he laughs and says he's privileged to be the first item ticked off. He tells me he couldn't take his eyes off me in the bar. The whole time, his free hand traces slow circles on the small of my back.

When he tells me he's leaving Sydney the next day for the Whitsundays, a pang of disappointment runs through me. He'll be working for six months crewing a yacht. 'You should come,' he says. 'We'd have fun.' I snort before I can stop myself.

'Don't be ridiculous.' *And yet . . .*

'What better way to start yer life over.' For a second, I think he has a point – after all, it's a terrible idea – but I baulk at the jump. Instead, I say that – while I appreciate the gesture – we don't need to do this dance. We don't need to exchange numbers and pretend we're going to call. And fantasising about sailing off into the sunset, well . . .

I say this because of the guttering flame deep down inside that repeatedly reminds me of how unlovable I am. It gasps for oxygen even though I've become practised at convincing myself it's untrue.

Liam says, 'think about it', and maybe I will. Then he asks me to turn over and curls behind me, echoing my shape. I've never been able to sleep like this, so I say, 'only for a minute'. He kisses my shoulder and sleepily whispers Dylan Thomas to me.

'*Do not go gentle into that good night, Old age should burn and rave at close of day; Rage, rage against the dying of the light.*'

Oh, God love him. I try not to laugh and decide he can hold me for as long as he wants. I lie awake with his arms around me for hours, his chest rising and falling against my back, his breath warm on my neck. I fall asleep as the sky outside my bedroom window starts to silver. When I wake up – he's gone.

14

no good deed

It's the first Sunday in years I haven't had to be up early for church, and it feels like I've missed an important appointment. I languish in bed for most of the day, replaying last night and ignoring the disappointment of waking up alone.

When I finally make it downstairs, there's a scrap of paper on the kitchen counter, held in place by a banana foraged from the fruit bowl. Written on it is a phone number and a child-like stick drawing of a sailboat. I try to resist the smile that starts in the pit of my stomach and quickly takes me over, but it's hopeless.

I lean into it, stretching and grinning like that proverbial cat, although I'm not sure which one – the one from *Alice in Wonderland* or the one that got the cream? *Grow up, you're not going to run off with a guy half your age.* In case I haven't got the message, every muscle in my body complains, punctuating the point. *Christ.* One good shag and I'm like the Tin Man. Reluctantly, I pick up Liam's note. *It was nice while it lasted.* Back to reality.

I look longingly at the little sailboat before scrunching the note into a ball and tossing it in the bin, catching a glimpse of myself in the mirror across the room. My hair is sticky-uppy, and my first instinct is to look away – but I stop. There's something different in my face. I move closer to the mirror.

It's in my eyes – they're both darker and brighter – and the set of my chin. It's the barely visible smile I know is there because it's threaded through every aching limb. It's the knowledge that something in me has split open and there's no stitching it back together. I'm not even sure I want to. It's as if – with every reflection before now – I'd been looking at myself through frosted glass and now it's clear – or more accurately, the glass is gone. There's nothing between me and whoever it is I am supposed to be.

This isn't a new version of myself. But I'm no longer the old me either. I haven't started fully living but – I tap it out on the mirror – I am *Not. Dead. Yet.*

I brew a pot of coffee, dig my phone and glasses out of my handbag, and head out to the patio. If I'm going to pick myself up, rejoin the world and deal sensibly with the fallout of my marriage disintegrating, I need to be caffeinated. Dexter circles me as I settle into an outdoor chair, eventually flopping at my feet with a contented huff. I turn my phone on. I'm immediately assaulted by a cascade of notifications. *This cannot be good.* I briefly wonder what might happen if I just threw my phone in the pool.

I steel myself. Things can't get any worse, could they? Although, repeatedly asking myself that is clearly jinxing things. Two missed calls from Abbey and one from Minette. I resolve to call Abbey back as soon as my coffee has kicked in. As for Minette – considering Daniel's instructions to stay away from Stars Fold – he can handle it. There are multiple texts:

Susie: I made your spreadsheet.

Susie: Speaking of spreadsheet, can you walk this morning?

In the light of day and sober, the Fuck-it List seems ridiculous. Do I honestly think visiting a sex dungeon or doing a nude run is going to help me find myself? Liam was a wonderful – what did Susie call it – circuit breaker? But I need to get on with my life like a grown up. I can make myself a priority without going nuts.

Her third text makes less sense:

Susie: Shit. Are you okay?

Why wouldn't I be okay? I scroll through the rest of the texts. Two are from Abbey:

Abbey: Mum, what the hell is going on? Is this true?
Abbey: I'm worried about you. Please answer the phone. We need to talk.

Daniel must have filled her in; nice of him to give me a heads up. The tone of her messages makes me wonder how he's skewed it. Annoyed, I click on the final message.

Liz: Nice photo. You left that tidbit out.

The hackles on the back of my neck rise. What's she talking about? What photo? Foreboding slithers around my neck as I remember Daniel's words. 'I have to figure out how to spin this.'

I punch the URL of the first news site I can think of into my phone's browser. *Shit.* What has he done? It takes only a few clicks to find it. The glib headline reads *NOW THAT'S A FALL FROM GRACE.* (I bet whoever came up with that thought they were *so* clever.) It sits boldly above an image of me on stage at the concert, dishevelled and mid scorned-woman roar. I scan the article. The words 'nervous breakdown' leap out at me and my fists clench in disbelief. I can't believe Daniel has played the 'crazy' card. A photo of me being bundled into a car – eyes half-closed and my underwear showing – comes next. Is that what Liz was talking about? I scan the words 'a family history of drug and alcohol abuse and mental health issues' and am instantly white-hot with fury. *Anything but that.*

It's a savagely low blow, but it's not over. Further scrolling reveals Daniel's sordid trump card – a photo of me and Liam leaving The Hip Joint late last night, our body language leaving no doubt as to what was going on. If I wasn't so stunned, I'd applaud the gall of him. Blood pounds in my head as I read the words *affair* and *toy boy.*

It's genius really. What better way to distract from your own wrongdoing than painting the aggrieved party as the bad guy. I've unwittingly given him everything he needs for a get-out-of-jail-free card. Now, it doesn't matter what I say – it's out there, and people love to believe the worst. How do I argue with public evidence, regardless of its veracity? I had a meltdown in front of thousands of people bombed out of my head. That's a fact. I slept with a man half my age last night – and I'm technically still married. Also a fact.

Nobody will care – or believe – that it was in response to my husband cheating on me for months, walking out and expecting me to toe the line. I'll appear like a jealous and deluded wife, a liar scrambling to cover my own hide. It seems he who gets in first, wins. I can already imagine him spinning it back to me: *'The church and the congregation are what matters. It's bigger than us. Bigger than me.'* I am the sacrificial lamb.

I dial Daniel's number and it goes to voicemail, so I hang up and try again. Eventually, when I can't stand the sound of his voice any longer, I leave a hissing message. '*This* is what thirty years is worth to you?' I ring off. 'Bastard.' It's all I can do not to hurl my phone across the yard, but instead I tap out a follow-up text:

Grace: Call me back. You owe me that.

I sit for several minutes, trying to settle the writhing, impotent fury in my belly. I'm having trouble locating the line between anger and panic. Control of my life is not slipping – it's being *yanked* out of my hands. I'm not ready to let go, but one thing is startlingly clear. If Daniel isn't going to consider me, I don't have to consider him – not what he thinks, not how things look, not how things impact the church or *our* reputation. There is no *us*. I'm done.

I make my way back to the kitchen, typing into my phone:

Grace: Suse, send me that bloody spreadsheet.

Then I go to the bin and fish out the note. You can't change a story once it's been told, but you can damn well write the next chapter. If I'm going to be accused of crazy things – I might as well do them.

I'm running my finger across the little sailboat when my phone rings. *Abbey.* I can't avoid her any longer. 'Hi, darling.' I try to make my voice sound as normal as possible but there isn't much point. Abbey launches without a breath.

'Finally! Mum, what the heck? I've been trying to get hold of you for days. Please tell me this is all a mistake.'

'I'm fine, honey, but it's been a rough few days. Have you spoken to your father?'

'Briefly.' She sounds wary – accusatory. 'He told me I needed to speak to you, that you'd explain everything. This is so unlike you.' Her voice cracks and I can't bear it. 'Just tell me, what's going on between you and Dad?'

In that split second, I make a decision. I'm taking back control.

'I'm leaving him, sweetheart,' I say. I don't tell her about Sasha, about Daniel twisting the truth. I tell her I haven't been happy and it's time to think of myself. I say that I'm sorry she had to see me that way, but what's done is done. The entire time I'm speaking, my brain is screaming *why are you protecting him?* But I'm not protecting him. I'm protecting Abbey.

She already believes the worst. Her voice betrayed her as soon as I answered the phone. And why wouldn't she? She's no different to anybody else; it isn't her fault. The seed was planted by an expert gardener. I could tell her the truth, but what purpose will that serve? She'll still doubt me, still be angry. Only she'll be angry at us both. Abbey isn't a child anymore, but she needs at least one parent as shelter.

'Christ, Mum.'

'I know it's not what you want to hear, but I promise everything will be fine.'

'Are you sure, because it doesn't seem fine? And to be honest, this isn't the greatest time for you to be having a mid-life crisis.' Something in her voice makes my spider senses tingle.

'What do you mean – what's going on?' There's a long silence – so long that I'm about to check she hasn't hung up. 'Abbey? Is something wrong?'

'Not exactly.'

'Abbey, I've had very little sleep, I'm not in the best frame of mind. It's not the time to be cryptic.'

'This is why I've been trying to get hold of you.'

'What is?'

Another silence, then—

'I'm pregnant.'

Just like in the car with Daniel, I think I've misheard. The rushing in my ears starts again. And there it is – the fist in my throat. Except this time, I know there's nothing that rhymes with *pregnant*. So I don't know why I ask her to repeat herself.

'I'm sorry, you're what?'

'I'm pregnant, Mum. You're going to be a grandmother.'

15

running up that hill

The rest of the phone call with Abbey is a blur. All I remember with any clarity is that the baby is due late November and Tobias's mother is 'beside herself'.

'You don't sound very excited,' Abbey says. I hear the disappointment in her voice and know what I'm supposed to say back, but the words won't come out. Because I'm not excited. All I feel is panic. Yet another part of my life is being wrenched out of my hands. I'm being forcibly frogmarched into the crone phase of my life whether I like it or not. *A grandmother?*

I manage to say, 'Darling, please don't think that. It's just a lot on top of everything else', followed by something about the doctor having given me valium because of all the, well, you know, and a general need to lie down. I'm fairly certain I suggest lunch tomorrow to talk before abruptly hanging up and commencing intense pacing of the kitchen while trying not to hyperventilate.

When the pacing makes me seasick, I find my way to the floor. It isn't much better. I'm stuck on the Gravitron – that horrendous fairground ride that spins so fast you're pinned to the wall by centrifugal force, helpless to move unless it's to turn yourself upside down in a redundant attempt to give the illusion of some modicum of control.

I can't be a grandmother. I just had sex with a twenty-five-year-old. *Oh, God!* I'm suffocating. I have to get out of the house.

Minutes later, I'm in the cupboard under the stairs, searching for running shoes I'm sure are shoved somewhere towards the back. Shoes I only bought because Abbey convinced us to do the Mother's Day Classic fun run five years ago. A truly hellish experience, namely because I don't run. Ever. I've always thought running makes no sense for human beings – unless something terrifying is chasing you.

The shoes are snug but I'm sure they'll be fine. I don't bother with socks. It's not like I'm planning to run a marathon – it's just a light jog to the end of the street to clear my head.

The first couple of hundred metres are a breeze. One foot in front of the other, a steady rhythm as I try not to think about the reason news of my impending matriarchal status has hurled me so violently over the edge. Left foot then right. Deep breath in; long breath out.

Isn't it joyous news? A *baby*. A brand-new little life.

I turn right and continue around the block. My ankles and knees jar with every step as my feet thud, heavy on the tarmac.

But me, a grandmother? Grandmothers wear cardigans and like being called Nanny or Grandy or Baba or some other nonsensical two-syllable word. They're dependable and well-behaved. They don't make plans to go to sex parties. Or get drunk and throw up in pot plants.

Left. Right. In. Out. My breath comes in panting bursts and my chest hurts. Daylight fades but still I run, eyes glued on the end of the long road. The shoes rub at my heels but it barely registers. Neither do the first few drops of rain. What am I supposed to do now? Take up knitting? Join other old ladies in their sturdy one-piece swimsuits doing water aerobics with those tiny, pointless hand weights? Grandmothers step up. All I want to do is step down.

The sky opens, rain dumping down and soaking me through. The unfamiliar shoes start to squelch painfully. I limp to a stop and slide them off as cars fly past me, tyres hissing on the wet road. My breath sucks in sharply as the sneakers take my skin with them.

It's dark now. I should go back. I glance towards home, breathing heavily, my hand pressed against my chest. *It's coming for you. Keep running.* I take off like a mad woman; bare feet slapping through puddles. Left. Right. In. Out. Breathe. But it's like running through quicksand, or like I'm sprinting with one of those stretchy bands looped around me – the ones masochistic personal trainers use – stopping me from going too fast. From running too far.

Left. Right. In. Out. Breathe. Don't cry. Try not to scream.

There's an intersection ahead. I don't know which way to turn. Either way I face a whole new version of myself. In one direction, a complete stranger. Frightening and unpredictable. In the other direction lies what looks like safety. How easy it would be – to lean in and take up a mantle that by definition makes my life about somebody else. At least I know how to do that.

But I'm terrified. Not only of losing myself, of abandoning the discovery of who I could be, but of failure. What if I can't be what Abbey needs – what her baby needs – because deep inside I don't want to be? There's something wrong with me. It should come naturally, shouldn't it? It's all horribly familiar, a creeping déjà vu. The clinching thought claws its way up – from where it's been gnawing deep in my guts – threatening to spill out along with the flood of tears I've been holding back for days.

What if I can't love it? What if it doesn't love me because I don't know what I'm doing?

I can't go through that again. But I don't have a chance to decide which way to run. At breakneck speed, I step on something small and sharp. A ferocious pain shoots through my foot and I stumble sideways, screeching, hoping to Christ it's not a rusty nail because I can't face a tetanus shot on top of everything else.

'What the—' I scan the pavement and find the offending object. It's not a nail. It's worse – a single red Lego brick. What is a Lego brick doing on its own in the middle of the street? My emotional trip-wire finally snaps.

Fists balled at my side, I scream with every breath in my lungs at the sky, at whoever or whatever is up there. 'What else are you going to throw at me? Isn't it enough?' The sky eats my words, my voice disappearing into the inky void. I get nothing back, not even an echo. Not that I expect to. Nobody's listening. The sobs build, rumbling and volcanic in my chest, and I turn in circles in the rain, still holding the Lego brick. I have no idea where I am. I wasn't paying attention.

'Do you need a lift?' A deep male voice comes out of nowhere and I turn to find a tradesman's van has pulled up to the kerb beside me. A muscular guy, with a shaved head and a tattoo on the side of his neck, is looking at me with what is probably concern, but I'm in no state to see it.

'Excuse me?' I shrink back against the fence.

'Sorry. Didn't mean to make you jump,' he says. 'You seem upset and look lost.' I gape at him, heart hammering. 'It's raining pretty hard, I thought you might need help.'

Deep down, I know he's being decent and making sure something terrible hasn't happened to me. Like he'd hope some other random person would do if they saw his mother or sister wandering the street at night, barefoot and crying. But that knowledge hunkers underneath mounting sobs; under Daniel and Sasha and the debacle of a concert; under Abbey and the impending baby and the fire and the reappearance of Susie in my life; under Liam and almost-Gerry and his stupid underpants; and those god-awful trashy headlines. Instead of saying 'thank you, I'm fine', searing anger engulfs me.

'I can bloody well see it's raining. Christ, can't a woman go for a night-time run in the fucking rain without some *man* harassing her? Are you some kind of *predator*?! Leave me alone before I call the police.' And then the crying finally comes. It tumbles out of me in a wail, loud and uninhibited; the way a two-year-old cries when they've skinned their knees.

Things are going to go one of two ways – the tattooed good Samaritan is either going to call an ambulance and tell them to bring a tranquiliser gun, or say *Screw you, lady,* and leave. His screeching tyres signal his departure, and I sink to the ground and howl, still clutching the Lego brick in my clenched fist.

Car after car drives past while I sit and cry in the rain. Occasionally one veers closer to the kerb – probably to figure out whether the dishevelled lump on the pavement is an unfortunate dog somebody has hit – before realising it's a crying woman and speeding off, sending a spray of run-off from the gutter in my direction – which I do think is a bit unnecessary. Not a single one slows.

The temperature has taken a nosedive along with the sun and I'm soon shivering. I need to get home. The problem is I haven't brought my phone, and I'm completely disoriented. Through the heavy rain, the light from a broad sweep of high-rises flares in the distance, sending a halo of light into the sky. I move towards it – certain it's the right direction.

Limping along the road, feeling hollow and more than a little scared, I finally see a taxi coming towards me. I flag it down and sink with relief into the back seat. Within minutes, I recognise streets and breathe easier. I have no idea how I got so turned around. I lean my head against the window, desperate to get home, shower and bury myself in sleep.

For the first time in years, I don't know what's coming. All of my carefully laid plans – sticking to the rules, doing what's right – and in the end, it hasn't made a difference. The life I'd worked so hard for was secure and stable one minute, now it's nothing but uncertainty.

I'd kept my promise to myself – and to Daniel and Abbey – with unwavering military precision over decades. I'd even convinced myself I was happy. People always say endings bring new beginnings. But what if it puts me right back where I started?

I wake to more horrible headlines and Susie's texts. She's annoyingly invested in the entire situation. Evidently, a couple of photographers were outside when I bolted in panic from the house. The photographs aren't pretty, and I'm not saying that out of vanity. I am wild-eyed and manic, bedraggled and shoeless. The headline? *IS THIS THE HIGHWAY TO HELL?*

Refusing to be a prisoner in my own home, I try reaching Daniel again. This is his fault. He can fix it. Although – knowing the media – once blood is in the water, all bets are off. Unsurprisingly, Daniel still isn't picking up my calls. I resort to donning dark glasses and stuffing my hair under a baseball cap, then inch the spare car – an old Volkswagen we keep for guests – out of the narrow gardener's entry behind the house. I head in the one direction nobody will think to look for me. West.

I hadn't planned on travelling down memory lane any time soon, but a lot has changed in the past few days, and despite my misgivings, Liz has me worried about Mum. The thought of driving down old streets – streets I've long tried to forget – has me nervous. I never know which memories are going to spring out at me.

Abbey has agreed to relocate our lunch, suggesting Westfield Penrith, which isn't too far from Liz's place. I'm not sure how Abbey knows that offhand; I didn't even know Penrith had a Westfield now. It used to be Penrith Plaza, but that was years ago. I guess everything gets swallowed up by the future eventually. I'll check in on Mum before meeting Abbey. I haven't told Liz I'm coming.

'Siri – call Susie.'

She answers on the second ring. 'So much for keeping a low profile. Since when are you trying out for the Olympics?'

'Since my daughter dropped another bombshell on me,' I say. 'I needed to blow off steam. Remind me to never run again.'

'Deal. So, what's the bombshell?'

'Abbey's pregnant.'

'Whoa! Congratu-fucking-lations, Grandma.'

'Less of the G word, please.'

Susie snickers. 'Sorry, *Nanna.*'

'I will hang up on you.' An unwelcome flush sweeps over me and I turn the aircon up, fanning the air towards my face. 'Honestly, I don't know how to feel. I can't get my head around it.' I sigh. 'Grandmothers are supposed to be *old*, Suse.'

'Nah.' Susie seems taken with the idea. 'It's exciting. You'll be a hot and sexy grandma.' She says it like a radio announcer, and it makes my skin crawl.

'Please never say those words again.'

'You're right. It sounds like a niche category on PornTube.'

'Yuck, did you have to go there?'

'What? Old ladies need sweet loving too.'

'I'm not an old lady.'

'I never said you were,' she says, 'but I think you've got a complex.'

'Whatever gave you that idea?'

'Because I can hear you shrivelling into a dried-up old raisin over the phone.' She laughs.

'Very supportive. Thanks a bunch.'

'That's what friends are for.' She switches tack. 'Hey, speaking of loving, are you still coming over tonight to set up your apps and go over the spreadsheet?'

'Do we have to?' I groan. 'I hate Excel and I'm not sure I should be dating this quickly. I'm still fragile.'

'Rubbish. You're about as fragile as Robbie Williams's ego.'

'To be fair, I think you'll find Robbie Williams is actually quite sensitive and hides his self-doubt behind a whole lot of bravado—'

'Whatever, dork. The point is, how are you supposed to have lots of sex if you don't go on dates? Come on,' she pleads. 'Let me live vicariously through you. Besides, I've already started planning your dating app profile. I was going to call you MILF77, but I guess I'll need to change that now. *GMILF77*.'

'What? No.'

'You know, Grandmother I'd Like to F—'

'I got it. Thank you. It sounds like a dragon from *Lord of the Rings*.'

'Suit yourself. I think it's hot.' The phone muffles and I hear the vague sound of voices and a PA announcement.

'Where are you?' I ask, puzzled.

'Nowhere. Just at a . . . thing.' Susie sounds like she's dropped the phone for a moment before it clatters back into clarity.

'Okay, cryptic.'

'Not cryptic. Boring work stuff. I gotta go. See you at seven?'

'I'm already regretting it.' I ring off as I merge onto the M4 and switch my CarPlay over to the Calm app. I need all the Zen I can get because – despite all best intentions – visits to my family never go the way I think they're going to.

16

christ on a cracker

July, 2005

Houses have long memories. You can't live a lifetime between four walls without it all seeping into the plaster. The good and the bad. Outside, it looks the same as ever, except Dad's garden beds look worse for wear, especially his bonsais. Mum's thumb isn't exactly green, but the state of the plants smacks of making a posthumous point as opposed to forgetfulness or lack of gardening skill. The heat breathes a dusty haze over the house; everything is faded but the things I remember – sharp and jagged as ever.

Inside will be different. Dad always took up so much space. I haven't seen anyone since the funeral and I'm nervous. A lot can change in six months. Mum hates celebrating her birthday, but it's her first without him and, despite everything, it's bound to be hard. Everyone's making the effort to be here today, even me. No doubt Mum will have made coleslaw and the pasta salad with the tiny peas and tinned ham. Liz said not to bring anything, but there's no way I was coming empty-handed.

Daniel lets Abbey out of the car and catches my eye over the roof. His look asks if I'm okay and I duck my head in answer and slide the platter of nibbles from the back seat. They tell me I'm distant. That I don't call or tell them what's going on in my life. That I have to be reminded of my nephews' birthdays. The subtext that is I don't care enough to make an effort. So, this platter is not just a platter.

Rolled prosciutto and salami nestle against piles of olives. Enough fancy cheese to cause a heart attack on sight: triple cream brie, camembert, and a pungent blue I'm sure Liz's twins will get a kick out of. Bell peppers, a gourmet salmon dip, and artisanal crackers that fan around the earthenware plate. It's an edible work of art. Of love.

Mum is smoking in the kitchen. I lean down to kiss her and can smell that she's already several bourbons in. Dad's old medals are on the counter; she's been cleaning them. I don't know why she insists on torturing herself.

'Happy Birthday, Mum.'

She looks me over. 'Did you get your hair done again? Looks nice.' My mother is the only person I've ever met who can make a compliment sound like you've done something wrong.

Out on the back deck, Nate is hunched over his Nintendo DS while Gus and Caleb run around shirtless in the heat. Nate barely looks up but makes room for Abbey to huddle in next to him. The twins crowd around as I set the platter on the table with a nervous flourish, offering it up for scrutiny.

'What's all that?' Liz raises an eyebrow.

'What does it look like?' My defences are quick to stir. 'It's French cheese and antipasto.' The boys poke at the peppers and lean down to sniff the cheese. They recoil instantly.

'PWOARR. That smells like Dad's feet.'

I knew they'd find it funny. I laugh and so does Abbey, but Mum leans out of the door, waving her cigarette at them. 'Boys, don't be rude to your Auntie Grace.' She glances sideways at me. 'That cheese is probably expensive.' The twins fall over each other, shrieking in disgust.

Mum stares them into submission, and I say, 'It's okay, it's only cheese,' but she shoots me a look that says 'See, I got them to behave for you.' I'm not sure what she thinks just happened.

I catch Liz rolling her eyes as she clears space around the platter. It stands out like a sculpture among bowls of chips, bottles of Coke, and the over-flowing ashtray.

'What happened to French onion dip and Jatz?' Liz says.

'I thought this would be nicer, seeing as it's Mum's birthday.'

She doesn't look at me but the tightening of her lips speaks volumes. 'Bit of a waste. You know we don't eat that fancy stuff.'

'You haven't even tried it.'

The platter sits untouched as I catch Mum slipping the twins twenty dollars in the kitchen. They hop on their bikes and fifteen minutes later they're back with a full shopping bag. Mum whisks my platter into the house as they empty the bag onto the table.

Liz opens the French onion dip and Jatz. The deli counter has yielded pre-cubed cheddar cheese and sliced kabana, wrapped in paper. Caleb flexes his skinny muscles, popping the lid off a jar of green cocktail onions. Everybody flocks to the spread like hungry seagulls. I look to Daniel for support but he's no help – he's too busy trying to fit a chunk of cheese, two Jatz and an onion into his mouth.

In the kitchen, Liz covers my platter with plastic wrap. I tell her I'm sorry nobody liked it but that I'd put a lot of effort into making it special.

'It's all good, Grace,' she says. 'Take it home for you and Daniel, there's no point it going to waste.'

'It'll go to waste anyway; it's a bit much for two people.' I glance through the back door to the table, annoyed, and I can't help myself. 'It's not like it was cheap.'

Liz stops wrapping. 'So invite some of your posh friends over.'

'Excuse me?' I bristle as Mum comes through the back door.

'Don't make it into a drama, Grace.' She empties the ashtray into the bin. 'It's just a bloody platter. Come and sit down. Enjoy some time with your family for once, hey?'

I peel the plastic back defiantly and take a large hunk of prosciutto, shoving it into my mouth and chewing hard as we all go out the back. I swallow it down and it sticks in my throat. A lot can change in six months, but a lot can stay the same.

17

go west

Liz and Colin bought off-the-plan in St Clair about fifteen years ago; a few suburbs down from our old house in Mt Druitt so they could stay close to Mum, who'd been on her own for a few years by then. It's a step up from their first house a few blocks away; a weatherboard two-bedder with a rickety enclosed verandah they called the 'sunroom'.

The upgrade is a nice, normal house, perfect for a nice, normal life, and they worked hard for it. Built over two levels, the apricot concrete render distinguishes it from its almost-identical neighbours. They put in a pool not long after moving in and built a granny flat. Mum moved in after her first fall and they found asbestos in the roof of the old house.

Liz complained about Mum whenever she got the chance, but I think she liked being needed – being the one who was always there. The boys have all moved out now – Gus is in Melbourne at university and Caleb is backpacking around Europe. Nate's got kids of his own, which still blows my mind.

I've only been here a handful of times. Daniel and my family never really clicked. They thought he was up himself. And Daniel, well, I remember him saying once that he couldn't understand how *they* produced *me*, and that he was proud of me for 'rising above my beginnings', for wanting more out of life. I defended them at the time, but in the end his opinion burrowed under my skin and crystallised into truth. Visits grew fewer and farther apart until I only really saw them on special occasions. I'd be lying if I said I haven't felt their absence. I just wish the anticipation of spending time with them didn't fill me with such anxiety.

I pull up out front and kill the engine. Liz's dogs – a pair of elderly cattle dogs named Bodie and Doyle – are already barking, announcing my arrival. Liz opens the front door before I'm out of the car. She steps outside wearing rubber gloves, denim shorts and a singlet. She's doesn't look happy at being caught off guard as she closes the door behind her.

I wave, grab the bunch of orange tiger lilies from the passenger seat and head up the driveway. She can't be mad at me if I bought flowers.

I underestimate my sister.

'What happened to giving me notice?'

I stop. 'I only decided this morning. I didn't think you'd mind.'

'You couldn't have texted first?'

'Do I need to make an appointment to see Mum?' I wait for a response. Nothing. 'Seriously?'

She peels her gloves off, lips pinched. 'The house is a bit of a mess is all, and Mum's just woken up. She's a bit—' She trails off and glances back at the door.

'I'm not here to check your house, Liz.' Her nostrils flare as she shoves the gloves in her pocket. 'I won't stay long. I'm meeting Abbey for lunch at Westfield.'

She smirks. 'Really? How long since you ate in a food court?'

I honestly can't remember, but I'm not telling her that. 'Can I come in or not?' There's a moment of stand-off, then she relents.

'You're here now.' She turns and heads inside, barring the door with her leg to stop the dogs escaping. 'Watch the dogs, they're temperamental with strangers.'

I bristle. 'I'm hardly a stranger. Your dogs love me.' I step over her leg and lean down to pat what turns out to be two young and over-excited bull terriers. Surprised, I pull back, in case they bite my face off. 'That's not Bodie and Doyle.'

Liz slips past me into the house, the unfamiliar pups trailing her. 'I had to get them put down last year – both riddled with cancer,' she tosses over her shoulder. 'Would have cost eight grand to sort them out.' She doesn't look at me, but I don't need to see her face to know her pragmatic tone is a front. She's an expert at it.

'I didn't know. I'm so sorry.'

She shrugs. 'Who puts their dogs through chemo anyway?'

Part of me wants to tell her I would have been more than happy to pay for the vet – that I know how much she loved her dogs. The realistic part of me knows she wouldn't have asked. The more salient – and unspoken – point though is I'm not involved enough to know it was needed. The awkwardness is mercifully swallowed by two rambunctious bodies careening down the hallway and launching themselves at Liz's legs.

'Grandy, Grandy! Can we go in the pool?'

Surely not. Nate's twins were barely crawling last time I saw them. They spot me and retreat behind Liz, suddenly shy. She ruffles their identical spiky blond crew cuts. 'Jaxon, Cruz – you remember your Great Auntie Grace.' She glances at me then adds, 'Auntie Abbey's mummy.'

The qualifier doesn't help. They stare at me with wide eyes that say they have no clue who I am. Liz crouches next to them. 'You need to have some lunch first. Go ask Pop-Pop to make you a wrap, then you can go for a swim.'

They tear off towards the living room – where I can hear some kind of motorsport on the TV – both yelling 'Pop-Pop!' repeatedly. Liz heads for the kitchen and I follow, skirting a mountain of clothes and bed linen spilling out from the laundry and a heap of camping gear piled next to the dining table.

'They're so big.'

'Grade 1 next year. Means I won't have them as much, which I'm not looking forward to, but they're ready for it. Clever monkeys.'

'Do you have them a lot? What's going on with Nate?'

Liz points to the kettle and I nod. 'Working as much as he can since him and Caitlin split. Trying to buy a house for him and the boys.'

'I didn't know they split.' I'm like a broken record.

Liz doesn't have to say anything. Her shrug says it for her. She looks towards the living room and smiles. I can hear the boys, now chanting, 'WRAP! WRAP! WRAP!'

'We don't mind. Col was born to be a grandpa.'

Liz passes my tea and I sip at it even though it's too hot, using it as a distraction from continuing a conversation that's too close for comfort.

'So you've spoken to Abbey?'

'What?' *Is she reading my mind?*

'You said you're having lunch with her, so I'm assuming you've talked to her?'

'Right, yes. Just quickly.'

Liz looks at me expectantly. 'And?'

I stall. There's no way I'm telling Liz that Abbey's pregnant and I'm panicking about it when she's playing Super-Nanna right in front of me.

'And what?'

'How'd she take it? She must be pissed at Daniel.'

Oh. 'Actually—' I quickly explain what I've told Abbey and why and ask her to keep it between us. Liz is unimpressed but doesn't seem surprised.

'Old habits die hard.'

'What does that mean?'

'It means maybe you need to let her see Daniel for who he is for once, instead of always being prepared to play the bad guy, then being a martyr when Abbey puts him on a bloody pedestal.'

'I don't do that.'

Liz's eyebrows shoot up. 'If you say so.' The air ripples with tension until Liz finally rolls her eyes and grabs the flowers. 'Anyway, your choice. I'll put these in water. Mum's on the patio.'

I reach for the flowers. 'That's okay. I want to give them to Mum.'

Liz ignores me, rummaging in a cupboard for a vase. 'They put that yellow pollen shit everywhere. I'll show her later.'

I silently count to five and unclench my jaw. 'No problem.' I glance at the back door. 'How is she?'

Liz looks at me briefly. 'It's been bad, but today's a better day.'

Mum is smaller than I remember. Twelve months can take a lot from a person. I tell myself it's the size of the wide sling chair that makes her seem tinier, but deep down I know furniture can't be expected to carry that responsibility.

I watch her through the screen door. Guilt whispers in my ear. *You shouldn't have left it this long.* She's wearing slippers with socks, even though it's not cold. An iPhone with a cracked screen is clipped into a mount on the arm of the chair so she doesn't have to hold it – she scrolls the screen with one finger, staring fixedly. Nothing captures her attention long enough to stop scrolling for more than a few seconds.

She doesn't turn when I open the door.

'Mum?' When she finally looks up, she gazes at me for a fraction too long before recognition hits. Then she smiles, her eyes widening.

'Grace, love! What are you doing here?' She struggles up and pulls me to her. I wrap my arms around her back – she's like a bird, all tremor and bones – as her cheek presses to mine. Her skin is paper thin, and I can smell cigarette smoke in her hair. She lets me go, her face dropping. 'Has something happened? What's wrong?'

I squeeze her again. I don't want to let go. 'Let's just say, it's been a bit—'

'Everything's fine, Mum.' Liz appears behind me and places a jug of iced tea and some glasses on the table. She shoots me a look. 'Grace was over this way to meet Abbey so she thought she'd pop in. Isn't that nice?'

Mum puts a hand to her chest, relieved, and sits back down. 'Good. You had me worried. It's such a surprise to see you.' She pats my hand. 'A good surprise.' Liz plonks an iced tea in front of me, glass clattering on glass, as Mum gives me the once over. 'How's Daniel?' She stops herself, quickly recalibrating. 'Wait. I think Lizzie said you might be having a few problems, be a bit stressed – sorry.' Her hands flutter in discomfort at the perceived faux pas.

Before Liz can chime in, I brush it off, assuring Mum it's nothing to worry about; we're simply working through some things. The lie rolls so glibly off my tongue, I almost believe it. It satisfies her enough that she relaxes, switching to regular programming. 'Well, it can't be all flashy cars and big houses now, can it love? Marriage is a job, like anything else. You have to work at it, and you don't always like it. Look at me and your dad.'

My neck prickles, but I'm saved from responding by the screen door ricocheting against the wall. Squealing at an excruciating decibel level – and now wearing nothing but matching Spider-Man underpants – Jaxon and Cruz chase Liz's dogs out of the house. The dogs crash against the table and it shifts, aluminium grating on concrete. I wince and Liz catches me. I morph my face into a smile, as if the chaos is adorable. I'm not a good actor.

If Liz bit her tongue any harder, it'd bleed. Maybe I should say something, smooth it over so she doesn't think I hate her hyperactive grandsons and replacement dogs – all four of which I'm sure are very sweet when they're asleep. Before I can, Mum snaps.

'Jesus Christ!' She grips the table. 'I can't think with all this bloody noise. Where the hell are their parents?' She looks around, agitated. I touch her hand; she jerks around to look at me.

'You mean Nate?'

She pulls her hand back, flustered. 'Of course I mean Nate. I'm not an imbecile.'

I blink at her, a sense of panic pulsing behind my ribs. 'Sorry, I—' I look to Liz for help but she's tight-lipped and already herding the kids towards the door.

'Go finish your wraps, otherwise no swim.' She swings them expertly through the door and they squeal again. Then she hollers, 'Colin! Can you get off your fat arse, turn the V8s off and occupy the twins please?' I wince again, this time behind her back.

Colin's jovial voice carries from inside. 'Last night you said you loved this fat arse. Oi – ratbags. Come 'ere.' The sound of the front doorbell is barely audible above their renewed squealing as he chases the boys through the house. Liz looks like she's about to explode and I can empathise. My senses are rapidly overloading, like they're being poked with a needle in quick succession from every angle.

Liz pushes her hair back from her face, exasperated and heads indoors, leaving me alone with Mum, who's back to calmly scrolling her phone.

'You okay, Mum?'

'Hmm?' She looks up, smiling.

I tread lightly. 'You seemed upset before – a bit confused.'

'Did I? Bit hot and tired is all. I am eighty, you know.' I must look worried because she huffs. 'You're as bad as Lizzie. Always making a fuss. I'm fine.' She pats my hand and repeats, 'How's Daniel?'

I try to smile but can't stop my chin quivering. I clear my throat, blinking and pretending to pick lint off my t-shirt. 'He's fine, Mum. Daniel's fine. What are you looking at on Facebook then? Anything interesting?'

Easily diverted, she turns the phone in my direction. 'I like all the animal videos. There's this one with a dog and a cow that are best friends, and – *Abbey!*' Her smile broadens and I follow her gaze, confused.

Abbey stands in the doorway, Liz behind her. She looks equally as surprised to see me. 'I thought we were meeting at Westfield.'

'How did you know I was here?' Our questions tumble over each other. It's been weeks, so I jump up to hug her as Liz ducks back into the house. Abbey stiffens but hugs me back, restrained and wary. I can't blame her, but it stabs at me anyway. I let her go and sit back down.

'I didn't. I was running early. I thought I'd pop in and see Auntie Liz and Nanna before lunch.' Abbey leans down to kiss Mum's cheek and she pats Abbey's face in return.

'She pops in all the time, when she's over this way. Don't you, love.'

She does? Since when?

'At least you don't have to worry about parking at Westfield now.' Liz emerges from inside with an extra glass and a large bottle of sarsaparilla. Abbey was addicted to the stuff as a teenager. I had no idea she still liked it.

'Actually, Abbey and I have some things we need to talk about.' I try to keep my voice even. 'We might still head over there, grab something to eat.'

'Don't be silly.' Mum waves a hand at me. 'Why would you pay for parking and food when you don't have to? You can stay for lunch, can't they Lizzie?'

Liz looks at Abbey then me. 'If they've got private things to talk about, Mum—' She doesn't get to finish the sentence.

'Private? We're family.' Mum shoots me a baffled look, shakes her head. 'You hold too much in, that's always been your problem.'

I clock Liz's eyes widening before she looks away and heat floods my chest and neck. *You don't know the half of it.* I catch Abbey's eye and she shakes her head almost imperceptibly. I peel my fingernails from my palms. *I am not being oversensitive.*

'It's fine, Nanna,' Abbey says. 'Me and Mum can talk any time.'

'Of course we can.' I force a smile. 'It's not that important.' *It's only my family imploding, an unexpected baby and my life spinning into some nightmare alien vortex – wouldn't want to bother anyone with the drama. I'll be over here pretending everything's fine and getting a blue rinse, shall I?*

I watch Abbey show Mum a video on her phone, laughing. There's an ease and lightness about her I don't often see, and it stings. When she's at home with us, she always seems vaguely on edge – the conversation a running commentary on how well her work is going, like she's trying to assure us of something. Whenever she's around Liz and Col, and Mum, she's different, relaxed.

I get a memory flash of her at ten years old, on Boxing Day – eyes shining, laughing hysterically with Nate as they tried showing Mum the dance routine from the Backstreet Boys' 'Everybody' music video. They'd been practising for hours.

Mum had no idea who the Backstreet Boys were. She thought they were trying to do 'Thriller' and made everyone's Christmas – even Dad's – when she got up to show them the steps, shimmying across the living room, swinging her clawed hands. The memory makes me chuckle and Liz catches it from where she's leaning on one of the patio posts.

She tilts her head, a flicker of paranoia. 'What's so funny?'

Before I can answer, Colin's husky frame fills the doorway, a wriggling twin under each arm. 'Go put your rashies on and wait by the gate for your floaties,' he instructs, trying for stern and not quite nailing it. Deposited on the patio, both boys tear towards the pool fence. Colin ambles past Liz, squeezing her bum as he passes, then looks my way, instantly awkward. 'Grace,' he says. Undoubtedly Liz has filled him in – probably shown him that damn TikTok. He quickly diverts his attention, spotting Abbey with relief. 'Crabby!' he booms – it's the pet name he's had for her since she was thirteen and horribly hormonal. 'How's that bun baking?'

What did he say?

Abbey stiffens, her eyes darting to me. Liz shoots him a

none-too-subtle look to shut-up. All it does is confuse him. 'What? You said—'

'Bun's baking fine, Uncle Col.' Abbey shifts in her chair, avoiding looking at me. She exchanges what she thinks is a surreptitious glance with Liz but it might as well be a flare gun. Abbey forgets that growing up in my family gifted both me and my sister with fluency in subtext.

Every inch of my skin prickles. *They already know.* Abbey must have told Liz she was pregnant – before she told me – and neither of them wanted me to know. I can't decide whether I'm annoyed, hurt, or both. I keep my face neutral. Mum is as confused as Colin.

'Did I miss something?' She looks from me, to Abbey, to Liz, then back to me.

I have two choices. I can point out that Abbey telling Liz about the baby before sharing the news with her own mother is incredibly hurtful, or I can pretend to be completely unbothered and blithely continue the conversation as though her pregnancy is common knowledge.

The problem with the first option is, no matter how I frame it, my hurt feelings will be taken as an attack – on both Abbey and Liz. Instead of understanding why it stings, the walls will go up, arrows nocked, bows at the ready. I'll be the one causing unnecessary drama and making it about me. I know this because I learned long ago – and the hard way – that my family is incapable of having honest, uncomfortable conversations about conflict without getting defensive.

The problem with the second option is that Liz and Abbey already know I'm upset. They knew pre-emptively – hence the subterfuge – and they can read it on my face. But knowing I'd be upset and allowing me to *be* upset are two different things. I take the path of least resistance and let it sink under the surface to stay there, unexamined. It's easier and less painful.

'Abbey's having a baby,' I say.

The delight on Mum's face is worth burying it, the next ten minutes a barrage of enthusiastic questions and unsolicited pregnancy advice. Abbey should sleep on her back, not her side; not eat soft cheeses; and she shouldn't be afraid to have a drink every now and then. Mum regularly had a glass of wine with dinner all the way through both pregnancies, and me and Liz turned out fine.

That's debatable. Liz and I lock eyes. I cross mine briefly and she stifles a smile.

'The rules are all too much, if you ask me,' Mum continues, on a roll. 'Women have been having babies for thousands of years without panicking about eating a bloody oyster.'

I stay out of it, neutral mask still in place. Abbey handles it all with aplomb. I'm not going to point out that up until a hundred years ago, women were still dying in childbirth by the truckload. Nobody likes a Debbie Downer, and besides, it's impossible to know exactly how many of those deaths were oyster related.

Abbey's excitement is palpable, but there's something else behind her eyes. It could be my own anxiety reflected, but I'm not certain.

'Are you feeling okay about it all, Abs?'

Her smile is too bright. 'Yeah, of course. Why wouldn't I be?'

'No reason. I just know how much you're juggling already, sweetheart.' I probably should stop there. 'Do you think it's the right timing?' *Too late.*

Liz has moved to the edge of the patio and is in the middle of lighting a cigarette. She takes a quick draw and exhales sharply, the smoke curling towards the table. She waves her arm through it, trying to divert it from Abbey.

'It's never the right timing, Grace,' she says. 'You and I know that.'

'It's not really the same thing, is it?' I say, trying to keep the edge out of my voice. This is not where I wanted to be having this discussion. I didn't think I'd find myself longing for a suburban shopping mall, but here we are.

Abbey shrugs. 'We think it's as good a time as any. I don't want to be having a baby in my thirties.'

'I didn't know you were that set on having a baby at all.' I regret the words as soon as they leave my mouth. Everyone falls silent. Except Colin, who's several metres away wrestling the twins into their swim vests and is oblivious.

'Have you decided what you're going to be, Grace?' he asks, over the top of the twins' heads. 'Nanna or Grandma?'

All eyes swivel in my direction. *Shit.* I already know there's no right answer. Not a truthful one anyway. My throat tightens.

'Neither,' I manage to choke out, and he laughs.

'You have to choose one. The kid can't call you Grace.'

Liz groans and rolls her eyes. 'Oh, God. Please don't be one of *those* women.'

My nails dig into my palms. 'I haven't had time to think about it, but Grandma and Nanna aren't really *me*,' I say.

Mum tuts loudly. 'For heaven's sake. It's not about you, Grace. You know, *I* couldn't have cared less what my grandkids called me, as long as they loved me and knew I loved them.'

Do not take the bait.

'I'm sure we'll come up with something, Mum.' Abbey smiles at me and it's the first connection I've had with her since she arrived. I return the smile. Maybe things won't be so tricky after all. If only we could get out of here and talk properly.

Mum starts on about how quickly pregnancies fly by, how much there is to organise, the dozens of items a new baby needs. Before I can offer anything, Liz has donated a bassinette, a cot, a convertible pram and a mountain of baby clothes – all from Nate and in storage from when the twins were babies.

'That's lovely of you, Liz,' I say. 'But I'm sure Abbey wants the experience of buying all her own new things. Right, honey?'

'But these are from family,' Mum interjects, as though Nate's double Bugaboo is some kind of heirloom. 'They've already been loved. That's much nicer than buying new things for the sake of it.'

Abbey scrunches her face. 'I mean, they are some of the big-ticket items. It would save us some money. And – *sustainable*. Bonus.'

I nod and say nothing, my jaw clenching and unclenching, because I know if I say '*oh darling, you know you don't need to worry about the money*' at this moment, it will be like blasting a flame across the table into my sister's face. It's also because part of me agrees. It is nicer. I just don't have anything to contribute.

Colin offers to get the bassinette out of the garage after he's taken the twins for a swim and work out when they can drop off the cot. Liz starts listing all the clothes she has boxed up, and I watch Abbey pull up the Notes app on her phone, ticking off item after item on a list I haven't seen yet. Mum starts googling trending baby names, tossing out, quite frankly, horrifying suggestions like 'Wednesday' and 'Maverick' and repeating herself, unaware that in all the excitement, nobody is paying attention. And I want to cry. It's all moving so fast. Eventually Abbey looks over at me, mistaking my expression.

'There's plenty of stuff still to get, Mum,' she says. 'I've got six months. Maybe we can go shopping and you can buy us some things?'

I bury my objections alongside everything else.

'Sure, sweetheart,' I say. 'I can do that.'

18

weird science

Susie lets out a low whistle. 'Whoa! That is way too bloody hot.'

'What? I think you need glasses. He looks like a potato.' I glance up from my phone, realising Susie has a mouthful of melted cheese and is not commenting on the unattractive man occupying my phone screen. 'Oh. You mean the pizza.' She nods, fanning her mouth. 'He still looks like a potato,' I say. 'Actually, they all look like potatoes.'

I poke the screen a few times, hoping it will magically make someone more attractive appear. My phone makes a *swoosh* sound. 'What just happened?' Susie peers at it and takes another bite of pizza.

'Woo! You got a match. Now he can talk to you.'

'But I didn't do anything.'

'You must have swiped right.' She leans over nonchalantly and refills my wine glass.

I'm horrified. 'But that was Potato Man. Why would I swipe right?'

Susie shrugs at me. 'You've gotta start somewhere.'

'I am not starting there. Can I un-match?' I take a sip of rosé and pull another slice of pizza from the box because this whole dating app thing is quite stressful. It's been about twelve years since I've eaten pizza. It's deliciously disgusting but I'm done worrying about what I put in my mouth. *Not a euphemism.* No more making myself small.

Susie makes an exaggerated sad face. 'But he's probably excited. Do you want to hurt his feelings?'

'You're enjoying this.' I throw my phone into her lap. 'Make him go away. This is your fault. I only agreed to this because you promised you wouldn't make me talk to weirdos, and that there were suitable options.'

Susie taps the screen a few times. 'Suitable options? You make it sound like we're shopping for a pantsuit. There, he's gone.' She hands my phone back. 'Man, you're brutal. I have no control over the quality of men out there. We have to work with what we've got.'

I slump back against the couch, disheartened. Earlier, Susie had proudly walked me through how to use my new 'Fuck-it List' spreadsheet, which for some reason came with an inbuilt algebraic formula for tallying sexual experiences vs non-sexual experiences and converting them into a percentage of the overall list. Looking at it hurt my brain. I hadn't wanted to disappoint Susie, so I'd exclaimed 'Yes, girl!' and made a mental note to pop to Officeworks ASAP. I'm thinking something much more analogue.

We'd spent the last two hours setting up my profile on Boom, which, according to Susie, is less sleazy than Tinder, less annoying than Hinge, and has more attractive men than Bumble.

'How do you know all this when you're supposed to be happily married?'

She shrugs. 'Rob was being a dickhead a few years back, so I told him to get stuffed for a couple of months,' she says. 'Trust me, I'm basically Yoda when it comes to these apps.'

We went with my middle name – Emilia – because apparently using my real name means I'm a Google search away from being stalked. I imagine Emilia to be enigmatic and sassy. She's sexually confident – definitely not a people pleaser. Basically, she's nothing like me. I chose a single photo with my face partially obscured.

'You know you're going to limit your options if they can't see what you look like,' Susie had objected.

'Don't you know who I am?' I was only half joking. The last thing I need is some journalist spotting my profile and plastering it all over the internet. Or one of the church husbands passing it on to Daniel as some kind of bro-code PSA. 'It's called *mystery*, Suse, and you can at least see a bit of cleavage.'

'Fine,' she'd huffed. 'But don't write any boring stuff about communication and shared values.'

'Why not?'

'We're trying to get you laid, it's not a job interview.'

'But I also want to be respected.'

'No, you don't.'

'Yes, I do.'

'No. You don't.' She'd slapped the back of my head for emphasis. 'You want to be thrown around, have your hair pulled, and be told you're a good girl.'

'Do I?' I'd glazed over, momentarily hypnotized by the erotic visual. *Good girl.*

We'd dedicated at least an hour to crafting the perfect bio in less than one hundred and fifty words, albeit fudging a few facts. It was trickier than I thought, because there are apparently lots of rules to consider: Don't sound needy or desperate, but remember hyper-independence is a turn-off. Men like to be needed, just not too much. You *could* be looking for a relationship – because *morals* – but you're also completely fine if he doesn't want one – because you're *so* chill. Casual's your favourite word, behind football. Be easygoing, but not easy. There's a difference. Which doesn't mean you're not still up for it, because you totally are. In a non-slutty way obviously. Because you're *classy*. Be cute and witty, but not too funny or too smart – you don't want to intimidate him. Say you like camping, even if you hate camping. And whatever you do, do *not* mention feminism, misogyny or the patriarchy. Doing so will immediately make the penis of any potential match shrivel up and drop off. Except don't make assumptions, because 'not all men'. *Bitch.*

'That all sounds complicated. I'm looking for one-night stands. Shouldn't I just say that?'

'Only if you want to be bombarded with sleazebags.' Susie rolled her eyes as if I was a moron. 'There's a *code*, dummy.'

'I don't get it. Can't I be honest. Be myself?'

Susie had reeled back in horror. 'Why would you want to do that? Nobody on there is themselves.'

'How does anybody connect and have sex then?'

'By not being themselves. Duh.'

'I'm so confused,' I'd admitted.

I've since realised that it doesn't matter. I doubt any of the men on Boom are taking the time to read it anyway. I haven't intentionally matched with anybody yet. So far, we've scrolled through dozens of men. All over forty – because I'm trying to be age appropriate – and all a little worse for wear. 'Why are so many of them holding dead fish?' I resume swiping left and grimace. 'Is it some kind of sex signal?'

Susie shrugs. 'Maybe they think it makes them look rugged. You know, *me hunter!*'

'Somebody should tell them we have supermarkets now.' I swipe again and stare at the screen. 'I'm beginning to think all of these men are delusional. There's no way Bill is forty-two.' I show Susie the profile of a heavy-set bearded man with missing teeth. He looks at least sixty-five. His headline reads *FWB only*. 'Sorry, Bill. I have enough "friends" and nothing you have to offer looks like a "benefit" to me.' I swipe left with a vigorous flick.

'You learned the acronyms!' Susie grins proudly.

'I'm nothing if not thorough when I commit to a project.'

'All of them?' She narrows her eyes, sly and suggestive. I know exactly what she's getting at. And I'm not biting.

'I can neither confirm, nor deny—'

Susie doesn't let me finish the sentence. She steeples her fingers, tapping them together with glee, channelling the Count from *Sesame Street*. 'One penis . . . ahahaaah! Two penises . . . ahahaaah!'

I cock an eyebrow. 'I think you'll find the correct plural term is pen*i*.'

Susie cackles. 'You know, you're really funny now you've had that pole-ectomy.'

'Thank you very much. I'm here 'til Thursday, try the veal.' I wave my phone. 'This is hopeless. You said this was a woman's market.'

Susie throws up her hands. 'You're being very picky for someone who's only had sex with two people in her life.'

'I'm sorry, but every man in my age range looks like Lurch from *The Addams Family*.'

'It is grim out there.' Susie nods, sagely. 'Older men do not seem to have mastered the art of moisturising. Unlike—' She snatches my phone and taps the screen.

'What are you doing?'

'Lowering your age filter.'

I attempt to grab the phone but she leans away. 'Suse, no – I don't want people thinking I'm some kind of desperate cougar.'

'Says the woman who's got a twenty-five-year-old's number tucked away in her purse, just in case. Anyway, "cougar" is on your list, remember? Look, it's simply for comparison.' She refreshes the app and hands the phone back. I blink at the screen, stunned.

'Whoa. What did you set it to – Paul Mescal?' I swipe left on the new profiles – because I'm not delusional enough to try matching with them – my eyes widening. *Hello*, Jake. *Hellooo*, Ryan. *Holy crap.* It's like a different species. One whose very survival has necessitated the evolution of defined abdominals and chin dimples. Maybe it's something in the water.

'I'm easing you in – thirty-five to thirty-nine. That's not creepy,' says Susie and I have to agree with her. Numerically it sounds perfectly reasonable for casual encounters. Realistically I'm less convinced.

'I can't imagine any of these guys would be interested in a menopausal forty-nine-year-old.'

'Younger men like experience.'

'Fairly sure we've established I don't have any.'

'Bloody hell, babes.' Susie's tone shifts gear into TED Talk mode. 'I don't know what you see when you look in the mirror, but from where I'm sitting, you've got a great rack and I've always thought you have very pretty eyes.'

'I appreciate that, but I can't do it. Anyway, they're not going to automatically be better at everything because they're younger.'

Susie makes a face. 'Here's my theory – men our age have a lifetime of being with women our age. We weren't taught to ask for what we want. We fake the majority of our orgasms. They don't even know they're shit. Younger guys are prepared to put the work in – they've *learned* – because younger women are different. Why shouldn't we reap the benefits?'

It's an impressive theory.

'What if not a single one swipes on me? I don't think I can take the rejection. It's a much safer bet to stick to men my age.'

She's not impressed. 'Fine. But everybody gets sick of potato eventually.'

I ignore her, click back into the app and find the age filter. I slide the upper range back towards fifty and sigh, thinking of FWB Bill and his missing teeth. Then I think of glorious Jake and his abs – abs I'm now realising I swiped left on and have relegated to the ether. *God damn it.* I surreptitiously slide the lower range down to thirty. There's no harm in keeping my options open.

There's something about arts and crafts that's therapeutic, no matter how old you are. I stick my home-made Fuck-it List to the wall in my bedroom and peruse it with satisfaction.

After mapping a grid in black marker on a big sheet of card, I'd filled in half of the list and spent an hour decorating it with coloured pens. A packet of gold stars sits on the dresser because my inner child is nothing if not reward-motivated. I'm also one of those people who writes things they've already done on their to-do list, because I've read it's good to start the day with a sense of achievement.

Vandalise a bus. Check.

Sing karaoke live on television (technically accurate and deserving of two gold stars because Alanis Morrisette is hard). Check.

Sleep with sexy Irish guitarist. Five stars. Check! Then I remember Liam's age and reluctantly place a star on the item beneath it: *Be a cougar.*

Four done already. *Excellent start.* The rest of the list is daunting. It's not even exhaustive, barely grazing thirty with space to add new things. But as I read it, my pulse escalates. Part of me wants to be exciting and sexually liberated, but my fear of judgment is deep-rooted. I've spent the past thirty years reading Bible verses that label any woman who claims her sexuality a 'disgraceful woman'.

To be honest, I've never really understood why sex is so 'bad'. It's the most essential of our natural urges. The human race would die out without it. But then it's not really about the sex, is it? The sin is in the desire – especially a woman's. It makes us unruly, and nobody wants that.

Panic presses in on me and I remind myself I don't have to do it at all. Susie might be disappointed, but I doubt she believes I'll go through with it anyway. This whole list sits outside my comfort zone – not just the sexy parts – and I'm scared. When I was a teenager, I mightn't have found these things scary, but I'm a different person now.

I wonder if remnants of the earlier version of me still exist – original programming buried somewhere under layers of propriety and restructured coding. Earlier versions don't go *poof* when life changes us, they're simply swallowed up and encased inside the updated version – like a set of painted matryoshka dolls. We're the opposite of spiders. They're forever expanding, outgrowing themselves, bursting out of their exoskeletons and leaving their creepy eight-legged shells behind without a backward glance. We carry our previous selves inside us, along with everything that comes with them, the good and the bad. Some of it buried deep, inside the smallest of the dolls, but always there – waiting.

It would be easy to envy spiders and their ability to let go of what's no longer needed. But maybe not everything that changes us should be discarded. Not every new version is an upgrade. Maybe the original me isn't dead, just dormant.

I study the list, trying to be realistic. I can't flip a switch and reboot my personality in an instant. I have thirty years of conditioning to unpick.

Then it hits me. What if I treat this like a science experiment? Experiments need research. They require objectivity. The scientist needs to approach things clinically. There's no room for fear, only facts. I can learn how to do this the same way I learned how to be a Christian, and how to fit in with the girls in high school. It's not hard; you just have to pay attention – learn the rules, then execute the behaviour. *Yes!* This is perfect. *This* is how I'll get through my Fuck-it List without freaking out. I face the chart head on, grinning.

I am totally getting top marks for this.

19

is that even legal?

Wayne – fifty-years-old, six-feet tall, divorced, enjoys theatre and the gym – is a lawyer. His photos give off a cocky Bradley Cooper vibe and he can spell, which makes him the pick of the age-appropriate bunch. I'm waiting for him in the lobby bar of a boutique hotel he'd suggested, just off Hyde Park. Wayne is already twenty minutes late.

Susie's insisted I text her his photo and drop a pin with my location if I go home with him, in case he's a serial killer. When I tell her she's not funny, she says, 'Neither is you being drugged and tied up in a basement.' She has a point.

I haven't been on a first date in thirty years, which means I've been on one first date in my life. Is dating the same now as it was in the 90s? Are there new protocols I'm unaware of? My nerves are making me sweat in all the wrong places.

My purse contains five condoms, which I realise sounds overly optimistic. It's not so much about repetition; mishaps happen, and it's best to think ahead. I didn't know there were so many varieties. I haven't seen one for years, I was always on birth control. I doubt I need to worry about pregnancy at my age, but Susie's graphic warning about chlamydia being 'rife out there' almost put me off the whole thing. The last thing I need is to emerge at the end of this experiment with a vagina like a Petri dish.

An unwelcome voice scratches at my brain. What does it say about me that I carry condoms in my purse just in case? In case of what? Some kind of random sexcapade that's so spontaneous there's no time to run to the pharmacy?

It says you're being a slut.

I flick the slur away. It's a horrible word and I would never, ever think it about another woman. But what we say to others and what we say to ourselves are two different things. I straighten my shoulders, my body rippling with indignation and rebellion. My inner voice can fuck right off.

And so, I have a ribbed one, a dotted one, a plain regular-sized one and something called a 'Magnum' (again, optimistic). I imagine it's all well and good to buy condoms for a boyfriend or husband – it's a familiar penis after all. But a stranger? What if I offer up a Magnum and the poor guy only has a piccolo? Men have such fragile egos at the best of times.

The fifth condom is glow-in-the-dark. I'm sure the brains behind this option were thinking about practicality in the dark. But I imagine the reality being more ridiculous – the condom, in situ, waving around like a lightsaber. *Zhhhhmm. Zhhhmmm. I will not be your father, Luke.*

When Wayne saunters in, I look twice to make sure it's him. His profile pictures don't do him justice – and that's not a compliment. He's at least ten years older, a foot shorter, and more Dennis Leary than Bradley Cooper. There is very little chance I'm having sex with this man. I'll be polite, have a civilized conversation, then make an early exit.

'Well, this is refreshing,' he says as he approaches, looking me up and down. 'You actually look like your photos. Very nice.'

I'm not sure how he can tell from my faceless photo, but I'll take it. He immediately orders two martinis without asking if I'd like one.

I tell him he looks different. He grins and says, 'Full disclosure . . . I'm sixty, and – now I know you're not a catfish – my name's really John.' My first thought is *why are men so obsessed with fish*, and my second is *did they not teach you the definition of irony in law school?* My third thought is *if you're going to choose a fake name, why on earth would you choose Wayne?*

He explains that women assume men over fifty-five can't get it up and assures me he most definitely can. His 'safety strategy' – a fake name and age – means less likelihood of a woman going all 'bunny boiler' and tracking him down online. I tell him it's fine, because my name's actually Grace. Wayne – sorry, *John* – has the temerity to look put out.

Three martinis in and he's asked me zero questions about myself but has told me all about his investment portfolio, his golfing prowess and his 'bitch of an ex-wife'. I don't mind. It saves me from making stuff up – I'm not good at lying on the fly.

Four martinis in, I'm pleasantly numb and have decided that John-not-Wayne is quite good-looking after all. Maybe I will have sex with him, to make him stop talking. I blink at him in a seductive manner, which probably looks like I've got something in my eye. He doesn't notice, he's too busy staring at my mouth.

I tell him I'll fix up the last round of drinks. He says, 'I like a woman who takes charge', as I wobble my way towards the bar. My card declines again and again. John-Wayne (because that's what I'm calling him now) doesn't seem surprised. He says, 'Riiiight', in a knowing voice, then winks and tells me he's sure we can work something out. He's got a room at the hotel, which is very convenient and explains why he suggested meeting here – but doesn't explain why he was late.

He kisses me in the elevator, sliding his hand up my skirt. He's not a very good kisser. We're both pretty drunk so I let it slide, but I push his hand away. He calls me a tease. A distant voice whispers that I should be annoyed, but I'm not. I kiss him again and say, 'All good things come to those who wait.' This isn't me – it must be Emilia. I can't decide if I like her.

The sex is terrible – and not because I'm drunk. We go through three condoms in the first six minutes because – despite his assertions – he can't stay hard. He keeps pulling them off and tossing them aside before working away at himself, grimacing with concentration. I'm not sure how to help, so I watch, my interest purely clinical. There's nothing arousing about this. It reminds me of somebody shaking an empty sauce bottle.

He catches me looking so he asks me to touch him while he rummages around between my legs like he's looking for something in the glovebox of his car. I oblige and do my best to get a rhythm going, but his poky fingers are distracting. He keeps asking, 'Is that it?' Short of providing him with GPS instructions, I doubt there's any hope of him finding my clitoris, so I reluctantly murmur *mm-hmm-mm-hmm*. It does the trick, and he abandons his excavation of my vagina, rips open another condom (not the Magnum, FYI) and climbs on top of me.

It's over quickly. He pumps away for about thirty seconds, growling in my ear, 'Yeah baby, do you like it when I fuck you like that?' while I look over his shoulder at the ceiling and think, *No, John-Wayne, not particularly*. The room is spinning. I'm not sure whether it's the thrusting or the dirty talk that makes a bit of vomit hit the back of my throat. I swallow it down as he rolls off me and heads for the bathroom. *I am never getting this drunk on a date again.* You'd think I'd have learned my lesson with Gerry.

I expect him to get dressed and hint that I should leave, so I pre-emptively start dressing. When I explain that I'm heading home he tells me to stay, because he 'doesn't want me to feel cheap'. He's quite firm about it and I don't want to argue with him – even though I didn't think about feeling cheap until he said that. I reluctantly agree, but I draw the line at spooning – that's a privilege that needs to be earned and John-Wayne has simply not put in the effort.

'I can't sleep that way,' I say, when he throws his arm over me.

'Suit yourself.' He rolls over and turns out the light, leaving me laying on my back, sheet clutched to my chin.

John-Wayne is snoring within minutes, and seeing as I'm not married to him, I don't have to put up with it. I inch silently out of the bed, and dress quickly. The door shuts behind me with a clunk and I scurry down the hallway, shoes in hand, in case he catches me escaping. As the lift doors close, I sag against the wall and start to laugh. I take out my phone, intending to send him a mature and polite message so he doesn't find I've left with no explanation. Something like '*Thanks for a good night. You're very nice but I'm not sure we're compatible*'.

John-Wayne has already unmatched me.

20

higher ground

Walking into Stars Fold, I'm on high alert in case I run into anyone. The morning service finished an hour ago so it's unlikely, but my nerves are frayed. The only person I want to see is Daniel – although *want* isn't entirely accurate.

Unsurprisingly, he's still not taking my calls. My bank card declined again in the taxi last night. Lack of available funds. Mortified – I hadn't felt that particular knot in my gut in what felt like a lifetime – I ran into the house to find some cash to pay the driver, who thought I was trying to dodge the fare and followed me to the door. The fact I was still carrying my shoes hadn't helped.

Had Daniel found a way to cut me off? He wouldn't stoop to that would he – he didn't have the right? We owned everything together, ran things *together.* I'd checked our online banking with a rising sense of panic – but everything looked fine, there was plenty of money in the account. *Calm down and call the bank. It's probably a glitch.*

Turns out I was right to worry.

This morning, a polite and robotic young man called Aaron answered my call and matter-of-factly informed me that a daily spending limit of two hundred dollars had been requested on our main account. By the account owner.

Adrenalin had spiked, flushing my skin. 'I *am* one of the account owners, Aaron. Can you please *un*-limit the account for me?'

Why would Daniel bother limiting the account if I could simply *un*-limit it? Was he trying to push my buttons? It's a joint account. Besides, if I couldn't access more than two hundred dollars, neither could he. Swallowing apprehension, I'd managed to say, 'Aaron, can you tell me if there have been any unusually large withdrawals in the past week?'

I'd held my breath, listening to the rapid click-clack of computer keys down the line.

'Yes, a withdrawal of twenty-five thousand dollars was made in branch yesterday.'

Bastard.

I stalk down the corridor and throw open the office door, ready to let loose with a stream of my new favourite expletives, to find Minette at Daniel's desk. She jolts when she sees me.

'Mrs Miller. What are you doing here?'

I bristle at her. 'Where's Daniel?'

Minette is usually unflappable. But right now, she seems pretty flapped. 'Uh . . . he's not here.' She pauses, clearly unsure how much information to give me. 'He went out,' she says. 'Straight after service.'

'Do you know where he went? You have access to our—*his* calendar.'

She shakes her head. 'I'm sorry, I don't.'

I study her, eyes narrowed, and she shrinks. 'Fine.' I gesture at the mobile phone on the desk. 'Give me your phone please.'

A look of panic crosses her face. 'Sorry?'

'I'm still your employer, Minette, and that's a business phone.'

'He said he didn't want any calls.' She looks like she's about to cry and automatic empathy surges. Old habits. *Remember, no more 'nice Grace'*. I raise my eyebrows, hand outstretched. She reluctantly passes me the phone.

'Mrs Miller, please—'

I steel myself – *ugh this mean-guy approach is hard* – and ignore her. I punch Daniel's number and hit speaker. He wants this public? I'll make it public. Daniel answers on the third ring. My pulse gathers speed, thudding in my ears.

'What part of "no calls" was difficult to understand, Minette?' He's curt and distracted. 'What's the emergency that can't wait?'

'It's me.'

His voice is curated and non-committal. 'Grace.'

'So it's only my calls you're avoiding.'

He takes a deep breath, like he's trying to work out how to manage me. He says, 'I think it's best we keep our distance while things settle down is all,' and then covers the phone. There's faint, muffled conversation. He's not alone, and the knowledge twists in my belly.

I snap. 'Do you think you could tell your girlfriend to fuck off out of the room while you're talking to your wife?'

The line clears. 'I will hang up on you if you swear at me again.' He's infuriatingly composed as heat rushes up my neck. Minette watches me from behind the desk, wide-eyed. She undoubtedly wants to be anywhere but here.

'I spoke to the bank,' I say, as calmly as possible. 'What are you playing at?'

'It's simple, I'm trying to avoid having to freeze our funds while we work through this. You can remove the limit, but I'll keep putting it back on. You're acting erratically right now. This way I don't have to worry you're going to empty our account out of spite.'

I'm rapidly losing my battle against fury, like trying to hold a door closed against the ocean. I push against it, knowing it'll get me nowhere. If I snap, Daniel will hang up.

'So, you're controlling my access to *our* money while pulling twenty-five grand out of the account to cover your own arse – and you're talking to *me* about spite?' I laugh sharply. 'You and Minette are the ones who have the media writing awful things about me *and* my family.' I catch Minette's flinch out of the corner of my eye. 'How could you do this to me after everything I've done? For you, for us – the church? I even covered for you with Abbey.'

A long pause – then he clears his throat and recites the expected spiel. 'And I appreciate all of it. But I have to protect Stars Fold. It's not personal, Grace.' *Not personal?* 'There was nothing in those articles that wasn't true in one way or another. I know it's not nice – and I'm sorry for that – but sometimes sacrifices have to be made.' He doesn't sound sorry at all, and he knows he's on loudspeaker. Daniel's not stupid.

I want to scream at him. I have the furious urge to kick the desk in front of me then sweep the computer from its surface, smashing it to pieces. But I can't do any of that without adding weight to his lies – also I'm not sure I have the hip flexibility to do one of those big karate kicks.

Minette stands witness this time. Daniel has pushed me to it, he turned on the gas. But striking the match and allowing myself to explode – *that* makes me unstable. Everybody will say there's something wrong with me. That I'm not okay. I'm crazy. Jealous. It's my fault. I should control myself. That kind of anger isn't very ladylike, is it? After all, Daniel's being *so* reasonable.

'Can you at least call off the paparazzi? It's stalking. I don't even know how they keep finding me.' I manage to say. He has the gall to chuckle.

'You think I'm some kind of puppet master, Grace? Here's a tip, maybe don't give them any ammunition. I'm not the one acting like a lunatic in public.'

'Who *are* you?' I ask, not expecting any real answer.

'I could ask you the same question,' he says. 'Look, I have to go. I'm in the middle of something.' *I bet you are.* 'And do me a favour – don't pull this stunt with the phone again. Text me. I'll call back if I think it's necessary.' He hangs up before I can respond.

I'm shaking with the effort of restraint, frustration zinging through every limb like high voltage with nowhere to go. I've never felt more helpless in my life. I manage to stop myself throwing Minette's phone at the wall. I place it on the desk, deliberate and controlled, as she eyes me. She looks terrified, and a tiny pang of guilt pokes at me. This is her job. I can't blame her. Daniel's used her as much as me. It doesn't mean I have to be nice to her.

'Thank you for letting me use your phone,' I say, heading for the door.

'Mrs Miller – Grace?' Minette's voice is tremulous, and when I turn back, she's in tears. *Ugh. I did not want to have to be nice.* 'I know you don't want to hear this, but I had nothing to do with the things they wrote.'

'Come on,' I say. 'It's your literal job, Minette.'

Her hands flutter at me. 'No, I mean, *yes*, it's my job, but all I said was that we needed to redirect the media's attention. Give them something else to focus on. Mr Miller called them himself. I had no idea he was going to say those horrible things; it's so unethical and unkind. I'm so sorry.'

'Yet you're still here, joined at the hip with all the bad ethics and unkindness.'

'I really need this job.'

I soften slightly – she's simply caught in the middle of an awful situation – and nod at her. 'Okay. But I'm not Mrs Miller anymore. It's just Grace now.' I move to leave before she tries to hug me.

'Grace? I have to tell you something else.' *What else could there possibly be?* She screws her face up and pauses before rushing the words. 'The photographers found you because Mr Miller told them where you were.'

'What do you mean? Was he following me?' My fists clench automatically.

'No. He didn't need to,' Minette explains. 'He was watching your bank account. He could see where you were spending money.'

Sunlight blinds me as I burst out of the service entrance into the back courtyard. Marching onto the grass, I fold inwards on myself and mutter vehemently, 'Fuck you, you fucking manipulative arsehole, I hope you catch syphilis and your dick drops off and then you die!' I growl, bear-like, and kick the nearest tree, hurting my foot and carving a chunk of leather out of the toe of my shoe.

Then I smell it. Marijuana. Not that I'm an expert, but it's hard to miss.

At the other end of the courtyard, one of our oldest parishioners – Margaret Symes – sits in her motorised wheelchair, smoking a fat joint and staring up at the trees. She hasn't seen me. I stare at her. *What is our saintly eighty-year-old organist doing getting stoned after church?* I step into her eyeline. 'Margaret, hello. I didn't see you there. Are you okay?'

She starts, then beams at me, putting a finger up for me to wait. She fiddles with her ears. 'Sorry dear, I turned my hearing aids off during the service. Forgot to turn them back on. I wondered why it was so nice and quiet.'

Relief washes over me. At least she didn't hear my rant. I'm not in the frame of mind for small talk, so I tell her it's nice to see her, but I'll leave her in peace to, uh – enjoy the greenery.

'Are *you* okay, Grace?'

There's no point pretending she doesn't know. I decide to be frank. 'No, Margaret. I am far from okay.'

She nods sagely. 'I'm not surprised. It's all a bit shit.' She catches my eyebrow twitch. 'You're not going to report me for profanity, are you?' In all the years I've known her, I've never heard Margaret say anything stronger than darn. I shake my head, too taken aback to respond. 'Cancer. Stage Four,' she says, by way of explanation. 'Liver, lungs, and now apparently up here.' She taps her head then takes a long draw on the joint, holding her breath. 'This is the only thing that helps,' she squeaks, eyes like slits, before exhaling slowly. I stare at her, unsure what to say, then sit down on the bench next to her chair, my heart hurting. I had no idea.

'Well. That's a bit more shit than what's going on with me.'

She presses her lips together, nods slowly again and passes me the joint. I'm about to refuse – it's been a lifetime since I smoked anything, let alone marijuana – then I think of the conversation with Daniel. The fury still vibrates through my veins. If ever there was a time for weed, this is it. *Extra gold star for me.* I accept the joint and take a big hit. It burns the back of my throat, but I don't cough. Nobody wants to be out-ganja'd by an eighty-year-old.

We sit in silence, the smoke puffing around us, a sweet and pungent cloud. My mum always said pain is relative. That someone else's problem being worse than your own doesn't mean you can't still feel bad about yours. Sitting here now, I can't help thinking there are some instances where that shouldn't apply.

Margaret is dying. Her family will be grieving soon. As for me – my husband slept with a pretty girl and is being annoying about all the money we have, and I'm freaking out about becoming a grandmother. *Boo-hoo, Grace.*

'You know what I've realised – at eighty-two-years-old?' Margaret suddenly blinks like an owl. 'Our brief life is a precious gift, but we only get the gift if we live our brief life. Do you know what I mean?'

Wow. She's really stoned. I nod supportively. 'Yes, absolutely.' *No idea.*

She smacks my shoulder – quite hard considering her frailty, which proves that weed is not as chill as everyone says – and leans earnestly towards me.

'It's important. I spent my whole life running around after my ungrateful sons and reading the Bible when I really wanted to be on Broadway. Now look at me – what a waste. It's all meaningless in the end. If you don't make decisions for you, do the things *you* love, your life isn't a gift. It's a burden.'

Margaret stares at me, waiting for an answer. It's like she's looking into my soul. It's a good job weed doesn't affect me, or I'd be really paranoid right now.

'I feel like Daniel's holding all the cards.' I don't know why I'm telling her that or where it's coming from, but nothing has ever felt so true.

Margaret puffs on the joint then waves it at me. 'So – play with a different deck.'

Whoa. She's like an all-knowing oracle. All this time, we had an oracle playing 'Abide with Me' on our organ and we didn't know it. Amazing, Grace.

'Ha!' *That's my name and a hymn.* I snort-laugh then realise Margaret doesn't know why I'm laughing. She probably thinks I'm stoned – which I'm not, obviously. What did she say? Play with a different deck? I try to retrace my thoughts, stitching them back together in reverse, but I take a wrong turn. Nope. It's gone, but it's fine. I'm sure it'll come to me.

Margaret eyes me. 'Can I show you something?' She pulls back the blanket on her lap, revealing a deck of tarot cards. 'Don't tell anyone. They'll have me burned at the stake. I know we're not supposed to believe in all this, but the closer I get to the end – well, it's been helping me more than all the Jesus stuff. Maybe it can help you too.'

I stare at her, surprised. 'Oh, Margaret, I really don't think tarot cards are going to fix my problems.' I know she means well, but the last thing I need is her telling me I'm going to come into money, travel the world, or meet a tall, dark and handsome stranger.

She makes a *psssht* noise. 'Come on, humour an old woman. Draw a card. Let's see what they have to say.'

I smile and put my hand out for the cards – mainly because my head is too foggy to articulate a reason not to. I'm hardly in a position to say I don't believe in a higher power. What's the harm?

She directs me to shuffle the cards, thinking about the area of my life where I most need answers. I weave the cards back and forth, closing my eyes and letting my mind run freely across the chaos of recent days. Snatches of random long-ago memories intrude – my wedding day; teaching Abbey to ride a bike; that terrifying day at the beach with Dad, when Liz and I were little kids.

'Now, split the deck.' Margaret's voice brings me back to the present. 'And choose a card.' I follow her instructions, hand her a card and stare at her, inexplicably nervous.

She turns the card and gasps. I lean over, looking for clues.

'The Wheel of Fortune. That's gotta be good, right?'

She squints her eyes at me. 'This is an exciting card, Grace. It means the future hasn't been written.'

I frown. 'So, it's an *I don't know* card?' I'm having trouble connecting the dots.

'The wheel represents everything in the tarot. Always turning, like life. It asks you to be open and adaptable, to take time to understand yourself. Don't try to know everything in advance.'

'But isn't knowing the future the whole point of—' I wave at the deck and she shrugs.

'The only thing certain about the future is that it will be a surprise,' she says, and I try not to get annoyed.

'So, literally anything could happen?'

'Your life is a blank slate.'

'That's not very helpful, Margaret.'

She smiles. 'You drew the card. I simply told you what it means.' I'm about to argue that she could have made it up, that tarot cards aren't real, when she sits back and pats my leg. 'The universe always has a plan, Grace. You've just got to have a little faith.'

What did she say? My head starts to spin and I lean back against the wall, Daniel's words from days ago echoing in my head.

Suddenly, Margaret grabs my hand. 'Here, take this.' She presses a fresh joint into my palm.

'Oh, I can't.' I try passing it straight back. 'It doesn't work on me. You keep it.'

She won't accept it. 'Grace, trust me.' She gives me a pointed look. 'It helps with the pain.'

Tears threaten out of nowhere. 'Okay.'

'Promise me, you'll save it for my funeral.' She smiles, her eyes half-closed and crinkled. 'I want it to be fun. I've already told my sons I'm not having anything stuffy or serious. They think it's the tumours talking, but I wrote it in my will, so they can shut up and do as they're told.'

'I promise.' I don't know whether to laugh or cry. A weird hiccup comes out instead as she takes my hand again – gently this time.

'You know, if Jesus was alive today—'

'Yes?' I squeeze her fingers, expecting her to share a tragically beautiful philosophical statement on the tranquillity that comes from being aware of your own impending death.

'—I think he'd really like marijuana.'

We dissolve into heady and hysterical laughter. As my mind wanders, aimless and unconcerned, it latches onto an errant memory – the last time I smoked. I was seventeen.

It can't always be weightless.

21

where there's smoke, there's fire

November, 1994

Dad has found a pack of cigarettes in the shed. St Moritz menthols, tucked between a pile of rusted-over tins of decking oil and several cartons of unlaid bathroom tiles. Our house is what people call a fixer-upper and Dad was gung-ho for a while after we moved in. But that was four years ago and barely anything has been fixed since then. Not much has been exactly on the 'up' either. He's assumed the cigarettes are Lizzie's.

Mum and Dad both smoke, but that's not the point. Lizzie is thirteen. Apart from it being illegal, she doesn't get to decide yet whether she wants to destroy her lungs. She has to wait until she no longer lives under this roof, which if Dad's attitude towards her is anything to go by, can't come soon enough. You're not supposed to have favourites among your children, but the disparity has always been clear. And not just to me. Mum's always trying to balance the scales – turning a blind eye to Lizzie's behaviour, hiding things from Dad. But it's a losing battle with her on the wrong side.

I've never understood why Dad and Lizzie don't get along. Mum says it's because they're too much alike. I'm not sure that's true but – for as long as I can remember – there's been a distance between them. A disconnect. I can't put a foot wrong if I try. Not that I ever do. I'm not sure where the line is between loving and hating my dad, I just know it's blurry and constantly shifting.

I'm scared of him but have known since I was little that his temper can be kept in check by good behaviour, his affection bought with achievements, reflected praise. Admiration by proxy. I've been a politician since I was four. The better I am, the more he loves me. It's not rocket science, and more than anything, it keeps the peace. If he's looking at me, he's not punishing Lizzie. Or Mum. I'm the eldest, it's my responsibility to keep them safe. It doesn't always work. Lizzie doesn't make it easy. I'm sure she does it on purpose. Fearless. Defiant. Unlike me. No wonder she hates me.

Dad is two six-packs in, and despite Lizzie saying the smokes aren't hers, he drags her roughly into the shed by the arm as Mum and I hang back outside the door. He sits her down on an upturned esky, hands her the cigarettes and a lighter.

'Tell me the truth, or you'll sit there and smoke every single cigarette until they make you sick,' he says. 'Own up now and it'll only be a week's grounding.'

'I am telling you the truth.' She smirks, sealing her fate. 'I wouldn't be caught dead smoking menthols.'

Next to me, Mum sighs. 'She shouldn't push his buttons like that.' She heads back into the house without looking back. There's no point in her stepping in; we both know it'd make it worse for everybody. Dad is fuming. He cuffs the back of Lizzie's head – not hard enough to hurt but enough to make a sound.

'Smart-arse. See how clever you are when you're puking your guts up.'

Lizzie responds by taking a cigarette out of the packet and lighting it, slowly and deliberately, looking Dad in the eye as she exhales. She'll smoke that entire packet before she admits the cigarettes are hers. Because they're not. They're mine and she knows it.

I don't know why she's more willing to piss Dad off than dob me in. I don't even know why I hid the cigarettes; it's not like I'm planning on smoking any more of them. It was stupid of me to buy them, but that Year 12 boy Susie's seeing – Dennis or whatever – called me a dumb kid. Turning seventeen apparently means you should either be screwing your brains out, drinking, or smoking. If you're cool, you should be doing all three. I chose the cigarettes because they were cheaper, less scary, and unlikely to result in something bad happening.

Guilt pushes me through the shed door by the time Lizzie lights the fifth smoke in the space of ten minutes. She looks like she could keep going all night, but I can't take it. Dad is on the verge of exploding, stalking back and forth in front of Lizzie, the force of a man three times his size radiating outwards – hot and intense. It'll go too far if I don't do something.

'Dad, stop.'

He growls without looking at me. 'Stay out of it, Gracie. Go back inside.'

'She's telling the truth. They're not hers. They're mine.'

He fixes me with a look of disbelief. I'm not sure whether the look on Lizzie's face is surprise, gratitude, respect or nausea. 'I mean, not actually "mine" mine, they're Susie's,' I gabble. 'I took them out of her bag at school because I've been trying to get her to stop smoking. I don't know why I hid them, I should have thrown them in the bin.'

My eyes dart to Lizzie in time to see any shred of grudging respect she had for me wither and die. Doesn't she get it? This is the easiest way to make it stop.

Dad folds his arms across his broad chest, still not believing me. 'So why didn't you own up sooner, instead of watching your sister get in the shit?'

'I'm sorry, Dad. I should have.' I step forward and cement the performance. 'I understand if you're disappointed in me.'

Dad rubs his face. He reminds me of the Hulk turning back into Bruce Banner. Shrinking. Softening. I breathe out. I did it.

Then he turns back to Lizzie; it's not over. 'Did you know they were Gracie's?'

Telepathically, I will her to lie and say no. It's a game of chess – sacrifice the truth for a better position. This is her way out. But for some reason I'll never understand, she nods – yes. Idiot. Dad shakes his head, as if he doesn't know what to do with his delinquent daughters. 'Good on you for owning up, Gracie,' he says. 'And for trying to help your friend. But you still watched your sister get in trouble for something you did. You're both grounded for a week.'

'What?' I jerk back, confused. 'Why is Lizzie grounded?' Lizzie isn't surprised in the slightest.

'For not being completely honest in the first place.'

'But, Dad,' I scramble, 'She was being honest. That's not fai—'

'Don't argue, I said you're both grounded.' His voice rises. 'Unless you want it to be two weeks. Now go to your rooms.'

Back in the house, I trudge up the stairs behind Lizzie and stop on the landing as she heads towards her room without a word. She must be mad at me.

'Phew, that was close,' I laugh nervously. 'I thought you were gonna smoke that whole packet if I didn't do something.' She looks flatly back at me, one hand on her door as I prattle on. 'I can't believe this, though – what an arsehole.'

'It must be nice,' she says finally.

'Huh?' I'm thrown. 'What must be nice?'

'Always being the hero.'

She shuts the door in my face.

22

pawno

Twenty-four hours after my unpleasant conversation with Daniel, I find myself back in Newtown standing outside a pawnbroker and clutching my handbag more tightly than I probably need to. *What the hell am I doing?* It's possible I've finally lost my one remaining marble, but the fear of losing my sanity is drowned out by the sound of my blood still boiling.

The small store is called Mickey's. The brick wall next to it has been graffitied with 'FUCK THE WOK AGENDA' in fluorescent green spray-paint. Underneath it, someone has written, 'It's woke, you brain-dead loser'. It's good to see meaningful dialogue in a community.

The metal bars welded to the door and windows are not instilling the feeling of security that's intended. I squash my misgivings and go inside, immediately enveloped by the cloying scent of antibacterial spray and the dulcet tones of Alice Cooper. The walls are a floor-to-ceiling riot of ski equipment, small appliances, DVDs and more Xboxes than I can count. The jewellery cases line the counter at the back.

Mickey – dressed in camo pants and a black tank top – stands behind them. I approach the counter and scan the jewellery, quickly and with a critical eye. Mostly yellow gold, small stones, nothing bespoke – nothing that comes close to the haul squirreled away in my handbag. I don't know if that's a good thing. I'd imagine most people shopping at Mickey's aren't in the market for opera-length South Sea pearls.

Mickey impresses me by unrolling a large piece of black velvet and popping a pair of black Prada spectacles onto his tattooed face, before spilling my wares across the counter. I'd gathered up every piece of jewellery Daniel had ever bought me and ferried it here in a large sandwich bag. It's all meaningless now, and most of it's been boxed in the wardrobe for years. If Daniel gets a nest egg, so do I. It means I won't need to touch our account. Daniel will have no way of knowing what I'm doing, or where – or with whom.

Mickey combs through the pieces and chews his lip. His mouth downturns into a grimace. 'I'll give you seven grand for the lot.'

What? 'Your ad says best prices in Sydney.'

He offers me an unbothered shrug. 'That is the best price in Sydney.'

'But this stuff is worth a fortune.' It comes out without thinking and makes me cringe. I've always been a little uncomfortable with how well-off we are, considering we lead a church. I'd be lying if I said I didn't enjoy the benefits, especially after how much Mum and Dad struggled to make ends meet, but I know how people – critics mostly – look at us sometimes, with a suspicious side eye. Like we're rorting the system, exploiting our congregation. But the church wouldn't have started without Daniel's inheritance; we'd worked hard, helped so many people. *Luke 6:38 – Give to others and God will give to you.*

I point to an ostentatious white gold choker, inlaid with sapphires. It was an anniversary gift I only wore once to be polite.

It's hideous, but it's worth as much as a second-hand Hyundai. 'That piece alone is more than that.'

Mickey is implacable, in the nicest way. His expression doesn't change. He simply says, 'Dunno what to tell you, love. This ain't Tiffany's.'

'No, of course. I didn't expect—' I trail off, embarrassed. He must think I'm a stupid old rich lady, slumming it, and waving my overpriced jewellery around like a twat. He's not far off the mark. How did I think this was a good plan? I start gathering it all up. 'Sorry to waste your time. I thought I'd get more than that and I really need—' Tears well and I sniff them back. *Oh god, don't cry in the pawn shop, that's pathetic.*

'What about that?'

I blink at him. 'What?

Mickey points at my engagement ring. 'It's at least 4 carat, quality princess cut. Even with my naked eye I can see its excellent clarity, good colour. I could give you decent money for that, if you're selling.'

'Oh, uh—' I clutch my left hand, a little thrown but mostly impressed. Mickey knows his diamonds. Mind racing, I twist the ring on my finger. I hadn't planned on selling it – I doubt Mickey's idea of decent money is even half of what it's worth, I'm not silly – but it's not like it's special. It's not even my original ring.

Daniel bought this sparkling monstrosity on our twentieth wedding anniversary saying I needed an upgrade. One that suited the life we'd built. Personally, I prefer the original – it was small, but it was beautiful. I'm taken back to the moment Daniel slipped it onto my finger. How full of hope and optimism I was back then. That's the one with sentimental value – the one I don't think I'll ever be able to sell, even with everything that's happened. It should go to Abbey – although it's probably cursed now.

'Take your time, love,' Mickey says gently. 'I know how hard these decisions can be.'

I hesitate, sliding the ring around my finger. 'What do you call decent money?'

Ten minutes later, I exit the shop with a hefty wad of cash tucked into my handbag and a thrill chasing its way up my spine. I turn my face to the sky and breathe. The sun feels good on my skin, and I feel the need to celebrate. A surprising thought flares to life as I head down the street.

You are going to be okay, Grace.

I'm beginning to like this side of the city. During the day, the streets of Newtown pulse with an earthy energy that's simultaneously relaxed and electric. The air thrums around me, thick with the buzz of a thousand different lives, chaotically butting up against each other. It's a welcome distraction.

Abbey has called several times to organise going shopping, but I keep putting it off. The thought of feigning excitement over booties fills me with dread. I know it probably makes me a terrible mother, but it's a visceral reaction, and I don't want her to see it written on my face.

Despite my feelings about impending grandmotherhood, I'm calmer than I've been in days as I wander towards King Street. Wrestling back at least a bit of control over my finances is a huge relief. I'm unhurried and fascinated by the streets around me.

Tattoo studios jostle for space with overcrowded thrift stores, minimalist book shops and tiny coffee nooks. A woman busks outside the cinema, the honking voice of her saxophone bouncing off the office windows opposite as I skirt around an artist's stall sprawling across the footpath, a cacophony of colour against the grey asphalt.

Newtown is alive, in myriad ways I've never experienced. Why, over a lifetime in Sydney, have I never spent time here? I suppose it's easy to march tunnel-visioned towards what you think is your ideal destination in life, when you're desperate to leave something behind – bypassing whatever sits in-between without realising it. Vaucluse – with its mannered air and prestigious addresses – is stark and rigid in comparison, while my memories of Mt Druitt are tainted by what was going on at home and at school. I got through it all thanks to Susie, but it's hard for me to look back on my childhood without remembering the burning need to escape.

I'd always thought I knew what I wanted and even convinced myself that I got it. What if I was wrong all along? It happens all the time – you go in thinking you've got it all worked out, only to come out of it with something completely different. There has to be some truth to the saying 'life doesn't always give you what you want, but it does give you what you need'.

The universe – I'm fairly sure at this point that it's not God – must be listening. As I turn the corner, I spot The Hip Joint across the road and it's open. I think back to laughing with Susie and meeting Liam. Clearly the place has good juju.

When I walk in, Travis is behind the bar. He clocks me immediately and calls out, 'Hey! If it isn't my favourite cowgirl. Come to get your jacket?' Not a word of that sentence makes sense. Does he think I'm somebody else?

'I'm sorry, what?' I sit down, flummoxed, as Travis retrieves my black leather jacket from underneath the bar. 'Oh, I didn't realise I left that behind. Why am I a cowgirl?'

'The shots you were drinking.' *Ohhh, those hideous cocksucker thingies*. 'Doesn't matter,' he continues. 'I'm not surprised you left the jacket. You had other things on your mind. Good night?'

I hesitate, but the smile that creeps involuntarily across my face says it all. Travis gives me a knowing look, lifting a hand to high-five me.

'Yeah, you did!'

I'm not sure I feel comfortable celebrating my brand-new sex life with a practical stranger, but I high-five him awkwardly anyway. The bar is mostly empty and once I order a drink, we settle into an easy conversation. I'm surprised to find out Travis doesn't just work at The Hip Joint – he owns it.

'Took it over from my brother eighteen months ago,' he says. 'Found out it was going under. Been trying to get it back into the black ever since.'

When he asks what I'm up to today, what feels like my entire life story spills out, including the reason I'm clinging to my handbag like it's my firstborn. He listens patiently, like every good bartender should.

'I know it probably seems silly, refusing to use our account – and I realise I'm in a privileged position to have money to refuse in the first place. . .' I trail off. 'God, I sound like an idiot.'

'Not at all.' Travis leans on the bar. 'Your husband is being a dick. That's like – what's it called – coercive control. I get it. You need to step away from that situation so you can move forward.'

I nod. 'Exactly. Now I just need to find myself a job for when this runs out.' I pat my bag. 'I don't even know what I'm qualified for anymore.'

'Do you know how to pull a beer?'

I snort. 'Do I look like I know how to pull a beer?' He shrugs and I backtrack. 'Wait, are you saying you've got a job going?'

'If you can pull a beer. My other bartender quit. She's moving to Melbourne with some girl she just met.'

Multiple thoughts run through my head at the same time. I definitely do not know how to pull a beer. Me? Work behind a bar? What if someone recognised me? This would really piss Daniel off.

Then I think, why the hell not? If I can run a multimillion-dollar mega-church and raise a functioning human being, I can figure out how to pull a beer. I remember the tarot card and Margaret's advice: 'Be open and adaptable. Your life is a blank slate.'

I smile and give Travis a shrug. 'How hard can it be?'

'Great. Cool, cool,' Travis's face lights up. 'You can start this weekend if you like.'

'Yeah, cool, cool.' Nerves flutter in my belly.

Travis hasn't pick up on my jitters. 'I don't know what's going on with your living situation – tell me if I'm overstepping – but I know breakups can be complicated. If you need it, there's a vacant flat above the bar. It's a studio and it needs a bit of TLC, but it's furnished. I've been using it for storage.'

I don't know what to say. I mean, I am *not* going to move into a flat above a *bar*.

'Why don't you live there?' I ask, stalling.

A shadow crosses his face. 'It was my brother's. Before he— left. I can't.' He leaves the explanation there and an awkward silence fills the space between us.

'It's kind of you to offer,' I say eventually. 'But my husband was the one who walked out. I've got a perfectly good house all to myself.' Then my brain serves me a vivid – and rather pitiful – mental picture. Me, alone in my kitchen, in a huge house filled with a lifetime of memories, without the people I made them with. Not to mention, Daniel can walk into the house whenever he wants. I hit the brakes and reverse. 'What's the rent, out of curiosity?' *I can't believe I'm entertaining this.*

Travis shrugs again. 'It could come with the job, in case things are slow and I can't give you enough hours. Like I said, it's basically a storage cupboard.'

I gape at him. 'Free? Are you crazy? This is Sydney. You could rent out an actual storage cupboard and people would pay a thousand bucks for it in the right suburb.' I shake my head, adamant. 'No, I'd have to pay some kind of rent.'

He's unfazed. 'If you like. Makes no difference to me. You could move in as soon as you want.'

I sit back, suddenly wary. 'What's the catch?'

'No catch. You sound like you're going through a pretty rough time, so—'

'But you don't even know me. Why would you do that?'

Travis studies my face for a few seconds before smiling. 'You're not used to people doing nice things for you, are you?'

There's a sudden lump in my throat. 'I guess I'm usually the one doing the nice thing for other people.'

'Ahhh.' He pats my hand then pours me another glass of prosecco. 'Let's call it karma, then.'

Less than an hour later, I'm standing in my walk-in wardrobe, trying to work out what to pack into a single suitcase to take to my new, sight unseen – quite possibly dilapidated – studio apartment. Dexter follows me anxiously from the bedroom to the walk-in, to the bathroom, and back to the bedroom, his tail wagging half-heartedly. He keeps bumping his nose against my hand for reassurance. Dogs always know when something strange is going down.

Keep moving, Grace. Don't stop or you'll change your mind.

It's baffling how something so completely bonkers can also seem like the sanest decision to make in the moment. I know I have no choice but to leave my old life behind and step bravely into a new one. It's not like any part of it has tried to hang on to me, I still haven't heard from a single 'friend'. Arriving home cemented it for me. Everything in this house feels like a lie and I don't see the point in delaying the inevitable.

Susie is on loudspeaker, trying to talk me out of it.

First, she warns me not to vacate the house in case it affects the settlement I know I'll have to face sooner or later. Then she gasps. 'Please tell me he didn't make you sign a prenup.'

'No, of course not,' I say. 'He's not *that* awful.' I hear her snort. 'Well, he wasn't back then anyway.' I assure Susie our finances are watertight, that it will likely be a clean split. Uncomplicated. 'He might be able to make things difficult now, but when the time comes, the lawyers will work it out, and there's nothing he can do about it.' To be honest I couldn't care less. It might sound reckless but I'm more than happy to walk away and wash my hands of everything.

'Do not put that in writing,' she yells down the phone, startling Dexter.

'Fine, I won't,' I reply, holding up two pairs of shoes for Dexter's opinion. He's no help at all. 'But I am capable of taking care of myself, you know.'

Then she tries to convince me that Travis is a serial killer.

'He's been holding on to your jacket for days, he offers you a job out of nowhere, now he wants you to *move in*, and you think that's normal? You're going to end up in six different buckets.'

'Why do you think every man is a serial killer?'

'Statistics,' she says, matter-of-factly.

'Well, stop it. He is being a decent person, and decent people don't chop their employees up. Besides, none of this is normal,' I say, exasperated. 'Isn't that the point? You're the one who started this whole "change my life" malarkey. You can't backflip now.'

'Don't blame me.' She sounds annoyed. 'I thought you were going to bang a bunch of people and maybe take me to Coachella, all expenses paid! This stuff is not on the list, Grace. I agree they're *very* bad decisions, but they don't sound like fun.'

Ordinarily this is where I'd back down, to save an argument. Like a good girl. *Like a nice, accommodating, good little girl.*

'Too bad,' I snap, more forcefully than I intended. Dexter whines and puts his tail between his legs, and I mouth sorry at him as if he can read human lips. 'The train has left the station and I'm on board, so you'd better buckle up. Okay?'

A brief stunned silence. 'Okay. Keep your hair on.'

'I can't stay here, Suse.'

She sighs down the phone. 'You're nuts, you know that?'

'So people keep telling me.'

In the end, I decide everything in my wardrobe is as unappealing as staying in this house. It all belongs to a version of me that doesn't exist anymore. I pack a few basic changes of clothes – jeans, t-shirts, underwear – and some clean bedding, figuring I can find anything else I need in those cool thrift shops near the bar. It'll be fun. A whole new me, in 90s jeans and ironic knitwear. I take down the Fuck-it List, grab my makeup bag and medications, then – on a whim – sweep my entire skincare 'cauldron' into the bathroom bin. *Fuck it.*

I immediately balk and fish out the French algae cream. That stuff's expensive.

The worst part of this is saying goodbye to Dexter. He's been my shadow for nine years, since he was a puppy. But I can't take him with me to a studio apartment, it wouldn't be fair to keep him penned in like that. Daniel loves him, I know he'll be okay. He gets under my legs as I bump the suitcase down the stairs, nearly tripping me, then follows me into the kitchen, watching me with his head cocked as I top up his water and fill his bowl with biscuits. I can't look at him.

Dexter usually bolts for his food bowl as soon as it's full, inhaling whatever's in it so fast you'd think he'd never been fed. But he ignores it, turning tail and heading for his bed by the door. He sits bolt upright, staring at me and quivering, ears flat.

He knows. And I falter. I kneel on the tiles next to his bed. 'Come here, boy.' Dexter shuffles in and hooks his nose under my chin, the very end of his tail thumping softly. I hold his ears and kiss his face, not even trying to hold the tears in check. He snuffles gently and licks them away, his tongue hot and raspy on my cheek. I grab him in a hug, burying my face in the golden ruff at the back of his neck.

I hold his head again, looking into his eyes. 'It's not forever,' I say, willing him to understand. 'I'll see you soon, I promise.' I don't know why I'm saying that – I'm trying to convince myself – but I don't know if it's true. I don't know what's going to happen. I just know I can't stay in this house.

I grab my phone and tap out a text to Daniel.

Grace: You can come home. I've moved out. Take care of Dexter for me.

I hit send before I can change my mind and tell Dexter to sit, the words sobbing out of me. 'Be a good boy. Stay.' I leave my door key on the kitchen counter and walk towards the front door without looking back. I hear his claws tip-tapping on the tiles behind me. If I turn around, I'm done for.

I'm still teary hours later, standing in the kitchen of my new home – which technically is also the dining room, living room and bedroom. It's not as bad as I expected – timber floor, off-white walls, and a bathroom that hasn't been touched since the 70s. There's a lumpy, brown couch, a double bed, a fridge and a small pine table with two chairs – all of which have seen better days. Two large curtainless windows look down on the street below. Late afternoon sunlight streams through them, illuminating clouds of tiny dust particles, still swirling from where Travis removed his boxes and swept the floor.

I've ignored two calls from Daniel. I don't have the energy to deal with whatever his dismissive take on my decision is. I've also made the bed but have realised there's no kettle, crockery or cutlery. No cooking utensils. No soap in the bathroom. No toilet paper. I have no washing machine. I did not think this through at all.

The chatter from the street below is intrusively loud. I tell myself I'll get used to it, like living under a flight path. Through the thin plaster walls I can hear the tenants of the flat next door, laughing. I get the urge to call out, to make myself known so I'm not so alone – like Diane Lane in *Under the Tuscan Sun*, when she stays at that horrible hotel, the one for sad and lonely divorced people. At least I'm one step up from her – I'm not curled on the floor in the foetal position. Not today anyway.

The Fuck-it List is pinned to the wall next to the bed – stark and bold, like it's laughing at me. I grab a pen and study it. 'This is your fault,' I say out loud, before sighing and filling in the blank lines with two new entries – *Get a ridiculously underpaid job* and *Move into own place* – before placing a tick next to each one. *Well done on making life harder for yourself, Grace. Two gold stars.*

It would be easy to stumble here, to regret my impulsive decision and frantically wind it back. Nothing's stopping me from repacking my bag and going home – except me and my refusal to have my every move tracked and controlled. And the thought of facing an 'I told you so' from Susie.

But if I've learned anything this past week, it's that no matter how well you plan your life, everything can change in an instant whether you like it or not, and sometimes you can't go back, no matter how much you want to. There is only forward. There is only the next step, and it's up to you how you move. I have two choices. I can chalk this up to a slight idiotic detour and reroute, or I can write myself a shopping list for tomorrow, take myself out for dinner, and continue to go all in. I look at the list again and force a shaky smile. That is not the list of a quitter – *or* someone who lives in Vaucluse. *All in.* It's not even a question.

I guess I live in Newtown now.

23

tantra, tantra, tantra

Joey's Boom profile lists him as an artist, a feminist, a sensualist, and a minimalist. I've picked him because I'm hoping he'll help me tick '*pose nude for an artist*' off my list – as well as the whole sex thing. He's moderately attractive and thirty-nine, which makes me a little nervous. His pictures give off a mature vibe, though – or at least, he's got his shirt on in his photos, which seems to be a rarity among the under-forty.

Our text chat was respectful but extremely flirty. I have high hopes for him on all fronts. Unless the minimalist bit is referring to his anatomy. I guess there's only one way to find out. He's invited me for drinks at his apartment. Susie says that's a terrible idea, but I don't see the point in being coy and, besides, bad decisions are the whole point. Maybe I should be more worried, but I'm certain Susie's being overdramatic. Surely not *all* men on the dating apps are psychos. Right?

'But you don't even know if you want to – you know – until you meet him in person,' she'd said. 'What if he doesn't look like his photos?'

'Been there, done that.'

'What if he has a squeaky voice? Or he's *vegan*?

'What's that got to do with anything?'

'Well, vegans are annoying, aren't they?'

I'd laughed. 'He looks pretty normal. But if I'm not feeling it, I'll be honest and leave. It's not hard.'

She was not convinced. 'You say that now.'

Joey frowns when he opens his front door and sees me standing there, clutching a bottle of wine. 'Emilia?'

I'm thrown for a second, then I remember who I'm supposed to be. 'Hi, yes. It's me. Definitely *Emilia.*'

'You look different,' he says, bluntly. It takes me a second but then I click.

'Oh, right. Sorry.' I wave my hand in the general direction of my head. 'Haircut. Bit of a new look.'

Joey studies my head for a few seconds as if the quality of my hairdo will make or break whether I'm allowed in. Then he nods, pressing his lips together in approval. 'I like it,' he says. 'Bold. Hard to pull off. I like a woman with that kind of confidence.'

I run my hand over my new dark brown crop. There's nothing bold about it. It's simply an attempt to throw off any potential photographers Daniel decides to send my way. I still don't trust that he's done with me. I allowed Susie the win when I wrote '*Cut my hair off*' on the list and awarded myself a star.

'Told you so.' She hadn't been able to resist.

There are four things in Joey's unnervingly spotless apartment. A soulless-looking beige modular couch facing a massive flat-screen TV, a low-slung Scandi-style bed, and a mountain bike. It's like sitting in an IKEA display room. We're only halfway through the bottle of wine when the conversation turns to sex.

It's honestly a relief. The small talk up until now has mostly been about the dangers of late-stage capitalism, whether I've read *The*

Ethical Slut (you really should, Emilia, it's seminal reading), and how he thinks all men should see a therapist because toxic masculinity is a scourge. I don't disagree, but it feels performative, which seems pointless because we both know where this is leading. I ask him what kind of art he does but he gets all vague and shifts the topic.

'What is art? It's subjective, don't you think?' He narrows his eyes, holding his chin, as if he's saying something insightful. 'Anything could be art, really. The act of giving pleasure, for example.'

I gulp at my wine, mainly because I don't know what the appropriate response to that should be. 'Mm-hmm,' I murmur, non-committal.

'There's nothing I find more beautiful than a woman experiencing pleasure,' he continues. 'Watching a woman orgasm is such a turn-on.'

'Really?' I drink more wine and he nods, earnest brow furrowing.

'Of course. My partner's pleasure is a priority for me. I pride myself on my generosity and skill as a lover.'

'That's, uh – good.'

He fixes me with an intense look. 'Do you come easily, Emilia?'

My eyes ping wide. 'Sorry? Oh, um—' I instantly think of Liam, but then of Daniel and the icky lawyer. '—it depends.'

'I'd lay money on the fact your ex-husband wasn't very giving. Am I right?' He doesn't give me time to answer. 'Comes from insecurity. Most men don't understand that every woman is different. A secure man will take the time to find out what works, you know?' He winks at me. 'You're tricky creatures.'

I manage to stop my eyes rolling and let 'Emilia' step in.

'I think we should move this into the bedroom,' I say, brazenly. 'You really like the sound of your own voice and I'd like you to stop talking and put your money where your mouth is.'

Joey is taken aback but recovers quickly. 'Ouch. I've always said one of the sexiest things about older women is they're not afraid to say what they think.'

Taking his hand, I lead him towards his sparse bedroom. I seem to be making a habit of having sex with men to stop them waffling on. I probably should examine that at some point. But not right now. I am about to be a priority to a very skilled and generous lover. Apparently.

Joey keeps his clothes on – which is a bit strange, but I go with it – and he tries, hard. Ten out of ten for effort and dexterity. It's not easy coordinating that tongue action with his left hand doing one thing and his right doing something else entirely. He should take up piano, I think he'd be quite good. Unfortunately, nothing he's doing is exactly the 'Moonlight sonata'. It's not even 'Chopsticks'.

Lento and pianissimo. Then andante, allegro, and a few frantic seconds of prestissimo. More fingers, less tongue, then vice versa. Nope. Nothing. I'm not even in the same room as a crescendo. It doesn't feel bad but not much is happening. If it wasn't for Liam, I'd still be convinced I'm defective. But I know for a fact I can orgasm.

'Tell me what you like,' Joey says, without looking up from between my thighs, and I assure him what he's doing is good because I don't actually know what I like. Satisfied, he returns to the task and finally the first stirrings of arousal begins. *Here we go.* Then he changes tack and starts doing something completely different. *Is he writing the alphabet?*

'Could you go back to what you were doing before?' I'm tentative, not wanting to seem bossy; after all, he is the expert. He obliges but not before he huffs – although it could be because he can't breathe down there. Too late. It's gone. I close my eyes and concentrate, slowing my breathing. *Relax, Grace. Enjoy it.*

'Are you close?'

'No, sorry,' I admit. 'Maybe I'm a bit tense.'

Joey kneels up and rolls his neck. 'It helps to get out of your head and into your body. It's okay. I think I need to bring out the big guns.' He hops off the bed and goes to the drawer. I watch with mild alarm. When he comes back, he's holding a bright pink dildo, a small gold 'bullet' vibrator, and a bottle of coconut oil. He catches my puzzled expression.

'It's organic, tastes better than lube.' *Fair enough.*

'You really don't need to go to all this trouble.' I eye the pink monstrosity. There's no way he's putting that thing inside me. What if he doesn't sanitize it between uses? 'I'm fine, honestly. We can move on from the buffet to the, uh – main course.' *What are you talking about? This isn't Sizzler.*

Joey is affronted. 'Not until I've made you come at least once.'

'Okay. But maybe just that one.' I point at the bullet. For the next twenty minutes, he employs every single setting on the vibrator. It's quite disconcerting having someone focus solely on your vulva with this level of commitment. I feel like a dissected frog in a science lab. For a minute it feels like it's working, and I scrunch my eyes, making encouraging noises. *Almost.* He switches settings from a *bzzzzzzzzz* to *bzz-bzz-bzz-bzz* – and it slips away again.

'I don't think it's going to happen.'

Joey doesn't look happy. 'Let me try one more thing,' he says, although I have no idea what else is left to try. 'I bet you're one of those women who needs a more intimate connection.' He lies alongside me and resumes working away at me with the little bullet while staring into my eyes. Then he kisses me, his tongue mirroring the action down below. I try not to think about the fact his mouth is all greasy from the coconut oil. Is this what he thinks women want?

The intense eye contact is weirding me out, so I close my eyes, but I'm getting bored and the vibrator is annoying. Why doesn't he want to have unsatisfactory sex, like a normal person?

'Stop.' I pull my mouth from his. 'That's a bit irritating. Honestly, you can give up now.'

He flops onto his back. I can't tell if he's annoyed or upset. 'This has never happened to me before. I can usually make any woman come, even if they're repressed.'

My eyes widen. *Excuse me?* 'I'm not repressed.' *Am I?* He responds with a deep sigh, throwing his arm over his face like a toddler. I shrug the brief worry away. I didn't come here for therapy. 'Look, don't worry about it. Like you said, women are tricky.' I run my hand down his chest. 'Your turn now.' It's the last thing I feel like doing, but I'd feel rude if I didn't at least offer after all that effort. It's not his fault my wiring is temperamental.

'There's no point. I can't come if I haven't got you off first.' He rolls away from me. 'It really affects me.' *Is he crying?* I'm getting crazy vibes now. God, I hate it when Susie's right.

'Oh . . . sorry.'

I expect him to say, 'It's not your fault', but he doesn't. He sits on the edge of the bed with his head in his hands. 'Maybe you have anorgasmia. Or it could be hormonal?'

I frown. 'Hmmm, I think I'm fine.' *This is starting to feel like a 'you' problem, Joey.*

'It must be something.' He sounds irritated. 'My technique was impeccable.'

I climb off the bed and pull my jeans on, sucking in a sharp breath. *Ow!* I think I'm swollen. This middle seam is not my friend. 'Maybe we should call it a night,' I say, as I pull my t-shirt over my head. 'I should go.'

Joey is staring at the wall. 'Yeah, that's probably best. I need time to process this.'

I slip my shoes on and stand awkwardly for a few seconds. 'Okay then,' I say eventually. 'I'll let myself out.' He waves over his shoulder without a word.

The short Uber ride back to the flat is intensely uncomfortable. Note to self: do not match with any man who puts 'feminist' on their profile, or wear tight jeans on dates ever again. I groan and sit with my legs sprawled apart, which doesn't help much but does make my Uber driver look at me funny. I avoid his eyes, sinking into the back seat as much as my puffy bits will allow. What a predicament. I think I'm going to need an ice pack.

24

rama lama ding dong

A week later, my injured labia are a distant memory but I'm still thinking about what Joey said. It's Saturday lunchtime and me and Susie are lounging in a cabana on the pool deck of the W Hotel. The sun is baking my bare legs and dancing off the water, as Latin jazz floats from tiny speakers hidden in the foliage. It reminds me of the time we took Abbey to Argentina. I don't want to think about that today.

Susie has decided – after the collective trauma of, well, *everything* – that I need to be introduced to the concept of day drinking. I don't bother reminding her that I've been well acquainted with daylight inebriation since childhood, because I don't want to ruin the vibe and apparently millennials rebranded it as fun some time ago.

'Do you think I'm repressed?' I peer at her over my sunglasses.

She sucks on her Aperol spritz until it slurps in the bottom of the glass.

'Yep.'

'So, because all but one of the men I've now had sexual relations with have largely failed to bring me to climax, that makes me repressed?'

She pulls her sunglasses down. 'Do you hear the words that come out of your mouth? No, you're not repressed at *all.*'

'Why is it my fault? Maybe they were terrible at it.'

'I didn't say it was your fault. It's entirely plausible they're all shithouse, except for the sexy leprechaun. But you're pretty tightly wound across the board.' She shrugs. 'It's who you are.'

I sit back and squint at the sun. 'You sound like Daniel and my family. I was trying not to think about any of that, remember?'

I'm experimenting with avoidance – with Susie's support – for at least one day. Maybe forever. Hence the fancy cabana. There'll be no dwelling on the multiple messages from Daniel telling me I'm being immature over the bank account, that I'm irrational leaving the house, and that I'm being unfair to Dexter, who he's not sure he has time to look after properly, so maybe we should think about rehoming him.

I'm not going to worry about the uncomfortable conversation with Liz over whether we should look at a care facility for Mum. I told her she was overreacting because Mum didn't seem that bad. If being forgetful and snappy was something to worry about, every woman over forty-five would be put in a home.

The Fuck-it List is also on hiatus today – even the most committed scientist needs a day off. I can think about my shoe-box apartment and my – as it turns out, quite stressful – job when I get back to Newtown.

My first shift at the bar last weekend was a debacle. I dropped an entire tray of glasses, managed to spray a patron in the face with the soda water gun, and I lost count of the number of men who said, 'You've given me too much head, love,' as I passed them their badly poured beer.

Somehow, I managed not to get fired. Travis was exceptionally patient with me, saying he'd seen worse and that I'd get the hang of things. I'm not entirely sure about that, but I've worked a shift every day this week and I'm exhausted.

More than anything, I don't want to think about the baby or feel guilty for continuing to put off shopping plans with Abbey. She called again yesterday. I told her about my new job and said I was working all weekend. I've promised to be there for her next ultrasound appointment – Tobias will be away – surely that's more important. Maybe I'll feel better about it by then.

For now, all I want to think about is fluffy things like, should I watch every season of *RuPaul's Drag Race*, or is Harry Styles too young for me now that he's a proper grown up? I throw my arm over my face to discourage further conversation, but Susie's never been good at reading signs.

'Abbey doesn't think you're uptight,' she says. I sigh and reluctantly re-engage.

'No, she just thinks I'm judgy and a hypocrite and have possibly had a psychotic break. And that I'm avoiding her.'

'She's so observant. Must be that lawyer training.'

'Whose side are you on?'

Susie throws her hands up in surrender. 'Fine, but you are avoiding her. You're going to have to get your head around it sooner or later. It's happening whether you like it or not. I don't even know why you're freaking out so much. Babies are cute, with their little startled faces and their screaming. They're kind of like goats. Everyone likes goats.'

My stomach tightens, anxiety starting to bubble. I don't respond, because I can't explain my panic. Even I know it doesn't make sense. But I feel it, and I don't know how to change that. I try subtly changing the subject.

'Enough about me. What's going on with you? Any news? How's the business coming along? How's Rob?' *Real subtle.*

Susie stalls, fiddling with her straw, then nonchalantly says, 'Same old, same old. I'm living vicariously through you, remember?'

I frown at her. Something's going on. 'We can't talk about my stuff all the time. Boring.'

She sits up suddenly and takes her sunnies off. 'Hang on . . . what did you say a minute ago?' *Also not subtle.*

'You might have to be a bit more specific; I said a lot of things a minute ago.'

She swings her legs off the lounger. 'That wordy thing, that made you sound like you'd swallowed a dictionary.'

'Is that a euphemism? I can never tell with you.'

'You said something like, all but one of the men you've bonked have failed to get you off. So that means—'

'Nobody uses the word *bonk* anymore, do they?' I lean away from her; she looks like she wants to slap me. 'Okay, that's what I said. So?'

Susie has done the (admittedly very simple) math and correctly surmised that – apart from Liam – there has been an almost complete orgasm drought for my entire adult life.

'What a selfish prick.'

'To be fair, it's not Daniel's fault,' I start to explain, 'I was very good at fake—'

She silences me with an aggressive hand gesture. 'Nope. Do not! Your husband not making you come for thirty years and being too oblivious to tell you were faking it the *entire* time, is absolutely his fault. Please tell me you at least had a good vibrator.' My look tells her everything. 'So you just flick the old bean – old school?' She wiggles two fingers at me. 'I mean, that's okay, whatever works.'

'I do not flick the old anything.' I wish she'd drop it.

Susie is looking at me like I'm an alien. 'But everybody wanks.'

'I don't.' It comes out primmer than I intend.

'Never?'

My mouth tightens and I shake my head. *Oh, God, I'm going to cry. Don't cry over orgasms, you weirdo.* 'It's not a big deal. I never worked out how to, you know – let go.' I roll my shoulders, like I'm trying to dislodge a big bug clinging to my back. 'It feels . . . uncomfortable.'

Susie is still staring at me, flummoxed. 'But I gave you that *Dolly* magazine in Grade 9. Dolly Doctor literally had a step-by-step masturbation guide.'

I frown at her. 'I thought you gave it to me because I liked Cameron Daddo – it had that poster.'

Susie moves and sits next to me, a little too close. 'This explains so much.' I raise my eyebrows at her and she puts her arm around me. 'This is why you're so tightly wound. You've got thirty years of pent-up orgasms in your body.'

'Don't be ridiculous.' *What if she's right? Maybe that's where all this rage comes from. I should really do something about it. I mean, I could explode.*

'Poor Grace, I had no idea.' She takes my hand and rubs my back, looking at me like I've been diagnosed with a terminal illness. 'It'll be okay. We'll get you fixed up in no time.'

Shopping for sex toys on Oxford Street at 3 pm, after a few too many Aperol spritzes, was not on my bingo card this weekend. But here we are. Susie – in her infinite wisdom – has decided the only way my life will improve is if I learn to please myself. Literally.

She says, 'You're all clogged up,' which doesn't sound erotic at all. 'Your tantric energies have shit the bed from not being used for so long.' She's really not selling this. She looks furtively left and right like a spy, then shoves me through a set of darkly tinted glass double doors.

To say the options are overwhelming is an understatement. Terrence, the over-eager sales assistant, doesn't help. It's bad enough having this conversation with Susie; I'm certainly not telling a leather-clad and moustachioed stranger whether I prefer internal or external stimulation, penetration, vibration or suction. Mostly because I don't have a clue.

There's an entire wall of dildos – although according to Terrence, the technical term is *faux phallus*. They're set out in rows, like shoes in the Nike shop.

'Feel free to try them,' says Terrence.

'I most certainly will *not*,' I say, relaxing somewhat when he takes a large and life-like one down from the wall and demonstrates, checking the weight and girth with his hands.

'Some are more realistic than others,' he says. 'Here, have a feel.'

Ten minutes later, we exit the store laden with discreet, black plastic bags. I couldn't decide between the *Womanizer Pro* – it features impressive-sounding air-pulse technology and looks like a tiny spaceship – and the intimidating and life-like dildo. So I bought them both. I tell Susie I'm going to call my new faux phallus 'Phil', because I like 'a-clit-eration'. She shakes her head like I'm a lost cause.

'How did I end up friends with such a dork?'

'What? That was clever!' I grin at her and lift my bags up with a squeal. Nervousness aside, this is empowering. Thrilling even. Maybe I'll finally become one of those women who are at ease in their bodies, unafraid to voice their desires, to feel good. *It's a lot of responsibility, Phil, but I have faith in you.*

Susie is already unboxing hers. She'd been gazing longingly at a peculiar green and gold dildo with bumpy ridges on it, like scales. It looked like a cross between a fish and a penis. I didn't see the appeal.

'Christ, I love Aquaman.' *Ohhhh.*

'Why does it have a suction cup on the end?'

'So you can stick it to the side of your shower.' She'd made a sideways stamping motion with her fist and smacked her lips together with a pop. Then she'd wiggled her fingers at me. 'Look, Ma, no hands.' She'd seemed so excited that I bought it for her on the spot. Nothing says thank you like a Jason Momoa–inspired dong. She pulls it from the packaging, right there on the street, and waves it at me, startling a little old lady and her miniature schnauzer. 'Don't expect to hear from me for at least two days.' Then she snorts as a thought occurs to her. 'Hey, do you want to see my impression of your ex-husband?'

Before I can respond, she licks the suction cup and thwacks the dildo to her forehead. It sticks there – held surprisingly firmly considering its weight – and bobs up and down as she cackles. 'Hello, my name's Dickhead!' We clutch each other, laughing as passers-by stare at us.

'Mum?'

I look up and over Susie's shoulder. Abbey is standing there, holding several large Baby Bunting bags and looking bewildered. *Oh, shit.*

'Abbey!' I let go of Susie, who turns around, spots my daughter and immediately sobers. She steps back, eyes cast down, trying to be inconspicuous. Practically impossible with a dildo on her head. Abbey looks at her like she's insane, then double-takes.

'Auntie Susie?'

'Hey, kiddo. Long time, huh?' She moves to hug Abbey, then remembers the dildo and changes her mind. Abbey's staring at us in confusion. The last time she saw Susie was that awful night fifteen years ago, when I took a scythe to our friendship. I smile brightly at Abbey as though nothing is untoward.

'What are you doing in the city? Is Tobias with you?'

'Shopping. I told you that. And no, he's in Dubai again, on business. What did you do to your hair?'

My hand flies to my head. 'Felt like a change. Do you like it?' Her expression says she's not loving any part of this conversation, let alone my hair.

'I thought you were working today?' Her tone is accusatory.

I think quickly. Lying to Abbey again is not great but it's preferable to telling her the truth. 'I was. But it was quiet, so Travis let me go early.' She's not convinced. At that moment I clock Susie, trying unsuccessfully to remove the dildo from her forehead. I stifle a laugh but I'm not quick enough. When I look back at Abbey, her chin is quivering.

'I see,' she says, and my stomach drops. 'Well, you two look like you're having a fun day, so I'll let you get back to . . . whatever this is.'

I try a too-bright smile and gesture at her bags. 'What did you get?'

'You don't need to pretend you're interested, Mum.' Her voice is chilly now.

'Of course I'm interested.' Even I can hear the lack of conviction. 'Why don't we go and grab a juice and you can show—'

She cuts me off. 'I've got to get back to the car. Parking's expensive and these bags are heavy by myself.' *Ouch.*

Abbey's already walking away as I say, 'Okay sweetheart. I'll talk to you soon.' My guilt meter ratchets up several notches. I am definitely a horrible mother. Susie steps up beside me, watching her go, the dildo still stuck firmly to her forehead.

'This is going to leave a mark,' she says.

I couldn't agree more.

25

would I lie to you

February, 2010

Susie's voice echoes through the house from the open front door, slurring and belligerent, ranting at Daniel. He's refusing to let her in, and I'm hiding in the kitchen, trying not to cry. I can't face her. She's caught me in a terrible lie that I can't explain away – the kind of lie that makes someone wonder whether you've ever loved them at all. Because if you did, well, how could you do it?

I did it because I'm a coward. I couldn't bear the thought of her hating me for choosing Daniel over her when she needed me.

The Bible tells us that to lie is a sin, and most people say they agree. Honesty is the best policy. But I don't believe that's true, and I think most people are lying. People ask for honesty but rarely want it, especially if it reveals an uncomfortable truth.

'I know she's here, you prick. Her car's in the driveway. Grace! GRACE!' I hear a scuffle; Daniel is physically barring the door. 'The least you can do is fucking talk to me.'

Guilt eats at me. I should have been in court with her today, adding weight to her story and holding her hand while a roomful of strangers judged her appearance and decided whether Andy almost killing her was 'that bad'. I'd told her we'd be on a flight to New Zealand for a conference. That I was sorry, but I couldn't get out of going.

The truth is: Daniel had forbidden me to be there. He said supporting a 'junkie' in an assault case was bad for the church, for our brand – I'd done enough already, involving myself in a volatile situation that could have endangered me too. We had a daughter to think of. I'd reminded him our 'brand' was compassion and that she was my oldest friend. 'Friends don't drag you down,' he'd said. 'You need to be smart about the kind of people you allow into your life.' Susie was a bad influence, a drug addict, and he didn't want me seeing her anymore. Things have been so rocky between us lately, I was scared to say no – but agreeing was a heaviness I didn't want to carry.

'He got off.' Susie's raised voice breaks. 'Can you hear me? The bastard got off.' I can't ignore her now. I rush out of the kitchen and across the foyer towards the door. Daniel tries to stop me, but I say I'll handle it. He shoots Susie a warning look then cups my face with one hand. I pull back, startled.

'Okay, darling,' he says. 'I'll be right here.' Then he hovers, out of her sight but in my eyeline. Watching me. Movement catches my eye from the top landing. Abbey is crouched behind the banister, her eyes wide. I jerk my head at her to get back into her room. She doesn't need to see this; she adores Susie. I can see tears tracking down her face as she scurries away. I turn back to the door.

Susie's a complete mess, mascara running down both cheeks. The bruises haven't quite faded, and the sleeve of her blouse is torn open and bloody from a fresh cut. She looks me up and down, swaying, then waves her arm around. 'Miss your fucking flight, did ya?' I take a breath, keeping my voice steady despite the thumping in my ears.

'What have you done to your arm?'

She looks down, blinking as though the blood's a surprise. 'Climbed over your stupid pointy gate. Figured you wouldn't let me in if I buzzed.'

'How did you know I'd be here?'

'Cause you're a shit liar.' She glares at me expectantly, waiting for an explanation. All I want to do is put my arms around her and say I'm sorry, but the words are lodged in my throat. 'You screwed me today, Grace. Nothing to say?'

I glance across at Daniel and he nods. Suddenly I feel them, the years invested, teetering precariously, and I think of Abbey and this house and the church and everything that comes with it. I can't lose this life. I can't go back there. I don't want to choose – it's like a fist in my chest – but if I have to, I choose this.

I ignore the fist and tell her I didn't want to hurt her when she was having a rough time. That I care about her, but I simply can't be there for her the way she wants. Things have changed, and I have to put my family first. I watch all the fight leave her body, and it crushes the breath out of me.

'I thought we were family,' she says softly.

'We're not fifteen anymore, Susie. You need to sort your life out.' The words feel like needles on my tongue. She scrubs her arm roughly across her face, sniffs, and sets her chin.

'Get a load of you. I only came here to tell you to go fuck yourself. Who needs you and all your fake bullshit anyway?' She sneers at me. 'Remember, I know who you really are.'

I harden myself. 'I think we're done here.'

'Too right we're done.' Susie backs out of the doorway, sticks her middle finger up at me then kicks a pot plant over, soil and rocks spilling across the pavers. I close the door and press my forehead to it, swallowing the sob that threatens. Then I lean on the intercom button to open the gate. Daniel moves in silently, wrapping his arms around me. He kisses my head and I stiffen.

'You did the right thing,' he whispers.

No. I didn't. I shrug out of his embrace. 'Don't touch me,' I say, before I walk slowly up the stairs and turn left, away from our bedroom and into Abbey's.

26

sticky feelings

It's been almost two months since my run-in with Abbey outside the sex shop. A lot can happen in that time. I've come to expect anything. I'm surprise-proof – although the speed at which Daniel stopped harassing me about moving out was unexpected. I also didn't envisage the pink running shoes that sit by my door. Turns out running is the only thing that clears my head, using up the anxiety and pockets of rage like a battery.

Mostly, I still feel like I'm going to die – which means it qualifies as a bad decision – but I fight the screaming lungs and heavy legs most mornings, stubbornly chasing the post-run high and dodging morning commuters on their way to the station. It might be masochism, but I find myself delighting in the continual soreness of my body. Every muscle complaining, feet tender, every inch of my body deliciously bruised – from running, from sex, from hours behind the bar – the sluggish ache of age and inertia traded for movement and momentum. I write '*Become a runner*' on my list.

The flat feels more like home, despite the quirks of an old building. The pipes clank if I try to run a bath and the power outlets are temperamental, but I haven't shorted a fuse and blacked out the building yet. I'd decided against raiding the house while Daniel was at the church. There's no point dragging my old life along with me. I'd raided Kmart instead, buying cheap tab curtains, a zebra-print throw rug, brightly coloured crockery and cushions, and too many tea-light candles.

By the window is an easel and a stack of art supplies – paints, brushes, pencils, some cheap canvases and a sketch pad. It's been a long time since I've done anything artistic – unless you count choosing our wallpaper with the decorator. It doesn't technically fit the definition of a bad decision, but when I'd thought about taking it up again, it gave me a thrill and I'd thought, 'fuck it'. I wrote '*Be an artist*' on the list then crossed it out and put '*Do art things*' – less pressure. I haven't given it a gold star yet because I'm too scared to open the sketch pad. What if it's gone – my ability, my imagination – what if God took it away because I wasted it?

Working with Travis has been . . . unexpected. The cocky flirtation from that first night in the bar with Susie has been replaced by an undemanding affability. We don't talk a lot – quick hellos in passing, easy banter at work, and reminders on things like how to change a keg or why you should never use a glass as an ice scoop. He never makes me feel stupid, recognising my frustration when I still get things wrong, and his routine presence is a comfort.

Apart from that, the Fuck-it List is coming along nicely. Over the past six weeks, five more gold stars have been stuck to my chart, although only two of the experiences were deserving of the reward. As far as non-sex-related experiences go, I decided to start with a splash and swim with sharks. Turns out organising it is pretty easy; you just have to buy a ticket at the aquarium.

Getting in the water is another story.

After a ninety-minute briefing and scuba lesson, it was time. I'd made the mistake of looking in the tank, hoping to see miniature sharks, the length of my arm. But the grey nurse sharks gliding through the water were huge, their mouths definitely big enough to take a chomp out of me.

I'd nervously signalled to the instructor, a surfie-looking guy in his twenties with scruffy blond hair and a deep tan. 'I've read sharks can sense fear, but can they sense pee too?'

He'd laughed. 'They couldn't be less interested in you. Just stick to the plan we went through – stay calm, no thrashing around – and we'll be sweet.'

As we sank slowly under the surface, the cold water cocooned me, enveloping my limbs and wrapping me in muffled quiet. A stingray drifted past, it's grey body rippling like fabric, and my heart rate slowed. It was the strangest thing. Although I was under water, I felt like I could really breathe – disconnected from what was going on above the surface.

A large shark swam above me – I could see every row of its teeth – and I stared at it in awe. There was a serenity about them I didn't expect. The instructor was right, the massive creatures had no interest in me. They were just doing their thing. I was fascinated. Sharks have been around for millions of years; they belong to something older and bigger, which puts petty human things into perspective. I hovered as though I was in slow motion, weightless and watching, for almost thirty minutes. When I finally rose to the surface, I felt like a Zen Indiana Jones.

It's a shame the thrill didn't follow me into my sexcapades, although things did get off to a good start. 'Get off' being the operative words.

Phil has been excellent company for an inanimate object, and whoever invented air-pulse technology needs to be awarded the Nobel Prize for services to humanity. By the time I'd peeled myself off the ceiling for the fourth time in two hours, on that very first day, it was clear my wiring is completely functional. I'd texted Susie, '*Liberation! Vive l'orgasme!*' and she'd responded in the only appropriate way possible – with a GIF of Jim Carey as Ace Ventura, doing a happy dance in a tutu. I'd written '*Learn to orgasm on demand*' in upper case letters on my list and ticked it off, triumphant.

The only remaining step was to release my orgasms into the wild, and that's where the other three stars went awry. I'd been cautiously optimistic. In hindsight, I should have stuck with cautious.

Alex was a flashy, very fit and funny, professional illusionist (yes, really) – thirty-five and all blue eyes, charisma and teeth. After bombing me over text for four days straight, with flirty check-ins, compliments, and sensitive emotional revelations, we'd finally made it to my bedroom. He'd watched himself in the wardrobe mirror the entire time he was inside me, body-rolling like Magic Mike and more turned on by his own reflection than by me. I was too amused to be aroused. Afterwards, while I was in the shower, Alex executed a brilliant disappearing act. At least I knew he was good at one thing.

Tom – a teacher, indeterminate age – was completely unmemorable. At least I think Tom was his name. I forget. *See?*

Derek – last week's date and a forty-two-year-old police officer – was quite pleasant. Pleasant looking, pleasant personality, pleasant kisser, refreshingly open about his pre-date nerves – and about the fact he had a prosthetic eye, thanks to an unfortunate firearm accident on the job. Unfortunately, I couldn't get it out of my head (no pun intended). All I could think while Derek was on top of me and about to climax, his face all red and his neck muscles straining, was 'I really hope his eye doesn't pop out'. I kept staring at it the whole time in uneasy anticipation. My possibly irrational fear not only meant I couldn't relax enough to get there, but I'm pretty sure I'm going to hell.

I bolt the double doors of The Hip Joint firmly from the inside after giving our chef, Connor, a wave goodnight. I lean against them with a groan, cracking my neck. Weariness hangs from my shoulders but my mood is buoyant because a bar shift give me no time to think. The simplicity of the work carries no lingering tension to take home, only a sense of practical accomplishment. I have a limit though and tonight I've hit it hard.

'I thought that last group of girls would never leave.' I head towards the bar, swiping a couple of dirty glasses from a nearby table. Travis is drying glasses, damp cloth over one shoulder.

'Take a load off. You were supposed to finish an hour ago.'

I hop onto a stool, grateful to be off my feet. 'I wasn't going to leave you with that lot. They looked like they were about to dance on the tables.'

Travis grins. 'Spoilsport. Perks of the job.' I throw my dish cloth at him as he tosses his apron on the counter. 'Hungry? You didn't take your dinner break.' He jerks his head towards the kitchen. 'Wanna raid the cool room?'

'Connor *will* kill you if you empty the pickle jar again,' I laugh but I'm aware of my stomach rumbling.

We eat in one of the booths, conversation initially light then cautiously personal. It's the first time we've done this and we're both guarded. Self-deprecating jokes test the waters until something shifts – *you're okay, it's safe* – and we both relax.

I check my phone several times to see if Abbey has texted me. She hasn't. Since the dildo incident, I've checked in every few days, hoping for her abrupt responses to eventually thaw, but so far they're still sub-zero. Her ultrasound appointment is going to be awkward if she's still angry with me.

'Everything okay?' Travis eyes me, quizzically.

'Oh, yeah,' I say. 'I was hoping to hear from my daughter. She's having a baby.' I steel myself, but Travis is the first person who doesn't make a grandma joke or congratulate me.

'That's big. How do you feel about it?'

'Blind panic,' I say, and he doesn't question me on why, he accepts it at face value.

'Are you and your daughter close?'

I'm unsure how to answer. It's a complex question. I tell him we're not *not* close but that, from the time she was small, Abbey seemed to gravitate towards Daniel – to patch a skinned knee, to watch her on the swings. I never measured up. I was the consolation prize, and only if Daniel wasn't around. It was understandable. With Daniel away a lot, I guess she felt like she had to grab all his time and attention. But knowing that didn't make me feel any less on the outer.

'I also think she could tell I didn't enjoy being a mother.' It's the first time I've said the words aloud – the first time I haven't buried the truth – and I'm instantly afraid. Of how it sounds, what it says about me, what Travis will think. What kind of mother admits that? I back-pedal. 'Don't get me wrong, I love my daughter.'

'Being a parent is hard,' Travis says simply and a flicker of anger sparks in me. To think that *parent* holds the same weight of expectation as *mother*. I try to stifle it – I can't expect him to know this. Most people would offer the same well-meaning platitude.

'Yes, it is. But motherhood should be as natural as breathing, you know? That's what we're told. It's what we're *for*. When you don't love it or don't want it – or you can't get it right – there's something wrong with you. You're defective.' It all tumbles out – there's no stopping it. 'So, you pretend. You go through the motions, and you do *all* the things you're supposed to. But no matter how hard you try to be the perfect mother—'

Travis frowns slightly. I expect him to come back at me with some kind of rebuttal or generic assurance that he's 'sure I'm a good mum'. But he doesn't.

'You're not good at not being good at things, are you?'

I stare at him, speechless and uncomfortably exposed, as though I've been skinned.

'No, I'm not,' I say eventually, and he nods.

'Do you resent your daughter, do you think? Maybe that's got something to do with how you're feeling.'

My skin prickles, hot and stinging. This cuts too close to the bone. It's one thing to admit to not being maternal; another to confess active resentment of your child. But he's right. It rankles me. The things I gave up. What I missed out on. How hard I worked to get everything right, only to feel like Abbey and Daniel share some special secret – a connection I'm excluded from – because, despite everything, I'm not enough. The realisation wraps around me like a python, muscular and certain, squeezing the breath from me.

When everything imploded, there was a brief moment where I thought, *now* – now I can find out who I am outside of being Daniel's wife, of being Abbey's mother. Outside of the things I've failed at. Things I never planned in the first place. The impending baby is like déjà vu. I'm tethered to motherhood again, by proxy, and I don't think I can do it. I don't *want* to do it, and I feel guilty because I love Abbey and want her to be happy. I'm failing her again – failing my grandchild – because I can't make myself feel the way I'm supposed to. It was my choice the first time – to make the best of it and bury my feelings. This time, I don't get a say in failure. And yes, I resent that.

I'm done with the amateur therapy session. 'Do you resent your brother?' I fire the words at Travis more defensively than intended. The look on his face triggers instant regret. 'Sorry. I meant, it must have been stressful being saddled with a failing business when he walked out.'

Travis takes a deep breath, exhales slowly. 'He didn't walk out. This bar meant everything to Max. He killed himself – not in the flat, don't worry – no note, no explanation.'

I blanch. 'That's why you took over the bar?'

He nods. 'I didn't find out about the financial problems until afterwards. I don't think he could face losing it – it was his dream since uni. After he was gone, I felt like I owed it to him to keep it open. But it's been tough, so yeah – I resent him.'

I don't tell him I know exactly the damage this loss does – the horror and helplessness, the sorrow and the anger – sometimes even unthinkable relief and the accompanying guilt. I can't revisit Dad's death, even out of empathy. I'll unravel. It's taken me too long to tuck the threads away, so they don't snag each time I think of him.

'I'm sorry, Travis. I didn't mean to—'

'You didn't know.' He fiddles with a coaster and smiles. It doesn't reach his eyes. 'I love my brother, and I miss him, but I'm still so pissed off at him.' Then he shrugs. 'Being human is confusing. Family is fucking complicated. But I think all the feelings can be true at the same time. It doesn't mean you're a bad person.'

I reach for levity. It's either that or cry. 'How'd you get so wise, Mister? Fortune cookies?'

'I watched a lot of *Dr. Phil* when I was a kid.' Travis laughs, the tension broken and we gaze at each other for a long second before he breaks eye contact. 'Well, this has been intense for a midnight pickle eating session. I bet you're glad you decided to hang out with me.'

I want to tell him I am, but I'm fighting an intense impulse to hug him – to *hold* him – feeling tender and bruised from the conversation. I grapple with the unexpected ache in my chest and tell myself it's not attraction I'm feeling. I'm craving comfort – solace, the kind of touch empty casual sex can't provide.

I pat Travis's hand instead, feign tiredness, and make a quick exit. The empty feeling lingers as I head upstairs, realising I have nobody left in my life to comfort me in this way. *I miss Daniel.* It's a sad little hunger and I don't know how to satisfy it alone. But I need to figure it out before I cave and do something inappropriate. The last thing I need is complication. It's the rules after all.

27

I see red

Tonight's date is with Cody, a fireman. Cancelling the date was a definite consideration because, when I'd gone for a run earlier, my traitorous body sprang an unwelcome surprise on me. Reaching the park where I usually turn around, I'd stopped to catch my breath and noticed a balding middle-aged man looking at me with distaste.

I was about to yell at him that a woman exercising is not a spectator sport when a teenaged girl tapped me on the shoulder. She'd surreptitiously pointed at my lower half and said she thought I might have sat in something. Startled, I'd glanced down at my crotch.

What in the menopausal fuckery? I had bled through my brand-new, white lycra leggings. It's always in the back of a woman's mind when choosing to wear white, but I haven't bled in almost a year. I've never even heard of a 'flash period'. It seems like an unnecessarily mean trick of nature, lulling us into a false sense of security: 'Congratulations on surviving forty-odd years of mood swings, excruciating cramps, bloating and ruined underwear. As a reward for your forbearance, no more periods for you ever again.'

PSYCH! Nature is an asshat.

I was mortified. I'd backed against a nearby lamppost, my hands in front of me like a soccer player during a free kick, while

I figured out what to do. I didn't have a shirt I could tie around my waist; I was miles from home, and it was peak hour.

It's a period, Grace. It's natural, more than half the population has them. There's no reason to be embarrassed.

It was easy to say, but most women don't walk down the street looking like their undercarriage has been chewed out by the shark from *Jaws*. We prefer to unobtrusively scuttle to the toilet with our tampons tucked in our bra, so we don't make men uncomfortable.

The longer I stood there, the more infuriated I'd gotten – at myself, at the needless shame. Finally, I'd gathered every shred of dignity I could muster and marched off down the street, head held high as I navigated hordes of city commuters, avoiding eye contact. My brazen period parade was a statement against the patriarchy, a protest – *Free the Flow!* Maybe by the time I got home, I'd feel empowered.

To be honest, I felt sticky and gross and humiliated and like I needed to inhale a packet of Tim Tams. But it was the thought that counted, and I wrote, '*Take part in a political protest*' on my list and ticked it off. I'd earned it.

By the time I've showered and thrown my leggings in the bin – let's face it, they'll never be white again – it's too late to cancel my date without being rude. No doubt it happens all the time, but if it was the other way around, I'd be peeved. I'm not in the mood, but at least it means I don't have to think about sleeping with him. But I'm giving myself a gold star on a technicality if I at least make out with him. It's my list, I can bend the rules.

Cody is thirty-two. I'm ignoring his age because, well, he's a fireman and I have a list to complete. It's pure practicality. Nothing to do with the fact he's featured in one of those charity calendars, all sooty and shirtless and cradling his hose. *I must remember to ask him how he feels about being objectified like that – poor thing, so demeaning.*

His profile is light on when it comes to word count. And by that, I mean there are none. But if a picture tells a story, his gallery tells me he likes the gym, tattoos, the gym, playing guitar, the gym, the beach – and holding kittens. At the gym. There's also a photo of him wearing satin shorts, bloodied and mid-kick, in one of those UFC fight cages. I'm not sure whether to be terrified or turned on. It's very confusing.

I meet him at a pub a block away, having learned my lesson with weird Joey, and realise quickly that Cody – all broody square jawline and previously broken nose – is made mostly of testosterone. He's as blokey as blokes come – stocky and muscular with a heavy brow and an abrasive five o'clock shadow. He appears to have come straight from the gym, so I needn't have worried about dressing down.

Cody seems genuinely decent, but we have nothing in common except an avid appreciation for his tattooed biceps. The conversation is simple and pleasant – he talks mostly about his job and how much he can bench press – but I can feel myself being prickly. I brusquely tell him about Daniel cheating. I even tell him about becoming a grandmother. I'm not being rude. I simply have zero patience and even less energy for trying to impress. I'm laying it all on the table. But the spikier I am, the more Cody seems to like it. *Men are so weird.* He thinks I'm not interested, so now I'm a challenge. The idea of it sends a thrill through me – there's no need to do the dance, to get him to want me. *Job done.* Even better? I don't have to be *nice*.

I tell him he's not my usual type. He asks why I swiped right. 'Because you're a fireman and you're attractive.' Cody doesn't seem surprised and leans closer. He's not wearing aftershave. I smell fresh sweat, musky and masculine. I pose the same question to him.

'I have a thing for older women.' *Okay then.*

I can't stop staring at his arms. Tattooed from shoulder to wrist, they remind me of those National Geographic photos you see of an anaconda that's eaten a goat. Not exactly an erotic visual, but somebody should inform my hormones because it's clear who's now in charge and it's not my brain. *Are you actually attracted to him, or are you just horny?* I tell my brain to shut up as a lazy heat stirs in my belly. *Stupid flash period.*

I look him in the eye. 'I'm not going to sleep with you.'

'Okay.' He doesn't break eye contact and I'm not sure he believes me.

'I want to kiss you. That's all.'

'Okay.'

He leans in and I put my hand out to stop him. He might as well be a brick wall. 'Not here,' I say. I'm not taking any chances with renegade photographers, and Cody is more than happy to come back to my flat. Thinking about it on the ten-minute walk home has me so turned on my legs are practically bowed.

We're barely inside before he's kissing me, his tongue thick in my mouth and stubble raking my chin. Pressed up against the closed door, my knees buckle. I kiss him back, hard, fingers tangled in his hair. One of his hands moves to my breast. Control is slipping.

I push on his chest. 'We should probably stop.'

Cody releases me straight away, puts his hands up. 'That's cool.' He grins. 'Look, I think it's obvious I'd love to fuck you, but you've made it clear you're not keen.'

Every inch of my skin is pulsing as I try to return my breathing to normal and collect myself, shaken by the intensity; I didn't feel this feverish with Liam. It's a completely different energy – out of control, dangerous.

'Oh, I'm keen,' I admit, my breath still ragged. I'm not surprised he looks confused. 'I'm just in a bad mood – furious at my ex. And, it's—' I make a face, '—that time of the month.'

Cody is unfazed. 'I'm a kickboxer, love. I'm used to blood sports.'

Did he really just say that? I'm not sure whether to laugh or be offended. Either way, I have never had sex while on my period. All I can manage to say is, 'Uh – okay.'

'No better way to work off anger.' He winks. 'Just saying. If that's the only thing stopping you, a bit of mess doesn't bother me. What's your flow like?'

My flow? Is this what young people talk about on dates now? I don't need to look in the mirror to know my cheeks are burning.

'Light to moderate, I suppose.' The words squeak out. I feel like a tampon commercial. Why am I so embarrassed? *Because you just met him.* I didn't even talk to my husband about my period, aside from acknowledging it was happening and getting him to stop at the pharmacy.

'Cool. We can put a towel down if you like.'

Daniel was never interested in sex during my period. He wasn't one of those extreme religious weirdos who think a woman bleeding is 'unclean', but he found the potential mess a turn-off. He said he was being considerate – I was bloated and cranky, he figured it was the last thing I wanted to do. Conversely, it was the time I wanted him most. Another spark of retroactive anger whips through me. 'Okay. Sure.' *Fuck it.* I'm never going to see Cody again and I'm turned on. Emilia wouldn't let a normal bodily function get in the way.

He checks in with me a second time. 'Only if you want to.'

I absolutely want to. But first I turn out all the lights.

We don't waste time on foreplay. The sex is hard and urgent. There is nothing tender about it and I'm never unaware of how much power snakes through his limbs. He manoeuvres my body like a ragdoll, pinning my wrists behind my head, his hands firm and certain. I've never experienced sex like it, but I'm starting to understand why bored housewives love those steamy alpha-male romance novels. Daniel wouldn't have known where to start making love to me like this, and I didn't know I wanted him to. Sex between us was always so polite.

When he tells me I don't have to be gentle, it's like firing a starting gun and all my carefully contained rage bolts free. The aggression that surges in me is so unfamiliar, I almost check myself. *Almost.* I slam my body against his, legs bracing, heels digging into the bed, my fingernails raking deep into his back until he hisses sharply. But he doesn't tell me to stop. My teeth close on his shoulder, on his bottom lip, and I taste blood. I have no idea if it's his or mine. I don't care and I don't apologise.

Cody picks me up and suddenly I'm on all fours and he's driving into me from behind. He's going to cleave me in half, but all I want is him harder and deeper inside me. I have no desire to quieten the guttural sounds filling the room. My body is no longer my body, it's something else. Something unbreakable, made solely of hunger and fury. I don't know exactly who I am right now. But it's not Emilia. This is me. I want this.

I don't come, but I'm bruised with satisfaction regardless.

When we're done, we clamber gingerly off the bed. The towel has shifted and the covers are damp, but it's hard to tell in the dark whether it's sweat or blood.

Cody makes the mistake of turning on the light.

'Holy shit.'

My bed looks like a crime scene. 'Oh, my God.' It's the first time in weeks, with everything I've said, that I feel blasphemous. 'I'm *so* sorry. I didn't think I was that—'

'Thought you said light to moderate—' Cody starts laughing, looking down at himself. It's a horror show. You'd think I'd eviscerated him. My own body is not much better. Hot shame taps at me, but I force myself to ignore it. *Laugh it off, it's fine.*

'Johnny Depp called, he wants his bed back,' I joke, a little too brightly. Cody looks at me blankly. 'You know, Freddie Kruger?' I waggle my fingers at him. He has no idea what I'm talking about. Because he wasn't even born in the 80s. Damn pop culture references – always a cruel reality check.

'Right. I might jump in the shower,' he says.

Once Cody's clean and dressed, I shoo him out. I don't need him sitting around making small talk while I hose myself off. Still unbothered, he tells me he had fun and kisses my head. I close the door, surprised to realise that I am also unbothered. I'm wildly exhilarated and spent and don't feel anything like an old woman. However, I am going to have to burn my sheets. Body aching deliciously, I start to strip the bed before the mess reaches the mattress. I reach across to tug the fitted sheet free. I hear a loud click and my lower back spasms. *You've got to be kidding me.*

28

transparent

'It can't be normal.' Two days later I'm on the phone to Susie while I wait for the chiropractor, my voice low. 'Should I go to the doctor?'

'Why are you whispering?' She's not providing the level of concern I feel is warranted when I'm fairly sure I'm haemorrhaging to death.

'Because the whole waiting room doesn't need to hear the gory details of how my surprise visitor has turned out to be a bloody tsunami.'

Susie huffs. 'You're one of those women who don't like saying "period" in front of people, aren't you? I bet you keep your tampons in a special box so nobody knows they're tampons.'

'I do not. And you're not helping. I'm worried, I think my uterus might be falling out.'

'Maybe he punctured something with his dick,' she says helpfully. 'You did say it was – what was the word you used – *vigorous*?' She snorts. 'Most people say they got railed. You're the only person I know who can make it sound like you fucked a thesaurus.'

My lips purse involuntarily. 'Railed sounds cheap and nasty.'

Susie cackles. 'Babe, you literally had a hot fireman blow your back out while you were on your rags. If that's not cheap and nasty—'

'Seriously? Don't call it that. What are you, twelve?'

'Geez, "rags" makes you uncomfortable. "Period" makes you uncomfortable. I can't believe you're such a prude.'

'I'm not a prude.'

'Then say, "I've got my period", without whispering. You're never gonna feel free unless you embrace your messy bits.'

'Stop life coaching me,' I hiss, although I have a suspicion she's right. 'I am not a prude.'

Susie laughs. 'See, you can't do it. You're a prude.'

'Grace Miller?'

I look up to see a man in a polo shirt staring down at me, holding a clipboard. 'I have to go.' I hang up and plaster on a serene smile, hoping to God he hadn't heard my conversation. 'Yep, that's me.'

The chiropractor – his name is Jim – is softly-spoken, wiry and wearing John Lennon–style glasses. A man of few words, I can't imagine him having the gumption to contort anyone into the positions needed to make that satisfying cracking sound people like so much – although I've learned people can surprise you.

After explaining that I hurt my back 'making my bed', Jim looks me up and down then agrees that the smallest things can do a lot of damage once you get past a certain age.

'Let's take a look.' He clips my x-rays up on the light box. There I am – from ribs to thigh – in grey-and-white skeletal relief. Spine and pelvis clearly demarcated, my body outlined in shadowy curves. It's the best photo that's been taken of me in years.

I see it first. In the hollow in my pelvis, angled off at two o'clock, is a shadowy object shaped like a large thumb. It's my tampon, but I don't understand why it's pointing in that direction. What's wrong with my vagina? Has it prolapsed from all the activity? Is that a thing? And why does nobody tell you that sanitary products show up on x-rays? *Maybe he hasn't seen it.* Jim's head tilts almost imperceptibly to one side. A hot flash sweeps my body as my inner monologue goes into meltdown.

It's just a tampon. I'm sure he's seen hundreds of x-ray tampons. How embarrassing. It's not embarrassing. I'm sure he's seen worse things on an x-ray than a tampon. People put all kinds of things up there. At least it's not a butternut pumpkin. Tell him you have your period. At least say something.

'Just so you know, I'm not smuggling drugs.' *Except that.*

Jim glances at me and presses his lips together, says nothing and goes back to studying the x-ray. I feel the need to elaborate, so there's no confusion. It could still be a Matchbox car for all he knows.

'It's a tampon, Jim.'

This time he blinks and doesn't look at me. 'I see.'

I'm still cringing on the inside but I'm not letting Susie be right. I'm a grown woman. I should be able to talk about my body without being embarrassed. *You are not a prude. Say it.*

I straighten, like I'm about to give a presentation. 'You know, because I've got my period.'

'Mm-hmm.' Jim is unruffled. Professional. And now I'm emboldened.

'Although it seems my spine's not the only thing that's crooked, am I right?' *Okay, that's enough.*

Jim – to his credit – completely ignores my attempt at stand-up comedy. He informs me that there doesn't appear to be any disc damage, instructs me to lie on his clunky table contraption, and deftly and silently snap-crackle-and-pops me. Then he tells me

I need to see their massage therapist as a follow up, to loosen the spasmed muscles. He hands me my x-rays.

'You can have these back,' he says. 'In case you want to frame them.'

Everybody's a comedian.

I'm not going to frame my x-rays, but I am hoping to one day have something more artistic to frame. Something I've created, from the heart. Creativity is supposed to be this wellspring that flows unfettered, a source of joy and catharsis. They say it's the best way to process your feelings. That, even if you don't think you're creative, you should journal, paint, sing – even bake – as a kind of release.

Unfortunately, I'm constipated – creatively speaking. I'm not sure which is more stuck, the joy or the catharsis, but my wellspring is barely a trickle. It's not that I haven't tried. While trying to rest my back, I've burned through half of my new sketch pad with misshapen houseplants, a portrait of Abbey that makes her look like a cone-head, and a drawing of Dexter that's so out of proportion you'd think I'd never seen a dog.

Which is why I'm standing nervously in front of an easel, in a backroom in Marrickville filled with strangers, at 6 pm on a Tuesday night. I'd seen a flyer for a beginner life-drawing class on the noticeboard in the supermarket. Craving direction – for someone to tell me how to find what I've lost – I'd swallowed the memory of how good I used to be. I was a different person then. Everybody here is learning and maybe that's what I need – to go back to the beginning.

The class was supposed to start twenty minutes ago. The teacher – a young woman in her twenties with henna tattoos and silver rings on every finger – keeps apologising and checking her phone as the students mill impatiently. My own phone pings.

Abbey*:* Checking you're still taking me to my ultrasound tomorrow? I have to be at North Shore Private by 10 am.

She's clearly still prickly, but at least she's talking to me. I hesitate. Seeing it makes it real. Then I force myself to tap out a reply:

Grace*:* Of course, darling. Wouldn't miss it for the world.

I add several appropriately excited emojis then delete them all. If I go overboard, she'll know I'm lying. Eventually, the teacher – I think her name is Gabrielle – calls for our attention.

'I'm so sorry. It appears tonight's model has been waylaid indefinitely.' A ripple of disappointment circles the room. 'I can set up a still life for those of you who want to stay, or we can reconvene next week.' Several students start packing up, grumbling under their breath.

It helps to get out of your head and into your body. My hand is in the air before I've fully processed the thought. 'I'll do it.'

'Sorry?' Gabrielle frowns at me. 'You mean set up the still life? That's very helpful, but—'

'No. I mean I'll—' I falter. *What am I doing?* '—you know . . . model. For the class. It's a life-drawing class. I'm sure everyone would prefer to draw an actual human person.' I'm babbling because I'm already kicking myself and wondering whether I've developed a disorder that makes you say the stupidest thing possible.

The room has gone quiet. Some of the students are looking at me like I'm bonkers and others with what I think is excitement – which makes me nervous because they haven't seen me naked yet.

What if they're disappointed? I'm not sure my ego can take it if they decide halfway through that they'd rather draw a banana.

Gabrielle is surprised but doesn't seem opposed. 'Have you modelled before?' Now I feel like an idiot. Of course you can't just *decide* to be a life-drawing model. People do this professionally, they know how to hold themselves, what shapes to make.

Get out of your head and into your body.

'Well, no. But I think it could be quite . . . liberating.'

Gabrielle asks if I'm sure; I'll need to sign a release form – *last chance to back out, Grace*. 'I'm sure.' Everybody stares expectantly at me as I move to the centre of the room, towards a single chair. I should have a robe so I can drop it dramatically to pose, like I do this every day and it's no big deal – isn't that how it works? Instead, all eyes are on me while I undress, painstakingly unbuttoning my blouse and removing each sneaker and sock. I pull my jeans down, standing flamingo-style to tug them off, praying I don't topple over. That would be mortifying.

Closing my eyes, I unhook my bra. *It's no different to sunbaking topless – not that you've ever done that either.* I take my briefs off before I can think too much and sit quickly, so my bits are at least partially obscured.

'Find a comfortable position, Grace.' Gabrielle is being helpful, but the only comfortable position I can think of is curled on the floor like a scared hedgehog. *Pretend you're someone else. Emilia. She'd love this.*

Leaning back awkwardly, I cross one leg over the other and hook my arm over the chair, arching my back and sucking my stomach in, fixing my gaze on a distant point on the wall. Then the ceiling. Anywhere but at the people studying me.

Gabrielle moves around the room, telling everyone they can either draw me or the negative space around me, seeing beyond the lines. She encourages them to be creative, to interpret my energy, which makes me wonder how exactly you draw a visual representation of abject terror. She approaches and leans down.

'Try to relax. You don't need to pose – imagine you're sitting watching TV or on a park bench, people-watching.' *Not helping, Gabrielle, I would never do either of those things naked.* She places a reassuring hand on my shoulder. 'Art isn't about perfection, it's about authenticity, what's real. Just be you.'

Be me. I'm not sure I've ever known how. The fabric of every memory I have is woven from the perception of who or what I needed to be at the time, for people to like me.

Get out of your head and into your body.

I take a deep breath and I shift, uncrossing my legs. My belly softens into folds, resting on the top of my thighs as I let go. *Exhale.* Leaning sideways, I rest my head on my arm, feeling the weight of my left breast slip towards my armpit, warm and heavy. I resist the urge to scoop it into a more appealing shape. I try to think only about the chair against my legs, my feet on the cold floor, the breeze from the window feathering my skin.

The scratch of pencils and charcoal against paper fills the quiet room. My eyes travel from student to student, watching them watching me. Expressions of concentration, thumbs held up with one eye closed for perspective. One man in a jaunty fedora makes sweeping strokes, before ripping his paper down and starting again. A kindly looking woman in her seventies keeps darting her head around her easel to look at me before darting back with a happy grin.

It hits me that it doesn't matter what I look like or the shape I make. Whether I'm beautiful or ugly, old or young, perfectly formed or not. My presence is the only thing that matters. That I'm here.

That I *am*. There's no judgment in their scrutiny, no appraisal, no opinion. This is simply what I look like. It's the first time in my life I haven't had to try to be something else, something better. And I'm okay. I wonder what I've been so scared of this whole time.

Exhale.

An hour later, once I'm dressed, I nervously ask if I can see their drawings. Not one of them is the same. In one, there's a defiant tilt to my chin. I radiate a certainty I definitely don't feel. Another embodies a sadness that makes me want to cry. One drawing makes me look more peaceful than I've ever felt, and another – scrawled in thick black lines – is taut with tension.

Without knowing who I am, they've all seen something different in me, found a truth, something that must be there even if I'm unaware. Stripping myself naked – getting out of my head and into my body – has somehow allowed a room full of strangers to see me more clearly than I see myself. I'm not sure what that means or whether I'm ready to be seen as exactly who I am. But I feel different, and that's a start.

Gabrielle thanks me for stepping in and asks if I'd be interested in doing it again, but I decline. As freeing as it's been, I'm not sure I want to make a habit of getting naked in front of a crowd of people.

'You'll come back for class though?'

I nod. 'I used to draw and paint a lot – I studied art, I was really good. But I stopped for a long time. I want to get back into it, but something feels off.'

'Maybe you haven't found the right subject,' she says.

When I get home, I'm too wired to sleep. It's late, but I excitedly put a gold star next to '*pose nude for an artist*' and pull out my sketch pad, scribbling for hours, my hand moving freely now – drawing the plant by my bed, the view through the window. I get stuck again on Abbey – unable to help the knot of tension that creeps in – and eventually call it a night. I need to be awake early to meet her. I connect my phone to the charger and set my alarm for 6 am, telling myself that tomorrow I need to recapture the feeling from the art class – all that matters is that I'm present. I can work the rest out later.

29

here and gone

A horn blares outside my window, dragging me from the first deep sleep I've had in months. I don't care what people say, I'll never get used to the jarring inner-city noise. Back at the house I'd be waking pre-dawn to the rush of the ocean and Dexter's morning grumbles to let him out, before I headed for the pool.

I squash the pang of longing and blearily open one eye. Sunlight streams between the curtains as I stretch, yawning. But something's wrong. The sun shouldn't be this bright before 6 am.

'No, no, no.' I bolt upright and reach for my phone, hoping the glaring sunlight is an approaching apocalyptic fireball. Which is preferable to the truth. My phone is dead. I've no idea what time it is. I disconnect and reconnect my charger, cursing the faulty power outlets. Nothing. I try a different outlet and glare at my phone, willing it to come to life. *Please, don't let it be after 9 am.*

Abbey will be furious. She already thinks I'm not interested in the baby. I pace the flat, berating myself for staying up late drawing.

My phone finally emits a gentle ping and I hurriedly punch in my passcode. *Come on, come on.* My heart sinks as the home screen flashes up the time in needlessly aggressive neon. It's midday. Abbey's ultrasound was two hours ago. I sink to the couch. This is worse than bad. Before I can dial Abbey's number, several voicemail notifications and four texts come through in a flurry, each escalating in concern from the previous. The final text stops me in my tracks:

Abbey: Don't worry about it. You're obviously busy. Auntie Liz is taking me.

What? Liz lives an hour away, how did she—? It doesn't matter. As long as someone was with Abbey. As long as she wasn't alone. I press a hand to my chest, trying to dislodge the knot that has suddenly appeared, but it won't budge. Of course Liz was there. It's another opportunity to showcase how close they are, like a punishment. *But this was not your fault.*

I fill a glass from the tap and gulp it down. Tears threaten, and I steady myself on the sink. Abbey has every right to be upset, and Liz did what any family member would do – be there for Abbey when I wasn't. I'm being unreasonable. *Are you?*

I try calling Abbey but it goes straight to voicemail. I don't trust myself to speak so I text instead.

Grace: I'm so sorry, darling. Let me explain. Call me back.

The message doesn't deliver. Her phone must be off. Calling Liz is out of the question. It would only take the wrong tone or a misplaced word from either of us to derail the conversation. I tap out a message instead:

Grace: Thank you for taking Abbey to her appointment.

I pause, then send a follow up message. I can't help myself.

Grace: It's a long way to come.

She texts back immediately.

Liz: No problem. I was dropping off the cot anyway. What happened?

I type a detailed response, then delete it. I'm not having Liz tell Abbey before I've spoken to her – 'your mother overslept' – making it sound offhand, unimportant. I need to explain.

Grace: I'll fill you in another time. I appreciate you being there for her.

The typing dots appear, and I watch them, steeling myself for a lengthy admonishment. I'm not sure I can hold back if she has a go at me. The dots disappear. Then start again.

Liz: All good. You can return the favour on Thursday. Need help with mum. If you're not busy, that is.

A pause.

Liz: By the way, she's having a girl.

Mum is in her usual spot on the patio, cigarette in hand and watching old clips from *The Graham Norton Show* on her phone. A half-full glass of bourbon and coke sits on the table. It's only 1 pm. Tight-lipped, Liz sticks several post-its to the fridge before hoisting a battered Gucci tote with peeling straps over her shoulder. She clocks me looking at the bag.

'Yes, it's a knock-off. Nate bought it for me in Thailand.'

'I didn't say anything.'

'We can't all afford the real thing as our gym bag.'

I'm not biting, and Liz looks disappointed. She's itching for a fight, a reason not to leave me alone with Mum. When I'd asked her if she's spoken to Abbey – who's still not answering my calls – she'd told me she didn't want to get involved. First time for everything.

'I'll only be a couple of hours.' She looks towards the back door. 'If anything happens that you can't handle, call me and I'll head home.'

I mentally tame the bristles that spike up my back. 'I think I can spend a couple of hours with Mum without the world ending. We'll be fine.'

Liz's nostrils flare. 'If she gets agitated, there's some diazepam on top of the fridge. Give her one and she'll calm down.'

I frown. 'Now you're scaring me. What aren't you telling me?' I peek outside, to make sure Mum can't hear me. 'If I have to give her valium, she shouldn't be drinking.'

The laugh that bursts from Liz is mirthless. 'You try telling her that. Look, she hasn't been good, and I wouldn't have asked if I wasn't desperate—'

'Right. Because, God forbid, I want to make sure my mother is okay. I mean, is there a diagnosis? Is she—'

'Grace!'

I stop short, noticing for the first time how exhausted Liz looks, and I get the same pang I did when we were kids, when she'd try hard to get something right and it slid by unnoticed. Her voice is flat as she rubs her face. 'I don't have time for this; I'm late. We can talk when I get back, okay?'

'Okay.' I soften, not just worried about Mum now.

'If you keep things easy, she'll be fine. Play cards with her, she likes that. Don't correct her if she gets confused.' Her voice breaks but then she stiffens, shoving emotion down. 'Just don't push her buttons.'

Me not push *her* buttons? There's so much I could say right now but I only nod. 'Got it.' After Liz leaves, I watch Mum from the door, still smarting from being told how to spend time with her like I'm a hired nurse. There's a war going on in the pit of my stomach, between guilt and defensiveness. I'm not sure who's winning. It's true, I don't know what's going on with my family. But it's not entirely my fault.

Family ties are bound up in countless proverbs. You can't choose your family. You always hurt those closest to you. Everyone says blood is thicker than water – and it almost always is – but how many times does a vein have to be opened before you have to find a way to staunch the bleeding?

Don't be so sensitive, Grace. We're just taking the piss. That's how my family has always 'shown love'. By poking fun. The thing about being sensitive, though, is you always catch the drag of the undercurrents.

It got worse after I met Daniel, when I started to change. In the end, I wanted too much. Tried too hard to be different. I know it wasn't just me who wanted to escape – but I was the only one who did it. Wanting more from my life insulted theirs, and I needed taking down a peg or two. It never occurred to them that my 'too muchness' was a mask I wore, so nobody would know I didn't think I was much at all. I guess the joke's on them.

The real punchline is I was also too much for Daniel and what he was building. Too common, too loud. I swore too much, dressed incorrectly, had too many opinions. He never said it in so many words, but I knew. So, I reconstructed myself completely, digging out the apparently offensive bits. I became what Daniel wanted because *that* was what our life required of me, and I was desperate to hang on to it. But the more I excavated to make room for a different version of myself – the more it built a wall between where and who I came from. I thought that was what I needed. Now I'm not so sure.

The first hour passes uneventfully. Mum is mostly lucid, aside from repeating herself a few times when we're talking about Abbey and the baby. I don't say much; I let her talk. She's excited, so there's no room for her usual passive-aggression. It's the first time I've been alone with her in years, and I'm enjoying her company; the way I did when I was small, when she'd read to me, brush my hair, or sing with me in the car.

A melancholy creeps over me. Those moments were rare once things got bad. When Dad and Liz were both home, the house was volatile. Not wanting to get between them, Mum closed herself off, busying herself with chores and errands so she didn't have to acknowledge the conflict. She was still Mum; she still did everything she was supposed to. *Except keep us safe. Except leave.* But she wasn't *there*. In her head she was elsewhere, away from him. And we could feel it.

We were almost adults by the time Dad got sober and found religion – the violence diluted and replaced by a burning guilt. Both Liz and I had moved out – me to university and Liz when she'd fallen pregnant with Nate – but I'd thought things would at least get better for Mum. Ironically, that's when she started drinking. Without us there, it was Dad she wanted to distance from – she couldn't stand how sanctimonious he became – but the bitterness of the bottle permeated everything. Even her relationship with us. Resentment chews through the melancholy. I squash it, and brightly suggest playing cards.

In between hands, Mum traipses inside to pour herself bourbon after bourbon. I can smell the alcohol from the other side of the table. I don't say anything – *you can't set her off* – but as her words start to slur, I'm increasingly uncomfortable. Liz says she's unwell, this can't be okay.

She calls me Liz more than once. I still don't correct her, but I'm having trouble gauging the line between whether she's drunk or something's wrong. Then she tells me she has to get dinner on because Dad will have had a hard day, and the last thing he needs is to come home and find us sitting around. I can't hold it together, and I say the worst thing possible.

'But, Mum. Don't you remember? Dad died. A long time ago.'

Confusion shadows her face. 'He— I don't— why would—' She shakes her head, and I can't make out the last few words she mumbles. She goes silent, staring fixedly at me for a few long seconds, then she blinks slowly, like her vision is blurred and she's having trouble making me out. Suddenly, it's like a light goes off, her eyes completely blank. The seconds stretch interminably as the first flutters of panic start behind my ribs. I reach out to touch her hand.

'Mum? Are you okay?'

Her eyes don't leave mine, but she jolts and slowly withdraws her hand, leaning away from me. I don't think she knows who I am. She closes in on herself, drawing her hands to her chest then avoiding my eyes. I'm frozen, with no idea what to say without making her worse.

I move my chair closer, trying to stay calm. 'Mum?' She looks back at me, confused. Her chin quivers and I nearly break. She reaches out towards me. Her hand rests on my cheek for a moment – 'Mummy?' – then she strikes me hard in the face.

I jerk back in shock. She's looking at me like I'm trying to attack *her,* and I realise that Mum is gone; there's nothing behind her eyes. My panic is full blown now. *Where the hell is Liz? I don't know what I'm supposed to do.*

'Mum, please. Don't do that.' I'm shaking, trying not to cry. I shouldn't upset her more. Mum hasn't said another word this entire time, as though she's forgotten how to speak. She struggles to stand, and I move to help her, unsure where she's trying to go.

Liquid spatters underneath the chair. She's wet herself and she clutches between her legs with both hands as though she's trying to stop it. Holding her arms, my face crumples and I dip my head, containing a sob so violent it nearly cracks my chest apart. I force a straight face and look at her – my antagonistic, survivor of a mother who is staring at me, eyes filled with tears, mute and holding herself like a toddler. How embarrassed she must feel. But looking in her eyes, I realise there's no space for shame – she's too frightened.

'Come on, let's get you inside.'

She resists for a second, then moves with me, her feet barely lifting from the floor. I guide her slowly, walking backwards, terrified she'll slip on the wet pavers and I won't be able to catch her. She fights me through the doorway and I catch her resistant hands. 'It's okay, Mum. Let me help you.' Her fingers curl around mine; suddenly docile. I can't hold the tears back. I keep my head lowered so she can't see them.

Managing to get her to the bathroom, I manoeuvre her towards the toilet, peel her soaked trousers down and help her sit. I crouch low, holding her hands. 'It's alright. Everything's going to be alright.' *It's not alright. Nothing is alright.* 'We'll get you cleaned up, okay? I'm here.'

I look at her face, now completely passive, and I feel that fist in my throat again, the same one from the car with Daniel. I can't breathe. I'm helpless and I hate it. There's nothing I can do to fix this. I flash back to the morning after the concert, when I woke disoriented, grasping for memory and finding only quicksand. Is this how Mum feels – all the time?

Then the strangest thing happens. One moment she's gone and the next, it's like a switch has been flicked. Electricity surges and the lights come on. Her eyes refocus and fix on me, on my knees in front of her. She registers that she's soiled and half-naked, and her expression twists. Mortification.

'What are you doing?' She pulls her hands away. 'For Christ's sake, Grace. Really?' She looks like she's going to hit me again. I lean back, wary.

'I'm trying to help you. Mum, you—'

She doesn't let me finish, shouting at me, telling me to get out, that this is not bloody on, that she's not an invalid. How dare I.

A door slams and Liz is in the bathroom. 'What the hell is going on?'

Mum's still yelling as I jump up and bustle Liz into the hallway. I explain that everything was fine, that Mum had too much to drink and got confused and was talking about Dad, and then she had some kind of episode and then— I crack open, my chest heaving, sobbing words incoherently. Liz throws a hand up. 'Stop crying. Just fucking stop.'

'What?' I gulp at air, trying to steady myself.

'How much did you let her drink?'

I stare at her. 'I didn't *let* her drink anything. She's a grown woman.'

'I knew this was a mistake. She's sick, Grace. You were supposed to look after her.' Liz tries to walk off and I grab her arm. She jerks it away, glaring at me.

'Don't put that on me,' I snap. 'You said not to stop her, not to push her buttons – and this is so much more than too much bourbon. She was talking about Dad like he's alive. Why didn't you tell me it was this bad?'

She rounds on me. 'Because you're not here, Grace. You're never fucking here. When would I have told you? You don't call, you don't visit. You're always too busy to talk. You're always there for everybody else – your friends, people you don't even know. But face it, you haven't given a shit about this family for years.'

It's a slap in the face, a figurative one this time, but she's partly right. Just not about the bit where I don't care. I bite down on the truth. If I try to defend why I've stayed away, she'll accuse me of making things about me. Again.

'That's not true.'

'Well, that's how it feels.' She takes a breath. 'Look, you should probably go.' She gestures towards the bathroom. I can hear Mum crying. 'This is going to take a bit to settle down.'

I wrap my arms around myself, feeling small. 'Okay. I'll call you later. Maybe I'll come back tomorrow.' *No, you won't.*

'No, Grace.' Liz's voice is sharp. 'You're not going to swoop in like you usually do – after staying away for God knows how long – thinking you can take over. That *you're* the one to fix everything.'

I jerk back. 'When have I ever done that?'

Liz points her finger in my face. 'You did it with Dad, *all* the time. Just to spite me. Even when he died. I've been asking for your *input* with Mum. Not for you to save the bloody day.'

I stare at her, stunned that she's got things so wrong. But instead of explaining, I bite. 'I'm sorry for ruining your life by trying to help.'

She sighs heavily. 'How about you sort things out with Abbey and let me take care of Mum?'

'She's my mother too.'

The fight drains out of her. 'Do what you want, Grace. Why change now?' She disappears into the bathroom, leaving me in the hallway. I hear her talking to Mum, soothing her. Part of me wants to barge in, to make them include me. But I'm in a tailspin. A familiar panic claws its way up my back again, wrapping its limbs around me and whispering in my ear, *You can't do this. It's too much. Run.*

Liz might think I have a hero complex, but all I want to do is get as far away from here as possible. And never come back. Because even I know this is not fixable.

Then again, neither were all the other times.

30

truth be told

January, 2005

Dad didn't want a funeral. He said they were a waste of money – all those people in black standing around being maudlin, half of them having not spoken to you in years, spouting bullshit about what a great person you were, then drinking free piss and eating sponge cake. 'Just stick me in the wheelie bin and put me out with the rubbish.' I was eleven the first time he said it, and I thought he was serious. All I could think about were the flies, and it haunted me for weeks.

The nave at Our Lady of Mercy is packed, Mum made sure of it, but I wonder how many of these people really knew him. She's wearing a red dress Dad hated; neither Liz nor I could convince her otherwise. 'Black washes me out,' she'd said. In an ocean of black and grey, she stands out like a fresh bullet wound, which I guess is appropriate. Scorsese would be proud of the symbolism.

The minister, new to the church, is dirge-like and solemn, and so are the chosen hymns – apparently Dad's favourites. I know he would have preferred Elton John's 'Goodbye Yellow Brick Road' or 'I'm One' by The Who. At every party – when Dad was just drunk enough but hadn't staggered across the inevitable line – he'd sing along, loud and off-key, using his drink as a microphone. Eyes closed and committed, imagining a life where he was a rock star instead of an army veteran turned beat cop, living in the suburbs with a wife and kids who hated him half the time. Mum and Liz were always embarrassed, but I liked it, even though it made me sad.

Mum is adamant she's not giving a eulogy, and I know Liz would rather eat sand than speak in public. Considering our relationship, I'm not sure I have the right to deliver Dad's eulogy; but I'm the eldest and somebody's got to do it. I'd taken the job off Mum and Liz's plates, along with a few other things, to lighten the load. They were dealing with enough, having been the ones who found him. I've received instructions not to embarrass the family – the way Dad went is shame enough. I don't know what they think I might say. Everybody knows a funeral is the one place you're supposed to lie, if only by omission. Don't speak ill of the dead.

Several people speak before me. The minister speaks of a man who knew his failings and sought forgiveness, who found refuge in God. I don't think he even met Dad, and I wonder who told him that. A craggy old man with a smoker's voice who I remember calling Uncle Peter when we were kids – not my uncle, but that's how it was back then – starts with a joke that falls flat. He served with Dad in Vietnam and talks of his bravery and mateship and how he could never beat him at pool, choking with emotion then clearing his throat, tucking it away with all the other feelings men like him and my dad bury until they get to be too much to live with.

A bullish man I've only ever known as Sergeant Baker brusquely lists Dad's finest qualities on the force: diligence, forthrightness, a sense of justice. Janet, the church treasurer, a bird-like woman in her sixties, tearfully rhapsodises about his volunteering, his compassion. She says, 'He was a pillar of the community and he'll be sorely missed.' Liz and Mum's faces are unreadable, but I feel them stiffen beside of me.

I wonder if any of them know about Mum's black eyes, his repeated infidelity, or the countless times he made me, and Liz, feel worthless. I wonder whether they'd think so much of him if they did. Probably. After all, nobody's without flaws, and what goes on behind closed doors, well—

Google says a eulogy should be heartfelt and honour the attributes and achievements of your loved one – but that only paints half a picture. My speech took days to write and another for Mum to approve it. She rejected anything negative, as though it reflected on her. What kind of woman stays with a man like that, and doesn't take her kids and leave? I've wondered it myself, struggling to understand how impossible it can be to walk away from someone who has failed you so hard.

The accolades skirt the reality – Dad was a good man to others, but he was a terrible husband and a bad father. Things weren't always awful – happy moments punctuated our lives. So how do you acknowledge the darkness without sounding bitter? Like there's no love lost when there is. Because despite it all, he was still my dad.

Standing at the pulpit, I'm nervous. Daniel smiles encouragingly, his arm around Abbey, who looks small and overwhelmed. He'd offered to have the funeral at our community church centre and to deliver the service, but Mum made no bones about the fact Dad would turn in his grave.

'Thank you all for coming, it would have meant so much to Dad,' I say, telling my first lie. I study the paper in front of me, wanting desperately to veer from the script. 'My dad was not perfect.' Mum and Liz's eyes bore into me – apprehensive – and I baulk. 'But . . . no one is.'

I follow the words on the paper to the letter, but for each story I tell, parallel truths run in my head like a movie, shimmering back and forth between shadow and light, the film catching on the reel.

'He was popular at Sydney Boys High, played on the rugby team.' Dad turning up drunk to my school play, heckling the girl who got the lead over me. Mum's embarrassment was accompanied by his slurring defence that he was standing up for me.

'He loved Japanese bonsais and collected them; he was meticulous with their care.' Dad sitting with Liz for hours, patiently teaching her how to prune them. Her breaking one with an errant ball, attempting to fix it with superglue

and Dad taking the belt to her legs for lying. 'He found joy in his garden.' Dad standing in the yard in his underpants, smoking, hose in hand and several beers in. When friends called for me, riding their bikes onto the grass, he'd spray them, yelling, 'Get off my fucking lawn!' Him holding the hose over the trampoline while we jumped, swimsuit clad, in the summer sun, and he shouted, 'Higher, higher.' Mum watching from the verandah, laughing.

'He was a family man, houseproud.' Wallpaper curling around fresh holes in the plasterboard, mapping Dad's rages; a vicious cartography of chair legs, fists and feet. Him building us a treehouse around the giant eucalypt in the yard, sitting in it with us after dark, telling ghost stories with a torch.

'He loved cooking Sunday morning breakfasts.' Dad, hungover and brackish, frying eggs and bacon and making me and Liz swallow every bite even though we were trying to be vegetarian. Him making me birthday pancakes and letting me play the new Madonna record all day. The same album thrown against the wall because I was playing it too loudly.

'He was a dedicated and loving husband, father and grandfather.' Mum crying when she found out about Cheryl from the RSL and the ensuing screaming match. Dad surprising her with a Fiji trip to renew their vows, both returning sunburnt and affectionate. Dad calling Liz a slut when she fell pregnant. The photo where he's grinning and throwing Nate in the air when he was two. Him teaching Abbey to fish.

My eyes swim. I put the paper down and look out at the sea of faces. I might not be able to explain the paradox that was my father, but I'm being disingenuous.

'Dad and I weren't speaking when he died.' Mum and Liz's faces drop. 'We'd fallen out. Anybody who met Dad knew he could be . . . intractable. I'll never know whether we would have sorted things out, so this is my only opportunity to make it right.' I look to the ceiling, closing my eyes. 'I love you, Dad. And we forgive you.'

When I sit down, Liz mutters, 'Still speaking for everyone else, I see.'

I can't look at her. 'It's literally the point of a eulogy.'

Mum squeezes my hand too tightly. 'Could have done without you airing our dirty laundry, but that was nice.'

Mum has her own way of resolving acrimonious feelings; she makes her points silently, and not always subtly. Dad had been on a low-sodium diet for years, on account of his kidneys, and it annoyed Mum more than it should have. 'Might as well eat bloody cardboard,' she'd said. Afterwards, at the wake, the food piled onto foil trays is so salty it's inedible.

31

weight of the world

Pulling into the driveway, I sit for a minute with the engine running, thinking how strange it is that the house now makes me nervous. But then, it's not just the house that's a potential minefield.

I'm only here to collect some things. Not wanting to drag my old life with me is one thing, but after visiting Mum, I was craving familiarity and comfort and arrived home to neither. My flat still feels like a stranger I'm being forced to make friends with. I have no mementos – no photos or ornaments to trigger happy memories, no books I've read a thousand times. I don't even have my favourite plant. When I packed up and left, I thought the flat was temporary. But things feel different now.

I'm relieved when it's Daniel who answers the door. I'm not sure what I would have done if it had been Sasha. I'm not ready to see her in my house. Daniel's juggling a set of keys, looking harried.

'Good, you're here,' he says. 'I'm heading out and didn't want to leave a key.'

I can't help needling him. 'Worried about burglars or worried I won't give it back?' His uncomfortable expression makes me laugh. 'Don't worry, I'm not going to keep turning up, and Dexter's a great guard dog.'

'Dexter's not here. He's at doggie day care.'

I frown. 'Since when?'

'Since I'm busy. It's not fair for him to be on his own all day.' *Ouch.* He glances at his watch. 'Sasha's picking him up then taking him for a walk.'

Jealousy ripples through me. Stealing my husband I can handle, but my *dog*? There are some things you just don't do to another woman. My nostrils flare, but I manage not to bite.

'*She's* bringing him back here?' It comes out strangled, and I hate that it gives me away. Daniel's eyes narrow.

'She'll be home around five.' *Home?* 'I imagine you'll want to be gone by then.'

My eyes roll so far back in my head I can see the driveway, and I hold out my hand. 'This is still my house, or have you forgotten? I'll need the keys to lock up.'

His voice is heavy with sarcasm. 'As long as you don't have any Tinder dates arriving.' I can tell he regrets saying it because he instantly flushes red.

The accusation knocks me off balance. 'What's that supposed to mean?'

'Don't pretend you're not seeing people.' The dismissive tone says he doesn't care. But I know how he holds himself when he's stewing, shoulders rigid, hands in pockets. 'Todd's brother saw your profile.' He's having trouble looking at me.

Is he jealous?

Gravity pulls me back to centre, a power shift. 'What I do with my time is not your business. You've made it clear we're no longer together. Also, you can tell Todd his brother's a dick.' Daniel's mouth twitches, struggling with control. 'Keys, please.'

He reluctantly hands them over, directing me to leave them in the mailbox. Then he shifts the power back, an emotional tug of war. 'Sasha put some boxes by the stairs for you,' he says. 'Five o'clock, Grace. Let's not have any childish confrontations.'

I want to poke the keys into his stupid eyes. I resist, smiling as he nods curtly and walks off, pressing my tongue so hard against my teeth that I taste blood. I can't, however, resist slamming the door once inside. I'm pacified by the brief flash of violence. Maybe this is why people go to those smash rooms, where you're allowed to destroy everything with a big hammer.

It's startling, the way love can alchemise so quickly into something else. Just days ago, my anger still rubbed inconveniently against the remnants of longing. But I detest my husband in this moment. The DNA of our relationship is irrevocably altered.

I exhale, put my bag on the stairs and look around. It's odd being here, even after only a few months. The house looks the same but feels immeasurably different.

I am still everywhere, as though I'm still living here. But then, I'm not dead, am I? My shoes on the rack in the hall, my trenchcoat on the hook. Photos dotted around of the three of us, of me and Abbey. I find myself searching for changes, like a masochistic version of *Where's Wally* – the new cushions on the couch, the kitchen stools shoved out from the counter, the air fryer that was the one appliance Daniel said we'd never get. *Stop it, Grace. This is pointless. You chose to leave.*

I grab two boxes and head upstairs. A cloud of perfume hits me when I open my bedroom door. It smells like she looks – sparkling and sweet, like sugar. I'm not surprised by that, I'm just surprised how much my room is drowning in it. Surely they're not sleeping in separate rooms already? Maybe she hates his snoring too. I smirk to myself. *Welcome to the dream, sweetheart.* But as I glance around, there are no other signs of her. My bed looks as pristine as when I left.

I check Daniel's room, curious, though I immediately wish I hadn't. His bed looks like it's hosted a wrestling match. A pair of high-heeled boots sit by the dresser and a lace bra drapes over the chair. *There goes that theory.* Annoyed, I march back to my room, coughing dramatically at the cloying sweetness.

I find the answer in the bathroom. My (former) abode is now her dressing room. The counter is strewn with hair products and makeup – a curling wand, multiple eyeshadow palettes, numerous brushes and lip glosses, and a set of hair extensions draped over the towel rack. *No wonder she looks so good. She's basically Barbie.* I'm fascinated – how does all this fit on one face? I spot familiar skincare pots next to her toothbrush. Didn't I throw all that away? Waste not, want not, I suppose, but it annoys me nonetheless. *The nerve.*

I stare at it all in irritation and an evil urge takes hold. Maybe I could pee on her toothbrush or dip her hair extensions in the toilet. *Grow up, Grace. You'll do no such thing.* Having a conscience is so annoying sometimes. Instead, I gather up the most expensive skincare – that *I* paid for – and toss it in a box.

Finally, I grab the framed photographs from the dresser, several books from the bedside table, and drag a storage box from the walk-in. I just need some touchpoints – something to remind me that my life before this one existed. That I haven't disappeared completely.

At least if I were dead, all this would have been done for me. When a person dies, their life is dismantled, packed up and put away – everything tied in a neat bow. Finished. Final. A lifetime of treasured belongings either fought over and divided between relatives or donated to charity. I think about Mum and wonder what we'll keep. What me and Liz will undoubtedly argue over. But I don't want to think yet about trawling through her things when she goes. It was supposed to be years away.

I spill photographs and thick envelopes onto the floor. I imagine when I do die, my family going through all this – to work out what Abbey or her kids will inherit. Things that hold sentimental value for me but, out of context, mean little to anybody else. The truth is, you can't inherit memories – no matter how special – if they haven't been shared.

Unless I tell them, my family won't know that this faded concert ticket is from seeing Debbie Gibson in 1989. I waited around at the backstage door afterwards, wearing a brimmed hat and too much eyeliner because I was obsessed with 'Lost in Your Eyes'. I was convinced that me and Debbie would be best friends – if only I could speak to her – and then everything would be okay, because if somebody extraordinary chose me, it proved I was worth something. But that never happened, I was just another girl in a hat. Until I met Daniel.

They won't know that the two handwritten love letters tucked into this packet of Abbey's baby photos were left anonymously in my parents' mailbox when I was sixteen. That I never found out who they were from, but I could never throw them away, because nobody had ever said such beautiful, poetic things to me. They're the only tangible proof I have that someone thought I was special.

I stare at the tumble of keepsakes, a wash of memories. Maybe this wasn't such a good idea after all. Shoving the box back into the walk-in, I sit on what is no longer my bed, gathering up the blue-and-grey blanket me and Abbey had made together when she was fifteen. She'd been obsessed with knitting – apparently it was an ironically cool thing all the girls at school were doing with their mums – so we'd sat every Wednesday for months, watching *McLeod's Daughters* and alternating rows of the blanket until it was done.

It nearly remained unfinished after she got upset at my insistence on unravelling a row if either of us dropped a stitch. In the end I let it go, but once it was done, our routine ended in favour of netball with her friends, and I sat through that awful episode when Claire McLeod died, by myself. I'll never forget the scene where Tess drags frantically on the rope attached to the truck – Claire inside – trying in vain to stop it tipping off the cliff. Away from her.

I hold the blanket up. The bottom half is dotted with holes, but I wouldn't have it any other way. I'd wanted our blanket to be perfect, not realising that Abbey just wanted time together. How is it a person can try so hard to get things right and still get so much wrong?

There's nothing else I want to take – and the familiar is not bringing the comfort I thought. I fold the blanket into the box, gather it up and leave the room. The click as I close the door has a finality to it. A full stop at the end of a very long sentence.

I don't belong here anymore. I'm in that liminal space between what was and what will be. I don't know where I do belong. All I know is the weight of guilt is too heavy, like a pack filled with rocks, digging into my shoulders, a reminder of everything I've done wrong.

Maybe the only way I'll be able to offload it and stop caring what other people think of me, is to let myself stumble, face down in the dirt – but the idea scares me. My self-judgment floats under the surface of my newly minted bravado, like a jellyfish, waiting for the perfect moment to snare me in its tentacles. *You're terrible. There's no coming back from this.* And maybe there's not. The old me would be making amends right now – with Liz, with Mum, with

Abbey, even in some ways with Daniel – setting things right, walking across glass to show I care and prove my worth. I know that's what everyone expects me to do.

But I won't. I have to stop being scared of who I might be if I stop pretending. My instinct tells me to run and for once I'm going to listen. Even if it's wrong, I'll get as messy as possible. After all, certain flowers only bloom in mud.

32

swing when you're winning

Number nineteen on the Fuck-it List reads '*Attend a sex party*'. Every time I walk past my chart, it winks at me as if to say 'Come on, pervy. Get your kink on. You know you want to.' Except I'm not sure I do.

I said I wanted to descend into the muck . . . but this dirty? It's all well and good to want to offload guilt and shame in theory, but I don't think it's that easy. Sure, this could be exactly what I need to break free of my self-imposed shackles, but I have a suspicion I'm more likely to end up with nightmares about that woman from *Game of Thrones*, with her clanging bell and grim expression, yelling *Shame!* every night until I die.

At the same time, I'd prefer not to put it off. Which is why I was intentional about the wording. *Attending* a sex party doesn't mean I have to join in. Then again, why go to a sex party if you're going to stand in the corner watching other people do it, like some kind of creeper? I'm aware watching is some people's *thing*, but I don't see the point. Couldn't you stay at home with all the porn on the internet?

Hence my dilemma. The thought of doing sex stuff with strangers, in front of other strangers, is fascinating – but it's also fraught with dangers. What if I don't find anyone attractive? I'm not good at rejecting people – I'm a recovering people pleaser – but I'd have to if they weren't my type.

What if people don't find *me* attractive? What if I make weird sex faces and I have no idea? What if I fart accidentally while it's all happening? Are there protocols I'm not aware of? Is it BYO lube? If not, I'm fairly sure communal lube is unhygienic.

Worst case scenario – it's sleazy, I satisfy my curiosity, have a cocktail, and go home. Best case scenario – the sexy vibe is a turn-on and all the gorgeous people want to take turns giving me orgasms. Either way, I get to stick a gold star on my chart.

I make my decision in the middle of a hot yoga class. My list says, '*Try one random new thing per week*', so I've dragged Susie along with me. We're hiding up the back because Susie took one look at the bank of mirrors and told me I was fucked in the head if I thought she was going to spend ninety minutes staring at her own face while trying not to die. She's wrapping one slippery leg around the other when I drop the bomb, and she nearly falls over.

'You're going to do it. Seriously?'

'Yep.' I studiously look ahead, hooking my foot around my calf and twisting my arms into a pretzel shape. 'I found one in Annandale that looks upmarket.'

She snorts. '*Upmarket?* What, is everyone carrying Chanel and drinking lychee martinis while they root each other?'

My foot slips and I lose my balance. 'Hardly. But it looks – you know – a bit glamorous. Not seedy.'

'Wow. You're for real. I thought you'd drop it from the list for sure.'

'Please refrain from talking.' The instructor's disapproving voice sails to the back of the room. 'This is a silent, open-eye meditation. Let's respect our fellow yogis.'

We make an effort to pay attention to the instructor's monologue and plant our feet wide, swan diving forward until our heads are hanging upside down.

'When are we going?' Susie's face turns red and I'm unsure whether it's blood rushing to her extremities or excitement. I peer sideways at her.

'Travis is giving me the night off on Friday. But you can't come.'

'Why not? I thought you wanted to get freaky?'

'Not *that* freaky. What if I decide to participate?' Susie makes a circle with her thumb and forefinger and pokes her other finger through it, silently mouthing 'par-tici-pate'. 'We only just reconnected. I think you seeing my hoo-ha in action is weird, okay?'

'No weirder than the time we made out at that uni party to get free drinks from the DJ. Do you remember? That was fun.'

I stand up, light-headed. 'That was not fun. It was like pashing my sister.' We lie down in savasana, but not before I clock the militant instructor frowning our way. 'The point is,' I whisper, 'I can look after myself.'

'Fine. Make sure you have a safe word.'

I roll on my side to face her. 'See, this is where I get confused. What good is a safe word unless I tell people what it is? Should I put it on a stick-on badge, or do I work it into conversations? Otherwise, it's redundant, right? I could change my mind in the middle of doing it and start yelling "*nectarine*" and people will just think I've got a fetish for stone fruit.'

Susie cackles so loud it makes the woman next to me – who I think had fallen asleep – jolt, her arms and legs flicking up like a marionette. I squash my face into my mat to muffle my laughter. Too late. The Yoga Nazi looms over us.

'Ladies, I'm going to have to ask you to leave the class. You're making the other yogis uncomfortable, which is not ideal when we're about to go into double camel pose.'

We stifle our amusement, roll up our mats and tiptoe between the rows of prone bodies towards the door. 'Sorry. So sorry,' I mutter as the instructor watches us go, her folded arms making her biceps bulge.

We reach the door and Susie turns back, bowing deeply.

'Namaste, motherfuckers.'

Secrets – officially termed a 'sex-on-premises venue' – is a converted warehouse, the entrance discreetly tucked away down a laneway. Before I get out of the taxi, I put on the feathered mask I bought yesterday. I've purposely chosen Secrets' masquerade night because I have no doubt that plenty of churchgoers are as kinky as hell behind closed doors. This is the last place I want to be recognised.

Inside, the light is encouragingly dim, the main room opulently decorated – gold patterned wallpaper, leather couches, tall bar tables and lamps. Sade's 'Smooth Operator' is playing on the sound system and a shiny metal pole connects the floor to the ceiling, right in the middle of the dance floor. *I am definitely not getting on that.*

Several couples and a few single women are dotted around the room, talking. Eyes swivel my way, assessing me. I straighten my shoulders – summoning Emilia – and stare back. I can't tell if anyone's attractive, they're all wearing masks, but at least everyone's well-dressed. Not that their fashion sense will matter later. So, how does this work? I spot a large sign, on one side of the room. *Rules. Excellent.*

Consent is key; No photography or video recording; Any guest violating the rules will be removed and reported to the police; Condoms and lube are provided in all rooms. At the bottom is written 'Mistress Ava will be overseeing The Dungeon from 10 pm.' A sex party *with* a dungeon? That's two stars for one.

I pour myself a glass of wine and loiter nervously by the bar. A few people are already making out – in various stages of undress – but nobody appears to have headed to the bedrooms yet, so it feels like any other bar. *This isn't so scary.* I try to relax and look approachable. *I can do this.*

I don't have to wait long. I'm approached by couple after couple in the first hour and quickly realise that single women are hot property. Sean and Megan are in their late thirties, hard-bodied, and regulars. They offer to take me under their wing and show me the ropes – *literal ropes?* – then Sean says he'd love to go down on me while Megan sits on my face. I politely decline. Trent and Julie – on holiday from Wagga, for their anniversary – are like over-excited puppies. Julie has nice boobs, but Trent has a bushy beard and dirty fingernails.

'Thank you, really. I'm flattered and you seem lovely. But I think I might spectate for now.' They look disappointed but within a minute they're talking to an amazonian blonde in the corner. They disappear down the hallway, leaving me feeling annoyingly interchangeable.

The main room empties out fast. The remaining single men eye me like vultures. *Nope, nope and nope.* Maybe this isn't for me. I empty the rest of a bottle of wine into my glass and head cautiously down the hallway. I can't claim my gold stars without at least checking out the action.

A couple in the first bedroom are going hell for leather and have drawn quite a crowd, several of whom are going hell for leather on themselves. In another bedroom, there's a threesome happening. It's Sean and Megan, enthusiastically executing their very specific proposal to me. I have no idea who the other woman is because I can't see her face.

The 'Orgy Room' is next and I approach the doorway with curiosity. There are at least twenty people in there, all still with their masks on. The pile of contorted bodies on the bed looks like a giant, panting octopus. I watch for a while – hoping to feel the sexy *Eyes Wide Shut* vibes – but I'm not turned on at all. There's no judgment – they all look like they're enjoying themselves. If I'm honest, it's anti-climactic. No pun intended. It's simply not as interesting as I thought it would be.

Unlike the dungeon.

A lone man is leaning up against the heavy double doors when I find it, watching through two small windows draped with red velvet curtains. He's forty-ish – average height and body – and wearing boxers, a singlet, and a black leather eye mask. It's nice to not be the only person with their clothes still on.

'Do you mind if I join you?' He turns with a start and looks me up and down, lingering on my feet in their strappy heels. 'Watching,' I add, in case he thinks I'm propositioning him, '—not *join you* join you. Like, not in a sex way.'

He laughs and moves over. 'No worries. Take a look, it's getting interesting.' *Oooh.* I approach with trepidation as we peer through the glass together. The room is bathed in red light and I see a bench and a heavy wooden chair, both complete with buckled cuff-straps, and a wall hung with assorted implements. I recognise the whips but can't imagine what you're supposed to do with the other things. They're all pointy and metal, that can't be fun. Someone could put an eye out.

On the other wall, there's a giant wooden crucifix – also with straps. The thought of doing anything sexual on that feels sacrilegious, even if I am currently ignoring God. I avert my eyes – resisting the urge to cross myself – and that's when I see it. In the corner of the room hangs a swing – scooped leather seat, some kind of stirrups, and handles dangling from the chains it's suspended from. *I knew it! Swingers' parties do have swings!*

'Yes!' I clap my hands, excited – because I like being right, no other reason. The man standing next to me mistakes my enthusiasm.

'I know where I'll be finding you later.'

'Oh, no. I just—never mind.'

There's no point explaining and it's not like he's judging. Let him think I'm into whips and chains. But I can't see myself actually going into this room. It looks terrifying. My interest is purely academic.

Trent with the dirty fingernails is lying face down and naked on a massage table in the centre of the room. Julie stands nervously over him with her boobs out, holding what looks like a small cricket bat. A striking woman in a PVC bustier and dagger-heeled, thigh-high boots is instructing her. Mistress Ava! I grin, thrilled. Not with watching Trent and Julie – but at the real, live dominatrix. *How exciting.*

Thwack! Julie paddles Trent's bare arse with the bat and he lets out a yell. The mistress praises Julie, who looks very pleased with herself. Trent not so much, but when asked if he's had enough, he shakes his head. *Thwack!*

I feel a jiggling beside me. *Oh God, is he masturbating? So what if he is – isn't that the point? Don't be judgy, Grace. I'm not being judgy, I don't want to get anything on my shoes.* I look down, apprehensive. He's scratching his thigh. I laugh in relief and he looks at me.

'Not finding it a turn-on?'

'I'm not laughing at them. I thought you were—' I jerk my hand quickly '—*you know*. I'm glad you weren't. I wouldn't have known what to do. This is all new for me.'

'No, watching's not really my thing.' He glances down the hallway. 'Doesn't look like it's yours either.' His voice sounds familiar, and I study what I can see of his face, trying to place him. He's studying me back and I duck my head, moving back to the window. Trent's arse is bright red now; Julie's putting her whole arm into it.

'I'm trying to broaden my horizons – have new experiences – but I don't think orgies or having an audience are my thing.'

'Me neither. Well, not orgies anyway.' He laughs and suddenly it clicks. Every Saturday morning for years, Abbey would sit in front of the TV watching *Round House*, a variety-style show for kids with games, music, and celebrities doing crazy stunts. The host – Patrick Wells, in his twenties at the time – had a distinctive laugh. The show's still running; I've seen pictures of him at the Logies. No wonder he's wearing a mask. Everyone's entitled to a private life, but I'm not sure the TV network would want news surfacing of their family-friendly star frequenting sex clubs. I decide not to say anything. If anyone gets it, it's me. Until he says, 'Have we met? You look familiar.' *Shit.*

I don't look at him. 'I bet you say that to all the girls.'

He clicks his fingers and points at me. 'I've got it.' Then he simply turns back to the window. *Is he going to put me out of my misery?*

'What?' I prod.

'Let's just say,' he eyes me knowingly, 'my ex-wife found God recently. Hence the divorce.' I must look panicked because he puts a hand on my shoulder. 'Don't worry, Secrets is very discreet.'

I decide to level the playing field. 'That's good for both of us.' I narrow my eyes. 'Let's just say, you've spent more Saturday mornings in my living room than I can count.'

He side-eyes me, then smiles. 'Ah – mutually assured destruction.' He puts out his hand. 'Grace, right?'

I nod and shake his hand. 'Nice to meet you, Patrick. My daughter is a big fan.' *That's it, Grace. Make it weirder.* We turn back to the window, but the spanking session is wrapping up. Trent is limping, which is understandable. I can't help myself. 'So, for the record, what *is* your thing?'

Patrick doesn't get a chance to answer. The doors open and Trent and Julie exit the dungeon. 'Okay, well I guess I'll leave you to your, um – whatever it is you're going to do in there,' I say. I'm not sure I want to know. *Liar, you're dying to know.* 'I promise I won't stand out here watching.' *Yes, you will.*

Patrick cocks his head. 'Maybe there's something else we can do for each other.' My eyes widen. '*Sleep with a celebrity*' is number twelve on my list. He's hardly Jon Bon Jovi, but still.

'You want me to have sex with you?'

'Not exactly.'

I frown. I'm not sure the celebrity one counts if we don't actually do it. However, if I smack him with something – in a sexy way I mean – technically I get three gold stars. Sex party, check. Sex dungeon, check. Try BDSM, check. And I don't even have to let anyone do anything scary to me. *Winning.*

'Look, I'm happy to, uh—spank you.' My face flushes. 'But I don't want to poke you with any of those spiky things, okay?'

'No spanking and no spiky things.' He looks down. 'But you have very pretty feet.'

'You want to have sex with my *feet*?'

He shrugs. 'You said you wanted to try new things.' *True.*

'Are you coming in?' Mistress Ava pokes her head out of the door holding a riding crop. I cannot believe I'm walking into a sex dungeon with *Patrick Wells!* Wait until I tell Abbey. *Oh, wait. Nope. Ugh, how annoying. It's such a good story.*

It turns out Patrick wants to do some unusual things with my feet, both of which I'm okay with. It feels oddly innocuous and danger-free, and I'm glad I don't have to get naked. First, he asks me to walk on him. I take my heels off, because I don't want to puncture his spleen and get sued by a TV network for damaging their cash cow.

Patrick strips off and lies on the ground, face up. The Mistress holds my hand for balance, looking bored, and I want to apologise for not being freakier. I tramp up and down, studiously avoiding accidentally stepping on his penis – *wait, would he like that? Surely not.*

Then he asks if I'd be comfortable sitting in the swing. *Note to self – add 'sex swing' to the list. That's FOUR gold stars!* I hoist myself in and hold on to the handles. Mistress Ava, sensing this is not going to get extreme, sits in the corner checking her phone and tapping her crop on her boot. Patrick stands in front of me, takes hold of my bare feet and squashes them around his erect penis like a hotdog bun. He leans on the chains, rocking the swing, and I try not to laugh. That would be rude, and he's been very nice so far. But this is ridiculous. *NW Magazine* would have a field day.

He finishes noisily and I plaster on an encouraging smile. 'Thank you. That was . . . interesting.' I glance around the room, holding my feet in the air, hoping to spot a box of tissues. There's no way I'm putting my shoes back on with sticky feet. They're Jimmy Choo.

Gold stars aside, I'm disappointed in myself. It turns out I am completely vanilla. *How boring.* One thing is for certain, though. I'm never going to be able to watch the Logies with a straight face again.

33

free falling

When life is hard, sometimes it's easier to convince yourself everything is fine – to focus on distraction and make excuses – than to see the uncomfortable truth. But life has a way of throwing things at you to circumvent your blinkers, peeling them back and forcing you to open your eyes. If only to realise you're lost.

Four weeks and several gold stars later, Abbey's frostiness is only just thawing. I've seen her once for an awkward lunch I thought I was prepared for. But the sight of her growing belly – the change in her gait, her centre of gravity shifted – made reality unavoidable, and the walls had closed in on me again. I was Princess Leia in that trash compactor, pushing back on the inevitable with all my might.

She could sense my panic. I pushed my food around, unable to eat, trying to connect by asking if there was anything else she still needed. But she quickly shut me down.

'Everything's covered now, Mum.'

'Maybe I could come to one of your antenatal classes?'

Abbey shook her head. 'Tobias is home for a while. He'll be there with me.'

'Of course. That makes sense.'

'Besides, I'd be really stuck if something came up again.'

It was fair to say, but it still stung. Out of ideas, I steered the conversation away from the baby and eventually Abbey cut lunch short, feigning tiredness. Trying to make up for it, I ordered her a fancy UV bottle steriliser online. She texted a day later.

Abbey: Thank you, but I'm committed to breastfeeding. I hope they accept returns.

I haven't been back to see Mum, but Liz has kept me in the loop, alluding to an unpleasant incident with Nate's boys and letting me know that she'd finally convinced Mum to get a proper diagnosis. It had come back swiftly – rapidly advancing vascular dementia. It's a gut punch, but knowing I *should* visit and *making myself* visit are two different things. I tell Liz I don't want to risk setting Mum off, but really, I don't know how to be around her.

Daniel has been unnervingly quiet, not that I've had any need to deal with him. I'm in no rush to sort out our financials; I'm managing fine by myself. My days are simple. I have freedom for the first time in ages, which is why – rightly or wrongly – I'm viscerally resistant to anything that threatens it.

Part of me thinks I should do something meaningful with my freedom – write a novel, volunteer, go back to school – instead of this list and working in a bar. But what's more meaningful than experiencing life? I try to ignore the feeling that I'm drifting without purpose. Ridiculous or not, the Fuck-it List is my anchor for now.

As for my recent gold stars – the empty slots on my chart had made me nervous – so I'd caved and written '*Skydiving*' down. Next thing I know, I'm at 15,000 feet wearing a pair of ugly goggles and strapped to a muscle-bound and attractively weathered skydiving instructor called Roger.

The ascent into the sky over Wollongong was swift, and I kept asking Roger to double check all the straps. I felt sick. Not even the feeling of his entire torso pressed against me could distract me. He edged me to the plane door – my eyes squeezed shut, arms crossed over my chest – and then my legs were dangling into space.

Don't look down.

We tumbled into freefall. *I'm going to die.* The air rushed past as we plummeted and somebody was screaming. It was me. Abbey's face flashed into my mind and the screaming stopped, my eyes opening involuntarily. Our freefall only lasted sixty seconds but felt like forever. There was no room for a single other thought. I was completely present – air buffeting my face, the clear sky, high above everything else.

The parachute deployed and the hard jerk upwards told me how fast we'd been falling. I think I was grinning, but I couldn't feel my face. I glanced down as we glided lower – the arcing infinite beach and the city, tiny in the distance – then I lifted my head, face to the sun and blanketed in blue. As close to seeing heaven as I'm probably going to get.

When we landed, I was exhilarated – heart pounding, limbs electrified. *I'm going to explode.* The energy was too big for my body; I didn't know what to do with it. So, I had sex with Roger. In the storage shed on a pile of parachutes. Two stars for one. The scratch of the canvas and Roger's stubble against my skin grounded me physically. In my mind though, I was soaring for days.

But it's impossible to stay on that kind of high, and the acquisition of yesterday's star proved it. Nothing like nearly getting arrested to put things in perspective.

I'd headed into the city, thinking I could at least pick up some baby clothes for Abbey as a peace offering. But as I wandered the baby section, I was drawn back in time to shopping for myself – heavily pregnant, newly married, overwhelmed and scared. Instantly, my chest tightened. *I'm going to have a panic attack.* I'd rushed towards the escalator, gripping the handrails tightly and trying to breathe as it carried me down to the ground floor and the lush serenity of the cosmetics department.

I should have gone straight home, but the perfume must have gone to my head. It's the only explanation for doing something that was categorically stupid – and illegal. I headed for the Chanel counter to fix my no doubt pale and sweaty face, finding the tester for my favourite lipstick and touching up my lips. I was about to put it back when the strangest urge came over me. *Put it in your bag.*

It *was* on my list. Nobody would miss a crusty old tester. I glanced around, then slipped it surreptitiously into my handbag. Hovering for a minute, I looked at a couple of others so I didn't look suspicious, then wandered nonchalantly away. My heart was hammering. I didn't even make it to the door.

'Excuse me, ma'am.' My stomach dropped. I turned to see one of the immaculate cosmetics girls – all severe ponytail and perfect winged eyeliner – staring at me disapprovingly, backed up by store security. *I'm screwed.*

I sat in the store manager's office, mortified, as she handed me another tissue. She was around sixty-five, with a salt-and-pepper bob and sturdy court shoes.

'So, it was a dare?' She was looking at me strangely after I'd babbled something incoherent about *having to do it.* 'Aren't you a bit old for that kind of thing?'

'Not exactly.'

Mum always used to say, 'I'd rather a thief than a liar.' I think she was trying to annoy Dad and I never understood her point, but if it was ever going to be apt, it was right then. So, I told the truth, offloading my entire story on to the poor woman. 'I'm trying to shake my life up,' I finished, lamely.

'My husband left me for my best friend,' she replied. 'I lost the house, and I'm still working here. I should be retired by now.' She leant back in her chair. 'What else is on your, er . . . *Fuck-it* List?' She leaned on her desk, enthralled as I rattled them off. 'You've done all those things so far? I think you're my hero.' *Huh?*

Before I was allowed to leave, she made me promise to update her and handed me a fifty-dollar gift voucher. 'Put it towards your next lipstick purchase. More women should have your guts. Bravo.'

Baffled, I scurried from the room before she changed her mind. I was horrified. There were bad decisions and then there were *bad decisions.* If I were still praying, I would have thanked God for salvation, but clearly it was dumb luck. I'm convinced there's nothing up there at all. We're on our own.

This morning, I woke with the intention of a reset. Life might not be perfect – my list might have swerved off track – but things could be worse, and I've come too far to let it get me down. *Today will be a better day.*

Why do I keep jinxing myself?

I'm setting up for the lunch rush when Lucinda walks into the bar. I haven't seen or spoken to her since the yoga class on the morning of the concert. In three months, she hasn't sent a single text to check on me. I didn't think anybody except Susie, Abbey and Liz knew where I worked – but if Lucinda knows, that means everyone does. *Great.*

It's too late to hide. 'Grace!' She rushes towards me, pulls me into a hug, then steps back, holding my shoulders. 'You cut your hair. It's so . . . chic.' *That's what she's leading with?* I clock Travis behind the bar, eyeing us. He can see I'm uncomfortable.

You good? he mouths. I nod but I'm not.

'It's been a while.' I give Lucinda a tight smile and she brushes it off.

'You know how it is, things get so busy and before you know it—'

I tell Travis I'm taking a ten-minute break, stressing the *ten minutes* and hoping she gets the hint. We sit opposite each other, and she takes my hand.

'So, how *are* you?'

I remove my hand, pretending it's to scratch my shoulder. 'I'm good. Really good.'

'Oh, *good.*'

'How are you?'

She prattles on about Chris and their kids. The more she talks, the more nervous she seems. Eventually she trails off into awkward silence.

'Why are you here, Lu?'

Lucinda hesitates before sighing. 'Because we're all worried about you.'

'Could have fooled me. So, what exactly are you worried about?'

She frowns – as if I should know – and when no recognition comes, she pats my hand. 'Well, you've clearly lost your way. I mean, *understandable*. It's all so difficult.'

'Difficult for who?'

'For everyone. We've all been beside ourselves. Daniel's been a wreck. The media attention was so stressful for him. The church is under such scrutiny, as I'm sure you can imagine. And your—' She waves her hand at me. '—well, it hasn't helped.'

It's been a while since I've felt the lava, but there it is. 'My what? I don't know what you mean.'

Lucinda lowers her voice. 'Your behaviour, Grace. Celia said you might have been on drugs, but that's not true, is it? And afterwards, with that boy? What were you thinking? Now you're working *here*—' She gestures around as if it's a brothel. '—and getting up to Lord knows what. I mean, people talk. We've heard things.'

Staring at her, I wonder how we were ever friends.

'You do know it was all rubbish? That Daniel was the one cheating?' My tone is frosty. 'I'm sure he's introduced her to you all by now.'

She shifts, uncomfortable, her hands clasped primly. 'We all saw you, Grace. Have you forgotten you were on TV? Men are weak, darling. They get tempted. We're supposed to be better, not go off and sully ourselves in retaliation.'

'So I'm supposed to just let Daniel destroy my life? Lucinda, he tried to cut me off financially, he was spying on—'

She cuts me off. 'You're being prideful. Daniel told us you chose to move out and refuse to use any of your joint funds.' She softens, taking both of my hands; which is good, because the look of pity on her face is making me want to slap her. 'This is not *you*, Grace. Aren't you ashamed?'

I stiffen, withdrawing my hands from her grasp.

'No, I am not ashamed.'

'Aren't you worried what Abbey thinks?' Her lips purse and she plays what she thinks is her trump card. 'Imagine what God thinks of you.'

I lean forward slowly and smile. 'Firstly – if you check your scripture, *darling* – God accepts us all, believer and sinner. Unlike my friends.' Her flushed face gives me a thrill, but not as much as my next words do. 'And secondly, I don't give a fuck what God thinks of me. I'm not even sure I believe in Him anymore.'

Lucinda gasps, laughably over-dramatic. I let her take a moment to recover, smiling sweetly. Eventually she covers my hands with hers, tearful now. I clench my fists under her fingers. 'Know that we're praying for you, Grace.'

I take a deep breath, unclench my fists and take her hands in mine, anger dissipating. *They can't touch me.* 'Thank you, Lucinda. But I don't need anyone to pray for me. I'm not lost. I'm finding myself, for the first time in years.'

For a moment, I think she understands. Then she pulls back, her expression laced with annoyance. 'I can see I'm not getting through to you. Remember, the devil only tempts the pure, Grace. The rest are already his. You've fallen prey to temptation, but I know you'll come back to us.'

I laugh, and she looks mortally offended. 'Are you honestly quoting scripture and judging *me*, when you haven't called once in the past three months to see if I'm okay?'

Lucinda pushes her chair back. 'We're going around in circles. This isn't why I came. I thought, seeing as I was here, I'd try to reach out.'

I'm confused. 'Then why *are* you here?'

'Daniel wanted someone to let you know in person.' She puts a hand to her chest, her mouth downturned. *Oh, no. What now?* 'Margaret Symes passed away.'

My stomach drops and I think back to the last time I saw her, when we shared that joint outside Stars Fold. I'd thought she had longer – if I'd known, I would have visited. But knowing it's coming never makes it easier. Death might herald its arrival, give warning – it might even be a blessing – but it still arrows your gut when it comes. *Rest easy, Margaret.*

Lucinda leaves and I busy myself, gathering glasses and ferrying them behind the bar, trying not to cry. Travis watches me, worried.

'That looked intense,' he says, and I respond with a non-committal *mm-hmm*. He stops what he's doing. 'Are you okay?' I dissolve into tears and before I can stop him, he's pulled me into an embrace – the first person to wrap their arms around me in comfort for months. I sink into him; his arms safe and warm. It's so good to be held. *Too good.* Travis's hand rests on the back of my head and I catch my emotions before they fly away with me. I extricate myself. 'I'm fine, Travis. It's just another door I have to close.'

34

faith, where art thou?

Margaret's funeral is at a parish church not far from the beach, in Dee Why. It's where her husband was buried a decade before she came to us. An old stone building, it reminds me of the church where Dad's service was held. It's been years since I've been to the Northern Beaches. Dad sometimes brought us over this way when Mum wanted us out of the house. I can smell the brine in the air, carrying memories I'd prefer to avoid. Unresolved feelings surface as I gaze at the stained-glass windows from the garden behind the church.

I'm hiding because Daniel's inside, along with dozens of our parishioners. I'll sneak in last-minute and sit up the back, for two very good reasons. Firstly, I don't want my presence taking attention from why we're here. Secondly, I have every intention of carrying out Margaret's final wishes with the joint. A promise is a promise.

People have been filing into the church for forty-five minutes, so it's almost time. Pulling the joint out of my purse, I huddle into a window arch and smoke the entire thing – it's what Margaret would have wanted – glancing around occasionally to make sure nobody catches me, waving the pungent smoke away. It hits faster than expected.

Music drifts from the open doors as I sidle around the building. I creep inside slowly and quietly – too slowly for a normal human. I feel like a Thunderbird as I step deliberately across the stone floor, glad I wore flats and not tappy heels. The door clunks behind me and every head in the room swivels. *Shit.* I freeze. Before I can decide between waving apologetically and diving headlong into the back pew, I spot Abbey down the front. I didn't know she was coming.

She beckons at me. *Nope, definitely not.* My head is already fuzzy. Maybe smoking the entire joint wasn't the best idea. I'm still standing like a statue in the aisle. *Move, Grace.* Most people have turned away, but a few are watching me, curious. Exasperated, Abbey stands and walks hurriedly towards me.

'What are you doing? Come and sit with us, I saved you a seat.'

I plant my feet. 'I'd rather not sit with your father.'

'Don't be ridiculous.' She rolls her eyes, tugging my arm. 'You can put your differences aside for Margaret.'

'I'd rather sit up the back.' My tongue is thick in my mouth. *Did that come out right?*

'You're being immature, Mum. Today isn't about you.' She's right, and it's not like I have to talk to anybody. I'm not sure I could even if I wanted to. I relent and follow her down the aisle, sliding into the pew beside her. Daniel glances briefly at me. He looks annoyed, but maybe I'm paranoid. Abbey nudges me. I face the front. *Focus on the service.*

Margaret's coffin is front and centre with a large, framed photograph on top. I assume it's of Margaret but then I look closer. It's Dame Judy Dench. *Weird.* What is Judy Dench doing on Margaret's coffin? *Did Judy Dench die? That's so sad – I love her.* Nobody else seems to have noticed. Maybe this is a dream. If so, I hope Ian McKellen delivers the eulogy. He could do it as Gandalf. *Margaret! You shall not pass!*

I'm having trouble following the service. My mind is like an errant goose, wandering off on tangent after tangent. The occasional word leaps out at me, and my brain plays the association game. When the Reverend says Margaret was a 'beloved *member*' and speaks of her 'passionate *organ* playing', all I can think is, *penis!* I swallow laughter, because Judy Dench is staring at me.

One of Margaret's sons gets up to deliver the eulogy and gruffly introduces himself as Rufus. *Did he just bark?* 'Ha!' It escapes my mouth and I quickly attempt to disguise it as a cough. 'Excuse me, sorry,' I say to nobody in particular. Every time Rufus mentions Margaret doting on her sons or how pious she was, the microphone feeds back sharply. I imagine her looking down and saying, 'Shut up and do as you're told', with every electric screech, and I get the giggles. Abbey elbows me but I can't stop. I cover my face, pretending I'm overwhelmed with emotion. Pulling myself together, I look up in time to see Rufus lean heavily on the crucifixion statue next to him. Jesus's head snaps off in his hand.

'JESUS CHRIST!' *Who said that?* I glance around. *Fuck, it was me.* '—our Lord and Saviour,' I add, making the sign of the cross in an attempt to cover myself, then resuming wheezing uncontrollably into my hands. *I'm upset, okay? He decapitated Jesus.*

Staring at me in consternation, Abbey leans in. 'You're making a spectacle of yourself.' *I'm not wearing spectacles, you're wearing spectacles.* 'Get a grip,' she says and she's right. I'm sure Margaret would find this funny, but I'm disrespecting her family. I really am a horrible person. *Why did they invite me? Didn't they see me on TV? I'm a loose cannon.* Breathing deeply, I centre myself and sit up straight. Calm, poised, pious. *I wonder if there will be pie.* But when a man in a kilt climbs the pulpit and starts playing 'Danny Boy' – red-faced and sweating, the bagpipes horribly out of tune – I lose the plot. Margaret wasn't even Scottish.

'I'm sorry, I can't.' Suddenly I'm on my feet, sniffing loudly. 'Losing dear Margaret, it's all too much.' *Somebody give this girl an Oscar!* I dash from the church, not caring that everyone's staring.

Abbey finds me sitting on the grass behind the church, still laughing. She stands over me, bewildered.

'What on earth was that?'

'Sorry, I'm just overcome.' She doesn't believe me. 'But did you see the little head?' I make a snapping motion, '*Bonk!*' and crack up again. She's studying me closely.

'Are you high?' *Uh-oh.*

'Little bit.'

'Mum!'

'It's not what you think.' I scramble up. 'Margaret asked me to. It was her last will and commandment.'

'You mean testament?' *Know-it-all.* Abbey shakes her head, forehead creased. 'I have no idea what's gotten into you lately, but this is . . . I don't even know what to say.'

'Just don't tell your father.' *He already hates me.*

'Oh, don't worry,' she snorts. 'I'll tell him you were extremely upset and went home. Which is exactly what you should do.' *Now Abbey hates me.*

'I don't think I should drive.' I'm shrinking, the way I did when Dad was angry, feeling stupid and small. *Everybody hates me.*

'Bloody hell, Mum.' She inhales and exhales, long and deep. 'Look, I came with Dad, so I can't drive you. I don't want him to see you like this. Sit here until you straighten out, and promise me you won't get in your car stoned.'

I have no idea how long it takes to get un-stoned when you've smoked a whole joint. I could be here until Tuesday. With one last disappointed shake of her head, Abbey walks away. My head is spinning, so I lie down on the grass to look at the sky.

And promptly pass out.

When I come to, the sky is ribboned with pink and orange. I've been out for most of the day. I stand up, light-headed and slightly put out that nobody spotted me lying unconscious on the grass. What if I were dead?

The church doors are still open when I head unsteadily for my car. It wouldn't hurt to stay a little longer. Besides, there's something I need to do. The lights are dim – a bank of candles flickering – and the church is empty. I sit tensely in the front pew, enveloped by the hush.

When I was little, we went to church every Sunday. My parents weren't particularly religious – Dad's revelation came later – it was a social thing, with Dad's colleagues in the police force. I found religion hard to understand. It was supposed to be about love and acceptance, so what was with all the wrath and nailing people to things? Did God want us to be frightened?

Confused, I'd asked to go to Sunday school, because I wanted to *know*. I put the pastor offside when I asked how he knew God was a boy. It didn't make sense. Ladies were the ones who made everything and took care of people. Maybe there were two Gods – a boy one and a girl one, doing different jobs like mums and dads do. It seemed obvious that the boy God did the angry, scary bits. The pastor told me God was the Father of us all and I had to trust in only that. I remember thinking he wasn't very smart and saying,

'But everybody has to have a mum, otherwise how could you get born?'

When I asked why ladies couldn't be priests and what was so wrong with Mary Magdalene, the pastor suggested I stop coming. Church attendance petered out when Dad's weekends began to drown. I doubt he wanted to spend his Sundays asking for forgiveness hungover.

I think I always wanted something to hold onto, something bigger than me. When things first got bad with Dad, I was reading CS Lewis, obsessed with checking the back of every wardrobe, just in case. I imagined Heaven to be like Narnia – where everyone was pleasant to each other, where they made mistakes but were told everything would be okay. Aslan, the giant lion, didn't want to frighten people – he was kind and fostered courage.

If God was real, why would he let Dad be so broken? Why couldn't he make Mum brave enough to leave? His failure to do so was a betrayal. So, in my childish wisdom, I stopped believing in God. For years, I prayed to Aslan every night instead. It didn't make things better, but it gave me hope. I re-read those books over and over. When I learned the truth, that they were allegory for Christianity, I was bereft. Betrayed again. That was the end of religion for me, until I met Daniel.

Dad was never on board with Stars Fold. By the time it took off, he was sober and seeking his own redemption. He said Daniel got his credentials from a cereal box, that it wasn't a real church. I thought he'd be proud of my success – *my little Gracie, didn't I do a good job with this one* – but our showy evangelical ministry, and the money, was apparently an afront to Jesus. We fought and I said I didn't need him in my life if he doubted my choices. But maybe he was right. Deep down, eight-year-old Grace always knew the truth. None of it was real. Haven't the past few months proven it?

It should be easy to shed it all then, like a costume I'm returning. Berating God for letting it happen made sense at first. Somebody to blame other than myself. But now – with everything I've done since – admitting he doesn't exist is the final step. I need to close this door once and for all. Except – what am I supposed to hold on to from here?

I gaze around the peaceful church. It's so different to earlier. With nobody here to fill the pews, or to preach or judge – no noise to fill the void – the space expands with a serene clarity. Maybe that's where divinity really lives. In the quiet moments.

Breathe in. Breathe out.

As the candles gutter in the silence, I realise I'd lied to Lucinda. I *am* lost. But not for the reasons she thought. I'm floundering from distraction to distraction, grasping for one thing that will show me who I am and where I belong. *I need to know.* A shuddering breath overtakes me and I slide to the floor, kneeling.

'Please, God. Help me.' My voice echoes back to me. A sob tumbles from my chest and I press my forehead to the stone in front of me. 'Are you there?' It's a whisper now. '*Please* – tell me you're there.' I cry quietly – feeling completely alone – until a run of silvery chirps breaks the silence and I look up. A starling has flown into the church. It darts past me in a flurry of iridescent wings and lands on the altar. I stare at it, and it stares back, fluffing its feathers.

As I watch the little bird, my angst subsides. I'm calm, expanding with every exhale. Is it a *magic* starling?

'Is that you, God?' I can't believe I'm talking to a bird. The starling doesn't reply. But then, as clearly as if someone has written it on my brain like a whiteboard . . .

You're asking the wrong question.

Watching the bird closely, I inhale slowly then settle into myself. 'Can you tell me who I am? Am I good person? Or am I a bad person?' I plead aloud.

I love you exactly as you are.

I desperately want the offered certainty to take root in my chest, but the answer has raised another question, and tears prick my eyes again.

'Then why did you abandon me?' The starling flaps its wings and I hold my breath – please don't leave me.

I have never abandoned you. You have abandoned yourself.

In that instant, a deep knowing pulses inside me, warm and vital. Yes. That's exactly what I've done. *Wait.* Does the God-bird mean I abandoned myself a long time ago? Or that I've abandoned myself since Daniel left? It's an important distinction. 'Uh, God? Can you be more specific?'

The starling studies me for a few seconds, annoyed. *I can tell.* It lets out a run of throaty clicks followed by a high-pitched whistle, beats its wings – then flies away. I guess I'll work it out by myself then.

I clamber back onto the pew. All but one of the candles have gone out. The last one flickers courageously, and I watch the lick of flame lengthen and contract, wondering if my imagination is simply telling me what I want to hear. It's more believable than talking to God through a bird. And who says it was God anyway? *Maybe it was Dad.* A lump lodges in my throat. I don't think it was my dad. He would never say that.

I can't overthink it. Whatever that feeling was, wherever the words came from, maybe I should accept that the bird was a sign I'm not alone. That the universe was letting me know I'm connected, so I could feel safe enough to listen to the source – to myself. After all, one of the only things I learned in Sunday school was that God is apparently within me.

I love you exactly as you are.

It doesn't matter in the end what I call the connection; calling it 'God' doesn't mean anything. When Dad first went to AA, he said some people struggled with the 'surrendering to God' part. They were told they could call it whatever they wanted – it was simply acknowledging a higher power. Some people made up their own acronyms. I wonder what mine would be? G.O.D. *Getting Over Daniel?* Maybe it's Great Organiser of Dreams. *I like that.* The point is, it's different for everyone and yet it's all the same thing – something bigger to have faith in. A human impulse since the dawn of time. I know I have no desire to return to the church, the noise filling the void. I might feel lost, but I can't go back. The only way out – to find clarity – is through.

I choose my own answer. I abandoned myself long before Daniel and the church, long before Abbey, long before my marriage ending and my list. I abandoned myself when I was so small I couldn't know the gravity of what I was doing.

I have never abandoned you.

I'm not sure what it means but I feel stronger – like someone or something is walking beside me. The path I'm travelling – paved with messy choices – is a little less scary. I have to believe it will lead me to myself. Because messy or not, the choices are mine and nobody else's. What the hell does a bird know anyway?

35

what goes up must come down

The middle of Monday afternoon isn't the ideal time for a date, but I figure there's less chance of things accidentally getting crazy at 2 pm. Mike's simply coming over for coffee. Every rollercoaster needs a lull, where it slows down or trundles along the straight, before it swoops another curve or throws you for a loop. I feel comfortable inviting him over because, well, he's a doctor. You can't get any safer than that.

I'm reining in my alcohol consumption as much as possible – hence the coffee. Lack of inhibitions and laughter aside, the hangovers have been brutal. It's been harder than expected, and that in itself is my wake-up call. I can say it's just 'taking the edge off' but I know what a slippery slope that is. I had a ringside seat as first Dad, then Mum, careened down it. My whole life, I've studiously avoided taking the same blurred trip. Until now. I guess it was inevitable – it's hard to fight DNA. But pain is pain – even dulled – and I don't want to be numb anymore. I don't want the memory blanks – they scare me, too close to home. Since the God-bird, I'm chasing clarity, even if it burns.

Mike is tall and blond, broad-shouldered with a swimmer's body. He's well-dressed and articulate and funny. We sit on my couch and sip coffee, the conversation dancing between politics and art, music and travel. We're honest and talk about break-ups and humanity and how life is short, and that more people should break the mould. He seems to find me as interesting and attractive as I do him. It's all very civilized.

'Would you like some MDMA?' *What?*

I blink at him. 'But you're a doctor.'

'That's why this is medical grade.' He reaches into his pocket. 'None of that street crap.' He clocks my startled expression. 'Safe as houses, don't worry.'

I tell him I've never done it, and he makes explosion hands next to his head. 'It accesses a whole other part of yourself.' Then he kisses me. 'And you feel *everything.*' He holds out his hand, two capsules sitting on his palm. I stare at them, unsure whether the fluttering in my belly is fear or excitement.

Get out of your head and into your body.

I take one and swallow it before I can change my mind. He follows suit. For the next thirty minutes we lie side by side on the floor, waiting for it to kick in. Mike holds my hand and keeps asking if I'm feeling anything. *Only panic.*

The rush starts in my toes and, as it sweeps my body, my skin crystallises. I'm shimmering and my ribs expand, like I'm filled with light.

'I think I'm feeling it.'

When he suggests shedding our clothes – he wants to show me something – it seems like the perfect thing to do. *Of course we should be naked, it's amazing.* We undress and sit on the floor. Mike traces my body with his hands, running his fingers up and down my legs, across my stomach, touching my face. He squeezes my arms, kneading me softly. Every nerve ending sings. His fingers thread into my hair, massaging my scalp, then tugging gently. My crystalline skin shatters – like glitter – and my eyes roll back in my head. I didn't know touch could feel this good. Then a wave hits me.

'I feel sick.'

He tells me it's normal and pulls me up before grabbing his phone. Music fills my apartment. 'Move your feet and breathe. Focus on the music.' He takes my hands and makes me sway. Another rush sweeps the nausea away, from my core outwards. I'm like a pulsing star, light streaming from the top of my head as I let it drop back. Letting go of everything. *Oh, my God.*

Mike fetches water from the fridge as I dance, naked and liberated. I'm bigger than my body. I hear all the musical layers, I can pinpoint each sound. I am the music. Every inch of me a melody – unknown and mysterious. Eyes shut, I drink and the cold travels my veins at light-speed; I see it in my mind – icy, blue lines, like feathered tree roots.

When I open my eyes, the setting sun is glimmering through the window. I move into it, laughing. I'm looking down on myself from above. It's the most beautiful thing I've ever seen. I'm connected to everything. This must be heaven.

Mike runs his hands down my back and turns me around. Everything's in slow motion and at high speed, all at once. We find our way to the bed and melt into a puddle of glowing limbs. It feels like hours before we finally have sex, too swept up in exploratory touch and ecstatic bursts of expressed thought – but eventually the peak subsides. Euphoria is replaced by cloudy desire and I'm lucid enough to remember a condom.

The sex is a chorus of sensation over arousal. It feels good but I'm removed, over-observant and hyperaware. It takes Mike a while to finish. I'm surprised I don't come close when my body is so sensitive, but I'm unbothered, heavy and content. We lie back, quietly staring at the ceiling. A minute later, I feel a trickle between my legs. Confused, I look over at Mike. His cock is bare. *What the hell?*

'Where's the condom?'

He glances at me, unperturbed. 'I took it off.'

I sit up. 'What do you mean you took it off?'

'I couldn't feel anything.'

Cold clarity cuts through the haze. 'But we just met. How do we—'

'I'm clean, don't worry. I get tested regularly.'

'That's not the point. I don't know you; you don't know me.'

'I said I'm clean. But I'm starting to worry you're not.' He laughs but I think he means it. My skin crystallises again but this time it's sharp and jagged.

'I'm not just worried about that. I'm not on any kind of birth control.'

Mike raises a disbelieving eyebrow. 'Can you even still get pregnant?' *Excuse me?*

I stare at him, speechless. He's got a point but the assumption – the disregard – slices into me anyway. 'I think you should go.' He sits up, laughing now.

'You're overreacting.' He kisses me quickly, before I can swerve. 'I can't drive. I'll go in the morning. Why don't you have a shower, you're still a bit out of it. The hot water will make you feel better.' When I don't answer, he pats my cheek. 'We've had a good time, it's fine. Trust me, I'm a doctor.'

I fix my eyes on the wall because I can't look at him, my breathing shallow, heart thudding in my ears. I don't know what to do. I want him out of my apartment – now – but what if he gets angry and won't leave? *You should have paid more attention. It's your own fault if you get an STD.*

Eventually I peel myself from the bed. My thighs are sticky and my lips curl in distaste as I lock myself in the bathroom. The crash is swift and opaque – the golden euphoria forgotten. I run the shower as hot as I can stand it and gulp mouthfuls of steam, trying to breathe – and trying not to cry – as I scrub him from me, feeling dirty and stupid.

When I come out of the bathroom, Mike is already asleep, sprawled in the middle of my bed. I don't wake him. I crawl under the covers on the very edge and curl into a ball, my back to him. I'm wide awake. I stay there until morning, not moving. Feeling it all.

Not long ago, at a church function, a man said to me – after his wife left him – that 'all women go crazy after the age of forty-five'. That overnight they become unpredictable, equally angry and sad about everything and nothing, and that – suddenly dissatisfied with their life – they up and leave their apparently great marriages to go off and teach yoga, become lesbians, brew kombucha and find themselves.

I'd smiled politely and tried not to say through gritted teeth that teaching yoga, becoming a lesbian and learning to brew kombucha sounded like his ex-wife was living her best life. But his description of menopause was not entirely inaccurate – although, it's not like we don't have a very good reason for it.

One of those online magazines wrote an article once that compared menopause to coming down off drugs. It claimed that when you're young and your oestrogen levels are high, it's like being on ecstasy. You're all lovey and nurturing – compliant and happy – but you're basically off your face on oxytocin. I mean, you need to be high. How else would you cope with screaming children, zero sleep and an equally demanding – and apparently incompetent – husband?

But once you've made it through the bloom of your childbearing days, your nurture drug dries right up. It's the comedown of all comedowns. Your eyes clear, your head clears – unclouded by happy hormones, you realise you've been fooled and now the curtain has been pulled back. Women don't go crazy; they just wise up.

It doesn't occur to men that it's anything to do with them. It's not as if *they've* changed, they're the same guy they've always been. It's simply that women go bonkers without warning, as though it's a biological design flaw in female DNA. Don't they say that about technology? What do they call it . . . 'built-in obsolescence'? Your iPhone starts glitching, so you're forced to buy the newest release. I guess that's how men explain away the urge to fuck the closest happy and compliant twenty-five-year-old. It's not their fault. The old model is broken. Apple made them do it.

Sitting in the unfamiliar waiting room, the fluorescent lights drill into me like I'm under scrutiny. My eyes are gritty from lack of sleep. The noise around me – the ringing phone, the TV on the wall, the toddler playing with blocks in the corner – bounces off my skin like hailstones. The drug-induced sensitivity lingers but I have contracted. Everything is a barrage instead of a delight.

My usual doctor, in Rose Bay, has treated me since my early twenties. I couldn't face seeing him – the inevitable questions, the barely concealed judgment. I'm too brittle – I might break. This doctor is a woman, about my age – efficient and friendly. I nervously explain the situation – omitting the MDMA – and tell her I'd like to be tested for everything. *Should I write 'Get an STD' on my list of bad decisions?* It would qualify. Even if it was involuntary.

'Does he have other partners?'

'I have no idea. I mean, I'm assuming—'

'He's not your usual partner?'

'No. It was, uh—new.'

'Do you have any other partners?'

I prickle with heat, unsure how much to say. Is it even relevant? I've been safe, every other time. She glances at me and smiles – open and easy. 'You're a new patient. I'm trying to get a clear picture.'

I fudge the numbers. 'Two or three in the last few months. But always with a condom.'

She types rapidly. 'And how long ago did this happen?'

I tell her it was last night, and she peers at me. 'Right. Well, I can do the screen, but it's unlikely anything will show up this quickly.'

I'm an idiot. Of course diseases don't spring up instantly. She tells me I'll need to keep an eye out for symptoms and come back if I notice anything – discharge, redness, sores. I should return for more tests in a few weeks, if I want to be sure. My skin crawls with disgust as I nod at her. *How could I let this happen?*

'Are you taking any kind of birth control?'

Can you even still get pregnant?

I push the memory down and force a laugh. 'I'm going through menopause. I don't need to worry about that.'

'How long since your last period?'

'Almost a year. Except, I had one of those flash periods a month or so ago.' The way she's looking at me is making me uncomfortable. 'You don't really think I could get pregnant?'

She makes a moue with her mouth. 'It's unlikely, but not impossible. Especially if you've had a hormone surge or increased sexual activity. It sounds like you're still in peri, so . . .' My stomach plummets. I can't have a baby. I have a brief mental flash – me and Abbey side-by-side at an antenatal class; then both of us holding babies. I can't be pregnant at the same time as my daughter. Or ever. *What if I am?* I can't face the thought of having to make that decision again.

'Can you write me a prescription for the morning-after pill, please?'

'You can get that over the counter now.'

I feel stupid. I'm almost fifty, I've been married and raised a daughter, but fifteen-year-olds on TikTok know more about sexual health than I do. What was I thinking, embarking on a sexual odyssey without a clue? I feign forgetfulness. 'Of course.'

The doctor sits back and takes off her glasses. 'There is one more thing. I don't want to pry, but it would be remiss of me not to say something.' She pauses. 'How are you feeling about it all?'

I frown at her. What does she mean? 'Uh – a bit gross. And annoyed.'

She leans forward. 'You do know what he did was sexual assault?'

My eyes widen. *What?* 'Oh, no – I think you misunderstood. I definitely consented to having sex with him. There was no *forcing*. I mean, up until then it was fine. It was great—'

'You agreed to safe sex, Grace. He removed the condom without consent. It's called "stealthing" and it's a criminal offence. Like any other form of rape.'

She's speaking a foreign language. *Rape? How can it be that if I said yes? If I liked it?*

'If you want to report it to the police, I can support that.' *Police? What are they going to do? I took drugs and willingly had sex with him for hours.* 'If you'd like to speak to a counsellor—'

I have to get out of here. I tell her I don't need to speak to anybody and that I'll wait a few weeks and come back. There's no point now and I'm in a bit of a hurry.

'Okay. If it makes you more comfortable, home testing kits are available now – for the more common STDs. Your pharmacy should have them.'

Now she tells me. I kick myself again. If I wasn't so naïve, I would have known all of this. I could have quietly gone to the pharmacy without telling anyone anything. Without having to go through this whole mortifying experience. *Without being told I've been sexually assaulted.* I thank her and leave, hurrying to my car and trying to shake it off. I sit in the carpark for ten minutes before starting the car. *Breathe. You're okay.*

The large pharmacy a few streets from my flat is busier than I expect, and it rattles me. I don't want to be around people. It's making me itch. All I want to do is get home, climb into bed and forget this has happened. The pharmacist – a portly young man with a serious face and thick glasses – is blank-faced as I tell him what I need. But I know what he's thinking. How could he not be? My order tells a sordid story. There's no 'more palatable' explanation for the items, no way I can pretend they're for something else. It might as well be written on my forehead. Shame sinks its hooks into me as I sit on a chair near the counter to wait.

I fold into myself – head down, eyes closed – concentrating on the song coming from the little speakers in the ceiling. It's 'What's Up' by 4 Non Blondes. The final line of the chorus is playing and

I'm right there with the singer, wanting to scream at the top of my lungs because I have no clue what's going on.

'Grace? A familiar voice breaks my reverie and I look up, startled. Daniel. He's wearing jeans and a t-shirt with sneakers. I haven't seen him wear jeans for years. I stare at him, gobsmacked. *This cannot be happening.*

'Hello.' It's all I can think to say.

'I've been meaning to call you. You left Margaret's funeral early.'

I'm completely thrown so I don't offer an explanation. 'What are you doing here? In Newtown, I mean, not the chemist.'

'We're going to a gig.' *We? And since when has he ever been to a 'gig'?*

Sasha chooses that moment to bound like Bambi from two aisles over. 'Found one.' She's holding a pregnancy test aloft and stops short when she sees me, but it doesn't dim her effervescence. 'Oh, hi!'

What the actual . . . ?

Daniel blanches but covers it quickly, thrusting his hands in his pockets. 'Grace, Sasha. Sasha, Grace.' I give him a look that says, *Really?* and he ripples with discomfort. Sasha beams.

'It's so nice to meet you,' she says, placing her hand on her heart. 'Big fan.'

Am I still high?

He shoots her a disapproving look and she falters, shrinking and dropping her eyes. An alarm bell reverberates through me at the familiar dynamic. I wonder how long it will take Daniel to dim her light.

'Grace Miller?' The pharmacist. *No, not now.* My feet are stuck to the floor, eyes locked on Daniel. The pharmacist repeats my name and I have no choice but to step to the counter, Daniel and Sasha hovering behind me.

'Are you taking any other medications?' *Does MDMA count?*

'No.' I will him to hand over my items quickly and quietly so I can take them and run. I don't know why I think I'll be that lucky.

'This one needs to be taken within seventy-two hours of sexual intercourse for efficacy.' *Shut up. Shut up.* 'You can expect mild cramping and some bleeding. If you're bleeding heavily for more than forty-eight hours, you should see your doctor.' *Kill me now.* My eyes are saucers, pleading for him to stop talking. He doesn't notice, he's too busy efficiently doing his job. He holds up the STD test, like he's on an infomercial. 'This will detect chlamydia, gonorrhoea and syphilis. If you're concerned about genital herpes, HIV or HPV – again, see your doctor.' *Give me an earthquake. A tsunami. A plague of killer bees. Anything.* 'Will that be all?'

'Do you stock cyanide?'

He blinks indifferently at me, then stuffs my items into a paper bag. I steel myself. I will not give Daniel the satisfaction of seeing me embarrassed – although, considering what Sasha is holding in her hand, he doesn't have a leg to stand on. When I turn, Sasha's pretty eyes are bugging out of her head as she glances back and forth between me and Daniel. His face is white, nostrils flaring, his mouth a hard, grim line.

Shaking internally, I meet his eyes and lift my chin, quirking an eyebrow as if to say, *What?* Daring him to say something. He deflates, taken aback at my expression. He was expecting the old me. *Sorry, darling. She's gone.* I tuck the paper bag under my arm. 'Nice to meet you too, Sasha. Enjoy your gig.' Then I stalk past Daniel, tossing over my shoulder, 'Congratulations.'

I spend the next week busying myself with work, starting early, staying late, and coping silently with the physical aftermath of the pill. It's so bad that I wonder if it's a conspiracy, to put women off using it. The idea of Daniel having a baby rolls furiously around in my head. I ignore calls from Susie and Abbey, unable to trust what I might say. I delete the dating apps from my phone. *Goodbye, Emilia.* I stare at the Fuck-it List and, after dutifully ticking off '*Try molly*', I contemplate tearing it down. But there are things I still want to do. They just don't involve sex. The thought of a man touching me makes my skin crawl. I'll have to come up with something else to fill the spaces.

Travis senses something's wrong, but I don't want to talk. When I'm not at work, I sleep. I can't let myself think – especially about that word. *Rape.* If the doctor hadn't said anything, I wouldn't have this gnawing feeling, spreading like a cancer in my stomach. I think I'm angrier at the doctor than anything, because only days ago – when I'd left that church – I'd felt empowered. Brave. Now a single word threatens to take that away. It's the first time on this whole journey I've felt dirty and ashamed. *I did not choose this.*

I refuse to be a victim – or a 'survivor'. Either term means something bad happened to me. It's my choice, whether to accept it at all – isn't it? I have that right – it's my body. So I push it down deep – deny it – and go through the motions while all my serotonin and dopamine heads off on a week-long road trip without me. Every physical sensation, every sound, remains harsh and dissonant. But on the inside, I feel nothing. I wish I could rewind, back to the euphoria. When the chemicals coursed through me, I was free – of care, of worry, of self-doubt. Cocooned but connected – feeling only good things. Nothing mattered, yet everything was vital. And I loved myself.

I try telling myself the shimmering high wasn't worth how I'm feeling. But I'm lying. I'd do it again.

At the end of the week, I finally take the STD test. *Negative*. But after working seven days straight – with the strain of holding everything in – I'm depleted, and it shows. Travis sends me home before closing, insisting I take a few days off. I don't argue, but I can't face days alone in my flat.

It's late when I knock on Liz's door. The lights are off in the house, and it takes her a while to answer. She's in her underwear and a t-shirt, hair mussed. 'Grace. It's ten o'clock. What are you doing here?' Then panic. 'What's wrong? Is Abbey okay?'

'She's fine.' *But I'm not.* 'Can I stay for a few days? Please?' I'm holding nothing but my car keys.

Liz stares at me in confusion. 'Why? What's happened?'

'Nothing. Everything. I didn't know where else to go.' My face crumples into tears. 'Liz, I think there's something wrong with me.'

She doesn't say anything. For once, she simply steps forward and puts her arms around me, holding me tightly while I cry. Suddenly we're back there – she's four and I'm eight – clinging together on those rocks as the waves crashed, thinking we'd been left alone, and all we had was each other. Just the two of us.

36

thicker than water

Liz lets me sleep for days, holed up in her guest room. She brings me food and doesn't ask me to explain. I wouldn't know what to say anyway; I don't understand it myself and barely know how I got here. She hasn't told Mum I'm staying, and I'm grateful. Liz tells me things have been bad, that adding whatever I'm going through into the mix is fuel on fire. I'm not the only one with limited emotional capacity. Col has been warned not to open his trap on pain of death.

On the second day, she comes into the room with a book and sits with me for hours, reading quietly and stroking my head. It reminds me of when we were small, still sharing a room – before she decided I was the enemy. On the nights Dad was at his worst, Liz would dangle her arm from the top bunk. I'd hold her hand until she fell asleep, making up stories to distract her from the shouting.

On the third day, she tells me I need a shower and that we have to talk. My walls go up immediately. 'About Mum,' she clarifies, and I relax. When she brings coffee up on a tray, I'm waiting cross-legged in the middle of the bed, damp-haired and pink. She joins me and another memory hits – this time I'm sixteen and she's twelve.

Liz wasn't allowed in my bedroom when I wasn't home – things would always go missing – clothes, jewellery, my *Smash Hits* magazines – followed swiftly by a snarky denial. I'd walked in to find her sitting on my bed and ordered her out before realising she'd been crying. She'd seemed so small when she said she needed my advice. A popular boy at school had embarrassed her in front of the class, reading out a love letter she'd written and saying he'd never date her because Dad was a pig and everybody knew he was a drunk.

Furious, I told her boys were not worth shit, that she was so much better than him. Liz spent the night in my room and we listened to Cyndi Lauper on repeat until she felt better. I doubt 'Girls Just Want To Have Fun' would work anymore. Music can only do so much.

Liz is tense as she tells me what happened with Mum and Nate's boys. Another episode, this time more violent. It had scared the hell out of them. After that, Mum had unthinkingly opened the pool gate while Liz was making lunch and Cruz had fallen in. 'She said she forgot they couldn't swim. If I hadn't come outside when I did—' Liz's voice breaks and I grab her hand. 'Mum was just sitting there, staring into space.'

'Jesus. What are you going to do?'

She gives me a pointed look. 'What are *we* going to do. Like you keep reminding me, she's your mum too.'

The barb is gentle, so I let it glance off. 'I know. That's what I meant.'

'The outbursts are every few days and I can't manage it. She's like a child; I have to be so careful. It's taking its toll on me and Col. Nate won't let me look after the boys, it's affecting his work—'

'I'm sorry, Lizzie.' I haven't called her that for years and it drives an unexpected lump into my throat. It catches her off guard too.

'Half the time, she's Mum, you know?' She trails off, her voice shaky. Then she clears her throat, reining her feelings in. 'I told her about you and Daniel.'

'What did she say.'

Liz shrugs. 'Not much, I don't think she was shocked.' *Right. Only me then.*

'Me and Mum have decided it's best if she moves into a care facility. They can look after her properly, we can visit whenever we want. There's too much that can go wrong here, Grace. I can't risk it.'

'You're doing the right thing. It's not just about Mum anymore.' I squeeze her hand. 'When? Is there a plan?'

When she tells me it's happening on Monday – three days away – I can't hide my annoyance. Why hadn't she told me sooner? Liz reminds me I haven't been answering my phone, that I haven't been reliable of late.

'You've been having a harder time than I realised, I get it.' She squeezes my hand in return, and I dampen the anger that threatens to spike – because she's right. 'But I'm sorry, I couldn't wait until you sorted yourself out and decided to be involved.'

'It's fine. It sounds like it's settled.'

'I need you there on Monday, Grace. I can't do it by myself.' I catch the echo of twelve-year-old Lizzie, reflected in her eyes as she looks at me.

'I'll be there.'

In the meantime, there's packing to do tomorrow. Mum needs help deciding what to take, so it feels like home. Abbey's coming over and Liz thinks it would be nice to do it together, that we could go through old photo albums, remind Mum of all the good memories, to avoid the whole thing being terribly sad.

I doubt driving down memory lane is the answer to that. But pointing it out will only rock an already unsteady boat. Before Liz leaves, she checks in with me again.

'You doing okay? Are you sure you don't want to talk about it?'

'No, I'm fine.'

'Suit yourself. But if all this is still to do with Daniel, you need to get past it. There are more important things to think about now. Move on, Grace.' *I'm trying.* 'He has.'

It's barely midday, but once Liz leaves, I bury myself under the covers and close my eyes, dreading tomorrow and the weight of the expected charade. Pretending the past was perfect doesn't change anything, no matter how hard you try.

Not many families make photo albums anymore – they're a relic of the past, like mixed tapes and Rolodexes. The temporal fragments we capture now are nothing but data. Multiple versions of the same moment; each shot taken repeatedly, erasing spontaneity to ensure the best light, the best smile.

But all photographs are inherently curated, aren't they? People have never pulled out their cameras for the terrible moments – their arguments, their grief or the tears over heartbreak. They don't record the mundane for posterity. Nobody thinks to capture the boredom, the harried mornings. It's new parents asleep with a baby on their chest; excited Christmas mornings in pyjamas; weddings and birthdays and graduation caps tossed skyward.

We parade the joyful, shiny things as proof of happiness. But forgetting the dark is impossible – it's coded into memory. Maybe we should photograph that too – proof of a life – because, in a hundred years, our grandchildren's grandchildren will pore over albums of long-forgotten images only to find history incomplete. The truth of a family lives in the margins, in the spaces between the photographs.

I make sure I'm downstairs before Abbey arrives, so she doesn't ask questions. There's no need for subterfuge with Mum. She sits alone in the backyard, face to the sun – her usual drink conspicuously absent. Whether she's introspective or unaware, she looks content. I don't want to ruin things. I still don't know what to say. I hover in the kitchen instead, watching Liz butter bread for sandwiches. Eventually she huffs at me.

'Bloody hell, if you're going to stand there, you can help. Here,' she shoves a sponge cake across the counter. 'Start on this while I take these over to the granny flat. The icing's in the fridge.'

Cakes I can manage, and I'm glad to have something to do with my hands. Grabbing the pink icing and a butter knife, I set to work, smoothing the mixture across the sponge, focusing on getting it perfect. The icing sticks to the knife, rolling upwards and taking a chunk of sponge with it. *Don't ruin the cake.* I clench my fists in frustration, load the knife and start again, trying to cover the crumbs. As I smooth the edge, another piece of sponge comes away. Fury flashes like dynamite.

'FUCK!'

I slam my fist into the cake as Liz walks back through the door. She stares at me, stunned and I stare back.

'I guess we're not having cake.' She laughs, but I want to cry. *I'm a lunatic. Who punches a cake?*

'I'm so sorry.'

'It's a cake, Grace. Don't worry about it.' She tosses me a dishcloth and starts chopping a tomato, then stops and eyes me. 'You know you can't avoid her all day.'

'I'm not avoiding her.'

'Yes, you are. She's not going to break. She's still Mum.'

When Abbey arrives, she's weird with me. I don't know what I've done to upset her this time. When she keeps looking at my eyes, it clicks.

'I'm not stoned,' I say quietly. 'If that's what you're thinking.'

Abbey smirks. 'Just checking.'

'Who's stoned?' Liz has ears like a bat.

I quickly say, 'Nobody' at the same time as Abbey says—

'Mum was. At a *funeral*.'

Liz stares at me, wide-eyed. 'What?'

'It's not how it sounds. It was a dead woman's final wish.'

Liz laughs. 'I didn't know you had it in you, Grace. My strait-laced sister – a stoner.'

'She yelled, "JESUS CHRIST", really loud—' Abbey's enjoying herself now, '—and then lost her shit, in the middle of the eulogy.' Clearly, it's more amusing in hindsight.

'You should have been here when she punched the cake.' Liz twirls her finger by her temple.

'Okay, but that cake was—' I grapple for the right word, '—stupid. And he decapitated Jesus!'

Liz snorts. 'Who decapi-what now?'

Abbey regales her with the entire story, complete with actions and sound effects. I interject with, 'Why was Judy Dench there?' and 'Christ, those bagpipes.' Liz looks completely bewildered. I touch Abbey's hand. 'I thought you were angry with me?'

Abbey sighs. 'I was surprised, Mum. You can't deny you haven't been yourself.' *Understatement.* 'But it's actually nice to know you're not perfect.' *What?*

I glance at Liz but she looks away. 'What do you mean? I'm not—'

'But you probably shouldn't make a habit of it.' Abbey interrupts, resting her hand on her stomach. 'You *are* about to be a grandma.'

I manage a tight smile back. 'Speaking of grandmas, we should probably get out to Mum.'

The granny flat is half packed up, several boxes sit by the door. We settle Mum into her recliner and share sandwiches as we box up books and wrap trinkets and framed photos in newspaper, holding them up for Mum's approval. She slips in and out of lucidity, watching us work with a bright curiosity.

Liz and Abbey are easy with her. Abbey chatters like nothing's wrong, even when the conversation goes awry. I watch Liz help her when she struggles to eat. Their roles are reversed, but then Liz has always been a natural. Far more than me. I don't engage with Mum much, discomfort snaking around me. Her usual brassiness is diluted. She feels like a stranger. Mum doesn't notice my distance, but Liz does. She jerks her head at a box of photos and I reluctantly pick it up.

'Would you like to look at some photos, Mum?'

She gazes at me as though trying to place me, then smiles. 'That'd be lovely.'

We show her photo after photo. Mum in her twenties, smiling and carefree. Me and Liz as little girls, as moody teenagers and again as adults, nursing Abbey and Nate. The first house and the second, long-forgotten cars in the driveway. Holidaying on the Gold Coast and that glorious day at Magic Mountain – until Liz was stung by a bluebottle at the beach and Dad got in a fight with a man at the Burleigh Beer Garden. Mum and Dad on her fortieth birthday; her smile was different by then.

We don't ask if she remembers. Liz had warned us it's the worst thing to say. Instead, we say, 'look at your chubby cheeks' and 'oh,

I loved that dress'. There's a run of recognition, where Mum is herself, and we laugh at our hairstyles and terrible fashion. I haven't felt this at ease with my family in forever, and for a split second, I feel like I'm home. But I'm fighting tears the whole time.

Mum picks up a photo of Dad, in his uniform. 'Who's this handsome man?' She turns to me. 'Is this your husband?' I stare at her, uncertain.

Liz puts her hand over Mum's. 'No, Mum. He's yours.'

Mum looks delighted and says, 'Well, aren't I lucky,' and for a brief moment I'm glad she doesn't remember. Then Mum gasps, noticing Abbey's bump. 'Grace, you're pregnant.' She lays her hand on Abbey's belly, then looks up at her. 'Be careful, love. That man of yours is no good for you.' Abbey looks startled as Mum reaches up and cups her cheek. 'You don't want to end up like me.' Abbey glances at me, confused and I'm reeling. Before Mum can say anything else, Liz steps in, touching her hand.

'That's not Grace, Mum. This is Abbey – your granddaughter.'

'It is?' Mum's face lights up like the sun, and she looks at Abbey again. 'Oh, she's beautiful.' Abbey's struggling to hold it together but she holds Mum's hand, with a watery smile.

'Hi, Nanna.'

Suddenly I'm on my feet. 'I can't do this. I'm sorry.'

I head inside and pace the kitchen, a riot of questions I might never get answers to racing through my mind. How do you resolve things with someone who's forgotten it all? *Why did she never tell me that? What did she see that I didn't?* I catch myself, because I did see it. I just didn't want to admit it. I push it aside as resentment bubbles with the one question I've never been able to ask her, that I've kept bottled up. *Why didn't you leave Dad?*

Liz and Abbey finally come inside. Abbey is as rattled as I am.

'I'll call you tomorrow, Mum.' She hugs me quickly then leaves and I grab my car keys, to follow. Liz huddles on a stool at the counter.

I try to smile at her. 'Not exactly the feel-good afternoon you wanted.'

Liz sighs. 'I know that was hard, but you'll still be there on Monday, right?' I nod and she squeezes my hand. 'At least say goodbye to Mum.'

She's sitting outside the granny flat and looks up as I approach, her face lighting up. 'Grace, I didn't know you were here.'

I crouch next her. 'Just popped in to grab something and thought I'd say hi.' She seems like herself and I can almost pretend this afternoon didn't happen. I wonder if she remembers where she goes – or if it's simply dead air, like static on a radio. 'I wanted to check you're okay. With everything – the move I mean.'

Mum takes her time lighting a cigarette. 'Don't tell Lizzie,' she says. 'She thinks I'm going to set myself on fire.' She takes a long drag and looks off into the distance. 'You know what I miss? Reading. I can't keep track of the pages and sometimes the words are all—' she waves her hand. 'It's a bit shit. I don't mind forgetting some of the other rubbish—' She looks at me. '—but I don't want to forget my girls.'

My eyes well with tears and she cups my cheek, the way she'd cupped Abbey's. 'No need to worry about me, love. Parents shouldn't be a burden on their kids.'

I put my hand over hers, wishing I could let it all go. 'No, Mum, you're right. They shouldn't.'

I sit in Liz's driveway for ages. The photos have triggered an avalanche of memories, good and bad. Things I haven't thought about in years. Things I've purposely buried.

It's been wonderful today to laugh, to remember that there *was* good. But it feels like the good memories were all a dream – one that makes the painful ones stand out in sharp relief. I think of all the mistakes Dad made – and Mum – and how they cling to me and Liz like smoke. The mistakes I know I've made with Abbey.

I've tried to do things differently, to *be* different, but here I am, wondering if it's inevitable in the end. That, try as we might, we're simply echoes of our parents, destined to repeat the same patterns. Duplicating our scars on our children.

Mum's words repeat in my head: *You don't want to end up like me.*

37

wake me up

April, 1988

Someone's playing music loudly in the house. That can't be right; it's not even 7 am. 'Wake Me Up Before You Go-Go' bounces from the hallway and my eyes fly open. If that's Lizzie playing Mum's Wham album, Dad's going to freak.

The music's coming from Mum and Dad's room. I push the door open to find Mum dancing in her nightie, holding Lizzie's hands while she jumps on the bed.

'Grace!' Lizzie's face is pink and her hair is sticking up. 'Mum said we don't have to go to school.' I stare at them.

'But we're not sick.'

'SO?' Lizzie squeals.

Mum laughs at my face. 'We're doing something more important than school,' she says, which doesn't make sense. What's more important than school?

'But I have to hand in my art project today.'

'Who cares about your dumb project? We're going on holiday!' Lizzie screeches at the same time as George Michael hits a high note.

Mum tells me we can drop my project off at school on the way. I can't argue with the compromise, so I leap on the bed and yell, 'We're going on holiday!' Then I stop. 'Wait, where are we going?'

She says Coffs Harbour, and when I ask when we'll be back, she shrugs and says, 'I don't know, we'll see.' Her smile wobbles for a second.

'What about Dad?'

Mum turns the tape player down. 'Your Dad's on double shifts all week, so he can't get away. It'll be more fun with just us girls, right?'

'Won't Dad be lonely?' Lizzie stops jumping. Before Mum can answer, I grab Lizzie's hand and swing it.

'Dad'll be fine. Grown-up men don't get lonely.' I don't know how I know that, or even if it's true, but Mum winks so I know I said the right thing.

'Okay, chop chop. I want you to get dressed and pack your favourite clothes. And be quick, we need to hurry.'

I frown. 'Why?'

She falters. 'Don't you want to see the Big Banana?'

Lizzie screeches again, repeating 'The Big Banana' over and over and I drag her off the bed to shut her up. We ferry clothes across the hall in little piles. Mum puts her favourite compilation tape on and turns the music up. Each time Lizzie and I walk through the door, there's a different song. It's like a disco, and we dance around in bursts to 'Karma Chameleon' and 'Footloose'. I pretend to play the keyboard for 'Take on Me' while Lizzie thrashes an air guitar.

When we're packed, Mum bustles us out of the house like it's on fire. She's wearing a checkered sundress and her hair is loose for once. It's weird wearing shorts and a t-shirt on a school day, but I don't care because the sun is shining, our frangipani tree is raining flowers and Lizzie isn't being a pain for once.

'Seatbelts on?' Mum turns around to check Lizzie, her cheeks flushed. She must be excited about Coffs Harbour. I nod and tug on mine like I've seen Dad do. Ten minutes down the road, I jolt. 'My art project!' When she says it's too late to turn around, I burst into tears. 'But I worked really hard on it. We're not supposed to learn about chiaroscuro until high school but Mrs Roden said I could if I get an A plus and—' Mum grabs my hand. We turn around and go back.

Dad is standing in the driveway when we reach the house. Mum hits the brakes, saying 'shit' under her breath, and we're stopped half in the driveway and half in the road. They stare at each other through the windscreen before she finally turns the car off. Lizzie jumps out before me or Mum can stop her.

'Dad! Dad! We're going on holiday.' She turns back. 'Mum, can Dad come too?'

We troop into the house and Mum tells us to occupy ourselves in our bedroom. Sitting on the bottom bunk, we can hear them talking, voices low and urgent. Lizzie says, 'I don't think we're going on holiday now.' I tell her to be quiet and creep out to listen. Their door is ajar, and I peek through the crack.

Mum is by the window, arms by her side, staring blankly at the wall. Dad's on his knees, arms wrapped around her hips, face pressed into her dress. I've never seen Dad cry, and it makes my stomach twist. He looks up and says, 'Please don't take them, Joy.' He must really not want us going on holiday without him. Maybe grown-up men do get lonely. Then he says something I can't quite hear. 'Kiss myself' maybe? Which doesn't make sense, but it must be that because Mum sucks her breath sharply and kneels. She puts her hands on his face and kisses him, and I back away from the door.

Dad drives us into the city and we catch the ferry to Manly. He says he remembers catching it with Mum on their first date. He buys fish and chips and we feed the seagulls, and he lets me and Lizzie bury him in the sand. Mum and Dad hold hands in the shallows while we swim. I've never seen them do that before.

On the ferry home, we sit at the back as the sun goes down. Lizzie's all sandy and pink-nosed and she falls asleep on Dad's lap. Mum stands at the railing, staring out at the wake. My tired eyes settle on Dad. He smiles at me. 'Did you have a good day, Gracie?'

I think about my project, still sitting on the kitchen counter, and wonder if we'll ever get to Coffs Harbour. I smile back.

'It was the best day, Dad.'

38

stark raving

One hour. That's how long I last in my flat. I try watching TV but all that's on is a documentary about trains, *Married at First Sight* and a re-run of *MasterChef*. I switch the TV off and call Susie. Her phone rings out, switching to voicemail.

'Suse, it's me. Do you want to come over? I know it's short notice and I've been off the radar, but I've had a . . . well, a rough week. Today was pretty crap with Mum. I'm back at work tomorrow but I could do with a distraction tonight.'

She must be screening her calls because she texts two minutes later:

Susie: Bit under the weather. Already in bed.

Something's off. I type half a response but delete it. If Susie wants to talk, she'll let me know.

I could call Liz or Abbey, but – apart from the fact I don't have the bandwidth to rehash today – Liz seems perpetually exasperated with me, like the things I'm going through are an irritation, distracting from the *real* problems. *You have to move on.* Abbey thinks I already have and why wouldn't she? She doesn't see that I'm still in pieces – and I don't want her to. *Parents shouldn't be a burden on their kids*.

There's nobody else I can call. Travis is working, but even so, I don't want to be *that person* and keep offloading my feelings on to him. Sitting in the silence, it hits me. I'm not just sad – I'm lonely. Constantly surrounded by people – in the bar, on dates, at art class – I've been slow to realise it. But I am.

My phone pings. Susie again.

Susie: Have you seen this?

Her next message comes through with a website link. I click on it. It's a news article about a fundraising gala for the Lord Mayor with a splashy photo of Daniel and Sasha. The caption on the photo reads: 'Stars Fold's new power couple?' There's more, but I click my phone shut. I don't want to read it. Going public is the final blow – I've been completely replaced. I expect the lava, but it doesn't appear. I'm hollow.

Within minutes, I'm dressed in my running gear and out the door. I don't care if it's dark; it's a Saturday night and the streets are busy. I take off, focusing on the rhythm of my feet on the pavement and my breath. I run for several miles and am about to turn back when I hear it. Heavy bass and a driving beat coming from a nearby club. It reminds me of the playlist Mike played in my living room. I jolt at the thought of him and swallow a shudder, crushing the sickened feeling that threatens to rise. I reach for the memory of the euphoria instead – the letting go.

Move your feet. Focus on the music.

The Fuck-it List says '*music festival*' – but this will do. Several dozen men have spilled out onto the street. They're all beautiful – some in leather shorts and mesh t-shirts, others shirtless; all as sweaty as I am. They don't look twice at me – I'm not their type – as I slip amongst them. Invisibility is exactly what I need right now.

Breathe out.

I tap my phone for the cover charge and descend down the stairs into a heaving throng of people, their movements wild and fractured under the strobe lights. Dark and fast and dizzyingly hypnotic, the techno is drone-like. The bass thumps hard in my chest, the volume making it impossible to think. *Perfect.* I grasp for the memory of that shimmering high as I'm swallowed up by the crowd.

I probably should have died last night. Apparently I dropped like an anchor, completely unconscious in the middle of the dance floor. I don't remember that bit. When I came to, the paramedics were crouching over me. I told them I was fine, but they weren't having it. Susie met me at the hospital – I figured she'd judge me less, considering her history. I felt bad when I saw the state of her. 'Wow, you are under the weather. You look terrible.'

'Not as rough as you, you dickhead,' she retorted, insisting on using my phone to take a hideous photo for posterity. She's not wrong. I feel like I've been run over by a train.

Half an hour later, Abbey raced into emergency in a panic. I glared accusingly at Susie – *you tricked me*. 'Pull your head in, she's your daughter. What if you died?' She had a point, but I wasn't happy. 'I can't stay. I'm not good with hospitals,' she added, before marching out. *Something was definitely going on.*

Abbey's pacing at the end of the bed, hands resting protectively on her bump as if being in the same room as my drug-addled stupidity will affect the baby. She occasionally looks at me with wide eyes, like she's going to say something, then chews on a thumbnail instead. Biting back everything she wants to say. She's been doing that since they brought me back from having an ECG an hour ago.

'Do you think they'll give me a new one?'

Abbey looks at me, startled. 'What?'

'If I've buggered this one up. Do you think they'll give me a new heart?'

She sighs. 'Can we not overreact and wait for the doctor's opinion?'

'This one's clearly broken.'

'I'm sure you haven't buggered it up, Mum.'

Abbey's no doubt wondering the same thing as me. Do they hand organs out willy nilly these days? Is my doctor like Oprah? *You get an organ! And you get an organ! Look under your seat! Everybody gets an organ!* There has to be some kind of quality control, right? I picture the families of organ donors, poring over a catalogue of potential recipients like those women whose biological clocks send them sperm donor shopping with a list. IQ. *Check.* Eye colour. *Check.* No major character defects. *Check.*

Luckily, it doesn't work that way, because I'm pretty sure – given the choice – the relatives of some poor dead person would prefer their loved one's heart go to someone much more worthy than me.

I doubt they'd be thrilled that their husband or daughter's untimely passing might help prolong the life of an emotionally defective forty-nine-year-old whose heart had given out at a rave after doing several large lines of coke off the rock-hard abs of a personal trainer called AJ. It's probably a good thing they don't write that level of detail on your medical chart.

Finally, Abbey sits next to the bed and takes my hand, her forehead creased with concern. 'What were you thinking?' I don't know how to answer that, because obviously I wasn't. 'What were you even doing at a rave?'

'Dancing. What else do you do at a rave?'

'Cocaine, apparently.'

I hate that I've worried her, but I hate the way she's looking at me more. I feel like an idiot. I mean, *honestly*. Who gets carted off from an underground rave in an ambulance wearing matching Lorna Jane? 'I was trying to blow off steam. Yesterday was pretty heavy, Abs.'

She releases my hand. 'You're nearly fifty, Mum. Blowing off steam should be going on a cruise with an all-you-can-eat buffet, not taking drugs at a dance party.'

'Excuse me, I'm forty-nine. I'm not dead.'

'You could have been.'

'I'm *fine.*'

I tell her she's overreacting and she's about to argue when the doctor walks in.

'How are you feeling, Grace?'

'Stupid.'

He glances up from my chart. 'I'm not surprised.' *Kick a girl while she's down, why don't you.* 'I mean physically – any chest pains, nausea or light-headedness? Any numbness in your arms?'

'No to the numbness, sort of to the rest,' I say. 'But I haven't eaten since yesterday and they gave me valium, so—'

He brusquely tells me the ECG showed no sign of a heart attack, then rattles off several long medical terms I don't understand. The upshot is that the continued chest pains are a concern. He wants me admitted until Tuesday to monitor and run more tests, to be safe and 'considering my age'. *Rude.*

'I'm alright, honestly.' I glance at Abbey then back at the doctor, 'I can't stay here. I have a family commitment tomorrow.'

The doctor is unbending. 'I wouldn't advise it, not until we get the chest pains under control. You're not out of the woods yet.'

Abbey's watching us both closely. 'It's okay, I'll explain to Auntie Liz. She'll understand. You're in the hospital.' Abbey doesn't know Liz like I do. This will be another example of making things about me.

The doctor says someone will take me to a ward shortly and leaves. I rub my face roughly with both hands. 'This is ridiculous.'

Abbey purses her lips. 'I'm glad we agree on something. What exactly will I tell Auntie Liz?'

'The truth.' I'm not going to ask Abbey to lie for me. 'I did something stupid and now I'm in hospital.'

'That's it?' I know Abbey's asking for so much more – wanting me to rationalise everything from the past few months – but any explanations I have bottleneck. When I shrug, she looks like she doesn't know whether to cry or yell at me. 'Fine. Do you want me to stay?'

'I think I'm going to sleep once they take me to the ward, so there's no point. You should go. I'll let you know when they're discharging me.'

She pretends to be reluctant, but I think she's happy to leave. She's looking at me like she doesn't know me at all. *It's okay, kiddo. I don't have a clue anymore either.* Once she's gone, there's nothing to do but stare at the ceiling and listen to the feverish child crying four beds down, and the tradie trying to explain how his eye got superglued shut. I'm more rattled than I'd let on to Abbey. Maybe this has gone too far. I've crossed a line. But – even as I think it – I can't make myself regret anything I've chosen to do.

What if I *had* died? I wonder what people would say at my funeral. Whether they'd skirt the truth (that'd I'd unfathomably gone off the rails at the end, reckless and irresponsible) in favour of propriety. Don't speak ill of the dead.

Here lies, Grace Miller, beloved ~~wife~~, mother, sister, daughter. She lived a good life and tried her very best to do everything right. Technically accurate, but like with my dad and with the photo albums, it paints only part of the picture. Omits half the story. Once upon a time I would have been happy with that; clean and neat and tied with a bow. Perfectly curated Grace. But now? It's not how I want to be remembered. I want the margins and the spaces in between. I want proof of a life.

I know I can count on Susie, who'll get up and tell all my worst – and funniest – stories, like the drunk sister at a wedding with an impromptu and inappropriate speech about the bride losing her virginity. She'll probably be struck down by lightning in the church. I can't imagine anybody's used the word *dildo* in a eulogy before.

39

crash and burn

On Tuesday I'm discharged with a clean bill of health, but not without a warning from the doctor and several pamphlets on drug addiction. Emerging from the hospital into glaring sunlight – holding only my phone and my door key and wearing my stale gym gear – I order an Uber, planning to call Abbey once I'm home. I leave the pamphlets on the back seat.

I texted Liz yesterday to apologise and see how Mum's move went, and she finally responded this morning with a terse, '*It went fine.*' I know my sister. Those three little words were weighted heavily with subtext.

Sitting on my bed an hour later, freshly showered and wrapped in a towel, I study the cascade of gold stars on the Fuck-it List. I count them up, surprised to find I've ticked off almost thirty things. So why don't I feel like a different person yet? I can tell myself I've changed as much as I like – summon Emilia, pretend I'm okay with everything, convince myself I'm learning something, even from the bad experiences – but maybe I haven't changed at all. Maybe I'm still the same insecure little girl I've always been.

I knew the list wouldn't be easy, but I wasn't prepared for how some of it would make me feel. I've found unexpected exhilaration – falling through the sky, letting myself be seen, even the sharks – but the sex, the thing I thought I needed most, hasn't delivered.

I'd hoped to find liberation in sexual expression, for casual connections to fill my cup. I wish I was that woman, but I can't lie to myself anymore. I hadn't felt *wrong*, or bad – but wanting them to want *me*, regardless of whether I really wanted *them*, had left me empty, even bruised. I've been chasing the high I felt with Liam. Chasing connection. I thought I was freeing myself, but I was seeking solace in the wrong place. I was searching for validation from men who didn't matter. There was no freedom in that.

I've given myself the gift of loving my own body – and when the time comes for me to share myself with someone, I now know what I need – but I have to accept that there are things left on the list that I'm simply not going to do. I might not have changed as much as I'd like, but the list can. Maybe I can rebrand it – instead of 'bad', what if all I need to focus on is 'new'?

I grab my marker and scrub through anything sex-related – sex on a plane, sex in a church, sex with a judge. Threesome and orgy. I hesitate over '*Fuck Jon Bon Jovi*' then decide to leave it. A girl can dream, and I should at least have something to look forward to. I cross out '*Get arrested*' with relief and tick off '*Music festival*' on a technicality. Then I write down '*Do cocaine*'. It's truthful, there's no point curating things. But I'm not sure it really deserves its gold star.

A knock on the door startles me. 'Hang on,' I call out. I drop my towel and grab my robe, running my fingers quickly through my hair before opening the door. Travis stands in the hall holding two takeaway coffee cups and a brown paper bag in his teeth. I laugh and usher him in. 'What's all this?'

'Pastries and a chai – you can't have coffee, right?' He holds out the bag. 'I thought the patient might need cheering up.'

I'd had to tell Travis I was in hospital. I missed a shift yesterday and I am not up to working tonight either. I'd left out the drugs – although I have a feeling it wouldn't faze him – simply saying it was a blood pressure thing. He accepted the story readily. *Probably because he knows I'm old.* I give him a quick hug. 'That's sweet of you. Did you manage to cover my shifts? Again, I'm so sorry.'

He waves me away. 'Don't give it a second thought.'

I rummage in the kitchen for plates as Travis turns about in the centre of the room.

'Place looks great. You wouldn't think it was the same flat.' Then he spots my list on the wall. 'What's this?' He leans in to read.

'Oh, you probably shouldn't—' I feel the first prickles of embarrassment. I can't talk to my boss about this. What if it violates some workplace sexual harassment rule?

'Is this like, a bucket list?' He grins. *I guess we're talking about it.*

'So to speak. It's a bit of a life reboot thing.'

'That's awesome.' He points to where I've written down '*ridiculously underpaid job*'. 'Is this you asking for a raise?'

I sit on the bed. 'I mean – if you want to take it that way.'

'I like the gold stars. Very . . . what's the word? Gratifying.'

'Exactly.' *Finally, someone who gets it.*

'You've done all these ones?'

'Yep.' I flush, waiting for judgment to fall. It doesn't.

'Whoa.' He points to the sex dungeon. 'Even that one? Cool!'

'Let's just say, not what I expected.' I make a face, then relax. Travis doesn't think badly of me at all. I don't need to be ashamed or explain any more than I have.

He points his pastry at me. 'You, Grace Miller, are full of surprises. I like it.'

Another knock on the door interrupts us and I glance at it, confused.

'I'll get it,' Travis says. 'You stay put. You're a patient, remember?'

I grin at him and take a bite of my pastry. Then he opens the door and I nearly choke. Abbey is standing at my door. With Daniel.

'Can I help you?' Travis smiles at them, oblivious.

'Hi.' Abbey's staring at him in confusion. Daniel looks him up and down, unimpressed. 'We're looking for Grace?'

I jump off the bed – in my *robe*. I know how this looks. 'Travis, this is my daughter, Abbey.' I grimace. 'And he's—'

Daniel interrupts, bristling with testosterone. 'Her husband.'

'*Ex*-husband.' I gesture at Travis. 'This is my boss, Travis.'

'Your *boss*?' Abbey's eyes ricochet between us.

Travis puts out his hand. 'And *friend*. Nice to meet you.' Abbey shakes it, still perplexed. Daniel ignores him.

'We need to talk, Grace. Alone.' He looks pointedly at Travis. 'If you don't mind.'

I stiffen. 'I don't remember inviting you here, Daniel. If Abbey wants to talk, she's welcome. But you—'

'Don't be silly.' He moves to walk inside and Travis steps in his way. *Oh dear.*

'She's just gotten out of hospital, mate. I don't think she needs to be upset.'

Daniel eyes him. 'I don't know who you think you are, *mate*. But we're Grace's family. And our daughter is also upset.'

'Mum, come on—' Abbey is pressed against the door frame, her arms crossed protectively across her body, and I relent.

'It's alright, Travis. I'm fine.'

He looks worriedly at me. 'You sure?'

I nod. 'I'll talk to you tomorrow.' I close the door behind him, turning to find Abbey and Daniel staring around at my tiny flat. Daniel looks like he's smelling a dead cat. Neither of them has spotted the Fuck-it List. There's no way I'm explaining it to either of them, so I sidle nonchalantly past them both, pick up the towel from my bed and yank the list down. I toss it into the bathroom along with the towel. Abbey frowns, suspicious.

'What's that?'

'Affirmations,' I say. *I am bold and fearless, unhinged and vaguely slutty. Namaste.* 'They're private. What are you doing here?' I fold my arms, defensive.

Abbey lowers herself awkwardly onto the couch. Daniel gestures for me to join her, looming like a disapproving schoolteacher. *Fuck him.* I perch on the arm of the couch to annoy him. I watch him battle not to snap and feel the petty thrill of satisfaction.

'This is an intervention, Grace.'

I laugh, incredulous. 'Excuse me?'

'First the drinking and now *drugs*?'

'We're worried about you, Mum,' Abbey says. 'You're not yourself.'

Daniel exhales sharply. 'Not herself? That's a bloody understatement, Abbey.' She shrinks back against the cushions. 'Grace, I don't know whether this is some kind of sad attempt to recapture your youth or get back at me—' *Oh, please.* '—but this behaviour has to stop. Not only could you have died, but the papers could have gotten wind. Haven't you embarrassed yourself enough?'

I manage to stay calm but the lava is dangerously close to erupting. 'I wouldn't worry, Daniel. The papers are too busy writing about Stars Fold's newest power couple.' I raise an eyebrow.

'Got any exciting news to share?' He shifts, looking uncomfortable. I've hit a nerve, but he recovers quickly.

'For Pete's sake, Grace. What's the matter with you?' Daniel's voice breaks and I'm thrown. 'Can't you see you're scaring your family? You might not care what happens to you, but we do.' He turns his head, pressing his fingers to the bridge of his nose. *Is he crying?* It's an act – it has to be – he's playing to the room and I'm not falling for it. Not anymore.

'Give me a break, Daniel. Nothing you've done in the past four months has shown a shred of care for me, so you can stop pretending for Abbey's sake.'

'Mum—' Abbey interjects, and for a second I think she's finally going to defend me. 'How can you say that? Of course Dad cares about you. You don't stop loving someone after thirty years.'

I recognise myself in her in that moment. Little girls and their daddies. It trumps everything. I'd done it myself – defended my dad when he was in the wrong, because I didn't want to upset him, didn't want him to stop loving me, even though Mum was the one who nursed me, advised me, comforted me. Understanding Abbey isn't hard. When love is hard won, you don't want to let go of it. She's never had to worry with me. I was always there.

Daniel straightens, pulling himself together. 'Gracie, please.' He softens and it confuses me even more. The hackles that were rippling from my back settle. *What is happening?* 'Listen to me. You're having some kind of breakdown. I think you should speak to someone—'

The hackles are back. 'So now I'm mental?' Abbey shifts as if to speak and I throw a hand up. 'Stay out of this, Abbey.' I stand, pointing at the door. 'Get out.'

Daniel stares at me as though I can't be serious and I repeat myself, fuming. If Abbey wants to stay, that's fine, but I don't want him in my flat for another second. He looks to Abbey for support and she finally backs me.

'I want to talk to Mum. You should wait in the car.'

Daniel hates losing and he can't leave without a parting shot. 'Fine. I'll wait downstairs and have a beer with your *friend* Travis.'

'Do what you want Daniel,' I say, my indifference infuriating him even more. 'I don't care.' Once he's gone, I have no idea what to say to Abbey. I bustle around and make us some tea. Her eyes follow me, watchful and worried. I can't stall any longer. I sit down and take her hand. 'That was fun.'

Her lip quivers. 'It's not a joke, Mum. I'm scared.'

I pull her as close as her belly will allow. She rests her head on my chest, like she did when she was little. Her hair still smells the same. 'I'm sorry I scared you, sweetheart. I really am.'

'I don't understand what's happening. You're like a different person.'

'Is that so bad?'

She pulls away from me. 'Yes. I need my Mum.'

And there it is. Need. Expectation. It runs through me like a shiver, and I try to shake it off – because I love her, despite the repeated urge to run.

'I'm here, Abbey. I'm right here.'

She's not buying it. 'But that's the thing. You're not here. You've been weird with me for months, every time the baby comes up. What's the problem? Do you think I'm making a mistake?'

I seize the window. *Steer her away from the truth.* 'I apologise if it's seemed that way. It hasn't been my intention, but I'm worried. A baby is a lot – Tobias is always away. How are you going to juggle your career and a baby when you're on your own half the time?'

Her brow furrows. 'I'm not. I told you that. I'm planning to stay at home, be a full-time mum. We decided that's best, and we can afford it, so—'

She did not tell me that. 'What? Why would you do that?'

A horrible sense of déjà vu creeps over me. *After everything I gave up for you.* I don't know what to say and she stares at me, my silence pricking her own insecurity.

'You don't think I can do it, do you? You think I won't be a good mother.'

'Don't be silly.'

'It's got to be something, because you are not on board with this baby. You shut down every conversation. You missed my ultrasound with no explanation. You lie to avoid plans.'

The familiar panic rises and this time I'm not sure I can shut it down.

'I'm sorry if I haven't thrown myself headlong into buying booties and sending you bassinettes and baby names, Abbey. I've been a bit busy trying to figure my life out and it's – messy.'

'Busy getting drunk and sleeping around, you mean.'

I can't pretend anymore. There's no point, she can see right through me. 'Fine! The baby sends me into a tailspin, okay?'

Confusion patterns her face. 'You used to say you couldn't wait until I got married and had babies.'

'It's what I'm supposed to say. I'm your mother.'

'I don't understand. What changed?'

How can I explain it when I barely understand it myself? 'I don't know. Me? My life. All I know is, it makes me want to run a mile. I don't know who I'm supposed to be now. I just got control of my life back and—'

'Oh yeah, you seem really in control.' Her tone is sharper, tinged with anger.

'I am forty-nine years old and I'm starting over. I've spent my whole life as a wife and a mother and there are things I want to do, that I want to experience. To figure out – as *me*.'

She shakes her head at me, slow and disbelieving. 'How the hell does being a grandmother stop you doing that?'

'It just does, Abbey,' I say, exasperated. 'It feels like the walls are closing in on me. I didn't ask for this.'

Abbey jerks back, eyebrows raised. 'This might shock you, but me having a baby isn't about you.'

Anger prickles and I try to damp it down, not wanting to argue. 'But it *is*. As much as it's about you, about Tobias. About your father. Don't you see? Your choice – that you are perfectly entitled to make – it *changes* me. It changes how other people see me, how I see myself. It changes me whether I like it or not—' Putting it into words centres it in my chest fully for the first time, like a dagger. My voice breaks, '—and I am allowed to have feelings about that, even feelings that might be messy and hard for you to understand. Because now it's like I owe something in return.' I'm struggling not to cry and failing miserably. 'There's an expectation of who I'm supposed to be now; to you, to her – of how much I'm supposed to give – and if I don't, I'm a bad person. Like, *I'm* the arsehole if I don't want to babysit and have my house filled with toys and mess, or if I want to be overseas at Christmas or move to bloody London.'

She's not getting it. 'What? You never go away at Christmas and you hate London.'

'That's not the point,' I snap, and the dam breaks. 'I couldn't if I wanted to. I'm stuck now, because what kind of mother walks away from her only child and her granddaughter? If I do, I'm a shit mother and a shit grandmother and I'm selfish. That's what everyone will say. But maybe I'm allowed to be selfish for once because – to be honest, Abbey – I have *always* been there for you. But I don't think I've got anything left to give. I've already given it all.'

Realisation floods Abbey's face. 'Oh my God. This explains your constant guilt tripping—' I jolt. *My what?* '—any time I didn't do what you thought I should or achieve what you expected.'

'That's not true. I've never been anything but proud of you.'

'Because I made sure you were. But all these years – you've resented me?'

I can't answer her. How can I explain that it doesn't mean I don't love her and that it doesn't mean I *won't* be there for her and the baby. I just can't make myself *want* to, and that's a different thing, isn't it? Maybe I am broken. This is not how mothers are supposed to feel. Knowing I've hurt her bites into me, but there's no point being dishonest now. John 8:32 comes to me once more: *And you will know the truth and the truth will set you free.* 'Yes. I think I have. I love you, but I don't want to be a grandmother, Abbey.'

The look on her face makes me want to reel the words back in, but it's too late. Her mouth settles into a hard line. 'Oh, you've made that abundantly clear.' She levers herself up from the couch. 'Well, I hope your drug-fuelled sex rampage around the world makes you happier than being my mother has.' She heads for the door and my heart drops into my stomach. Another guilt rock to add to the pack.

'Abbey! Don't say that. Wait—'

'Dad was right. You have gone crazy. You need help, Mum.'

With that, she's gone, and I sink back on the couch, my hands to my face. What have I done? *You've been honest, that has to count for something.* She'll see it one day, given enough time – after countless sleepless nights and demands, her own sacrifices and a stalled career. But I don't wish these feelings on her. Knowing Abbey might eventually understand doesn't help because, right now, my daughter feels abandoned. The irony is crushing. I don't know how to fix this.

I pick up the Fuck-it List from the bathroom floor when I go to splash my face and stare at it. It's no longer just a list. There's a flow on effect I didn't expect, wasn't prepared for. *But if you toss it now, this will all have been for nothing.*

I pin it on the back of the bathroom door.

40

ask no questions

Friday morning. The hot sun slicing through the window when I woke up was offensively bright and in stark contrast to how I'm feeling. The past month has been flat and sallow because Abbey's still not talking to me. Not that I've tried. I'm too scared – that there's nothing I can say to make it better. I'm hoping she'll call me when she's ready but the more time passes, the more I worry things are irreparable.

Susie is avoiding me; sporadic texts, too busy to catch up. I've no idea what I've done. *Maybe taking drugs is not great when your friend is a former addict?* A couple of weeks ago, I'd invited her to see an 80s tribute band at the local RSL, thinking it would be nostalgic fun, but she declined.

Susie: Not my thing. But have a good time.

I'd tapped out a swift response:

Grace: Come on, it'll be like we're fourteen again. I miss you and I need this.

The typing dots appeared then disappeared. Finally:

Susie: Not everything's about you, Grace.

I'd stared at my phone, annoyed. Why did everyone keep saying that? I cared about other people; it didn't mean I wasn't allowed to have needs. Then I remembered one of my lecturers at university talking about creative feedback: 'If one person says something's wrong, feel free to ignore it, but if multiple people say the same, you should listen.' Discomfort rippled through me. *Is that really how people see me – how I am?*

More typing dots appeared . . .

Susie: I'm going camping for my birthday the weekend after next if you want to come with. Just the two of us. It's a bit of a ritual. I reckon it'll be good for you.

A pause, then another text.

Susie: I miss you too.

I'd wrinkled my nose – *ugh, I hate camping, it's all bugs and dirt* – but it would give us a chance to talk, for me to find out what's going on.

Grace: Sign me up.

The camping trip is this weekend and I'm dreading it, even though I need the distraction.

Feeling adrift without Susie and Abbey, I've been keeping a low profile – wake up, run, work a shift in the bar, eat, go to bed. The routine gives me something to hang on to. It also stops the intrusive thoughts. Scrubbing myself clean after Mike. The shame afterwards. The rave. The fear I felt waking up disoriented.

The Fuck-it List has been neglected. I've tried keeping up with doing '*One random new thing a week*' – a singing lesson (bad), a boxing class (better) – but I'm not feeling it like I was. I'm wondering if it's time to quit completely, that maybe it has done its job. But the competitive voice in my head can't help itself: *You're not finished. Don't fail at this too.*

Liz has thawed somewhat, texting me regularly with updates on Mum, but our connection is glitching again. She says Mum is declining rapidly, that I should visit her. I don't know what she wants me to say. Deep down, I know she's right. I've been digging through my memories, trying to collect the good ones of me and Mum, like shiny pebbles. Hoping if I collect enough, they'll outweigh the resentment. One memory keeps rising to the surface – occasional days when I'd be home sick from school. Mum would set me up on the couch with a blanket and bring me soup. In the afternoon, she'd join me and we'd watch *Days of Our Lives.*

Mum never missed it, so she'd fill me in on the ridiculous storylines – which characters were having affairs, which ones had died or mysteriously come back from the grave. The opening credits echo in my head, and I can't help thinking the sand trickling through the hourglass has almost run out. The difference is, I won't be able to turn it over and start again once it stops.

Mum is sitting by the window when I arrive at the nursing home. I'd sat in the car outside for twenty minutes, staring at the low blonde-brick building and willing myself inside. It didn't look like a home; it looked like a hospital. I'm nervous to see her – which is ridiculous, she's my mother. But being alone together didn't go so well the last time.

'Mum?' I step tentatively into her room. It takes her a moment, but she recognises me and I breathe easier. I sit down and she pats my hand, saying she didn't know I was coming, that she would have made lunch. I'm tense and unsure what to talk about so I keep it light. I tell her I went skydiving and that I'm taking an art class.

That my job is going well and that Abbey's belly is getting so big. Mum watches my mouth as I talk, but I don't know how much of it she's following.

'I thought of something nice.' I pull my battered copy of *The Lion, the Witch and the Wardrobe* from my bag. 'You said you missed reading. Maybe I can read this to you?'

She smiles and nods her head, her gaze drifting out the window as I read. I gradually relax. I'm not sure why I chose this book other than it felt like the right thing. Revisiting the familiar pages is like coming home after an arduous trip. I read for almost an hour and at one point I think she's fallen asleep. When I stop reading, she opens her eyes.

'What happens next?'

Some of the words stick in my throat. I'd forgotten them, although I've read the book dozens of times. The narrator explains – if the children ever remember their life through the wardrobe, it will be as if it were only a dream. I falter, my eyes flicking to Mum's face. I get to the part about not understanding that things can be good and terrible at the same time, and I have to close the book. I can't see the text.

I look up and Mum is staring at me, puzzled. 'Are you here to see family, love?' She has slipped away from me again, the neurons in her brain confused and untethered. Where do her memories go? They can't just disappear – we're taught in school that energy doesn't stop, it only changes. Are they floating around out there somewhere, unrecognisable and lost, waiting for someone to catch them?

I scrub at my face, not wanting to upset her. 'I am. I'm visiting my mother.'

'You're a good daughter. Do I know your mum?'

'Maybe,' I say, swallowing the lump in my throat and forcing a smile. 'You know, you remind me of her.' That seems to delight her. I ask her, innocently, 'Do you have children?' But guilt pricks at me. *Don't do it, Grace.*

Her forehead creases and she twists her hands, hesitating. 'Daughters, I think.' A smile as the memory connects. 'Yes, two girls.'

I can't help myself. 'What are they like?' Nerves churn as she digs for the answer then laughs softly.

'I think they're a handful. But good girls.' She studies my face. 'My Grace—' I start, *does she recognise me?* '—tries so hard. I wish she knew—' She doesn't elaborate, the thought gone.

'I'm sure they love you very much,' I say, and she brightens suddenly.

'She's having a baby.'

'Congratulations.' I smile. 'A grandma.'

'Mm-hmm.' She nods slowly. 'I have to make sure I . . . it's—' she trails off, confused, staring through the window again. Murmuring so low I can't be sure I've heard correctly, '—my second chance.'

I can't let it go. I know I should. 'Second chance?'

When she turns, her eyes are red-rimmed. 'He . . .' she searches for the words, '. . . was not always good.' And there it is. My chance to ask the question that has beat itself against my ribs like a caged bird for a lifetime.

'Your husband? Why didn't you leave?'

Her face drops and so does my stomach.

'I tried . . . twice.' The unexpected answer cuts in to me as she trails off. 'I couldn't leave them.'

'Grace?' Liz stands in the doorway. I don't know how long she's been there or how much she's heard. 'What the hell are you doing?'

Clearly enough. She hauls me out of the room. 'Are you *trying* to upset her?'

I shrug her off. 'Of course not. I came to read to her, and we were talking. I didn't expect the conversation to go there, but it's fine. She thinks I'm somebody else.'

'That makes it better how?'

'You don't own her, Liz. I know you think you do, because of your whole *co-dependent* thing, but you don't get to decide what I talk to Mum about.' I know I've overstepped by the look on her face and I attempt to reel things back. 'Don't you want some answers, before it's too late?'

'No. It doesn't matter anymore. I've made peace with the past.' *Liar.* 'I can't get over your selfishness. First you bail on moving Mum in here—'

'I was in hospital, I—'

She throws a hand up. 'Don't even get me started with that. And now this – grilling your sick mother for information because *you* want answers?'

'I wasn't grilling her. She's fine.'

'How would you know?' We glare at each other – a standoff – until I break. I can't do this now. I'm too rattled.

'Fine, I'll go.' I head back into the room to grab my bag and the book. Mum doesn't even notice me. I stalk past Liz into the corridor. 'See, she's perfectly okay.'

Liz sighs, her hostility already tempered. 'I know what it's like to want to run away from your life, you know.'

The sudden shift throws me. 'What? Where did that come from?'

'The year after Nate was born, he spent more time with Mum and Dad than with me because I was out every night, blind drunk.

I'd drop him off and not come back for days. Mum and Dad put me in rehab, remember?'

I nod, but I'm still puzzled. 'What's your point?'

'I can see what you're trying to do. You think if you run fast enough and distract yourself, all the shit stuff will disappear. That's not the way it works, trust me. It catches up with you eventually.'

'I don't know how many times I have to say this, but I am not lost or running away from my life. I'm running towards it.' I waver. 'I'm just not sure which direction it's in.'

'So, you *are* lost.' Liz smirks and I want to slap her.

'I'm going.' I throw my bag over my shoulder and march down the corridor.

'Come on. I was kidding,' she says. I ignore her and keep walking. 'You've got to let it all go, Grace.'

'Yeah, because we're all *so* good at doing that.'

I stalk to my car, unable to shake Mum's last words. They're under my skin, like shards of glass.

I couldn't leave them.

41

not drowning, waving

November, 1985

Mum's not well today. She says she has a headache, but I think it's more than that. I heard Dad shouting at her last night. He'd had lots of beer, and it always makes him sick. I don't understand why grown-ups do that. After I drank all that creaming soda at Trudy's eighth birthday party and vomited in the pool, I stopped drinking it forever.

He shouted so loud last night that he woke Lizzie, and she got into bed with me. It makes us both feel better, so I don't usually mind, but then she wet the bed. Mum was crying by then, so I didn't want to go out and tell them. I put our pillows on the floor instead. Lizzie said it was like camping and wanted to tell stories but all I could think was: how can you love somebody and still be so mean to them?

Dad's taking us to the lagoon at Curl Curl because when you have a headache you need to lie down in the dark and everybody needs to be quiet. I'm good at doing that, but Lizzie's not, because she's only four. Curl Curl is my favourite. There's this rockpool with little crabs and those funny enemy things that have a hundred fingers, and you can see all the fish swimming around. Lizzie doesn't like them touching her legs, but I don't mind at all.

Dad's putting our things in the car – a big esky with sandwiches and cheese sticks and a bottle of Fanta. I don't know why his fishing rods are in the boot because you get in big trouble if you catch fish in the lagoon. Dad should know. He says if we're good he might buy us a Paddle Pop – but only if we don't act up in the car.

When me and Lizzie say goodbye to Mum, she's staring into her wardrobe wearing her sunglasses. I think the light is hurting her eyes. I hope I don't get headaches when I'm old. She doesn't notice us in the doorway at first. When she does, she closes the wardrobe in a hurry. She looks sad, so I don't want to leave her at home by herself.

'Are you sure you can't come, Mummy?' Lizzie's holding my hand, watching Mum closely. I think she's going to cry. I tell her not to be a baby, we'll be back in a few hours. Mum says she's going to take some Panadol and have a sleep, and then do something important. She pulls us both in, squeezing us tightly.

'Bye, my beautiful girls. Remember, I love you very much.'

Lizzie falls asleep in the car because Curl Curl is a long way away. It's so hot the back seat sticks to our legs and the radio's up louder than Mum is allowed to have it. Dad taps his hand on the steering wheel, shouting, 'Whoa-oh-oh,' and singing something about going to April which doesn't make any sense, but most grown-up songs don't, if you ask me.

I brought a book with me so I won't be bored – it's about some rabbits that go on an adventure to find a new place to live and then this bad rabbit comes, but I have to stop reading because I'm getting car sick around the bends. I ask Dad if I can open the window and he says, 'Tell me if you're going to be sick so I can stop, Gracie. I don't want to have to clean it off the car.' I stick my head out of the window and suck in the air, but I don't feel any better.

Dad pulls into a carpark. It doesn't look like the lagoon at Curl Curl. Lizzie wakes up, blinking in the sun. 'Where are we?'

Dad says he thought he'd surprise us because we've never been to Bondi and there's good fishing on the rocks. He wants to teach us how to cast a line.

He unpacks the boot and makes us wait by the car while he runs across the road. He comes back with bait and a carton of beer, but no Paddle Pops.

He says we can swim before learning to fish, which is good because I don't want to touch the worms. Lizzie's holding the bag of bait, and she squeezes it to make the worms wiggle. Dad sets up between the flags, cracks a beer, and tells us to paddle in the shallows. I ask if he remembered sunscreen. He shrugs and says, 'You'll be right, mate.'

The waves are too high, the wash tugging at our legs. Neither of us likes it very much. The lagoon is way better, I don't know why we couldn't go there. Dad drinks more beers while we build sandcastles and dig a big hole, until he says we're digging too deep and it's a good job there are no dunes at Bondi anymore, because they're prone to collapse. He tells us the weight of the sand forces your guts out of you with no time to scream and it scares Lizzie and makes her cry. I don't know who the Beaumont children are, but Dad says he wouldn't be surprised if that's what happened to them.

We follow Dad up the path away from the beach and around the rocks, salty and sunburned. Lizzie's legs are tired, so Dad swings her up on to his shoulders and she's laughing, but I'm a bit worried because Dad is all wobbly, and we're pretty high up. He finds a good spot to fish from – big black rocks over the water, cold, salty spray shooting in the air.

'Don't try to climb down the rocks,' Dad says. 'Those bloody waves'll take you before you even see 'em.' He doesn't need to worry, there's no way I'm going near the edge.

Lizzie keeps accidentally breaking the worms in half. She thinks it's funny, so Dad smacks her leg hard, leaving a print of his hand on her skin. I want to yell at him to leave her alone, but I don't. 'How about me and Lizzie sunbake while you catch us some fish?' I hand him another beer and press the Fanta bottle against Lizzie's leg, pointing out two seagulls fighting over a chip.

When Dad's line snags, he tells us to stay put and climbs down to free it. We wait as wave after wave crashes against the rocks, the spray falling on us like rain. But Dad doesn't come back. I'm worried but Lizzie doesn't notice for a while, she's too busy squinting into the sun, trying to keep her eyes open. Eventually she gets bored.

'Where's Daddy?'

There's only one explanation. 'I think the big waves got him.' I thought I'd be sadder.

She looks at me wide-eyed. 'He's gone?' I nod and she accepts it without question.

'I think Mum's gone too,' she says. I ask her how she knows, and she clings to me and says she just does. 'Who's going to look after us?'

I'm scared and trying not to cry, but I hold her shoulders. 'I will. I'm your big sister. I'll never leave you on your own. I promise.' She grips my hand as I march us back down to the beach and across the sand to the road. I ask a lady at the crossing where the police station is, and she points up the street.

'Where are your parents, sweetheart?'

I tell her we might be orphans, because it sounds dramatic, and she gasps as the crossing beeps. At the station, I tell a nice policeman with a moustache that we came to the beach with Dad but now he's gone and we need to get home to see if Mum is gone too. He scratches his head. 'Where'd your dad go?'

'The bloody waves took him,' I say.

The policeman takes us back down to the beach. Dad's storming up and down the sand in his speedos with a cut on his head, yelling our names. I wave and call out and he runs, arms outstretched, scooping us up. Then he shakes us hard and says he thought someone had taken us.

Dad's not allowed to drive the car. He's had too many beers. The nice policeman drives us all the way home in his car, even though Dad is rude to him. The police station phoned the house, so Mum is waiting for us when we get there. She's still wearing her sunglasses, even though it's dark now. Dad staggers into the house and straight out the back to his garden and Mum doesn't say a word. She takes the sunglasses off once the policeman's gone and her eye is all puffy and purple.

I don't say anything because I don't want to be rude, and maybe she's embarrassed at looking ugly. Lizzie stares at Mum, puts her hands on her face and says, 'You've got an ouchy', then kisses her finger and gently pokes the purple mark.

Mum makes us have a bath and silently puts calamine lotion on our sunburn. I think she might be mad at us for going to the police station. I tell her I'll help Lizzie get ready for bed. Maybe that'll make up for it.

Once I've brushed Lizzie's hair, I go across the hall to Mum and Dad's room. There's a big suitcase open on the bed. Mum's taking clothes out of it and putting them away in her wardrobe.

'What are you doing?'

Mum doesn't look at me. She takes a big breath and closes the wardrobe doors.

'Something important.'

42

isn't it ironic?

Daniel is waiting outside my flat when I arrive home, with Dexter panting at his feet. I stop short on the stairs.

'What are you doing here?'

'Grace!' Daniel pushes off the wall, smiling broadly and I step back automatically. Dexter struggles up, wagging his whole body at me.

'Is Dexter okay?'

'He's fine. I was passing by and thought you might like to see him.'

'You were *passing by*? In Newtown. With Dexter?' My face is a puzzle. Daniel thinks for a second then relents.

'I wasn't passing, I wanted to see you. We need to talk.'

I push past him – giving Dexter's head a quick scratch – and shove my key in the lock. 'I'm not in the mood, Daniel. Maybe some other time, when I'm not busy being a mentally unstable drug addict.'

I turn to slam the door in his face but I'm not quick enough. His hand is on the door frame and Dexter already has his paw across the threshold. Both of them yelp at the same time.

'Bloody hell.' I open the door and crouch down to comfort the dog.

'My hand is fine, Grace. Thanks for asking,' Daniel says, flexing his fingers.

'Don't be a baby. You shouldn't have tried to force your way into my flat.'

'I wasn't *forcing*—' He stops. 'Can we start over? Grace, may I come in? I'm not here to argue, I promise.'

'Fine, but can we make it quick? I'm going away for the weekend and I need to pack.'

Daniel follows me in. He lets Dexter off his leash and he immediately jumps on the couch. 'Get down!' Daniel instructs. Dexter ignores him.

'He's fine. He's allowed on the couch.'

'Oh.' Daniel shuffles his feet. 'So where are you going?' I fix him with a cold stare, and he puts his hands up in surrender. 'You're right. None of my business.'

'What do you want, Daniel? If you're here to tell me your little girlfriend is pregnant, I'm not interested.'

Daniel flushes. 'No. You'll be happy to know that was a false alarm.' He tries for a laugh. 'God, can you imagine? At our age?'

I glare at him. 'I couldn't care less.'

'Look, can we sit down?'

I glance at Dexter, who's stretched the length of the couch. He looks so comfortable. I reluctantly gesture to the bed, but position myself as far away from Daniel as possible as he takes a deep breath. *Oh, God.* I'm reminded of that moment in the car when I thought he was going to tell me he was terminal. *Don't tell me he wants to marry her?*

'I've never apologised for the way everything happened, for not considering your feelings. I've been awful to you.' He reaches out and takes my hand. I gawp at his fingers around mine like they're an alien creature. 'I miss you, Grace. I miss our family. I know you'll never forgive me, but I'll regret it if I don't try—' The whole time he's talking, it's like I'm back in the car with him – with the rushing in my ears – but everything's in reverse. He says something about *being lonely . . . under pressure*. He's looking earnestly into my eyes. What is going on? . . . *behaved so badly* . . . If he thinks I'm going to forgive him this easily, he's got another thing coming . . . *I was stupid to lose you.* My chest expands and I breathe in. The rushing stops. His fingers are woven through mine. How did that happen? 'I've made a mistake.'

'Huh?' I stare stupidly at him as he shifts closer. I can't move because I'm so bewildered my nervous system appears to have shut down.

'Watching you move on, the thought of other men touching you – my *wife* – it's been torture.' He cups my face. 'I still love you, Gracie.'

I look into the eyes of the man I spent thirty years of my life with – made solemn vows to, raised a child and built a home with – knowing I should pay attention to the voice in my head screaming that he dismantled my life, humiliated me. But that voice is battling for airspace with another that's whispering, *'You can have your old life back. You can forget the past few months, forget about the list. Everything can go back to normal. Wouldn't that be nice?'* I know I told Susie I didn't want my old life back, but that was when it was being held to ransom. Now it's dangling in front of me like a carrot, and all I have to do is take it. *He loves you, Grace.*

Daniel kisses me, and I freeze for a second before I kiss him back, ready to fall willingly into the reboot. It only takes a minute for me to realise something's off. I expected to feel relief, or at least comfort in the familiar. I don't feel anything. I keep going and start unbuttoning his shirt – *maybe we're rusty* – but when he puts his hand on my breast, I pull back.

'Stop.'

'Why? What's wrong?'

'I don't think this is a good idea. I need to think about this.'

'Come on, Gracie.' He reaches out to touch my hair. 'It's *us.* What do you need to—'

'Daniel.' My voice is firm but calm as I shift my head away from his hand. 'I said I need to think.'

He stares at me as I flop back on the bed, trying to gather my thoughts. Then he lies down beside me, giving me a lingering look before he stares up at the ceiling, unsettled.

'You're different,' he says.

'I know.' *I don't think this is going to work.*

We lie there in silence for a while. I'm trying to work out what to say, how to tell him that I can't do it. I don't want my old life back, even if it is easy and secure. Even if he loves me, because I don't think I love him. Not anymore. *Clarity.* Suddenly Daniel groans and puts his hands over his face. I look at him in alarm. 'What's wrong?'

'I feel guilty.'

'For which bit? There's been so many things,' I say wryly.

He shakes his head. 'No, guilty for being here. I feel like I'm cheating on Sasha.' *Hang on, what?* I sit up.

'Firstly, we're still technically married, and you can't cheat on your mistress with your *wife*. And secondly, I thought you broke it off with her.'

'When did I say that?'

'I think it's a natural assumption. You just told me you still love me and want to get back together.' He puts his head in his hands.

'I'm confused, Grace. This is all so hard.' He glances up at the ceiling. 'I've been asking the Lord for guidance, but—'

Laughter bubbles out of me because, honestly, this is so comical. Daniel is watching me almost fearfully.

'What's so funny?'

'You are!'

'I understand if you're angry and upset—'

'Do I look angry? And I'm not upset.' I'm surprised to realise I'm telling the truth, and I actually smile at him. 'But I don't want to try again, Daniel. I'm sorry. Now, if you don't mind, I need to pack.' I half expect him to fly off the handle or try to persuade me, but he doesn't, as though my laughter severed the final cord. He knows he has no power over me anymore. I climb off the bed and attach Dexter's lead, cuddling him and letting him lick my face while Daniel buttons his shirt. He doesn't say another word to me as I walk them to the door. 'Goodbye, Daniel.' He stares at me for a second then nods.

'Bye, Grace.'

I shut the door and lean against it. *Did that really just happen?* I'm emotionally drained. I need to sleep for a week. The last thing I'm in the mood for is roughing it in a tent. But a promise is a promise. I drag a bag from under my bed and start to pack.

Susie had better not snore.

43

let it go

Susie has insisted on driving her old Holden, even though the suspension is shot and the aircon is on the fritz. By the time we get there – after being subjected to Cold Chisel's entire back catalogue (road-trip rules, apparently) – I'm tired and sweaty, my spine is out of alignment, and I've developed a deep hatred for 'Khe Sanh'.

Things appear to be back to normal between us, but I'm worried about her. She's lost weight and seems preoccupied. I hope she's not having problems with Rob.

Her 'secret camping spot' is a small clearing, circled by several tall eucalypts. A sandy path leads down to a tiny, secluded beach.

'Are you sure we're allowed to camp here?'

'Nah,' Susie snorts, pulling on a straw hat. 'But as long as nobody sees us, we'll be sweet.'

'Seriously? We could get fined.'

She rolls her eyes. 'Relax. Haven't you ever done anything a little bit illegal? Trust me. I come here every year and I've not been busted yet.'

I decide to trust her, and we unload the car. Susie is impressively prepared and puts me to work assembling the tent, barking orders like I'm in the army. I do as I'm told; if it was left to me it would probably fall on us in the middle of the night. Susie high-fives me when we're done.

'So, what's the plan?' I ask.

'The plan—' Susie reaches into the esky and pulls out two beers. '—is we're gonna bloody relax.' She cracks them open and plonks herself into one of the chairs, letting out a sigh of contentment.

'We're just going to sit here? Not go for a walk or anything?'

'Grace, love. Considering the last few months, don't you want to just stare at the water . . . *do* absolutely nothing?' She has a point. I sit down and take a sip of beer. 'Atta girl. We're doing fuck all until it's time to build the fire for the ritual.'

My eyebrows go up. 'There's an actual ritual?'

Susie leans over to pat my leg. 'You'll love it, I promise.'

'You're not going to make me dance around the fire naked, are you?'

'Babe, if you want to get your tits out, don't let me stop you. Now hush up and enjoy the quiet. Wake me up when the sun starts to go down.' She puts her beer down, pulls her hat over her face, and promptly falls asleep.

Susie's right, I haven't stopped since everything happened. I don't know what to do with myself, with nothing to do but sit. After months surrounded by the clamour of the bar, the quiet is disconcerting. But I close my eyes and breathe into it, realising it's not quiet at all.

The sound of thousands of leaves rustling with the wind comes into sharp focus; the faint buzz of a cricket, the rush of the ocean. I open my eyes as the trees sway, the sun bouncing off the water in glittering slices. *Divinity lives in the quiet moments.*

Tension lifts from my shoulders. For at least an hour I sit still, listening to the waves rolling, watching a small lizard wriggle its way up the trunk of a nearby tree, a lone seagull pinwheeling over the water.

When the sky starts to blush pink and gold, movement above catches my eye. I look up and gasp. A massive flock of starlings swoops above me, rolling in perfect precision like a swirling black net, changing direction and making shapes in the sky. *A murmuration.* It reminds me of warm lips to an ear, whispering comforting words.

Abbey would love this. Before she decided to study law, she talked of being a wildlife photographer. We'd bought her an expensive SLR camera for her sixteenth birthday and she went everywhere with it for years, until corporate life swallowed the creative, separating her from miracles like the one above. *I wish she was here.* The force of missing her hits me like a fist and I whisper, 'Help me fix things, please,' as the flock of birds drifts into the distance.

Seconds later, a starling lands on a nearby tree-stump. 'Bloody hell, not you again.'

'Well, if that's the way you feel—' Susie rouses from her sleep.

'Not you. I was talking to Go—' *Don't say God, you'll sound insane.* '—that bird.'

'What bird?'

I turn around. It's gone. 'There was a bird there a second ago.'

'If you say so.' She pushes herself up and stretches. 'Right, time to get sorted.'

'Are you going to tell me what this ritual is?'

'Nup. When will you learn to trust me, babe? Have I steered you wrong yet?' I make a zipper motion across my lips and Susie flips me the bird. 'I'm gonna make us some sausages. We need to fortify ourselves.' *Now I'm scared.* 'You can collect wood for the fire.'

I look at her uncertainly. 'Are you sure a fire is a good idea? We're in nature.'

'On the beach, dummy. The fire pit is in the boot of the car.' She puts her fingers up like a girl scout. '*Leave no trace*!'

Heaving the metal tub out of the boot, I struggle with it down to the beach as Susie starts the barbeque. The next half an hour is spent peacefully gathering driftwood, sand scrunching between my toes as the sky darkens. Susie wanders down as I'm standing admiring my pile of sticks, feeling accomplished. She's carrying a plate of sausages and bread in one hand, a basket in the other.

'We make fire?' I say in a caveman voice, and she laughs.

'You're a dickhead.' She plonks the basket down, hands me the plate and sets to work on my sticks. Minutes later, we're munching happily around flickering flames.

When she asks how things are with Abbey, I take a moment to answer, chewing slowly.

'It's all a bit of a mess. I've been trying to wrap my head around it all, I really have, but I'm still struggling.' I shrug. 'I think it's because I don't know who I'm supposed to be now.'

'Why do you have to be somebody else?'

I frown at her. 'Because there's expectation, of how I'm supposed to act. Grandmothers are supposed to be all . . . grandmotherly.'

'Says who? Why can't you be whatever kind of grandmother you decide to be? I don't think it's like being a parent, where I imagine you have to be everything all at once.' She takes a bite of her sausage. 'Being a grandmother doesn't have to replace who you are. It's like an extension on a house. Build extra space.'

'I never thought of it that way.'

'And listen.' She waves a piece of bread at me. 'You've spent months intentionally not giving a fuck what people think of you, so why care about other people's expectations now?'

'I don't know, actually.' I'm startled to realise she's right. 'Probably because this is scarier.'

Susie nods. 'I'm sure it's just as scary for Abbey. Sometimes, the only thing you need to do is tell people you love them and that you'll be there. Figure the rest out later. Life is short, babe.' I get the sense she's not just talking about me. She slaps my arm. 'Speaking of . . . how's the list going? Anything juicy to share?'

My face scrunches. 'Do I need to answer that? You were at the hospital. I think it's fair to say the train slid off the tracks.'

'That's kind of the point. You can't tell me it hasn't been fun. Come on—'

'Yeah, of course. Some of it's been amazing.' I shrug. 'But—'

'No *buts*. Do you know how proud I am of you? Your life crashed and burned and look what you did. You came out all guns blazing. I don't know if I could have done that. I certainly couldn't have done any of the stuff on your list.' *Now she tells me.*

I well up immediately. 'Thank you. I'm glad I'm doing it, really. But a few things have happened that—' I pause, and she looks at me with concern. '—never mind.' Maybe I'll tell her one day, but not tonight. It's her birthday. I don't want to ruin it. 'Anyway . . . what's been going on with you? I was starting to think you were avoiding me.'

Susie stares at me for second, chewing her lip, and worry ripples through me. Then she looks up at the sky. 'Look, the moon's up. Time to get our witchy magic on.' The subject change gives me whiplash and I watch in confusion as she rummages in the basket, producing some paper and two pens.

'Uh . . . okay.'

'So, this is called the "Full Moon Releasing Ritual".' She hands me a pen and paper. We're to think of three things we need to let go of and write them down. Then we'll speak each thing out loud, to 'take the power out of it', and hurl the paper into the flames.

'What if I don't know what to write?'

'Just focus on the moon and think about your life. Go deep and you'll know.' But that's the last place I want to go. *It's where all the monsters are.* 'It helps to put your hand here and here.' She motions to her chest and her throat. 'Your heart and throat chakras. Love and compassion, for yourself and others. And speaking your truth.'

My eyes widen. 'I had no idea you were this woo-woo.'

'I told you I've been doing spiritual development. There are a lot of things you don't know about me, Grace Miller. You're not the only one who's changed.' She's right, and I feel a sudden sadness at having missed out on her journey. 'Anyway, it's not woo-woo. It works, trust me. Just go with it. If there's anybody who needs a bit of releasing, it's you.'

I do as I'm told, and we sit in silence for a few minutes. I imagine I can feel light pulsing underneath my hands. *Maybe the woo-woo is catching.* I try to be as open as I can. I'm not sure if the three things I write down are right, but they feel real. Even if they're hard to say.

Susie turns to me. 'Okay, remember, this is a safe space. Are you ready?'

'Not really.' I'm oddly nervous. I shouldn't be, this is my oldest friend, but I've never said all this out loud. 'You go first.'

Susie clambers up and faces the fire. 'I'm letting go of regret.' I smile at her encouragingly. 'For the years I lost to drugs, and what it did to my relationships. Regrets are pointless. I have to accept the things I've done are part of my journey.' She crumples the paper then tosses it into the flames. It curls into ash and disappears.

She talks about her feelings of resentment – against people who hurt her and let her down – and letting those go. My face burns and I can't look at her, even though I know she's not only talking about me. Her third item puzzles me. 'I'm letting go of fear.'

A laugh burbles out of me. 'Don't be silly. You're not afraid of anything.'

Susie gives me a funny look. 'I have breast cancer, Grace.'

I stare at her in shock. *What the fuck?* I scramble to stand up but she stops me.

'No, don't. I need to do this.' I sit down, trying not to cry as she gathers herself. 'I have breast cancer!' She shouts it, as though the wind can carry it away. 'And I'm shitting myself.' Suddenly she pulls her top off. She's not wearing a bra. 'This is the last chance I've got to wave these beauties around before they lop 'em off.'

I can't stop the tears as I watch her turn in circles with her arms out, baring her breasts to the sky, to the ocean. She crumples the paper in her hand. 'I'm letting go of fear!' Her yell echoes across the sand and into the fire it goes. Then she plops down onto the sand and gives me a small shrug.

'How bad is it?'

Susie brushes me off. 'I don't want to talk details. Another time, okay? That's not what tonight's about.' She punches her fist into the air. 'Letting go of fear, remember.' The bravado doesn't land.

'Why didn't you tell me?'

'Doesn't matter. I'm telling you now.'

'Nope. We're not doing that.'

She shuffles uncomfortably, mulling it over. 'Honestly? I didn't know whether you were gonna bail on me again once you sorted your shit out. I'd rather do it by myself than worry about whether you'll stick around while I'm dealing with it.'

Guilt scissors into me. 'I understand that. But I'm not going anywhere.'

'No offense, but you've said that before.'

I rub my face and take a deep breath. It's now or never. If we don't clear the air, it's always going to be a sticking point. 'Can we *please* talk about what happened?'

Susie shakes her head. 'Ancient history, babe. Leave it.'

'I can't, Suse. It's clearly still on your mind – as it should be – and I want to apologise. I never should have let you go through it alone.' Her mouth is a thin line. I explain how Daniel thought there was too much at stake, that things had been rocky, and it had felt like an ultimatum. 'I should have stood up to him, Suse. I should have been there for you. I'm so sorry.'

She offers me a tiny smile. 'I reckon it's harder when you've got so much to lose. Honestly, I forgive you, Grace. We can let it go.'

My own smile comes out lopsided. 'If it makes you feel better, I stopped having sex with him after that.'

She grins. 'Helps a bit, yeah.'

'I did nearly have sex with him the other day, but I don't think that counts.' Susie's arm shoots out and whacks me on the side of the head. 'Ow!'

'Are you mental?'

'I said *nearly*!'

Susie shakes her head in disappointment. 'This is why you're supposed to tell me everything, so I can stop you doing stupid shit.'

'I hate to tell you this,' I laugh, 'but if that's the case, I think I need to fire you.' I reach out, taking her hand. 'I'm so sorry you're sick, Suse. I don't know what to say.'

'Yes, you do. It's your turn.'

'Oh, I can't. Not after all this. It's not about me.'

'You're not getting out of it that easily. Up you get.'

Standing slowly, I face the fire, clutching my pieces of paper. I glance at Susie and she gives me a little nod.

'I'm letting go of guilt,' I shout out to the water, feeling silly. 'Because for some reason, I'm still carrying the weight of every mistake I've ever made.' I scrunch the paper and toss it into the fire.

'That was good. See?'

I roll my eyes and keep going. The next one is harder, and I pause, tears pricking my eyes. 'This one is for shame.' My voice wobbles. 'Because I've never felt like I'm good enough because of how I grew up. Because I haven't loved being a mother and if people knew, they'd think I'm a terrible person.'

'Oh, honey.' When I look at Susie, she's crying, and it nearly topples me. I stare at the paper in my hand. I'm not sure I can let it go. *You can do it, Grace.* I hold it in the flames, watching it blacken and curl until it burns my fingers. Then it's gone. 'One more, babe,' says Susie. 'You're doing great.'

I face her. 'This one – this thing I want to let go of . . . it's that I think I might be selfish.' Susie's eyes widen. 'I didn't think I was, because outwardly I put other people first – but not always the people who mattered. I did that so people would think more of me, so they'd love me for being a good person. So, it must really have been for me.' My voice cracks. 'I've let people I love down – because I've chosen myself over them.'

Susie wrinkles her nose. 'Nah, you can't have that one.'

'What? Why not?'

'Because everybody's selfish sometimes, and that's okay.' She shrugs. 'Everyone has a shadow. You can't pretend it doesn't exist. There's duality in everything, light and dark.'

'See, now you just sound like Yoda.'

'Sorry. You have to choose another one.'

I cross my arms. 'You can't tell me what I want to let go of.'

'Yes, I can. It's my ritual. You can do better than that.' She's annoying me now.

'I don't have another one.'

'Yes, you do.'

Anger flares before I can stop it. 'For fuck's sake, Susie. No, I don't!'

'And there it is.' She smiles serenely, opening her hands, and it hits me like a brick. I gasp. *How did she know?* My mouth settles into a hard line, my fists balling, fingernails digging into my palms as I look up to the sky. It's so obvious.

'I am angry.'

'That's it.'

How had I not realised? *Because good girls aren't allowed to be angry.* I've never let it all out, not since I was too small to remember. Good little Gracie, always polite, always keeping the peace. I've held it in my entire life. Daniel leaving me has ruptured something,

'What are you angry about, babe?' Susie's voice is gentle.

I'm breathing heavily as I finally open my hands and let go. Pent-up rage pours out of me in a torrent. 'I'm angry at Dad for hurting us, for making me feel like I had to be better for him to love me. I'm angry at him for killing himself and abandoning us.' My voice gets louder. 'I'm angry at Mum for not leaving him and for being bitter – and now I'm angry I'm losing her. I'm angry at Liz for making everything so hard all the time and acting like nothing I do is ever right.' I'm closer to the fire, the heat licking my skin. My throat tightens as I shout louder and faster to get it all out. 'I'm angry at Daniel for throwing me away like I didn't matter. I'm angry at losing control of my *entire* fucking life.' I yell into the flames like they can answer back, but they ripple and absorb it all. 'I'm angry at men because *fuck them*, fuck the lot of them!' My voice lowers to a growl. 'I'm angry at the world. I am angry at God.' Then a realisation strikes so deep it almost guts me. 'I am angry at *myself*.' Then I whisper it, only to me. 'I'm angry at myself.'

A cry erupts from my chest as I crush up the paper and hurl it into the flames. I scream, loud and guttural, until there's no air left in my lungs. I'm a volcano, and all the lava that's threatened but never spilled spews out of me. I never imagined screaming could feel so good.

Susie's on her feet beside me, tears streaming. She balls her fists and screams with me. I stare at her in shock for a second before it takes me over again and we scream together, our eyes locked, a violent chorus of two. Then she grabs her bare breasts and throws her head back. Her scream becomes a howl. Our voices echo into the sky and it's no longer pain and fury but liberation.

Then she's stripping her pants off and I start to laugh, a hysterical rolling laughter.

'What the bloody hell are you doing?'

She grins at me through tears. 'I'm going for a swim. You coming?' She takes off, running towards the water. In seconds I'm naked and racing behind her, my feet digging into the soft sand. We dive through the waves, the water icy and delicious. As we swim out beyond the break, I'm not sure if we're laughing or crying, but it doesn't matter.

I arc over backwards, the cold air kissing my skin, swimming under in a loop. When I surface, Susie yells, 'You're like the little fucking mermaid.' We grin stupidly at each other as we slowly calm. Then without speaking, we float onto our backs, buoyant and still. My hand finds hers and we drift, boobs to the sky and staring at the stars.

Eventually, Susie jerks upright. 'Ow. *Ow.* What the fuck? Something's biting me.'

I panic immediately. 'Oh my god, is it a shark?'

It turns out Susie has been stung by sea lice. Back on the sand, she stands with her legs apart, inspecting her crotch and raking her fingers up and down her thighs.

'Why didn't you get stung?' she asks accusingly.

'I don't know. Maybe they only like salty people?'

She grimaces. 'I'm gonna go find some bottled water.'

'I'll come with you.'

'No, I don't need you watching me rinse my bits. Stay here and chill by the fire. That was pretty intense.'

I watch her stagger up the path like she just returned from battle, then I sink to the sand.

I'm light and limp, like a dishcloth someone has wrung out so completely that not a single drop of dirty water is left. I wonder if I'll ever be angry again or if I've used it all up.

I lie back, the sand cold against my skin. But underneath it is something else. I can feel the earth beneath it humming, warm and alive. I feel held and protected – like I did in the church – and I know now, with utter certainty, that it's maternal.

I lie there for an age, staring at the sky. When I finally wander up the path, Susie is already asleep. I creep quietly into the tent and curl beside her. She rolls over and throws her arm around me, spooning me. I sink into her and exhale.

I don't remember the last time I felt this safe.

44

it's no secret

We don't speak much on the drive home, aside from Susie telling me that road-trip rules mean the return-trip music is passenger's choice. As we pull away from the dirt road, I connect my phone and open a music app. Punching '80s' into the search bar, I click on the first playlist and crank the volume. Life wasn't perfect when I was a girl, but it was simpler somehow.

Song after familiar song plays, and I smile because I think I've discovered the missing ingredient for time travel. I don't know whether the secret's in the melody, the lyrics or something else, but there's something magical about music. Something indefinable, with the ability to transport you with pinpoint accuracy to another place and time. The years drop away and I'm her again, at seven and ten and thirteen and sixteen. Who I was before life had its way with me and who I was when it started to bruise. Who I was before I remade myself as someone else. I'm the melody again, but this time I know it by heart.

I lean against the window for hours, listening as the scenery flashes by. As each new song plays, they string together my story, as though the playlist has been curated just for me. I tap my fingers to 'Tainted Love' and sing softly to 'I Think We're Alone Now'.

'Girls Just Want To Have Fun' reminds me of Lizzie, and I listen silently to 'How Will I Know' and 'I'm Still Standing', lost in memories of Mum and Dad and trying not to break.

As we near Sydney, we both sing loudly to 'I Will Survive' and 'Don't Stop Believin'' – because it's physically impossible not to, and maybe this playlist is not only for me. I laugh as Susie unexpectedly pretends to play guitar like George Michael when 'Faith' comes on.

Driving over the Harbour Bridge, Bonnie Tyler's rasping voice on 'Holding Out for a Hero' rattles me like thunder. The words pulse through me and I'm crying silently, because nobody's coming to save me – but I finally know I don't need them to. I am okay. I breathe deeply, eyes closed, as an unmistakable guitar riff wraps itself around me and Tears for Fears sings about no turning back. They have one thing wrong through. I don't want to rule the world. I simply want to love my life. I've only got one shot at it and who knows how long I've got.

Finally, as Susie turns the car onto King Street, close to home, a funky bassline and familiar keys kick in, as if to confirm that a higher power is indeed controlling this playlist. It's 'We Are Family', and I know in that instant what I need to do.

I could never have imagined I'd come away from this weekend feeling like a changed person. But I *am* changed. Letting go has made space inside of me, so I won't be needing to build that extension. I see Abbey's face in my mind and, for the first time, imagine the baby. *It's time to stop fighting so hard, Grace.*

After Susie drops me off, I leave Abbey a long, rambling voicemail. I tell her I'm sorry, that I want to fix things, and that I've thought long and hard about my reaction to the baby. I'm petrified, but that's my problem. I want to be there for her, and I love her.

It takes her a whole day to respond by text and when she does, it's not the response I'm expecting.

> **Abbey**: I don't think you know what honesty is, Mum. I know you lied to me about what happened with Dad, that it wasn't you who left. Is there anything else I don't know?
>
> **Abbey**: Oh, that's right – you almost gave me away to Auntie Liz.
>
> **Abbey**: Explains a lot.

It's as though someone has poured ice over me. I call her straight away. She doesn't pick up, so I tap out a frantic response.

> **Grace**: I understand you're angry, but I can explain. Please call me back.

I stare at the phone for almost twenty minutes – my nerves bottoming out – before the text dots appear.

> **Abbey**: I'm not angry, Mum. I'm hurt and I don't want to talk to you. I need some space.

I start typing back, close to tears, then stop. There's no point pushing. If she needs space, I'll give it. Then I close my eyes and take a deep breath because, from the moment her text came through, I've been holding another feeling at bay, and it answers another burning question: Yes, the anger stocks do replenish.

45

the gift

October, 1999

I can barely see through the windscreen. Rain is coming down so hard the wipers can't keep up. There's a torrent of thoughts in my head that are just as blinding because I've been fighting panic ever since we left the shopping centre. Trying to stay calm. I can't believe I left her. How could I do that?

Abbey's been screaming bloody murder for most of the drive, since she dropped her sippy cup and it rolled under the seat. I can't reach it, and I can't pull over.

'We're nearly there, sweetie. It's okay.'

Nothing is okay.

It's not her fault. She's still feverish, and probably hungry. No. She's traumatised, Grace. You abandoned her.

Taillights flash red in front of me and as I tread the brakes too hard, we jerk forward. Abbey screams louder then starts to cough, as though she's choking on something. I can't see her properly in the rear view, so I crane my neck to look back, trying to keep the car straight. She's red-faced and covered in snot, pushing her body against the harness, then she relaxes and lets out a high-pitched wail.

'Mummyyyyy.'

A sob breaks from me as I hunch over the wheel, hands shaking. Her screams vibrate through me and pressure builds in my chest, in my head. I'm still fifteen minutes from Liz's and I'm not sure I'll make it because I can't make her stop. What if I snap?

Abbey cries herself out and falls asleep a few minutes before I get there. I stand in the rain in Liz's driveway, staring at her, not wanting to wake her. Eventually, I slide her gently from the car. She lets out a small cry but doesn't open her eyes as I carry her to the door. She's a dead weight on my shoulder and I'm scared I'll drop her. My whole body shakes as I wait for Liz to answer the door.

'Grace. What on earth . . . ?'

'Take her. Please, just take Abbey.'

Liz is wide-eyed. She peels Abbey off me and cradles her as I walk inside and stand in the hallway, trembling. 'What's happened? Are you alright?'

I stare blankly at her. All I can do is shake my head. I don't trust myself to speak.

'Okay.' Her voice is low, gentle. 'I'll put Abbey down in my room. Go sit down and try to breathe.'

I glance around in panic. 'Where's Col?' I don't want anybody to see me like this.

'He's at his parents' place with Nate. It's just me here.'

She finds me a few minutes later, pacing in the living room. 'What's going on?'

'I can't do this. I'm not coping.'

Liz steers me to sit down. 'Take a breath. You're fine.'

'No, I'm really not.'

She takes my hand. 'Honey, I know you've been struggling with Daniel away, and this is a rough age, but trust me – you're not going through anything most mothers don't go through. You should have seen me when Nate was born.'

I pull my hand away. 'You don't understand. She's not safe with me.'

'Don't be silly. Come on, you need to calm down.'

It comes out of me in a rush, my voice high and strangled. 'I left her, Liz. I walked away and left her at the shops. I don't even know how long for.' I can't breathe. I'm choking on tears. 'Someone found her and took her to centre management.'

Liz tries to hide her shock but it's obvious. 'Oh, Grace—'

'What kind of mother does that? Anything could have happened to her—'

'Okay, okay. But it didn't. She's fine. You're fine.'

'I am not fucking fine.'

I tell her things haven't been okay since the day Abbey was born. That I'd hoped to feel that rush of maternal love everyone talks about, but I didn't. That I've been going through the motions ever since – doing all the things I'm supposed to – but I find myself staring at this small, very dependent human, wondering what the hell is wrong with me. It's not a wonder Abbey is always on edge. She can feel my panic leaking from me, soaks it up like a little sponge. I've been trying my best, but it's not enough. I just feel . . . empty.

I grab Liz's hands. 'I want you and Col to take her.'

'What?' Liz reels back. I don't know what I'm thinking. It's only been a year since they lost Chloe, how can I ask this? But it feels like the only solution.

'You love Abbey, and she loves you. I know we've had our differences, but you are amazing parents.' I'm desperate. 'You'll be better for her, don't you see? I'm not a good mother, Liz. I'm broken.'

She's staring at me, dumbfounded. 'You can't be serious. You don't know what you're asking, Grace.'

'Yes, I do.'

'There's no way Daniel—'

I'm almost hysterical as I remind her that Daniel is away more often than he's at home. There's no way he'd be prepared to be a single father. That this is the only way Abbey will have two parents who can raise her properly. I have no idea if that even makes sense. I haven't thought it through. My hands are knotted so tightly together that I feel my knuckles crack.

'I'm scared I'm going to hurt her. She deserves better than this. Better than me.' I'm sobbing now. 'Please, Lizzie.'

A tear slides down her face as she watches me, her mouth tight, her mind racing. Then she pulls me close, wrapping her arms around me.

'Okay. If this is what you need, Grace. I'll talk to Col in the morning.'

An hour later, we're still on the couch, my head in Liz's lap. The tea she made has gone cold on the coffee table. I've simply been staring at the wall. I don't feel panic. I don't feel sad. I'm numb.

A pitiful wail comes from the bedroom. Abbey. I turn my head and look up. Liz has dozed off. Standing slowly, I make my way to the bedroom.

Abbey is sitting up in the middle of the bed, still half asleep and disoriented. Crying in little hiccups. Exhausted, I crawl on to the bed and lie down, putting my arm around her. She flops back on the pillow and curls into me, quietening instantly.

'Shhh, baby,' I say, and she snuggles closer. Her skin is hot against mine. I rest my face on the top of her head and inhale – baby shampoo and calamine lotion, her own particular smell underneath, warm and familiar. And I'm crying again, fat silent tears into her hair and onto the pillow. 'I'm sorry, Abbey. I'm so sorry.'

Pulling her closer, I place my hand flat on her back. I can feel her heart beating, fluttering against my palm. The same heartbeat I carried inside of me, alongside my own. Abbey puts her chubby arm around my neck, tangling her fingers into my hair and holding on tightly. As I breathe her in, I feel a rush of love move through me, like something coming in to land. It centres in my chest, clicking into place – the thing that before now hadn't quite found its seat.

Abbey lets out a sigh and murmurs, 'Mummy.'

I kiss her soft head and whisper, 'It's okay. Mummy's here.'

By the time morning comes, I've changed my mind.

46

jigsaw

Memory is malleable and the truth is never absolute. We reshape remembrances over time, softening or sharpening the edges to suit us. We remember events differently depending on where we were standing at the time. What really happened is ground zero – but each of us orbits it separately.

Liz isn't surprised to see me. All she says is, 'Hi, Grace,' when she opens the door. No defensive fire, no fight. But it's fine – I've got enough for us both.

'How could you tell her?' My eyes are blazing and I'm surprised Liz's head doesn't burst into flames. Being in the wrong usually makes her come out swinging. But she doesn't.

'It wasn't my intention and there was a good reason.' Her composure inflames me even more. 'Come inside and let me expl—'

I stalk past her into the kitchen without letting her finish, leaning on the counter to glare at her. 'There's no good reason, Liz. She was never supposed to know. Can you imagine how that makes a kid feel – to think your mother didn't want you?'

'She's not a kid,' she says, and I can't believe *that's* her comeback. My face says it all and she puts her hands up, acquiescent. 'Grace, please. I know I did the wrong thing.' It throws me. I don't have the manual to operate this dynamic. 'You can keep yelling or you can let me explain. Believe it or not, I was trying to defend you and make Abbey feel better.'

'Well, you failed spec-fucking-tacularly at both things.'

'I'm aware.'

Abbey had visited for lunch a few weeks ago – *she's known for weeks?* – still upset over our argument and needing Liz's shoulder. She was apparently going on about me having some kind of breakdown, that I was being selfish and not thinking about anyone's feelings.

'I couldn't listen to that,' Liz says. 'She was being unfair, and it made me angry. I told her you'd done nothing *but* think about her feelings and that you lied to shield her from Daniel's shitty behaviour. Because you're a good mother.'

I'm taken aback and it dampens my fury – briefly. 'What did she say?'

Liz rubs at her face. 'I don't know what happened; she took it all the wrong way. She was angry you didn't think she was capable of handling the truth. Then she said she wasn't surprised because you didn't think she was capable of handling a baby either. I told her that wasn't true, but she said you would know, because you're the perfect mother or some shit.'

'I've never said I'm perfect.' *This is all my fault.*

'Come off it, Grace. You're like a robot, you always have been.'

'Excuse me?'

Liz folds her arms, unable to help defensiveness creeping in. 'She was crying and scared she's going to be a shit mum. I love her, Grace. I wasn't going to watch her beat herself up for not meeting some perfect standard that's not even true. I told her you're not as perfect as she thinks. That you struggled with being a mother. She refused to believe me and it just came out.'

My eyes narrow. 'You've been waiting for this.'

'What?'

'You've been waiting for the right moment, all these years, to get back at me.'

She's staring at me, stunned. 'Get back at you for what?'

'For changing my mind.' I'm raging now. 'What? It's not enough to constantly remind me of it – going out of your way to show how close you and Abbey are, how much better a job you would have done?'

'What are you talking about?' She looks baffled. 'Why would I want to get back at you? You're her mother. You don't think I was glad for her – for you both?'

'I think you were upset I took her away from you.'

Liz leans forward, her face pained. 'For fuck's sake. Of course I was *sad*. It was a huge thing to agree to after Chloe.' She hesitates. 'I was angry at the reason.'

Now I'm the one confused. 'I don't know what you mean.'

'Cut the bullshit, Grace.' She's twisting and clenching her fingers, the same way I do when I'm tied in knots. It's the first time I've noticed any similarity between us. 'It's obvious, it always has been. You didn't think we could give her a good enough life. We didn't have money or a nice house, we didn't speak all fancy. You thought she'd end up just like me – not finishing school, stuck out west with all the other bogans, popping out a bunch of kids to a bloody diesel fitter. And you think that's a shitty life.'

Her words slice into me, because part of me knows how the view appears from where she sits – even if she's wrong. 'Is that why you think I kept her?' She nods, attempting to hide the hurt and failing, and my anger tangles with the echo of old remorse. The feelings fight for space behind my ribs until the anger retreats and

I finally sit down. 'I wouldn't have asked you if I didn't think you'd give her a good life.' My voice breaks unexpectedly. *It's okay, you can say it.* 'If anything, I was jealous. You were so good at being a mum – and I couldn't get a single thing right. But I changed my mind because I realised I was in love with my daughter and I wanted to try. I told you that.'

'I didn't believe you.'

'I couldn't do it, Liz. Even if I stuffed everything up, I couldn't give her away. It had nothing to do with you.'

Confusion washes over her, and she blinks at me, small and uncertain. 'Then why did you stop coming around? You stopped visiting unless you had to. You barely called. It was like you wanted to get away from us – away from me.'

I'm unsurprised we're still on opposite sides of the glass. It's been a lifetime since we've been shoulder to shoulder. Probably because it's been decades since we've been honest about how we really feel. We've been too busy playing defence, trying desperately to keep the other from scoring.

'That wasn't why, Liz.' I study the floor to avoid looking at her. 'I didn't want any of you knowing I was still struggling. I *was* embarrassed, but not of you. I won't apologise for wanting to change my life. You can't blame me for making sure Abbey grew up differently to us.' She's chewing her lip, listening. 'But then – when things got better for me – every time I saw you, I felt like I'd done something wrong simply by existing. I was some "snotty rich aunt" to make fun of – and if I got upset or offended, I was making a drama. Everything I did was taken the wrong way. Why wouldn't I stop visiting?'

Liz sighs. 'Grace, has it ever occurred to you that *I* was jealous? I just wanted them to see me. You might not have been around much, but trust me, you were there – ‘*Grace this, Grace that. Grace’s big house, Grace’s church, Grace’s beautiful daughter, hasn’t Grace made something of her life*’. Whenever you visited, it was like the bloody Queen was coming.’

‘I didn’t realise you felt that way. I’m sorry.’

‘They were always proud of you – you know that.’

I stare at her, puzzled. ‘See that’s the thing, I don’t. They never told me they were proud of me after I left home. Dad told me the church was rubbish, they’d never call or come to the house. I had no idea they even knew what was going on in my life.’

Liz’s face loses any last trace of antagonism. ‘You’re kidding.’

‘No.’

We study each other, not saying anything. Finally seeing each other, understanding our unique orbits.

‘Well, our parents fucked us up good and proper, didn’t they?’

‘I don’t think they meant to, Grace. I mean who does? One day you’re a kid, the next you’re a parent, and nobody gives you an instruction book.’

‘How do you do that?’

‘Do what?’

‘Forgive them. Dad was so awful to you, for so long and for no reason.’

‘Honestly, it took me a while,’ she says, ‘but Dad was broken. I think he felt like a failure, and he took it out on me, on Mum, on you – even though he loved us. I realised a long time ago that it wasn’t my fault.’ Liz softens. ‘It wasn’t your fault either. How could it have been? You were perfect.’

‘It wasn’t enough though.’

She looks confused. ‘What do you mean?’

‘You always thought I was trying to make out that I was better than you. But I knew if Dad was distracted, if he was *pleased*, he left you and Mum alone.'

It takes her a few long seconds, but finally she twigs. 'Oh, Grace.' She grabs my hand back. 'It wasn't your responsibility to protect us. You were a kid.' I pull my hand away to scrub at my face and another realisation hits Liz. 'That's why you're the way you are with Mum. Because it should have been her responsibility.'

'Did you know she was going to leave him?' I say. 'She told me, that day you got angry at me.'

'Her memories are all mixed up, Grace. You can't—'

'No, she knew what she was saying. She didn't know who I was, but she said she tried – twice. I've been wracking my brains, trying to figure it out.' I lean forward. 'Do you remember that whole weird Coffs Harbour thing?'

Liz thinks for a few seconds then gasps, the pieces falling into place. 'You made her turn around to get your homework.'

I nod at her and cover my mouth, fighting tears. 'I can't help wondering how different things could have been if I hadn't cared so much about every little thing.'

She squeezes my hand. 'When do you think the second time was?'

'I think it was that horrible day at Bondi, when Dad fell off the rocks.'

Confusion patterns her face. 'But we were with him that day.'

'I know.' I will her to catch on, so I don't have to spell it out. 'But once we got home, I went to Mum's room, and she was unpacking a suitcase.'

'That could mean anything.'

'No. Mum said something else to me the other day.' I know the meaning of Mum's words on the surface. *I stayed.* It's the context that cuts and now I know what Abbey is feeling. 'She said, "I couldn't leave them". Not *him,* Liz. *Them.*'

I watch her knit it together in her head. *Mum was going to leave us.* We sit silently, letting it sink in.

'We can't blame her for wanting to run, Grace. We both did, at one time or another. But in the end she couldn't, because she loved us.'

I smile at her. *Exactly.*

She studies me. 'You know, it might be hard for you to believe, but me being close to Abbey has never been about you. I love my niece, and she loves me back. It's that simple. I think you're seeing something different because you still feel guilty.' She takes my hand again. 'It's time you put it down. You're nearly fifty, you're gonna hurt your back.'

I laugh and hiccup at the same time. 'Shut up.'

'Let it go, Grace. I have, and so will Abbey.' I nod and squeeze her hand. 'Right,' she says. 'Where to from here? What do you need?'

'No idea, Lizzie. I still don't know what the hell I'm doing.'

She stands and surprises me by patting my cheek, like Mum used to. 'It's called life, love. None of us know what the bloody hell we're doing.' My little sister wraps her arms around me and I cling to her, the way she clung to me on the rocks all those years ago.

Thank God, I'm not the only one.

47

stuck on you

The street is dark as I grab the chalkboard stands from out front of The Hip Joint. If anybody had told me months ago when I walked into this bar for the first time that I'd come to love working here, I wouldn't have believed them. But it's been good for me. And it's been a needed distraction this past week.

I've tried giving Abbey space, but I'm desperate to make sure she's okay, to try explaining. She refuses to pick up my calls and won't call back, despite leaving numerous messages. All I can do is wait.

Susie's on my mind constantly. As is Mum. I've been replaying her words in my head over and over. Holding on to resentment has created such distance between us. But knowing that she tried to leave, something's shifted. She might not have managed to protect us, but what if she was doing the best she could – like I have been?

Travis is wiping the bar down as I head inside and grab the last few glasses from the tables. I watch him for a moment, smiling. It's startling how people can come into your life so unexpectedly and end up being such an integral part of it. Who'd have thought that Travis, with his flashy tequila pouring skills and cheeky flirtation, would have provided me such stability – a rock to cling to while

I was buffeted by the storm – without expecting anything in return. He looks up and grins, catching me staring.

'What? Have I got something on my face?'

'No.' I put the glasses down and lean on the bar. 'Just thinking . . . I want you to know how much I've enjoyed working here.'

'Uh-oh. That sounds like there's a "but" coming. Is this your way of telling me you're breaking up with us?'

I laugh. 'Not at all. Simply being appreciative. I'm not sure you realise what this has meant to me – the job, the flat. You're a good friend, Travis.' Leaning across the bar, I pull him into a hug. He squeezes me and when I stand back, he's blushing.

'Don't be silly. I mean, I didn't expect to write-off so much beer in the beginning.' He winks. 'But you're pretty good company, so I think I can let it slide.'

'You're welcome.'

Travis tosses his dishcloth over his shoulder. 'I'm nearly done here. Do you want to celebrate your not-resigning with a snack? Connor had the pickles restocked today—'

'Sorry,' I shake my head. 'Raincheck. I'm popping upstairs to grab some supplies, then I'm heading out. There's someone I need to see – and I need to make a good impression.'

Susie opens the door and looks at me like I've got two heads. To be fair, she's not expecting me, and I am wearing a party hat. I'm also holding a bunch of coloured balloons in one hand and two enormous shopping bags in the other. I blow hard on the party horn I'm gripping between my teeth. The paper uncurls with a wheeze and a sad little *parp*, flies out of my mouth and lands at her feet, trailing saliva.

'Are you on drugs again?'

'Nope. No drugs.' Her expression says she doesn't believe me. 'We're having a party.'

She pulls her dressing gown around herself, looking tired and drawn. 'Not in the mood for a party, funnily enough.' I maintain my celebration face even though my stomach is weighed down by nerves – and potential stupidity. This could be the perfect medicine, or it could fall completely flat.

'You will be for this one.' I hand her a foil balloon that says '*Bon Voyage*'. 'It's a going away party for your boobs.' I hold my breath, smiling so wide that my top lip sticks to my teeth. She doesn't say anything, but I've seen those eyes before. She's trying to decide whether to kick me. 'You know – *Ta-ta to your ta-tahs*,' I add before stepping back, out of reach of her feet. Finally, she blinks at me.

'You're a fucking idiot.' Then she laughs. 'I bloody love you.'

I start unloading a bag onto her coffee table. 'I didn't know what treatment you might be on, so this wine is alcohol-free.' I present a bag of broccoli chips and some hummus. 'And these are organic. Mmm, yummy.' She doesn't look impressed.

'What are you doing?'

'I'm being thoughtful. It's what friends do.'

'If you were my friend, you wouldn't have brought that shit. Grape juice is not wine, mate – and what the fuck are broccoli chips?' She gags.

'I thought you might say that. Which is why—' I reach back into the bag, '—I also brought these, just in case.' I plonk a bottle of vodka, real potato chips and a huge block of chocolate on the table.

'That's more like it.'

I pour us both a vodka and Susie flops on the floor next to me. I'm not sure what to ask. I don't want to upset her but it's not like we can pretend it's not happening.

'So, when's the, uh—' I circle my hand in front of my chest, '—procedure?'

'You can say "chopping my tits off". It's what they're doing.' She points at her left boob. 'I've only got it in this one but they reckon I'll get it in the other one too. I wouldn't want to be lopsided, so it's all good.' She takes a big swig of her drink. I recognise the bravado for what it is and raise my eyebrows. 'Fine,' she says. 'Next Friday. Probably be in there for a couple of days.'

'I'll be there.'

'You don't need—'

'I'm not taking no for an answer.' She gives in more easily than usual. 'You're just going to have to deal with it, because I'm never going to let you down again.'

'That's a big call. I mean—' She holds up the broccoli chips and I laugh.

'I'm serious. I'm not letting you go through this alone. Okay?' My chin wobbles and she pats my hand.

'Yeah, yeah. I get it, *Ride or die, bitch.* It's getting soppy now.' She sits back and points at the other bag. 'Are you going to tell me what all that is?'

'I thought you'd never ask.' With a flourish, I pull out two sheets of white cardboard and several small pots of paint. 'You know how in kindergarten they get kids to make handprints? We're doing that, but with your boobs. I'll help you paint them – we'll do a pretty pattern or something – and I'll do it too. It's for posterity.'

'How does making titty prints bring us money?'

'Not prosperity. *Posterity.* To remember them by.'

'That sex party made you kinky, didn't it?'

I waggle my eyebrows, 'You have no idea. Come on then – get 'em out.'

We strip off our tops and open the paint pots. Susie sits up straight, shoulders back and looking down at herself, while I paint swirls on her skin in red and blue and yellow. It's hilarious and poignant and powerful, and I'm reminded that my friend, with all her jagged edges and the big heart she keeps tucked away for special occasions, is truly beautiful.

Susie paints my boobs blue, with white angel wings on the left one, and red devil horns on the right. I look down at them, confused.

'It's to remind you that you're not just one thing. You contain multitudes.'

I bow, laughing. 'Thanks, sensei.'

By the time we're both done, the paint sticky on our skin, Susie's more excited.

'What now?'

I hadn't thought about the mechanics. I hand her a sheet of cardboard. 'Maybe we should smoosh it against ourselves?'

'So like, smoosh and press?'

'I guess? I've never done titty-prints before, I'm winging it.'

'I think we'll get a better print if we put it on the floor and kind of – *Ooof*.' She mimes flopping on her belly. 'But you're the artist.'

It could work.

We lay the cardboard down and hover over it on our hands and knees. On the count of three, we drop with a wet splat and dissolve into hysterics. Susie peels herself off the floor first and starts wheezing.

'They look like cauliflowers.' The colours have merged and formed one big, funny-shaped glob. It looks like a lopsided eight. I clamber up and look at mine.

'Speak for yourself,' I say, still laughing. 'Mine look very nice.'

Susie side-eyes me. 'Still gotta win everything, huh?'

'Nah.' I pick up my titty-print and proudly show it to her. 'I can't be bothered hating myself anymore. Too much hard work, mate.'

She sits back on the floor and goes quiet. Her eyes don't leave the cardboard. 'I'm really fucking scared, Grace.'

I drop my print and shuffle over on my knees, wrapping my arms around her from behind. 'I know. But you're not alone, okay?' She grips my arm with one hand, squeezing it tightly and we stay like that for few moments. Then she pats me.

'It's gettin' weird now. Get your tits off my back.'

I peel myself off. Her naked back is now plastered with two amorphous blobs of paint. I start laughing. 'Sorry, I think you're stuck with them.'

She snorts and twists her head to look at me. 'Babe, when are you going to accept it. We're stuck with each other.'

I wouldn't have it any other way.

48

beautiful little things

If I drew a timeline of my life, most of my memories of Mum would be clustered together along the first half. I'm sure it's similar for most people. You spend your childhood under your parents' wings and when you finally leave the nest, a distance occurs. Inevitable but natural. Independence is how a parent knows they've done a good job.

But this is different. The years since Abbey was born are dotted with only sporadic memories. Birthdays. Christmases. Funerals. Time spent for the sake of it was sparing. I had my reasons, but with time proving finite, I'm no longer sure they were good enough and I'm regretting staying away.

I touch Mum's arm gently, not wanting to startle her. She's sitting in the communal lounge near a bookcase, a blanket over her legs, watching the other residents – some playing cards, others chatting over tea.

Mum looks up, questioning. 'Yes, love?' *She doesn't recognise me.* I should be used to it by now, but I'm not. I feel a pang, deep in my chest, each time it happens.

'I thought you might like some company,' I say, and she blinks at me, trying to work out if she knows me, but the thought drifts quickly. She says that would be nice, and I sit opposite her. She watches me with vague curiosity, serene and weightless.

I think about how the way our lives play out ends up shaping who we become. We start life like a single Lego brick, simple and unbroken. But over a lifetime, our memories click together and stack up – the things we've done, had done to us, the choices we've made – building a person, complex and unique and unavoidably breakable.

Reaching into my bag, I pull out my art supplies. 'Would you mind if I drew a picture of you?' She asks if I'm an artist and I tell her I am.

'Why do you want to draw me?'

'Because you're beautiful.' She's taken aback but doesn't touch her hair or ask how she looks. I imagine it's because all that pressure and pretence has fallen away along with the rest. I take a pencil and begin drawing.

I focus on what's in front of me, the obvious surface. I want to get this right, but I can't help the niggle in the back of my mind, the fear that ruined my drawings of Abbey, stopping me from visualising the reality of her.

Breathe out.

She's empty of memories, but as I trace the parts of my mother, my own recollections fill the gaps between the lines. They're not all good, but they're truthful. I outline her eyes and think of all the times she looked at me with love *and* with disapproval. I remember watching her put on mascara, fascinated by the way she'd blink against the brush, her mouth open like an 'O'. I see her eyes bruised, too many times.

I draw the lines of her mouth and see her laughing when me and Lizzie would do something silly or when Dad would tell a terrible joke. Smiling down at Abbey when she was born. Spitting bitter words because she'd forgotten how to be happy. Her hands make me think of every time she brushed my hair. I see her knuckles, grazed bloody from weeding the concrete path in front of our house because, if it looked perfect outside, nobody would know the inside wasn't.

I trace the lines of the arms that carried me, arms she threw up in front of her face to deflect Dad's fists. The shoulders we cried on and that carried all that weight for years. As I draw the curve of her lap, I see Lizzie perched on it for a story and me at her feet.

As my picture takes form, I finally understand why the people in my art class all saw something different. It's right in front of me, if I choose to see it – strength, weakness, fear and sadness, and every little moment of joy. I'm seeing her properly for the first time in my life and she's not only my mother. She's a woman just like me.

Movement catches my eye across the room and I look up to see Liz standing near the door, watching us. She's crying. I put my pencil down and move to stand, but Liz stops me with a hand. Then she nods, smiles and walks away. Leaving me with Mum.

If our memories make up who we are, who is our mother now? Unburdened by her stack of bricks, I wonder if the reason Mum looks so peaceful is because she's returned to her original shape – simple, unbroken. I'm not sure it's worth the cost of losing the good along with the bad – because there *was* good. But maybe it is.

I wish I could forget some things. So many memories keep us stuck. But we can't forget intentionally. All we can do is try to let them go. The memories she never shared are lost to time. But the rest, we'll hold for her – me, Liz, Abbey, Liz's boys. We can remember and remember and remember. And I can choose which of mine I let go of, before it's too late.

Mum gazes towards the window as I fill in the shadows and smudge the hard lines, softening her story. She starts humming and I recognise the tune, she used to sing it to me and Liz sometimes. 'Que Sera, Sera' by Doris Day. I sing quietly along with her as I finish drawing. When I look up, she's smiling delightedly. She sings too, looking at me the way she did as we drifted off to sleep, and I choke up. How does she remember these words and nothing else? Although, after the road trip home with Susie, I don't know why I'm surprised that music lingers long after all else is forgotten, etched so deeply it transcends memory. Anchoring us to all the things we feel, that we've ever felt.

I wipe my eyes, dust my sketch pad off and kneel beside Mum to show her. Her fingers flutter to her mouth, then she touches the paper. 'Grace, love, you're so talented.' I jolt at my name and look up into her face. 'I'm so proud of you.' The recognition fades in front of my eyes, a momentary snatch of clarity. But it's enough.

I lay my head on her lap, tears streaming, and Mum's hand rests on my head. She strokes my hair and I realise I don't need to forgive her. She's my mother and she's perfectly imperfect. She did her best, just like I have, and there's nothing left to forgive. I have to let go, not only of the past but of my grip on the future. *Whatever will be, will be.*

Mum hums again and my mind wanders. I think about that playlist, how it felt like it was telling the story of my life and wonder what Mum's would be now, with so much forgotten. I think about Susie and what songs might give her strength, unable to bear the thought of losing her along with Mum. I remember the songs Dad loved and the story he wanted for himself but didn't get. As for me and Liz – our stories might be similar but we've been discordant for most of our lives. Maybe it's not too late to find the harmony. My thoughts turn to Abbey. What songs will she teach her daughter? Will I sing my granddaughter to sleep sometimes, the way Mum did?

My brain switches tracks and the opening bars of 'We Are Family' play in my head. I'm flooded with warmth and a sudden revelation. I've been trying so hard to separate myself from who and what I am to other people. But I realise now, it's an impossible extrication.

After Mum dies, she'll live solely in the way we remember her, in the memories we carry. One day – when I too am gone – all that will be left is who I was to the people who loved me. Mother, daughter, sister, friend. The memories of me. The things I did and said, the things I gave and took. When I'm gone, nobody will know or care who *I* thought I was – it's the imprint I've left that matters. It doesn't mean I shouldn't be my own person, keep things for myself. I can know and nurture the little red Lego brick of me. But you can't build anything with a single brick.

49

bloom

I wake in the same position I fell asleep in, my bedcovers barely disturbed. I'd slept like I'd been shot with a tranquilizer gun, but I'm anything but sedated. I'm more clear-headed and relaxed than I've been in months. I even sing in the shower, which is weird, but I blame it on the earworm from last night because driving home from seeing Mum, the DJ on KISS FM clearly had a thing for Yazz. *Maybe you're happy, Grace?* But how can I be when I've hurt Abbey, and when Mum's so sick? I reach automatically for guilt, then stop myself. *You're allowed to feel good.*

I towel off, humming 'The Only Way Is Up' and study my list. It's still pinned to the bathroom door, but I haven't touched it since camping. It's given me so much, but it's also taken. Maybe that's the point, because it's taught me to stand my ground but also shown me how to let go.

I count up the things I've ticked off – not even forty – and an invisible bird lands on my shoulder chirping, '*that's good enough*'. I don't argue because I already know – I'm done with the list. Letting go has to mean abandoning my quest for perfection. I might not have hit my target, but I've got what I needed. It's time to wrap it up. I can still try new things – but I don't need to try so hard anymore. I don't need the gold stars.

I write '*Let it all go*' in the space at the bottom, tick it off and yank the sheet of cardboard down. As I'm about to slide it under my bed, I remember something that I missed. I re-scan the list and there it is, sitting neglected among all the gold stars. *Maybe you can do one more thing.*

Elemental Ink, a few streets away from the flat, is all white walls, exposed brick and shiny metal surfaces. The tattoo artists' work revolves on an oversized flat screen and the counters are loaded with thick design books. A petite and heavily tattooed Japanese woman sits behind a computer at reception.

When I ask her if they take walk-in appointments, she looks me up and down as though I'm the last person who would simply 'walk in'. Maybe I look too boring for a tattoo. What if being cool and interesting is a pre-requisite for an appointment? *That makes no sense – tattoos are supposed to make you cool and interesting.* I wonder if I should tell her I've done molly and been to a rave *and* a sex party.

She saves me the trouble.

'Danik has space today, but it depends what you want.' Her voice is lacklustre and nasal. 'If you're looking for something new school, watercolour or blackwork, they're not his thing. If you want realistic or portrait, you'll need to book and come back. Neo-traditional is fine, if it's not too big. Minimalist, you're good to go.'

I show her the design I'd drawn earlier, certain the simple linework qualifies as minimalist. Tattoo terms can't be that different to art, right? I don't want to have to come back because I know I'll chicken out. It's now or never.

'Yeah, that's easy. Where are you thinking?'

I run my hand between my breasts. 'Uh, here? What do you think?'

'Sure. It'll look sick.' She hands me a consent form and takes my drawing out to the studio area, so the mysterious Danik can prep the design.

I wait nervously for almost forty-five minutes before a man emerges from the studio in a tight singlet, his entire arm encased in plastic wrap. He looks pale as he proudly shows the receptionist. All I can see is a riot of colour and traces of blood – but she looks impressed. I'm less and less sure about this whole thing. Maybe I should—

'Grace?' *Too late.*

Danik is six foot five and in his forties, with a hipster beard, a thick eastern European accent and stilted English. His hands are huge. He looks like he'd be more at home chopping down trees. He ushers me into the studio and sits me down in the chair. A stencil of my design sits on a metal tray nearby.

'You draw this?' he asks, and I nod. 'It is good. Very nice. You want it here?' He points vaguely at my chest. 'Also very good. Okay!' He makes a whistle sound and circles his finger.

I gawk at him then the penny drops. 'Oh, right.' I strip down to my bra then hesitate. Do I sit here topless? I'm not particularly self-conscious but this is different. It's intimate – especially this design – and I feel exposed and vulnerable. But it's not like he can tattoo around my bra. I put my hands on my breasts, uncertain. He clicks immediately.

'You are shy? No problem. I give you sticker.' He holds up two round promotional stickers with the studio logo on them. 'You do this—' He mimes attaching them to his nipples and pops his lips.

I guess they'll do.

Stickers firmly in place, Danik tilts me back in the chair then puts on fresh gloves before prepping my skin and his tattoo gun.

'Is this going to hurt?'

'Of course. But you are tough, yes?' I'm not sure what the correct answer is, but I figure if I can survive the last five and a half months, I can get through this.

The gun buzzes into life and the needle makes contact. It vibrates into my skin and I think, '*that's not so bad*'. Then it bites. I breathe slowly and try to focus on the ceiling.

My new tattoo is a lotus flower with an Unalome curling from the centre. I'd spent hours on Google, trying to find a perfect way to represent where I've come from, where I'm going. The lotus blooms from dark and muddy waters and Buddhists say it represents the potential of life. The Unalome is a single line, spiralling upwards, its twists signifying hardships and lessons, the line straightening as we become our authentic selves. At the top are three little dots for eventual enlightenment – the final destination. I'd remembered what Susie told me about my heart chakra, in the centre of my chest. *Love and compassion, for myself and others.* It was the perfect place.

Gradually, the sharp vibration becomes a dull burn. Danik stops to reload the needle with ink and wipe the excess from my skin. As he starts again, I look down in fascination, watching the delicate black lines taking shape. It's part of me forever now – indelible. Exhilaration floods my body and my skin hums as it hits me. *This* is where divinity truly resides – in our choices, in living. It's in expansion and experience, in creating and letting go. It's in the sublime and the mundane, the special and the ordinary. It's in allowing yourself to *be.* To really live.

Danik has finished the twisty bit of the Unalome and started the straight line that's taking me home to myself when my phone rings.

It's Liz and I ignore it – I can call her back later. She calls a second time, but Danik is engrossed and I don't want to interrupt him. When my phone rings a third time, I know something's not right.

'I'm sorry, I have to take this. It might be an emergency.'

He sits back, unfazed. 'It is no problem.'

I answer the phone, worried. 'What's wrong? Is Mum alright?'

'Mum's fine,' Liz says. 'Abbey's in labour and Tobias is stuck in Dubai.'

I bolt upright in the chair. 'But she's not due for two weeks.'

'What can I say – unborn babies aren't great with calendars. And before you say anything, she only called me first because of how she left things with you.' She's choosing her words carefully. 'She wasn't sure you'd come, with everything that was said.'

My heart cracks open. 'Does Abbey actually think I'd stay away when she's giving birth, because she was hurt and angry at me?' *How did things end up such a mess?*

'I guess you can talk to her about it at the hospital, It's moving fast apparently – her waters broke before she called the ambulance to take her in – so you should probably hurry.' Liz says. 'Keep me posted, okay?'

'You're not coming?'

'I don't think I should, Grace.'

'Rubbish. We both need you there. I'll see you at the hospital.' I hang up before she can argue. 'I'm sorry,' I say to Danik. 'My daughter's having a baby. I have to go.'

'But your tattoo. It is not finished.'

I hop off the chair, yank the stickers off my boobs, pull my t-shirt on and stuff my bra in my pocket.

'It's okay, Danik – neither am I.'

50

amazing grace

It's never too late to be what you might have been

– George Eliot

I sprint the two blocks to my flat and race upstairs to grab my handbag, car keys and spare clothes, in case I need to stay with Abbey. I'm halfway out the door when a thought strikes. I dart back inside, grab a pen, and drag the Fuck-it List from under the bed. I write '*Become a grandmother*' in huge letters at the bottom. Sticking a gold star next to it, I smile with satisfaction, then fly out the door.

The GPS says twenty-two minutes, but it must be on drugs. It's not peak hour but the traffic is already sluggish, and it takes me forty minutes just to reach the bridge.

'Come on, come on.' The cars in front of me are moving at a snail's pace and I bang the steering wheel. I cannot let Abbey down. Not this time. *Hello, God? So, I know we've had our differences, and I know I'm being a problem child questioning everything – but the thing is, I need you right now and I promise I'll figure it all out and be less selfish, if you'll—*

The car in front of me swings out and around a set of hazard lights and I see a car that's rear-ended another. As soon as I pass them, the traffic opens up. I press my foot down on the accelerator with relief. *No need for divine intervention after all.*

Ten minutes later, I'm running into the maternity unit at North Shore Private Hospital and looking for the birthing suites. I follow the receptionist's directions and round the corner to come face-to-face with Daniel, sitting outside Abbey's room.

'Tell me I made it.'

'You made it,' he says, as I hear a low moan from inside.

'Why aren't you in there? What are you thinking, leaving her alone?'

'She doesn't want me. She's still angry, and I get it. Anyway, she's not alone.'

I head inside. Abbey's leaning on the bed, circling her hips. Liz is on the other side, holding her hand. I stop, surprised. 'How did you get here before me? You live an hour away.'

Liz looks up. 'I was at DFO at Homebush, Col needed new boots and won't let me pay full price.' She lets go of Abbey's hand. 'I'll be right outside sweetheart, I'm going to leave you with your Mum, okay? You've got this.' Abbey hasn't looked up but she nods, her breathing heavy.

'You don't have to wait outside,' I say to Liz, and she grabs me in a hug.

'Yes, I do.' She kisses my cheek. 'I love you, Grace. You be with your girl.'

I dump my handbag and take Abbey's hand. 'How are you doing, honey?' She looks up as a contraction starts and any answer is lost as she squeezes my hand and exhales, lengthy and guttural, rocking from side to side.

'That's it, Abbey.' The midwife bustles in and gives me a quick smile. 'You're doing great.' The contraction subsides and Abbey's grip on my fingers relaxes. She takes a few long, deep breaths as I stroke her hand.

'I'm glad you're here,' she says. 'I'm so sorry, Mum. I shouldn't have gotten so mad—'

'Shh. It's not important. You need to focus on getting my granddaughter born.'

Abbey looks up at me again, through a curtain of sweaty hair, and gives me a small, scared smile. 'Okay.'

Another contraction hits within minutes and this time Abbey doesn't moan, she cries out. The midwife moves around the bed. 'That's only a couple of minutes apart. Do you feel like you need to push?' Abbey nods and says she doesn't think she can stand. I help the midwife get her onto the bed. She examines Abbey quickly. 'You're fully dilated Abbey. On your next contraction, I want you to bear down, alright?'

I sit at the side of the bed clutching her hand and, in this moment, I am only mother. I know it's not all I am, but it's who I need to be right now. Maybe that's the secret, knowing which version of yourself you need to be for the people you love at any given moment. When the next contraction hits, Abbey tucks her chin and pushes, crushing my fingers. Several contractions later, she cries out again, saying it's all in her back.

'Abbey, sweetheart,' I say, trying to be useful. 'I don't know if this helps, but when I was in labour with you and it was all in my back, I had to get up on my knees.'

She doesn't look at me. 'I'm not being rude, Mum,' she growls, 'but I really don't give a fucking shit.' She sounds like she's possessed and it's the politest abuse I've ever taken. I shut my mouth and try not to laugh as the midwife shoots me a look, stifling her own smile.

An hour passes. Abbey's still pushing, her screams splitting the air. She flops back exhausted and crying in between. I keep repeating, 'You're doing so well, you're doing so well'. It feels redundant but I don't know what else to say. I hate seeing her in this much pain when I can't do anything. I'm standing out of her eyeline so she doesn't see me crying.

'I can't do it,' she gasps, turning her head to look up at me and it breaks my heart.

'Yes, you can, Abbey. You can do anything,' I say. 'Except be an Olympic gymnast, it's probably too late for that.' I don't know why I'm trying to be funny, but Abbey laughs despite herself, through gritted teeth. It turns into a cry as she bears down again. A second midwife has joined the other and she says the baby is crowning.

Another push and her head is almost out, but two pushes later she hasn't progressed. 'Abbey.' The first midwife's tone changes and my stomach drops. 'Your baby's shoulders are stuck. We're going to need to get you in a different position to help her out, okay?' She explains that they'll push Abbey's knees to her chest to shift her pelvis. The second midwife bustles me out of the way so they're on either side of her. I stand back, helpless, as Abbey's hand reaches out to me, grasping air for a few seconds before the final contraction takes her over.

The midwives force her knees up and back and tell her to push. One of them reaches inside her to free the baby. Abbey sounds like she's being torn in half and time slows down. Then it catches up in a rush and the baby is out and all I can hear is Abbey's ragged breathing. Her head is on the pillow, eyes closed. I'm not sure what's happening but shouldn't the baby have cried by now? The midwife is holding her across her palm, purple and chest down. Rubbing her back gently but firmly saying, 'Come on, sweetheart, come on,' and I'm frozen. I can't breathe. I can't do anything, except—

Please, whoever is up there. Let her be okay. This time it's not flippant or making excuses. This time – as the seconds stretch – I'm reaching out into the universe and desperately hoping somebody or some*thing* is listening. Praying for divine intervention. *Please.*

Finally, a tiny mewl from the baby. Then another. Relief washes over me as the cry gathers strength and the midwife plops her on Abbey's chest. I watch my little girl open her eyes and reach up to hold her own and I realise I'm crying and whispering under my breath.

Thank you. Thank you. Thank you.

An hour later, Abbey and the baby have been cleaned up and checked over. Liz has paid a quick visit and already left so Abbey can rest. As she departed, she'd given me a teary hug and said, 'Congratulations, whatever you're going to be called.' Which is her way of saying whatever I choose is all good with her. Daniel still paces outside, uncertain and not wanting to intrude. I feel kind of bad for him, but I'm also happy to keep my girls to myself for a little longer. Abbey is sitting up, cradling her daughter in her arms, as I sit on the edge of the bed.

'Do we have a name?'

Abbey smiles. 'Stella. And her middle name is Joy – for Nanna.' *It's perfect. She's perfect.* The lump in my throat makes it hard to speak but I lean over and touch my granddaughter's tiny hand. I don't know what I was so afraid of.

'Hi, Stella.' As I look down into her face, she's sucking on her bottom lip, and I see Abbey in her already. Which means I also see myself, and I see Mum.

I hope Mum gets to see Stella, in a moment of clarity, to know she won't only be carried in our memories when she's gone. She'll live on through me, through her granddaughter and now her great-granddaughter. I think that's what faith must be, in knowing that we continue. Because it's not only our multitudes that we contain within us. As women, we belong to a far bigger set of wooden dolls.

When we carry our daughters, we carry our granddaughters too. And when our daughters carry their own daughters, the granddaughters they might one day have are already waiting. The potential of all the different versions of ourselves is already seeded, like a trail of tiny stars, reflecting who we could be, who we will be, in a hundred different ways. Links of a chain, overlapping three by three. Mum carried Abbey unknowingly, when she carried me. My grandmother carried me along with my mother, years before that. And I carried Stella, along with Abbey. Three little dots. I was already her grandmother before I knew it.

Abbey grabs my hand. 'Can I say sorry now, Mum?'

'There's no need, Abbey. I'm the one who should be sorry, and I owe you an explanation.' She looks up at me and she's my baby, and it seems impossible that she's holding her own. 'I hope you know I love you. So much. I was young and scared and I thought I couldn't be the mother you needed. It was a moment of panic, that's all. I could never be without you. Ever.'

She smiles at me. 'I figured that much out. I think I just needed to process it on my own. I've been scared too, so I get it. And I know it's all connected – why the idea of being a grandmother freaked you out so much.'

'Well, aren't you a smart cookie.' I lean down and kiss her head, the way I did when she was little. 'I am *so* sorry I haven't been there for you. I was so scared of history repeating, but you're not me, you're your own person. I wish I could rewind the clock.'

'It's okay, Mum. Honestly. You're here now.'

She's right. And that's all that matters.

'Can I say something, though?' I pause. 'Being a mother is complicated, because you don't stop being a person in your own right. But that's what's you're expected to do – sacrifice yourself completely.' I squeeze her hand. 'But promise me you won't do that. Hold onto yourself, don't be afraid to make mistakes, you'll be a better mother than I was if you do.'

'You've been an amazing mother, what are you talking about? I know you haven't always found it easy, Mum. Believe it or not, I do see you. I love you . . . even if you have been messy and weird.'

My heart squeezes, hearing her say it out loud. 'Speaking of messy and weird, you probably should let your Dad in to see you.'

'Fine, but he's been a dick.'

'Abbey!' I laugh despite myself. 'He might be a dick, but he loves you.' Abbey chews her lip, looking away and fussing with Stella's blanket.

'Mum? Do you really think I can do this?'

'Of course you can.'

'What if I can't? If you found it hard—'

I take a breath as I look at my daughter's face, flushed with exhaustion and elation and shadowed by the fear of what's ahead. I look down at the scrunched face of my granddaughter, who has just come flopping and protesting into being – and honestly, I've never related to anything more in my life – and I smile. I push Abbey's hair back from her forehead.

'Don't worry, Abs. It'll all be okay. And even if it's not, you'll get through it.'

'Are you sure?' she asks in a small voice, and I laugh.

'I'm living proof. Maybe once you and Stella are settled, we can get away somewhere for a while, the three of us? Maybe Auntie Liz can come too, even Susie – like a girl's trip.'

'That sounds lovely, Mum.' Abbey smiles up at me. 'Where will we go?'

I'm still holding her hand and I squeeze it tightly.

'I hear Coffs Harbour is nice.'

Daniel is standing outside the nursery window when I come back with coffee. I watch him from a distance. He seems older somehow. They're monitoring Stella closely; there are no further complications, but her birth was considered traumatic. *Aren't they all?* None of us come into this world quietly and we spend the rest of our lives trying to find peace. It pains me that her first experience is trauma, but I'm certain being cocooned by love from all sides will prevent it from imprinting.

Abbey didn't want them to take her. I assured her it was best and that she should take the opportunity to rest. I didn't want to leave her. I wanted to keep holding her hand, the same way I did when she learned to ride her bike. Afraid to let go in case she fell. But I know I have to now because, if she doesn't fall sometimes, she won't learn to get back up.

I join Daniel at the window and hold out his coffee. He starts and I wonder what he was thinking about. We stand in silence watching Stella until it's uncomfortable.

'What a little miracle, hey, Grandma,' he says finally. 'Despite *us*, we did a good job with our girl, didn't we? Shame Tobias isn't here – you know, to smoke the old cigar, father to father.'

I side-eye him. There's so much I could say to that, but I don't have the energy or the inclination to be combative. The fury and the hurt has dissolved into mild annoyance and an odd affection – the kind that has you rolling your eyes but you're not really that mad. The realisation surprises me. I'm not sure I *like* him, but I don't hate him and that's something.

Five months ago, I couldn't have imagined feeling this way, but everything has changed, including me. So much has happened that might not have if Daniel hadn't left me. I wouldn't have found Susie again, meaning I wouldn't be by her side through the battle ahead. It's unlikely me and Liz would have been open with each other, or that I'd have finally reached a place where I understood Mum and Dad.

I might never have picked up a sketch pad. I would never have met Travis, or done any of the crazy, awful, beautiful things on my list. I wouldn't have even *had* the list. If none of those things had happened, I might never have been truly honest with Abbey, which has meant we have a chance to be closer than we've ever been. It's the greatest gift out of all of this.

I'd thought everything crashing down around me meant my life was over. But it was the opposite. The walls crashed down to open it up – to make space. That ending was the beginning of the rest of my life.

I can't help wondering, if Daniel hadn't cheated and left, how much longer I would have stayed, pretending everything was fine – that I was fine? Probably until the end. I would have lived out my life without learning about myself – about my body, my heart, my strengths, and the broken parts I'm on my way to putting back together. I would have told myself I was complete when I wasn't. That's the real tragedy.

How can I stay mad at Daniel when my life has changed so profoundly? Besides, it's not like I'm ever getting rid of him, especially not now. I turn to him and bump my coffee against his. 'She's a miracle indeed.' I impulsively kiss him on the cheek, pulling him into an embrace. 'Congratulations, Grandpa. And thank you.'

He looks mildly disconcerted at the new moniker and confused by the affection, quickly untangling himself. 'Uh—Grace. We probably shouldn't.' *Huh?* 'I know it's easy to fall back into things when emotions are high, but I still have a girlfriend and I don't want to lead you on.'

Oh, my God. Abbey was right. He really is a dick. I let his stupidity slide and decide that he's definitely being called Grandpa, whether he likes it or not.

'Thanks for letting me know, Daniel.' I try to keep a straight face. 'I guess I'll have to control myself.'

I stay at the nursery window watching Stella long after he leaves, remembering how tiny Abbey was when she was born – her rosebud of a mouth, the unusual amount of hair for a newborn, like she had a little blonde mullet. I'm drawn back even further, to the day Mum and Dad brought Liz home from the hospital. It's hard to believe it was forty-five years ago. The memory's as clear as if it were yesterday.

Liz had been delivered prematurely by caesarean, so Mum had been in hospital for a week. I hadn't been allowed to visit and Dad fed me baked beans on toast every night. I didn't tell him I hated them, because he was clearly trying. When they'd arrived home, I remember waiting in my room as Dad paid the babysitter, scared and not knowing what to expect.

'Are you ready to meet your baby sister?' Mum had sat on my bed, patting the covers next to her. I wasn't. I was worried

I wouldn't like Liz and wondered if they could put her back if she was horrible. But I'd climbed up anyway and Mum had shown me how to hold her. Her face was all pink and I remember her fingernails. They were like tiny shells. As I'd looked down at her, Dad had stood in the doorway and asked what I thought of her, and I'd started crying even though I didn't know why. I remember telling him I loved her a lot. And I did, instantly.

Dad had sat on the bed then – on the other side of me – and put his arm around all of us, kissing Mum. I think I remember it so clearly because everything felt so safe in that moment, like nothing bad could ever happen. 'Being a big sister is a really important job, Grace,' Mum had said. 'You always have to look after her, okay?'

I remember the way Liz's skin smelled and the downy softness of her skin as I'd leant down to kiss her little head. That was the moment I made my first big promise. I've made so many promises since – time goes so fast – and I've kept as many as I could, broken more than I wanted to. But maybe that's just life, we do the best we can. It's all we can do in the end, isn't it? I'm still not sure how to do this whole grandmother thing but I'll figure it out. I promised Abbey I would and this is one I won't break. I can't promise I'll get it right, but I'll try. For both of them.

One of Stella's tiny hands is sticking out of the blanket. It twitches by her face and her eyelids flutter. I can't keep my eyes off her, thinking about the words Mum said under her breath. *Second chance.* People always say there's a reason for everything. I don't think that's always true – some things are too horrible and inexplicable to have a good reason. But sometimes things do make sense, only you can't see it until long afterwards, looking back at all the sliding doors that got you here.

And I am *here.* I am present – not thinking about the past or worrying about the future. I'm here, today. Tomorrow I will do whatever Abbey needs me to do. I'll find a way to be whatever this beautiful baby will eventually call me. And if anyone calls me a crone I'll take it as a compliment, because this is my chance to be wiser.

Maybe I'll explore my shadow side, but I know I'll keep reaching for the light. I'll undoubtedly do more stupid things. Sometimes I'll pray and sometimes I won't; and I'll get lost again I'm sure, but then I'll be found – or some version of me will be. And maybe I'll spend Christmas in London – but I'll always come home. To Abbey. To Stella. To Liz and to Susie. To Mum. To all the glorious women in my life, because their love is the only validation I need. Which means I'll always come home to *me*, because it has finally sunk in that I don't have to choose one thing. All of these versions of myself – all the things I am to the people I love – can co-exist. I am everything and everything is me.

I don't know what's coming next, but I don't need to. I can stop trying so hard and holding on so tightly. Most of all, I can trust that, no matter what happens, everything will eventually be okay. Some things are out of my control, and I think that's fine with me. After all . . .

Life always has a plan, Grace. You've just got to have a little faith.

Acknowledgements

Seeing this very personal book realised has been a long time coming, and it's the first I've written where I've literally had to 'sit down at the typewriter and bleed'. It was difficult but cathartic, and I don't think I could have done it without the support and encouragement of so many people. There are many of you to thank from different phases of this often torturous – but always exhilarating – writing trek.

Firstly thank you to Varuna, The National Writers' House. This book was born there and nurtured there, over several stays, including a Varuna Fellowship in 2023. The magical energy there, the space to breathe and think and dream, as well as write, will forever be woven into these pages.

The incredible team at Simon & Schuster Australia – my publisher, Anthea Bariamis, and editor, Shannon Grey, who supported and guided me through the tricky (and confronting) editing process and allowed me the space to learn but also to fight for my story. Julia Kathro and Dana Anderson for making sure the world knows about this book. And anybody else behind the scenes who was a part of bringing *Disgraceful* into being and getting it into the right hands and into bookstores. Shout out to Coco McGrath for helping me be brutal and kill some darlings. And a special thank you to Cassandra Di Bello, who may have moved on from S&S to another adventure, but who fell in love with Grace from the first page and is the reason this book was acquired. I will be forever grateful.

Team Ninja – the incredibly talented writers Emma Grey and Nina D. Campbell and Anjanette Fennell (my fabulous agent). Between us, the unwavering support through incredible ups and downs, the thousands of pages read, and the endless cheerleading. has been a life raft in the sea of uncertainty that is trying to make it as a writer. I am so blessed to call you my friends and to be riding the rollercoaster of inspiration, passion, inevitable disappointments and equally as inevitable successes with the three of you.

Divorce Crew – my ride or dies. Sommer Tothill and Matthew Lowe. Thanks for the mems, the memes, the laughs, the tears, the gossip, the wine, the dirty talk – and most of all, the friendship. To say I might not have made it through all the ups and downs without you is a gross understatement. Except you're not gross. You're hot AF. Just saying. *D.C. Forever!*

Random, but important – to author Nick Earls for reading my early writing years ago and telling me to keep going. I kept going. Screenwriter and showrunner Vicki Madden whose brilliant take on character changed everything for me (and for everyone I talk to about character). To all the friends and friends of friends who offered up their dating horror stories as inspiration or shared their heartbreaks with me. A particular thank you to my friend, Cristin Symes, who shared her Nanna with me. I've no doubt Margaret is laughing as hard as we always do.

My family – my sisters, Kylie and Clare, and my mum – who are all voracious readers and have devoured everything I've written since primary school. To my dad, who is not a voracious reader but who passed on his wannabe rock star vibes to me, and that's gotta be worth something. Family is not always easy, but if you're lucky enough to have a family like mine, it's where you know you can always come home to.

My clever, funny and kind daughter, Nikita, whose love for books and stories – even the trashy ones (actually, mostly the trashy ones) – fills me with motherly pride. And I don't generally do motherly anything. Thank you for being willing to read all the things that come out of your mother's brain – you know, the dirty things you don't want to think about your mother thinking about. I hope I haven't scarred you. I'm sure you'll be fine. Thank you for being you, for showing me there are different ways to be a good mother, and for being proud of me. I clearly did something right. And, Peyton and Maggie, my beautiful granddaughters – for teaching me to be open to life's unexpected changes and, of course, for the cuddles. Mimi loves you.

Finally, thank you to the universe for showing me that, even in your darkest moments, when you feel as though your life has been thrown to the wolves, if you keep the faith and keep putting one foot in front of the other, you'll eventually make it out the other side. And maybe even turn what you've been through into something beautiful. My biggest hope for this book is that all the women out there who have felt something similar will see themselves in Grace and her story – and know that they're not alone.

Sensitive Themes

Readers should be aware that this novel contains themes of sexual assault, suicide, domestic violence, coercive control, abortion, postpartum depression, terminal illness, and alcohol and drug addiction. If you are sensitive to these subjects, please use this information to make an informed decision about whether to proceed with this story.

About the Author

Rachel Fox McLeod is an award-winning fiction writer and screenwriter. Her film and television credits including *Wanted* (Matchbox Pictures), *Mako Mermaids* (Disney/Netflix) and *The Bachelor*. Rachel has also been awarded the Josephine Ulrick Literature Prize and the Griffith Review Emerging Writers Prize. Rachel likes tattoos, pop culture, the F word and cheese. Not in that order . . . cheese always comes first.

To find out more about Rachel head to:
therealzerofox.com
Facebook.com/realzerofox
Instagram/Substack/TikTok @therealzerofox